THE MAIDEN & THE UNSEEN

BOOK ONE
IN THE
LOVE & FATE
SERIES
BY
JEANETTE ROSE & ALEXIS RUNE

ROSE & STAR PUBLISHING

Cover Design by Fae Lane
Editing by Shannon Cave
Art by Cebanart

To Kelsey:
For the original title of this book: Balls & HR.
Love,
Jeanette & Alexis

Authors' Note

This is not a mythologically accurate retelling of Hades & Persephone, not only is it placed in the modern day, but we took many liberties with the source material. Including the birth order of Hades, Poseidon and Zeus. We also changed the family tree so Persephone is not related to Hades at all.

Chapter One
Hades

MY CLAWS FLASH AS I DIG THEM into the marble of my desk at the constant bickering of my brothers' voices in my ear. Thousands of years old, yet nothing has changed. I'm still the referee for my brothers' squabbles. I don't know why I even participate in these conference calls anymore. But, I'm the dutiful brother.

Which, when you compare me against my two siblings, is not exactly a sign of praise. Yet I am now stuck in the middle, *permanently*, with Zeus's new directive.

The gods are getting bored on the mountain. They want to go among the mortals again. Make them comfortable.

Somehow, because I had the business acumen to not withdraw from the mortal world completely two thousand years ago, I'm now the bank for all the gods descending the mountain.

I'm a glorified tour guide. A bank with a pulse. Many thought Midas had the golden touch? I'm the God of *Wealth*. In other words, *bitch, please.*

Poseidon whines in my ear about a dolphin conspiracy to dethrone him as King of the Seas. I barely bite back my scathing retort at that.

Hades, God of Biting His Tongue.
Hades, God of Middle Siblings.

I don't have time for this. Unlike my idle brothers, I have a fucking *job.* Not just downstairs, but also during the six months I'm outside the Underworld. Yet, Zeus allows gods off the mountain, and suddenly I'm footing the bill. Only a handful have taken him up on his offer, several actually trying to live here *and* on Olympus. The tiny pocket realm that's only accessible for those with divine blood. Though I suppose most mortals in the modern day find it humorous that their ancestors used to believe we lived on top of a very climbable mountain.

"Unlike you two, I have a job to get back to." I suddenly snap into the phone. Unlike them, I've *always* had a job. Gaia divided the realms after the Titan War. To my older brother went the seas and the pocket realm of Atlantis. To my younger brother went the skies and the pocket realm of Olympus. To me went the land beneath and the pocket realm of the Underworld. My brothers had nothing that was required of them from their realms except occasionally mediating a conflict. My realm? Constant vigilance and ordering. A job I do half the year; the other half I spend here in the mortal realm.

Both my brothers go silent for a moment, surprised at my sudden outburst. I'm usually so patient with them, for the past thousands of years. But today, I snap.

"Damn, what's up your ass?" Poseidon snickers. His lackadaisical voice is laced with both humor and surprise. I can practically see him leaning back in one of the dry rooms in Atlantis, the gold beads in his wild curls clinking as he moves. No doubt he's wearing a pair of swim shorts and nothing else.

"Someone doesn't like sharing," Zeus adds. I can hear him shifting on his throne. The fact that he set up a landline in the throne room of Olympus tells you pretty much everything you need to know about him.

I slam the phone down, running a hand through my hair, tossing it. No one knows how to rile you up like your siblings. I can't even figure out what it was about today that made me lose it.

I take a deep breath, getting control of my anger, before looking at the list in front of me. Newly de-mountained gods were required to come through me, so we could establish them in the mortal world without causing alarm. It's a little *shocking* how many of them think it's so easy and that these things just *happen*. The first group from the mountain was full of disasters and near misses. I'd learned my lesson. Each small group of those who wish to descend must follow my carefully outlined and strict rules. Or I send their ass packing. To live among the mortals is to follow them. More than one god had thought to push my boundaries, and paid dearly for it.

My eyes scan the list, looking for anyone I feel might *bend* the strict rules I have in place. My eyes wander to the bottom of the list, frowning when I notice there's one name fewer than there should be.

When I picked up the list, there were eighteen names. Now, there are only *seventeen*. My teeth grind. Fucking gods. Someone's trying to slip past the procedures but still enjoy the benefits. Oh, they'll fucking learn. Think they can bypass my rules? My precautions and protections?

I grab my phone, my lips twitching. Think to hide from me? *Me?* Wonder how good they'll feel when the Bank of Hades suddenly dries up? If their name appears on this list, an account is instantly attached to my name, with a monthly allowance, most in the tens of thousands, provided to them. But when I pull up the list of accounts, the names attached to all eighteen keep shifting. *A concealment charm, clever.* These accounts were their only source of income. Zeus drew the line at me forcing the gods to *work* for a living. *Chaos forbid, they actually get jobs and become functioning members of the world they want to enjoy.*

8

Apparently, I was the only one regulated to that. If I froze their accounts, and stopped giving out allowances, how tragic it would be for them. One by one, gods would be beating down my door to get their money back. Cross their names off my list, and I'll have the person hoping to slide past my protocols. Then I can properly decide on a way to punish them for their attempt.

My lips twitch with amusement. There's nothing I love more than a game of strategy, and the longer it takes, the better the reward tends to be. This will be a diversion to occupy my mind in the meantime. Away from work.

I open my computer and freeze the first account, the first name on the list.

The phone next to me rings a minute later.

Let the games begin.

Chapter Two
Persephone

THE STEADY HUM OF THE COFFEE MA-CHINE SOFTENS the sound of the rush hour traffic outside, just audible through the open window. Such a contrast between the two. I lean idly against the counter, the rich smell of the brewing coffee already starting to awaken my drowsy senses.

Four hours of sleep...

I yawn, glancing out of the window, grateful once again for my sixteenth-story apartment, allowing incredible views of the city and providing undisturbed access to the most incredible sunrises.

This morning, the sun looks as lethargic as I feel, her shine muted as she reluctantly rises.

Mood.

I tilt my head, watching her lazy ascent, my mind drifting to the sunrises of my past. How different my life is now...

I walk to the window, gazing out at the concrete jungle, and I can't help the comparisons to my home charging to the forefront of my mind. Buildings litter my view, stretching high to the sky. Cars and trucks crawl down the busy streets. Humans bob and weave as they hurry along the sidewalks, in the midst of their daily rat race. So unlike the view from my lonely balcony on Olympus, vibrant, grass-covered, rolling hills as far as the eye can see. Birdsong filling the air, trying, but failing, to drown out the sound of my thoughts. A serenity afforded to so few, wasted on me, the female who desires...something else.

This isn't exactly what I imagined when I fantasized about this realm. They say the grass is always greener, a concept I could never wrap my head around from my ivory tower, but the reality is, nothing is ever perfect.

How easily I could slip back into my old routine at home. My mother loves a strict schedule. From before I can remember, my every move was timetabled, leaving no room for even an errant thought.

I sigh, glancing at my laptop. It's not as if I don't have any ties here. While I don't have the endless menial chores, I do have a job. I groan inwardly, thinking of the emails that await me, even though I only stopped working four and a half hours ago. While I don't have my mother here, I do have clients, clients who are somehow even needier than her. Then, there is the other human stuff I have to deal with: bills, taxes, rent, mansplaining.

My mother warned me. I was so wrapped up in the romance of it all that I disregarded her, and there was no way I was going to let her win by stalking back to her, hat in hands.

Don't be a fool, P. She always *wins.*

I scoff, shaking my head. It's not as if I hadn't paid the price to come here. For 228 years, I begged and pleaded. Trying to convince her that it would be beneficial, not just to me, but to her, as well.

The truth is, I've never fully understood my pull to the mortal realm. But, from an early age, from the moment *Navigating the Mortal Realm* fell into my lap, I've been obsessed. It felt like something was tugging at an invisible string in my chest, pulling me, a feeling that had not eased since arriving here two years ago.

To this day, it surprises me that my mother finally relented. For years, she kept me locked away, hidden from the world. So much so that I'm not even a household name.

I'm the Goddess of Spring, for fuck's sake.

She would never tell me why she was so protective over me, why I was never allowed to have any friends or meet the other gods and goddesses. My life was so sheltered. My whole family system consisted of me, my mother, and some trusted servants. My first encounter with a god happened by chance when Hermes, Herald of the Gods, delivered a message to her. My mother's furious bellows down the marble corridor provided me with his name, and the one book on Greek gods in the library gave me the basics on him.

Upon meeting him, I decided I wasn't missing much by being kept from them. He seemed arrogant and tricksy. Not someone I'd want to befriend. But I did yearn for a friend. For someone to speak to about my dreams.

My mother's kindness in freeing me, of course, came with rules. Limiting rules. Even though I was expecting them, my excitement plummeted with every limitation.

I can still see her catlike smile as she gazed at me, that was the moment I knew I would never be completely free of her. I might be in a different realm, but the control would always be with her. Gods forbid, I would ever be in control of my own life.

Rule 1: Absolutely no fraternizing with other divine beings.

Not a problem.

Rule 2: Mother will check on me every six months to ensure rules are being followed.

Annoying, but okay...

Rule 3: No men. That is completely inclusive, friends or...otherwise.

The hardest rule to follow.

I've always been a romantic, and while rule three was not as limiting as she thought, it still frustrated me. I hated that she was dictating who I could date, who I could be friends with.

Fortunately for me, I've been successful in concealing my life from her, enough that she has no idea who I spend time with. As expected, she only attended the first of the four check-ins I've had, sending nymphs in her place the subsequent times.

The coffee machine huffs as it finishes pouring the life-giving nectar, saving me from my thoughts as much as from the gnawing fatigue. I glance at my laptop again, thinking about the day of work ahead, about the emails, the conference calls, the international meetings.

Some would say my life is just as tedious now as it was on Olympus. The only difference...

Now I'm free. And I wouldn't change a thing.

Chapter Three
Hades

ISNARL IN ANNOYANCE WHEN YET AN-OTHER GOD comes complaining to me about their card being declined. If any of them bothered to get actual *jobs*, they would have an income to fall back on. Rather than relying on the monthly stipend I provide them.

Five fucking years since the gods came off the mountain, two years methodically shutting down one account, then another, and I'm no closer to finding the one who eludes me. I shut off one account, wait for the god to complain, then check them off my list. But more gods have come down from the mountain, and the concealment charm does its job well. With all the accounts are mixed, there are more places to hide.

I'll find you, little rat.

I'd forgotten how many of us had descended the mountain. So many had grown bored of the relentless tedium of the city of gods. Nothing to do but think, eat, drink, and fuck. *What a chore.* Not that those who descended, living among the mortals, did much differently here. Same event, different venue. Just drinking and eating and fucking. But I suppose they could avail themselves of a different taste. The same nymphs likely grew boring after a while. Even for the depravity of Olympus.

There's only so many ways to do the same thing over and over. I suppose most wanted something *new* and *shiny*. And they hated having to walk all the way to my massive building on Wall Street to speak to me, face-to-face, in order to get their funds back. As if it was such a pleasure for me to see gods and goddesses going in and out of my office for the six months I'm topside.

Doesn't help that each god cries to me about the unfairness of this entire situation. Putting my head back on my office chair, I try to force a sense of calm on my shoulders. It's never difficult for me to control my emotions. A soothing wave settled down, allowing me to return to a state of serenity. *Control.* Get control.

Hades, God of Good Counsel.

Hades, God of Listening to Other Gods Bitch.

A moment of calm flickers through me, gazing out the window of my office. I'm complaining about the fickleness and distracted nature of the gods, and yet, they're doing what I'm not. They're *living*. I've been among the mortals since the time they worshipped us. Working, developing, building the future the rest of Olympus now benefits from. But I've never been like them. I've never hosted the elaborate parties, the luxurious hunts, the frolicking orgies and debaucheries. I've always preferred to be alone. I've never experienced what the other gods sought in this day and age. I've been the downer, the rule maker, the obedient and dutiful god. Have I become the old man who tells kids to get off their lawn?

When did I last feel *young?* Which I suppose is pretty fucking rich for me to think. Half of the year, I spend devoted to the souls of those who never got even a fraction of the years I've had. I sound like a miser. How many times have I heard souls beg for one more day, one more minute, one more second, of life? And I've wasted eternity. Being dutiful. Being unseen.

Standing from my chair, I stroll to the window

overlooking the city, leaning my arm against it, staring out. Wall Street is laid out beneath me, tiny specks of life, of *mortality*, weaving in and out. It's late, so most have gone home for the night. But there are a few, like me, who never really leave work. We live our lives for other people.

Look at these mortals. So full of life and whimsy. Valuing each moment, knowing it could be their last. I let out a soft chuckle. I suppose Homer did get that part right. I envy them.

Their ability to see the world. So different from mine.

Pressing my forehead to the cool glass, I watch them below. Barely quirking a brow when I see a woman fight with a thief as he makes off with her purse. Does he feel desperation? Despair?

What has driven him to this?

I sigh audibly, my breath fogging the window. Moving away from it, I tuck my hands into my pockets, ignoring the work waiting for me on the desk, going to my penthouse upstairs. The entire two top floors of my building form my home when I am topside, only accessible by a keycard for mortals, and various wards kept the divine out. Even my brothers. *Especially my brothers.* The interior is sleek and modern, every convenience built in and prepared for. Massive windows compose most of the penthouse, allowing me to watch the never-sleeping city outside. *Watch.* But never touch. Kept apart.

Undoing my suit jacket, I toss it over the back of a chair, unbuttoning my shirt. I should call someone to fuck. Pulling out my phone, I scroll through the contacts, looking for someone to simply pass the time.

Too clingy.
Asked for my social security number during dinner.
Goddess.
God.

Nope. No and no.

Damn. Maybe I should do as the mortals do. Download one of those dating apps. What have I to lose? I smile to myself, download one of the hookup apps, and establish a profile. What should I put in my bio?

God of the Underworld looking to make you feel out of this world? Gods, that's terrible. Plus, Zeus would likely frown heavily if I suddenly announced that the gods were real and living among mortals.

Lonely business magnate looking for someone with no strings. That sounds like I'm planning to murder them.

Fuck. Why is this so hard? A bio on a hookup app isn't rocket science. *God of the Dead looking to feel alive.* Maybe I should go without a bio?

Can I go without a bio?

When the app doesn't prevent me, I pick three photos of myself at work, and put my phone down, getting into the shower. I get out of the shower, feeling better about my chances, going to check my phone.

I blink at the alert.

YOUR ACCOUNT HAS BEEN CANCELED DUE TO SUSPICIOUS ACTIVITY.

I blink repeatedly at the alert. Suspicious activity? I just made it! It's a hookup app! Everything about it is suspicious!

I toss my phone to the side. Maybe it's a sign. Gods and hookup apps apparently don't mix. Fuck.

I should really just keep my focus on finding the god who's not supposed to be here rather than finding someone to bury my cock in. The game is posed for a killing blow, and the list of potential culprits gets smaller and smaller. *See you soon, little rat. Very soon.*

Chapter Four
Persephone

I LOOK DOWN AT MY BLACK CARD, BROWS FURROWED. This is the third store in a row it's been declined in. The shiny black plastic seems to stare up at me, mocking me. *Plutus Bank,* engraved in gold, contrasting beautifully against the light swallowing background. I hurry back to my apartment to check my account.

I always have money, always save from my paycheck. The web page seems to take hours to load, and when it does, I stare at the blinking cursor, blanking on my username and password in my panic.

I look down at the keyboard and the letters blur into a mess of shapes. My mind races as I consider my last meeting with the nymph. It was only last week...did she find something incriminating and report it back to my mother? I look around the apartment, trying to identify any signs of Jackson but find none. I'm always so careful, making sure he doesn't leave any of his belongings here.

Surely, if my mother knew I'd been casually seeing someone for the past six months, the penalty would be higher than the extraction of my finances...

I take a breath, trying to calm my racing heart. I force myself to think calming thoughts and try to take comfort in the fact that I've probably not been found out, and this is just an error.

Once my heart rate slows and my mind is able to return to a somewhat more rational place, I easily recall my username and password. Once again, the wait is torturous, as I stare at the loading screen. After what feels like an eternity, the page loads, and I click on my main current accounts, readying to see that, financially, I'm fine and that I just need to call the bank to unlock my account.

My eyes go wide at the balance.

$0.

Every single account.

What the fuck?

My heart starts pounding again, and the room spins as I'm seized by panic. I grip the sides of my chair, trying to take deep breaths to stop myself from spiraling. This is a mistake. Must be a mistake. How could I have no money? I squeeze my eyes closed, hoping that, when I open them, my reality will be different. But when I open my eyes, my gaze locks on the number again.

Fuck fuck fuck.

Wait…Helios…he'll know what's going on.

I stand from the chair, making it topple over, and practically run to his apartment a few blocks away.

The second my gaze lands on his apartment building, relief fills my chest, burning from my run here. I can practically see his smiling face, lounging on his balcony, sunning himself, his already tanned skin even more golden brown and sun-kissed. I roll my eyes at the thought of him, but my chest swells in gratitude for him.

Helios, the Sun God, was one of the first people I met when I arrived on Earth. The irony doesn't escape me that I had been in this realm for mere minutes before I broke Rule 1, and after a few hours, when we became friends, also Rule 3.

He was kind, attentive, and helpful, showing me the ropes and teaching me the intricacies of blending in with the humans. To this day, he is the only person in the realm who knows my identity. He is also the only god who knows that there is a "Goddess of Spring." His surprise made me realize the lengths my mother went to, to hide me from everyone. Helios and I have always had an easy relationship. He is the first friend I have ever had, and the idea that I was not allowed such for so long still fills me with anger, especially now that I know what I was missing.

I greet the doorman as I rush into the building, the elevator already waiting for me. When I arrive at his floor, I brace my hands on my knees as I catch my breath and pound on his door. He answers a few moments later.

"Helios…Mother…Money…"

Helios lifts his eyebrows at me, his white teeth flashing, a stunning contrast next to his golden hair and skin. "Slow down, petal."

He stands from his sun lounger and places his hand on my elbow, easily guiding me into the house. Helios's house suits him, full of rich tones, earthy colors, terracotta pots. There are pops of color throughout, blues and greens. He gestures for me to sit down at the kitchen island and pours a glass of water, placing it in front of me.

"Drink."

I gratefully accept the cool water and drink deeply, draining the glass completely. I pull my long, brown, wavy hair into a messy bun, hoping it'll help me cool down, my skin slick with sweat. Running has never been my favorite, but running in New York City, at the height of summer? Absolutely not.

Helios fills my glass again before placing his hands

on the counter. I can tell the interrogation is about to begin.

"So...?"

I take another sip, delaying the conversation until I'm finished organizing my thoughts.

"All of my money. It's...gone. Do you...do you think my mother—"

Helios laughs, cutting me off. I glare at him. There is nothing funny about losing all of your money. I doubt he would be this relaxed if it were *his* bank account that had been looted.

"Oh, you've been taxed. It's going around."

My brows draw. "Taxed? I pay my taxes..."

Helios walks to his fridge and grabs a protein shake, chuckling again. "Not federal taxes. You've been taxed from on high, you know, the God of Taxes."

I roll my eyes, frustration building. "Enough with the riddles, H. What are you talking about?"

Helios pauses. "Wait, do you really not know where all of our money comes from?"

I blink at him, perplexed. "I assumed it came from my job."

He rolls his eyes. "You can't think your job is paying you millions a year."

My cheeks heat with embarrassment. "I..."

Stupidly, I'd never really thought about it. While I've been here two years, I'm still not sure about the intricacies of money, and it's not something mortals openly discuss with one another. I get paid what I get paid, and I never think any more about it.

Helios lets out a weary sigh, his hands returning to the countertop. "Right, I forgot. Your mother is terrible and set you up to fail."

My lips twitch despite myself. Helios has never been shy about his feelings toward the Goddess of the Harvest.

21

"All gods have an account with the Rich One. He's responsible for sponsoring all of us. You'll need to talk to him to have your money reinstated."

I worry my brow at his moniker. I feel my lip curling at the thought of having to speak with another god, someone who sounds like an egotistical, arrogant asshole. "The Rich One? How do I find him?"

"His office is on Wall Street. You can't miss him."

I stand from the stool. "Alright. I'll go now."

Helios laughs. "You just want to pop by and say 'hi'?"

I shoot him a glare. "I have no money. What else can I do?"

Helios holds his hands up. "I'm just saying, he's not a fan of…spontaneous meetings."

My fists clench, patience wearing thin at Helios and his attempt at banter. "Are you going to tell me how to talk to this guy or continue to be a dick about it?"

He smirks. The asshole *smirked* at me. "I'm debating…"

Exasperated, I spin on my heels and leave his house, storming to the nearest subway station. *Helios is such a fucking asshole.*

My leg shakes the whole way there, nerves setting me on edge. I sigh at the small mercy that my monthly subway card had just been renewed, so I didn't have to worry about being allowed on the subway. The anxiety sits heavy in my stomach, and waves of nausea roll through me as the train blasts through the city.

Wall Street is bustling, and I quietly curse myself for not being more patient with Helios, to try and get more of a description about where to find this "Rich One" or some insider information. I try to remember that book about Greek mythology. The second I found it, I hid it under my mattress, knowing my mother would disapprove of me trying to educate myself about this particular subject. I curse my childhood self for only ever rereading the same page, over and over. I curse again that I can't even recall the name of that god, like it's been locked away so well, never to be accessed. All I can remember is the darkness of the writing, the shadows that curled around the corners of the page and two single words. *"The Unseen."*

I struggle down the sidewalk, bodies brushing past me as everyone rushes to grab a quick lunch. I sigh, frustrated, not knowing how I'm going to find this building that I have no knowledge of, when my eyes are drawn to a large building, easily fifty stories high.

Plutus Industries.

There is something about the building that draws me in. I can't decide if it's the elegant but bold script of the sign or the way the windows perfectly catch the light of the midday sun...or the fact that it's just the name of my bank. Either way, I'm drawn to it. That ever-present tug in my chest intensifies as I look up.

The main reception is large, busy. Expensive-looking furniture and decor artfully litter the room, making it the perfect balance between "workplace" and "comfortable." The plush cream leather sofas look comfier than my bed.

I walk to the directory and glance through it.

Plutus Industries Bank – 48th floor.

"Can I help you?" I turn to the voice. A stunning, blonde woman sits behind the reception desk, her gaze judging me in my denim shorts and crop top. I silently curse, knowing my hair is scraped up in a bun, and the only makeup I'm wearing is mascara with a red gloss. Of course, she looks like a perfectly preened Barbie.

I plaster a smile on my face and walk over to her. "Yes, I'm looking for...um... Who leases the 48th floor?"

She raises a perfectly manicured brow. "No one, *leases* any of the top five floors. They belong to the owner of the building."

Oh.

My gaze hardens as I begin to lose my patience. I chalk my fiery mood down to the heat…and my new lack of finances. "Who *owns* it then?"

"Do you have an appointment?"

It becomes clear that she's not going to give me any information. I sigh. "No."

"Well, unfortunately, there's nothing I can do for you."

I smile blandly at her and turn, readying to leave, when I feel a sharp tug at my chest. I turn to face the elevator, my gaze going to the swipe card system.

No way to infiltrate then.

My feet start moving on their own accord toward the elevators. I frown, hearing heels click against the marble floor behind me, as the receptionist trials me.

"Miss, you can't just—"

The elevator opens when I approach, and I enter, turn, and press the button for Floor 48. My gaze locks on Ms. Perfect, and I smirk in satisfaction as the elevator door slowly closes and it lurches into action.

The second I'm hidden from view, my brows furrow again. Why had the door opened for me?

I get lost in my mind as I start ascending the floors. I've made it here, but what am I going to say? Will they see reason? I'm pulled from my thoughts when the elevator dings. The doors open, not to a typical office as I was expecting, but a plush living space.

I step out, rolling my eyes at the grandeur.

Who the fuck am I meeting with?

Chapter Five

Hades

TODAY'S A NEW DAY. Finishing a punishing workout, I strip off the shirt I've sweat through, striding to my kitchen for water. There was little that was not provided for me in my penthouse. In addition to the massive chef's kitchen, there's a study, a full library, a state-of-the-art gym, even a guest room. Though that last has never been utilized.

I open the fridge, grabbing the bottle of water, sucking on it as I turn, the fridge door softly shutting next to me. My feet stop in place when I see a woman standing in my living room.

I blink for a moment, stunned. How long had she been standing there? How did she get in? My protocols? My security? *Bypassed.*

"Oh…I…" she begins. Her voice is soft, but husky.

I blink again. A young woman is standing in my sanctum, my *home,* a place she never should have been able to enter. I slowly lower the water bottle from my lips, locking on her. Her eyes flare, and she takes a step back, almost on instinct at my focus. Sensing the predator's den she's just stumbled into?

I pin her with my glare. "Who are you?"

She blinks at me, her gaze trailing down my torso. Damn, I'm still dripping sweat, and the soiled shirt is hanging on one of the chairs by the island. "I…uh…"

I storm closer, annoyance shimmering. "Who are you?"

This close, I can take in the things I took for granted when I noticed there was someone in my penthouse. Immediately, I regret not trying another of those hookup apps last night. Without the release I needed, I'm very aware of how *breathtaking* this woman is. Her hair is dark and messy, in a bun, but with the flicker of light, a deep red lurks in the dark brown. Fire beneath a tame image. Her skin a golden tan, shapely in all the ways I like. I stop myself from letting myself drool a little when I see how her hips flare out. I bet her ass is *life changing*. Her lips are shining a battle red, and I'm already picturing them trailing along my skin, my mouth, my…

Okay, need to focus. Head out of cock.

I shake my head almost imperceptibly, but her scent floods my nose. *Roses in a cold, crisp fog.* Fuck, she even *smells* amazing. This is unfair. Half mysterious and half sweet.

"Persephone," she hisses. "I want my money back."

Her face flushes perfectly with her anger, even as her hands curl into fists at her side. *Her money.* Fuck, she's a goddess? I've definitely never seen her before. But, that explained how she got into my penthouse without a key-card and bypassed the wards. She must have a conceal-ment charm or something similar, likely the same item which enabled her to appear on my list and vanish a moment later.

I tilt my head. "Hm, my plan bore fruit." *Luscious fruit.* "May I change before we have this meeting?"

She narrows her vibrant eyes on me. "It seems, since you hold all the cards, I have little choice but to wait."

Someone doesn't like having their choices taken away. I smirk slightly down at her, enjoying how I tower over her. I'm not above using my height to my advantage,

26

along with other things. "And it's *my* money."

Not hers. It's all *my money.* Welcome, little rat, I've been waiting for you.

I hear her cursing as I spin on my heel toward my closet to change. Not to mention gather my wits. *She's a goddess, dude. They're always beautiful.* Thankfully, she wasn't *today's* beautiful. She was curvy, her hips flaring out, her breasts heaving with anger as she glared at me. Not like she'd crack under the weight of my body after I fucked her into the next realm. Then the one after that too.

Stop that. Goddess means off limits. I should have tried another of those mortal apps. Then I wouldn't be so aware of the fact that I'm going through a bit of a dry spell.

Pulling on the first suit I grab, I try to reach for that calm, clear head. I would need it to figure out this mystery. I put on the black slacks, starched white shirt, and matching suit jacket in a haze of muscle memory. I even tie on my shoes without even registering it.

Persephone. I've never heard of her. I'm out of touch with the rumor mill of Olympus, but surely I would have at least *heard* of her. I would remember having seen her before. She has a body and face I'd not soon forget.

I walk back to her, covering my own curse when I see she's pulled her hair out of that messy bun, softening the curves of her face. *Fuck.* Her face is flushed slightly, no doubt from her rage at me, and I can't help but think of other things that might get her *flushed.*

I gesture to the elevator. "Shall we?"

She storms to the elevator first, leaving me to trail behind, giving me that first full view of her backside. *Fuck. Life changing. I knew it.*

Even in the less-than-a-minute ride from my floor to the office, the small mode of convenience crackles. Again, she doesn't wait for me, stomping off the elevator, unerringly turning into my corner office without guidance, her head held as high as a queen.

I move to my desk, sitting in my chair after she takes a seat across from me.

"You took my money," she hisses. Her eyes locked on mine. Not even flinching from the intensity of my stare. Her eyes are a light blue, a ring of gold around the pupil, a sun in the clear sky. Even as they fire with barely contained rage, they give me the sensation of lying in a field, surrounded by flowers swaying in the breeze.

I should not like that she's not backing down from me. I really *should not* like that.

"*My* money," I correct, continuing to watch her.

She throws back her head, laughing humorously, the sound grating my ears. "How do you figure?"

I scan her again. "You're a god living off the mountain. Did you think your living arrangements and spending funds just *appear?*"

She blanks for a moment before covering it.

I smother a smirk. *Got you.*

"Fine. But the money that I earned from my job?"

My lips twitch. Nice try. "Your *job?*"

Gods don't have jobs off the mountain, except for the few who work for me. They are content to laze about and let me provide. Those who do usually end up in jobs that bring them fame and fortune, without revealing their true identity. A strict provision of them rejoining the world of mortals.

Her jaw clenches. "Yes. My *job.*"

"You mean as an influencer?" I sneer. "Actress? Model?"

Careers befitting the indolent goddess.

Her eyes narrow. "Why would you say that?"

"You're a goddess," I add, humoring her. "You're not exactly made for *real* work."

She visibly bristles. "Are you this misogynistic to all

women or just goddesses?"

I pause, before letting out a loud laugh. She's full of snark, I'll give her that. "Just goddesses."

Goddesses are vain and cruel creatures. As are gods.

She sighs, her lips pursed with her annoyance. "I think you have offended me enough today. If you just give me my money back, I'll be on my way."

Not happening.

I steeple my fingers, putting my elbows on the desk, leaning closer. "Do you even know how much money you are asking for?"

She blanks again, before covering herself with a confident smirk. "Difficult to know, considering you have apparently been giving me money also."

I smirk back at her. "I'll take that as a no." I open the folder my assistant placed on my desk for another business matter. I look at the numbers, tsking as if something has been found. "Hmm, fascinating."

"What?"

I look up at her. "You can't afford your rent on your salary."

Her eyes blaze at me. "You're lying."

"I don't lie." *I'm totally lying.*

Her gaze ignites even more, her fists on the arms of her chair. It takes her visible moments to put her face into a sweet smile. "Look, Mr....?"

"Hades."

She clears her throat. "Hades. You are obviously a very busy man. So why don't we cut the bullshit and come to an agreement?"

Should not find that hot. Should not find that hot.

"An agreement?" I tsk. "I hold all the cards."

Her saccharine smile falters. "What do you want?"

I laugh, humorouslessly, just like she did. "I have everything I want."

She crosses her legs, drawing my gaze to her. My

mouth drying at the flash of her thigh. Fuck. She clearly knows how to play the game. "So what do you suggest?"

I suggest I break my "no divine" rule and fuck you on this desk.

Focus.

"Tell me about your job."

Her lips purse, drawing my eyes again. "Why?"

I shrug, feigning nonchalance. "You're the first goddess with a job. I'm curious."

"I'm a social media manager for a number of high-profile accounts." She purrs.

I was not expecting that. Social media manager is a thankless job that requires hours of work and constantly communicating with both your client and the masses. They work behind the scenes to promote others. Very rarely are given any kind of credit.

How…odd for a goddess.

"And you…enjoy that?" I ask, my voice low with skepticism. All the goddesses I knew wanted to be in front of the camera, not behind it.

She rolls her eyes at my tone. "Yes."

"Then, congratulations," I say, "you've found a use for yourself and a new job."

"Oh?" Her tone turning lethal.

"Unless you want to be evicted."

"You want me to work for you?" She laughs humourlessly.

I nod. "Do you have an issue with that?"

"Doesn't seem like I have much of a choice."

I stand from my chair, adjusting my suit coat. "You don't."

She gazes up at me, still in her seat. "Why are you doing this?"

Because I can. "Monday morning. 8:00 a.m. Don't be late."

She stands slowly, her eyes flambéing me with her

rage, and storms out of my office. Through my glass walls, I see her giving me the middle finger over her shoulder.

I smirk wickedly, alone in my office.

I'll see you soon, Little Goddess. Real soon.

Chapter Six
Persephone

MONDAY MORNING ROLLS AROUND IN THE BLINK OF THE EYE. I curse myself for wasting my entire weekend seething about my encounter with *Hades*. Even when I was out for lunch with Jackson after the meeting, our encounter ran through my head over and over, my blood boiling anew every time.

His dismissal and complete disregard for my career and the assumptions that I'm some...vapid, desperate party girl? *Is he fucking kidding?*

Even more frustrating was how my body reacted to him. His misogynistic words did nothing to dampen my need. *Did they heighten it?* My fists clench as I remember how my gaze snagged on his sweat-covered chest, his muscles tense from his workout. How I imagined running my tongue up his neck. Even thinking about it now makes my stomach flutter. *Get your head out of the gutter, P.*

Any unsavory thoughts are easy to combat when I consider my current financial situation. Jackson left on Friday night, and I didn't even consider asking to stay at his place. Not that I would feel comfortable staying at his house. It may have been six months, but I wouldn't even class us as being in a relationship.

When I woke on Saturday to no food in the house, I found myself heading back to Helios, ready to beg him to feed me. His behavior from the day before was quickly forgotten when he graciously invited me into his home, fed me, and asked me to stay all weekend. Every stray moment I was not being distracted by Helios, my mind wandered to "the Rich One."

I sigh, looking at myself in the mirror of the elevator. Granted I look better than I did at our last meeting, but the anticipation of his intense gaze forced me to try on at least four outfits before settling on this deep plum, fitted dress, which now seems to be the wrong choice too. The cotton hugs my body too tightly, the hem sitting too high on my thigh. The only part of my outfit I'm content with...the sky-high black heels. Heels scream confidence. *Fake it 'til you make it.* Plus it'll lessen the height difference. He must be at least six and a half feet, compared to my five and half feet.

I run my fingers through my hair, fluffing it slightly, and touch up my bold red lip. *Here goes nothing.*

The sound of the elevator ding sends a jolt through me. I turn and look at the already bustling office. *Am I late?*

I walk to the main reception desk, a busty blond sits, her thumbs furiously tapping on her phone. I clear my throat. "Excuse me?"

She looks up, her gaze bored. "Yes?"

I smile at her brightly. My reputation with receptionists in the building needs to change. "I'm Persephone. I believe I'm expected?"

The receptionist's head tilts in recognition at my name. She sweeps her eyes over me, taking me in. The receptionists in the building must gossip with each other. I didn't exactly make a good impression on the one in the lobby.

"The social media *expert?*" She practically spits at the

33

last word.

My gaze hardens. *Well, this one isn't going to be a friend either then.* "Yes."

Her lip curls as she looks me over again. "Your office is down the hall. Don't bother the boss." She absently hands me a folder and slowly moves her gaze back to her phone, but as I walk away, I get the sense she's still watching me.

The office is just as ostentatious as the rest of the building and his apartment. The individual rooms have floor-to-ceiling windows and all offer a glorious view of the city, putting shame to the one from my apartment.

I feel the eyes of everyone as I make my way down the seemingly endless corridor. *Right, I'm the new girl.*

My first encounter in my new job has done nothing to ease my knotted stomach.

I locate my office, right at the end of the corridor. It feels like it was done on purpose, so that everyone could look their fill of me. No doubt a power play, or a move to see if I shrink under scrutiny. *You'll have to do better than that, Hades.*

I close the door of my office, the desire to hide unmet due to the glass.

The room is beautiful, a white desk sits in the middle with a white, leather, high-backed swivel chair tucked under it. A potted plant with browning leaves sits on the floor in the corner. I peer out of my office, satisfied everyone has grown bored with assessing me. I twist my hand slightly, and the plant gets a jolt of life, the leaves turning a vibrant green. Pink flowers sprout all over it.

Sitting at the desk, I open the laptop.

Welcome, Persephone Prosperina.

My lips twitch. I received a warmer welcome from a computer than I did from any of my "colleagues."

It surprises me to see that I already have a busy inbox full of ideas, tasks, and projects. The heavy workload eases my anxiety, the thought that I'll be able to throw myself into work.

For being at the end of the corridor, there is heavier foot traffic in front of my office than one would expect. I don't lift my eyes to look at them, but I hear their commentary. Occasionally complimentary, mostly not, they circle like vultures eyeing their prey. I hit the keys on the keyboard harder, trying to drown them out. *How long until I'm old news?*

"You do eat, don't you?"

My fingers still at that voice. Deep, arrogant, self-assured, entitled. *Sexy.*

I slowly lift my eyes to him, schooling my face into a look of disdain, which wavers the second I take him in.

His crisp black suit is perfectly tailored, hugging every muscle. The sight is borderline obscene. His bright white shirt contrasts sharply, drawing my gaze to his broad chest, the top button left undone, giving the smallest glimpse of the skin beneath. Just from that sliver of skin, my mind immediately flashes back to our last encounter, his shirtless torso gleaming with sweat, my gaze utterly captivated by a single bead of moisture rolling teasingly over his muscles.

Focus, P.

I give myself an internal shake and force my gaze to lock on his, pushing out those infernal thoughts.

"Usually. Unfortunately, some asshole emptied my bank account for absolutely no reason."

He leans against the doorframe. I can't help but appreciate how his powerful muscles strain as he shifts. "*My* bank account." He tucks his hands into his pockets, pushes off the doorframe, and walks over to me, confidence oozing from him. *Confidence* and *arrogance.*

Rounding my desk, he closes in on me, stopping behind me. My body tenses as I feel the heat from him seep into me, and my breath hitches slightly. He leans over my shoulder, and I'm surrounded by his intoxicating scent, sandalwood and citrus. There's something so familiar about it.

"Hm."

I lift an eyebrow and look over my shoulder at him, my face inches from his. "Yes?"

"Inspecting your work. Is that allowed?"

"I could just…email it to you."

He leans in closer, putting a hand on the desk, partially caging me in. *Oh fuck, his smell* is *intoxicating.*

He turns his head to look at me, his breath tickling my lips. "I prefer a more hands-on approach."

It takes everything in me, but I don't shrink away. Not allowing him to intimidate me. I can feel him assessing me, testing me, asserting his dominance.

"And how often am I to be under this scrutiny?"

His eyes roam over my face, searching for…something.

Did he just…glance at my lips?

"As often as I want to."

My eyebrow quirks, and my lips pull into a half smile. *Is that how you want to play it?* "I don't think it requires you to be this close."

The bastard smirks, his eyes roaming over my face again. "Do I make you nervous?"

I lean in even further, the movement pushing my breasts together slightly. I'm going to win this game of chicken. "You wish, Hades."

His eyes dart to my chest, and he growls. The sound is low, threatening, and…arousing?

Fuck…

I give in to my desire and lean back into him, biting back a groan at how his hard muscles feel against my back. "And what about you, Hades? Do I make you nervous?"

He moves away, straightening behind me. I almost

36

shiver at the lack of his warmth.

"Why would you?"

I grin. "There is something so poetic about the God of the Underworld being nervous about the Goddess of Spring, don't you think?"

He steps away, his hip hitting the desk. "What did you say? The Goddess of…"

My brows furrow. I turn to face him, his reaction throwing me. "Spring."

He takes another step back, looking at me like…he truly *does* fear me. He turns from me and storms out of the room, leaving the door wide open.

I stare after him for long moments. *What the hell was that? Not everyone likes spring, I guess. Maybe he has hayfever.*

Chapter Seven
Hades

G **ODDESS OF SPRING.** Spring is a time of renewal, of the ground coming back to life after the death of winter. *Coming back to life.* Goddess of *life*. Fuck, fuck, *fuck*. This is why I stay the fuck away from divine. Because every single goddess can be interpreted as being close enough to being a goddess of life to make me sweat. Though, no goddess has come as close to being a goddess of life as the Goddess of Spring.

Fuck. I really fucked up this time.

I make it back to my office, shutting the door, and misting the glass walls to give myself some privacy. When I designed the offices, I thought the glass walls would enable me to see the rest of the office and keep tabs on everyone. The frosted switch was a later addition, when I saw someone trying to pick a wedgie in an adjoining office without revealing it, very aware of the glass walls. I felt the collective sigh of relief at the installation. There are some things you need privacy for. And with her here… *Fuck.* I can't stop thinking of all the ways I might take advantage of the soundproof and misted glass in the near future.

I land hard into the plush desk chair, the well-oiled hinges not even protesting as I lean back in it. I grab the phone, forcing my hand not to shake, as I dial the number by memory. How many times have I made this exact call over the years? It will be the same call I always have. They'll tell me they can't say if it is or isn't her.

Doesn't stop me from still calling though.

A smoky, throaty voice answers immediately. "Your One True Destiny Services, how can I direct your call?"

"It's Hades," I snap, before she can go into the whole spiel.

"Oh." The voice pauses, the throatiness vanishing instantly. "Let me see if they're in."

The receptionist puts me on hold for a moment, and the recorded voices go into the entire list of prices for everything from phone sex to high-class escorts. I rub my forehead hearing the list. I suppose I can't really complain. They were one of the few divine individuals that were actually *employed.* I once mentioned that sex work was not *work,* and was summarily lectured for hours after. I have since come around to their way of thinking. *Even a very old god can learn new tricks.*

"Yo," the first gruff voice says, followed by the sound of two other people connecting.

I rub a hand down my face, already bracing myself for this conversation. "I need to know whether the Goddess of Spring classifies as a goddess of *life.*"

All three voices suddenly synchronize. "The King of the Dead will meet his match in the Goddess of Life. With the culmination of their union, the goddess becomes the Queen of the Dead, bound to the Underworld, even more tightly than her husband."

I roll my eyes. "Yeah, thanks, I know all that. My question?"

"Goddess of Spring is a Goddess of Life, dumbass," Atropos snaps, having broken out of the prophecy thrall with her sisters.

I blink in surprise at the actual confirmation. I expected some sort of cryptic bullshit. And it doesn't surprise me at all that Atropos is the one to deliver it; of the three Moirai, she's always been the most curt.

"Spring is a time of renewal and new beginnings, where things come to life," Clotho adds.

"Did you finally meet your match?" Lachesis asks.

I rub a hand down my head, a headache looming. Talking to the Fates was a trial for even my great amount of patience. It's impossible to get a straight answer out of them, and most of the time they only tell you enough for you to fall into their predictions.

"Persephone, Goddess of Spring. I just hired her, is she…the one?" I gulp, pulling at my collar, undoing my tie.

"Ooohhh, I like that name. *Persephone,*" Clotho trills. "Very unique."

I groan. "Is she the one?"

Atropos audibly starts filing her nails, the sound of her heels hitting the top of her desk. "Does she *feel* like the one?"

This is exactly why no one talks to the Fates anymore. It's like trying to extract a sore tooth from a feral dog. And they're avoiding my question. *Again.*

"She feels like she could be a menace," I hiss back.

Lachesis snickers. "Sounds like she's already under your skin."

"Big bad God of the Dead, completely undone by the goddess who redefines *flower power.*" Clotho giggles.

I slam my fist on the desk, squeezing the phone. "So, she *is* the one." I stop myself from breaking the fragile electronic. This is more than they've stated in any other call. It's easy to deduce what they aren't saying. "How do I stop the other part?"

"The *culmination?*" Atropos laughs, the sound of her nail file grating through the speaker.

Patience. A necessary trait when dealing with the

40

Fates.

"It doesn't mean you can't slip her the pickle, if that's what you're asking," Lachesis hums.

I blink in surprise. "It doesn't?"

I always thought culmination meant having sex with her. Was I wrong? What the fuck else could *culmination of their union mean*?

"Culmination, in this case, means, well…your…you know," Clotho creaks.

"Your sperm, baby batter, the liquid thunder of your thighs," Atropos finishes.

I blink repeatedly, making sounds with my mouth, but no words come out. I…I wasn't expecting that. Maybe this is why no one talks to the Fates anymore, because…of the things that come out of Atropos's mouth.

"So, long as you don't come inside the Goddess of Spring, you won't activate the second half of the curse," Lachesis says.

"Anyway, we got to go, you know. Busy and all," Atropos adds, hanging up.

"I…" I squeak, trying to form a sentence, a question, anything. *Liquid thunder of your thighs.* Traumatizing.

"Bye!" Clotho calls, hanging up.

"See ya!" Lachesis states.

And then I'm listening to nothing but a dial tone.

I don't know how long I sit there, holding the phone to my ear, completely stunned, before I put it back in its cradle. Just staring at it, trying to figure out what I just heard.

Chapter Eight
Persephone

I SIT BACK IN MY CHAIR, MY BROWS FUR-ROWED. The plush, white leather groans under my weight as I move. I rack my brain, trying to recall any of the information I found over the weekend on Hades, *God of the Underworld, King of the Dead.*

The search allowed me some insight, but I still felt as though my mother had done me a disservice by not educating me about the Olympians. *I feel like I barely know myself.* Every time I had gone to ask Helios about him, I changed my mind at the last moment.

I replay the moment in my head. His warmth, his smell. And then his…change in demeanor. It was as if we were enjoying a game of cat and mouse, and the second he caught me, he got spooked. But I was never running from him…I was provoking him. I wanted him even closer, and was desperate for him to turn his head and press his lips to my neck.

I wince at the memory of the fear on his face after he found out who I am. Why would that have affected him? Spring meant new beginnings and life. Nothing to be feared. And yet, the title "God of the Underworld" would invoke terror in even the fiercest of gods. So why would I frighten *him*?

I force myself to focus on work. Since I arrived on the mortal plane, work has been my solace. While living amongst the mortals hasn't been the breathtaking experience I planned, I still enjoyed it. But experiencing their daily anguishes has been challenging, and I've found that the most effective way to cope is to throw myself headfirst into work. I open up my emails, and my day becomes a blur of analytics, social media, and Photoshop.

When 5:00 p.m. rolls around, I'm more than ready to go home. The appraising gazes and snarky comments make me feel tense and on edge. Plus, no matter how much work I buried myself in, Hades still took up the forefront of my mind.

God of the Dead living there rent-free.

I turn off my laptop, stowing it in my bag, and grab my coat, hoping my coworkers will be too invested in heading home for the day to pay me any notice.

I let out a sigh of relief when I reach the elevator without a single gaze falling upon me. But my relief is short-lived when the blonde approaches me, the sneer from earlier still plastered on her face. *Maybe that's just her face.*

I inwardly groan as we both enter the small, confined space of the elevator. I reach forward and press the button for the ground floor a little too quickly.

"Hades is taken." Her shrill voice is like nails on a chalkboard.

I turn to her, my lips pulled into a bland smile. "Why would I need that information?"

Her eyes flash. I can tell she's imagining relieving my head from my body. "Everyone saw the way you were looking at him."

I lift an eyebrow at her. "Oh? Is that so?"

"Yes. He is taken," she hisses.

I turn away from her, facing forward once again. "Understood."

The rest of the short elevator ride is silent, tense. Why would she feel the need to mention this to me now?

Did I look at Hades in *that* way? Surely not. I couldn't stand him. His arrogance and lack of awareness of others. His demeanor and the fact that his ego filled the room, suffocating all life inside it.

His rippling muscles and the way his ass flexes as he walks. The scent of sandalwood and citrus sending a pang of desire straight to my—

No. Absolutely not.

The second the doors slide open, she rushes out, as if she'd been trapped in a small, enclosed space with someone infected with the plague.

"Oh, before you go…" I say, not being able to stop myself from antagonizing her.

She pauses, her shoulders tense.

"If you see Hades, tell him I look forward to seeing him tomorrow."

She glares at me. Obviously, there will never be any love lost between us.

I smirk, feeling satisfied, and hold my head a little higher.

I knock on Helios's door, guilt sitting heavy in my stomach. I can't keep staying with Helios, but I still have no money, and my pride is not letting me demand it back.

The door swings open, and Helios grins at me, his cheerful presence easing the strains of the day immediately.

"How was work, petal?"

I sigh, my lips twitching. "Everyone hates me, including my new *boss*."

He gestures me inside. "Drink?"

I brush past him and head straight for the kitchen. His apartment is so welcoming, it's easy for it to feel like home. "Please."

Helios practically glides to the bar and pours two glasses of ambrosia. He hands me one of them, and we both sit at the kitchen island. "I told you that you should have just told your mom about the money. Everyone's scared of her."

I scoff. "And give her a reason to pull me back to my mountainside prison? I don't think so."

Helios shrugs and tosses back his glass, draining the golden liquid. "But...you wouldn't be working for someone you hate."

Do I hate him?

Yes. Of course, you do.

I follow his lead and down the remnants of my drink, needing a moment to formulate a response. "This is...temporary."

He snorts. "Is it?"

"Why wouldn't it be?" I lift an eyebrow at him.

He looks into the bottom of his tumbler. "How do you plan to get out from under his thumb?"

I saunter over to the bar and grab the bottle of ambrosia. I pour myself a heavy-handed measure. "I'm only there until I make another plan." *Keep telling yourself that, P.*

Helios rolls his eyes, pouring himself a glass of scotch. "The only job you're getting that will pay for your current apartment is as an escort." He pauses. "High end."

I chuckle, slamming my drink. Since I left the mountain, consumption of alcohol is not something I've taken to. I always feel too excited to take in everything, to experience everything. Plus this world still seems too unfamiliar to me. It's always a consideration to keep my wits about me. But here in the safety of Helios's place, after an extraordinarily shitty day, I indulge. I look at my now-empty tumbler. Ambrosia, so potent, so delicious. I wink at him, smirking as his cheeks flush. "I think I'd do well as an escort."

My heads starts to swim as the alcohol begins to affect me, and I take another three shots in quick succession.

"Your mother would kill you…and then probably me."

I take a deep drink straight from the bottle before strutting over to him and grabbing his hand, my head swimming, loving the way my body moves while under the spell of the sweet wine.

"Dance with me."

He smiles and starts spinning with me, our bodies close. I let out a squeal when he dips me. I tilt my head back, giggling at the feeling of the blood rushing to my head, making the walls seem to move.

I feel him tense and glance up at him, his gaze roaming my face before settling on my lips. *Uh oh…*

"Persephone, I—"

I reach up and pinch his cheek hard. "You're so handsome, Helios. Have no gods or goddesses caught your eye yet?"

He tries to hide a wince, but even in my liquor-addled haze, I catch it. His cheeks redden as he stands us up once more. "You should go to bed."

I nod and kiss him on the cheek. "Goodnight, Helios. Thanks again for letting me stay here."

He smiles fondly at me before helping me to the guest room. I quickly settle into bed, not enjoying the feeling of the room spinning. Thoughts of Hades consume me, hoping I don't see him tomorrow. There is nothing I want more in the world than to not see him for the rest of my immortal life.

Lie.

Chapter Nine

Hades

I AVOID PERSEPHONE FOR THE ENTIRE WEEK, *deliberately* avoiding her, keeping my office walls misted so I'm not tempted to look at her or see her walking down the halls. I have my lunch delivered to my office and keep my hours in the extreme. Anything to avoid seeing her. If only I could find a way to make the glass walls of my office scent-proof in addition to soundproof. Only a whisper of roses, and my body is racked with need. I need to get an air purifier for my office. Or demand that she stop wearing that hauntingly beautiful perfume. Doesn't she know how much damage she does to a person's self-control?

Finally, I can get some work done on the weekend, alone in my office. I frown down at the numbers on my desk. I haven't left the building at all this weekend, poring over spreadsheets and memos, hoping to get my mind off of my new hire. Not to mention what the Fates said. *So long as I avoid culmination, I can fuck her?*

Okay, why am I even considering that? She's my employee. I can't have sex with her. Not to mention she's a goddess. Oh, and also, I'm cursed. Yet, my nose is still remembering her bouquet, and the way her nipples seemed about to cut through her shirt earlier. Or the way her eyes hooded, the vibrant color darkening. The golden sunburst around her pupils vanishing as they expanded.

I need to fire her.

I pull my gaze from my desk, my eyes going unerringly to her office, the glass walls that divide each area doing little to dissuade my eyes. I'm on my feet before I realize that I'm moving, walking the short distance to her office. In the doorframe, I pause. *What the fuck am I doing?*

But rational thought is checked out, as I'm overwhelmed by her scent. Why is her perfume so fucking addicting to me? I've started keeping fresh roses around my penthouse like the absolute pathetic man I am.

My eyes catch on the cardigan she's thoughtfully left on the back of her chair, in case it gets chilly in the office. A soft, pale pink. In my mind, I can see her shivering from the chill of the room, sliding her arms into the fabric. The soft material gliding across her skin, able to touch her when I can't. Stepping forward, my finger trails along the soft fabric, which forces a plume of her enchanting aroma to fill the room. Fisting the material, I pull it off the chair, lifting it to my nose, groaning. *Roses can't even compare.*

Her fragrance makes me lose reason. *Fuck.* My cock strains for release, and I'm unable to deny it. My free hand drops to my belt, undoing it, my zipper following. I take a deep inhale of her cardigan, fisting myself at the same time. My eyes slide closed, supplying the fantasy that keeps me constantly rushing for a frigid shower. Which keeps me in my office with frosted glass, avoiding the Goddess of Spring.

We're in my office, the glass misted, and she's wearing those deadly heels and nothing else. She's sitting on my lap, bouncing on my cock, begging for more. Her breasts are flushed and heaving, with each thrust. She's facing away from me, on display, while only my cock is revealed and buried in her cunt.

49

"Please, more," she begs.

I fist her hair, yanking it. "I should make them all watch me fuck you, see that I own this body, that you're my little plaything."

She whimpers, her slick release staining my slacks. I couldn't care less at that moment. I reach for the button to clear the glass, allowing everyone to see her—

I let out a choked yell as I start to come. Without thought, I use her cardigan to catch it. My roar is cut off, as I come onto the little piece of clothing. The very piece of clothing that gets to touch her skin, while I can't.

It takes a long moment before my mind finally clears, and I realize what I've done.

I did not just come all over my employee's cardigan, in her office, imagining that I was fucking her for all to see.

This is the kind of thing that harassment attorneys dream of. Fuck, fuck fuck.

I panic and toss the cardigan into her trash bin, before pulling it out and taking it to my office. Leaving it in her office? Could I be more of a dumbass? Is this how Bill Clinton felt? Yet, instead of a blue dress, I'm cradling a soft pink, cashmere cardigan. I am not about to be drawn before a Senate hearing to analyze just how much I've violated some law. Gripping it tightly, I bolt to the elevator, pacing for the small amount of time it takes for the elevator to arrive, and the even shorter amount of time it takes to rise one floor.

I rush to the sink, using some dish soap on the stain, scrubbing it vigorously in my kitchen sink. *Come on, Come on.*

The material suddenly turns to nothing but a handful of soft yarn in my hands. *Fuck!*

She'll notice if there is suddenly a giant rubbed hole in her cardigan. Not to mention, every part the soap touched continues dissolving in my hands. I toss the cardigan in the trash, but my stomach twists, and my mind ignites on the idea. I pull it out of the trash, frantically looking for the label of the designer. Once I find it, I have a new, identical one on its way to my office. It took a lot of money and more than one name drop to get it on a Saturday, but, by the time the sun begins to set, a brand new cardigan is sitting on her desk chair, waiting for her on Monday.

Chapter Ten
Persephone

SEVEN DAYS. It has been seven days since I last saw Hades. Every morning when I arrive, the glass in his office is already misted for his privacy. Every lunchtime, he gets food delivered. And every evening, when I'm heading home, his office is the same as when I arrived.

The weekend came and went, and I spent most of it avoiding my gracious host. *And thinking about Hades.*

Jackson facetimed me on Saturday evening, and I was hit by another wave of guilt when he asked me why he had barely heard from me this week. The excuse I gave him about being busy at my new job and wanting to make a good first impression wasn't a strong one, but was accepted by him. For all we've been dating for six months, there's always been something…missing. *Really, P? Blaming Jackson for your nightly fantasies about your hot-as-fuck boss's head between your legs?*

And they *had* been nightly. Every evening, when I climbed into bed, my thoughts immediately drifted to Hades, and my fingers found their way to the slick skin between my thighs.

As I walked into the office, my stomach knotted. Surely he couldn't avoid me for another week. Stuck in the paradox between not wanting to see him and being desperate to see him.

"Persephone."

I halt in my tracks, halfway to my office. I turn to face the blonde who was quickly achieving enemy status. "Minthe."

"You've been moved to another office."

I lift an eyebrow. Was this another ploy by Hades to avoid me? "I have? Why?"

Minthe smirks. "Boss's orders. You're in the basement with IT now."

I roll my eyes at the pettiness and continue walking to my office to pack my things up. The only items I have to collect are my revitalized potted plant and my cardigan.

I walk to my chair and pick up the cardigan. When my fingers brush the soft material, my brows knit. Does it feel softer? Newer? I pick it up and look at the tag. I tilt my head when I notice the price tag. I definitely already removed that. The cardigan has been worn and cleaned many times. I look around, through the glass walls of my office, my gaze snagging on Hades's fogged windows.

No one is paying any attention to me. *A nice change.*

I fold it over my forearm and grab my plant before making my way down to the basement.

The second the elevator opens, I'm once again the subject of everyone's perusal. *Fuck, I only just became old news upstairs, and now, once again, I'm fresh meat.*

"Um…are you lost?" A whimsical, slightly accented voice pulls me from my thoughts.

When I look up, my gaze it met by an unusual set of eyes. One iris like onyx, the other steel. It takes me a moment before my gaze starts to wander, taking in the rest of this unusual woman. Her features are large, and yet, they fit her face perfectly. Above each eye is a perfectly sculpted brow, one dark, one light to match her eyes. I notice she has continued the theme with her hair, styled with the perfect middle part, separating the starkest of

53

black and the brightest of white, tied into high space buns. She looks to be in her late twenties, and she holds her tall, slim build awkwardly. She wears a spiked choker around her neck, and her outfit looks to have been taken directly from an early '90s copy of *Rolling Stone*.

I smile at her, her kind face making me feel at ease immediately. "I'm Persephone, Social Media Manager. I was told my new office is down here?"

She blinks repeatedly behind her large spectacles. "Oh…uh, okay. I'm Melinoë. People call me Mellie."

I immediately like her, Maybe I am going to make a friend—

A chill runs down my spine, and I regard Mellie again. When I'm in the same room as another divine being, I can feel their presence. It's not always easy to pinpoint who it's coming from, but there is a distinct awareness. Standing beside Mellie, I feel something, not the same as being with a goddess, but…she's not mortal.

"So…um…you're from Olympus, right?" Mellie asks, as she starts guiding me to my office.

I tense slightly, not used to people asking me questions about my divinity, but I suppose my sense was right. What is she? "Uh…yes."

Mellie leans in, lowering her voice. "I'm from… um…the other place." She flushes and smiles awkwardly. "Anyway, this is your office. I'm down the hall in the pit if you need anything."

I nod absently, my mind elsewhere. *The other place?* I close my door and sit at my new desk. It's evident the time and money that was spent on decorating the upper floors was not afforded down here. The space is comfortable enough, but more similar to a regular office than the plush environment I was in last week. One pro. The rooms has four walls and barely any windows.

My mind wanders to Mellie again. Where is the other place? What was that sense I got from her? Was Hades forcing her to work for him too?

I consider the feeling I got from Mellie. It wasn't unpleasant. Not as stifling as being near a divine, but it was...different. It felt like a blanket was wrapping around me, a beckoning, dark cocoon. Such a familiar feeling and yet...I can't place where I've ever felt it before.

The noise increases from outside as people leave their cubicles to make lunch plans. I hear a soft knock at my door.

"Come in!" I barely look up from my laptop.

"Um...do you want to join me for lunch? Or not, you don't have to..."

I glance up at her, finally pulling myself away from my work. "I...I can't. Thank you for the offer though."

She visibly flinches and her face drops. "Oh...okay." Her shoulders slump dejectedly, and she scurries off.

There's that guilt again.

I pull my cardigan on and quickly immerse myself in work, barely noticing when my coworkers noisily return from lunch.

My head snaps up when the building trembles. I grab the desk, my knuckles turning white. I try to remember earthquake protocols. Fuck, do I know any?

New York doesn't have earthquakes. It's one of the reasons I chose this city.

The building continues to tremble under the force. A loud rumble of thunder echoes outside. I grip my desk for dear life, waiting for it to pass. When the building finally stills, I stand from my desk on shaky legs and walk to the door. I open the door, expecting to see the office in a panic, expecting people running, crying, screaming and yet...when I peer outside, everyone is going about their business. As if the building didn't just shake violently. As if I...imagined it.

I look around for Mellie, hoping she has an explanation for me, but she's nowhere to be found. Maybe she's up on the 48th floor. I walk to the elevator, trying to justify my decision to go up there. I press the button repeatedly, impatient. I need to get up there to check on everyone.

Lie.

I have friends there, and they might be scared or injured.

Lie.

I am *not* going to see Hades. I do not *want* to see Hades.

Lie.

I'm not going because I need to lay eyes on him today.

Lie. Lie. Lie.

The elevator is, thankfully, still working, although even this forces me to pause. Was I the only one who felt it?

I pull on my fingers the whole way up, nerves knotting in my stomach. Taking an elevator post-earthquake is probably not the *smartest* plan in the world. That's why I'm so on edge.

Lie.

I catch myself fixing my hair and checking my makeup in the mirror. Giving myself a mental slap, I look away, frustrated with myself.

The second I reach the floor, Minthe's eyes snap to me, her lip curling. "What are you doing up here?" she hisses.

I glance behind her to Hades's office, hearing a commotion behind his fogged windows. Once again, no one seems fazed by the earthquake or the argument currently going on in the boss's office. Disappointment sits heavy in my stomach that I can't see him.

"The earthquake…" My eyes trail back to Minthe's scowling face.

She flushes slightly. "Go back to your floor, *Perse-phone.*"

Chapter Eleven
Hades

I DON'T KNOW WHAT I EXPECTED WHEN I WAS CALLED AGAIN TO MEDIATE MY BROTHERS. Zeus glares at Poseidon, both sitting in front of my desk, the two chairs both seeming to barely contain them.

Zeus is filling the entire chair, his six foot eight frame practically making the *extremely* expensive armchair groan. I suppose it was a form of divine retribution that not only was Zeus the youngest, but also the tallest of us. The silver white hair and beard were his choice; I know for a fact that he picked the color because he thinks he looks more *distinguished.* As if being taller than most gods, and firmly packed with muscle, really is negated by *white hair.* His eyes are the same as mine though, as are Poseidon's, a deep, sapphire blue. Though Zeus's are currently flashing with barely contained lightning, while Poseidon's appear as turbulent waves slamming on shore.

Poseidon's hair is a dirty blond, matted curls, several of them ending with golden beads, moving with each of his angry inhales. It's easy to see the similarities in the three of us, the similar face structures, even the crackling arrogance that marks us as siblings. A relation I'm sorely wishing didn't exist at the moment, as I'm being dragged into another of their little debates. As if I don't have other things to do. As if there isn't less than three months left before I head downstairs and so much work to be done before then.

I sigh at them both, even as they both stand, continuing their argument, not even looking at me as I follow behind them. The ever dutiful. The unseen.

Zeus storms into my office an hour ago, sparks coming from the bottoms of his shoes. Every step leaving a singe on my floor. I barely stop myself from sighing in annoyance. Did they have to have all their squabbles in my office? I can't keep up with the constant maintenance. Between the sparks Zeus throws off naturally, forcing the electricity and cellular to go haywire in his presence, and Poseidon making the bathrooms suddenly flood and causing earthquakes in the building, it's a full-time job just to keep up with them. Another job, on top of the other ones I already have. *Ruler of the Dead. CEO of a Fortune 500 Company. Glorified tour guide. Borderline pervert when it comes to a single goddess.*

Fuck, I'm definitely trying not to think about her when my brothers are present. They have the uncanny ability of picking up on me even being remotely interested in *anyone.* They claim it's my lot, as the only unmarried brother. I say they're just a pair of assholes who love to meddle.

"You are being irrational, Brother," Zeus snaps at Poseidon.

"ME?!" Poseidon scoffs.

I rub a hand down my face, exhausted already from this small interaction. "Just go home, you two. I'll take care of it."

Like I always take care of everything.

Hades, God of Cleaning Up Other Gods Messes.

Zeus and Poseidon storm to the elevator, continuing their bickering, almost plowing through Persephone.

Her eyes follow them until the doors close, before trailing to me. Seeing her for the first time in over a week is like drinking water after days of thirst. She's dressed in a midnight black pencil skirt, and a deep purple button-up, emphasizing her curves. *Fuck*. As always, the sight of her red lips has me hardening.

I force my feet to shift, concealing my reaction. It's bad enough that I shamefully violated her cardigan, and even more shamefully, still have the pieces of it in my penthouse, unable to throw it out. But to let her *know* what she does to me? Unacceptable.

I glance at the clock, raising a brow. "Finally decided to show up to work?"

She lifts a dark brow at me, glancing at Minthe. "I was informed this morning that I was moved to the basement. I have been working there all day."

The basement? Why in the world would I send her there? The basement is for most of IT, keeping the servers cool and stopping them from overheating. A sea of men who barely know how to speak around women. Well, and Mellie, I suppose. I worried, initially, about placing Mellie down there, but I shouldn't have. Apparently, she mentioned someone's nightmares *once*, and the rest of them knew to be wary of her. Persephone didn't look worse for wear at all.

I flush and try to school my features when I see her wearing the replacement cardigan I put in her office. She must not have noticed that the original was…*misplaced.*

"You're supposed to be up here, so I can keep an eye on you. Make sure you're not pulling a *goddess*." Cashing a paycheck without doing any of the work. Though, in the week she's been working here, I've heard nothing but compliments on her work ethic.

She walks closer to me, smirking, her scent whirling around me, trapping me like a vice. I almost go to my toes in reaction, my body trying to close the distance between us. *Fuck this hold she has over me.*

"Then maybe make sure you're not getting your wires crossed with your assistant."

I glance at Minthe, noticing her long red nails are curled into the desk, her smile brittle and forced. "I'm sure she meant well."

Minthe nods, smiling at me brightly. There must have been a mix-up. Minthe was a dedicated assistant. She wouldn't deliberately sabotage anyone.

I glance back to Persephone, gesturing to the office she usually uses.

She rolls her vibrant eyes at me. "I'll need to retrieve my laptop." Her smile turns saccharine. "Maybe your assistant would be so kind as to assist me?"

I gesture for Minthe to follow, turning on my heel and returning to my office. My shoulders slump with exhaustion as another earthquake rocks the building and the echo of thunder follows.

A middle sibling's job is never done is it?

Chapter Twelve
Persephone

BEING EATEN BY A CYCLOPS, DROWNING IN THE RIVER ACHERON, LISTENING TO A MAN EXPLAINING NFTS. All things I would rather endure than spending any time alone with Minthe. As we walk to the elevator, I can feel the hatred seeping from her. She walks on teetering heels, barely stumbling as a second earthquake rocks the building. My own steps, not nearly as confident as the foundation shakes.

The journey to my office is tense. I know I didn't *need* her assistance with this, but there is something so satisfying about Hades demanding that she help me, at my request.

I want him to order me around. Would he punish me if I didn't submit?

My cheeks heat at the thought, and I hastily push that thought to the back of my mind.

Minthe storms ahead of me the second the elevator doors open, and almost in the blink of an eye, she's entering my office. I sigh, following her. No sooner have I entered the room than she rams my laptop into my arms. I point at a box of files that someone brought to me earlier. "Just those boxes and my plant, and I think that's everything."

She shoots me a glare before picking up the box,

grunting at the weight.

"You're leaving?"

I turn to see Mellie standing in my doorway, her expressive eyes wide.

"Move, dweller," Minthe hisses, her narrowed eyes fixed on Mellie.

Mellie seems to flinch at the name, then lowers her eyes in submission.

I don't think so.

I step closer to Mellie. "Would you like to hang out with me this Friday?"

Her wide eyes snap to mine. "M-me?"

I smile warmly and nod. I can practically feel Minthe's eye roll before she barges past Mellie and stomps to the elevator.

"A-are you sure?" Mellie's cheeks flush. "I'm sure Minthe would be more fun."

Being eaten by a cyclops, drowning in the river Acheron, listening to a man explaining NFTs.

I grab a stray business card that fell from the box, thanks to Minthe's careless handling, and hand it to Mellie. "Text me."

"Oh, uh, okay," she stutters.

I smile at her again and head to meet my "helper." She's rapidly pressing the elevator button, as if the number of presses directly corresponds to the speed it reaches you. It's clear that the basement is a deplorable environment to her. I can't help but enjoy every moment of her discomfort as the elevator slowly descends, floor by floor, making multiple stops on the way down, prolonging the torture, as we stand side by side, waiting for it to arrive, not speaking.

Her tapping heel on the thin carpet is the only sound in the whole office. Obviously, her presence here is not a welcome one. Not even the near-constant sounds of typing can be heard, almost as if the whole office is holding their breaths, in stasis until she leaves.

The second the doors open, Minthe hurries into the small chamber. I feel her glare turn to me as the door starts to close. "You shouldn't talk to her."

I snort. "Thanks for the advice."

"I mean, don't you know what she is?"

I move to the back of the elevator, ignoring her. I lift a hand up in front of my face, grimacing slightly at my desperately-in-need-of-a-manicure nails. *The second I get my money back...*

I push off the wall when we reach our floor, heading for my office. I don't even check where Minthe goes with my box of documents. I don't care. I just need to be alone in my space again. I'm vaguely aware of her hissing at me as I walk away from her.

I place my plant back in its corner. It appears to sigh in relief as it basks in the sunshine that my windowed office provides. My lips twitch as I wonder who dislikes the basement more, my plant or Minthe. I sit at my desk. As much as I hate to admit it, I missed my desk chair. I slide my hands over the arms, smiling at the satisfying sound of my skin against the quality white leather, the buttery feeling of it caressing my fingers.

Opening my laptop, I dive back into work, trying to not let my mind wander to Hades. Distraction works... for a while, until the image of him gazing upon me for the first time in a week flashes into my mind. The briefest of flickers in his gaze before he corrected his face into his usual, arrogant, bored, indifference.

Not letting your mind wander to Hades, hm?

While he avoided me, it was easier to pretend that he isn't as...perfect as he is, that my memories of him were false. It was easier to imagine him with a red face and bright green hair, teeth missing. But then I saw him today. All six and half feet of his perfectly muscular build. And once again, my traitorous brain reminds me of our first encounter where that six-and-a-half-foot, muscular body was shirtless and sweaty. How many times I've revisited that particular image, the fantasy always ending the same…him pinning me against something and thrusting inside of me…

I squeeze my thighs together at the thought, bringing my pen to my mouth and gently biting on it, unconsciously submitting to my thoughts.

That shirtless sweaty body over me, his weight covering me, his sandalwood and citrus scent surrounding me, his c—

Absolutely not, P.

I clear my throat, my legs still clenched beneath my desk, my clit aching. Needing friction. I shake my head and look back at my laptop

Back to work.

After another hour or so of staring at my computer, I vaguely hear a knock at the door.

"You spoke with Mellie?"

The ache between my thighs increases and a curl of heat sits low in my stomach, twisting deliciously. I glance up, desperately hoping my torment is not evident on my face…

Oh look, it's the six-and-a-half-foot, muscular frame you were grinding against your chair thinking about earlier. Nice one, P.

I feel my cheeks heat slightly as I take in every inch of his perfect build. The way his tailored suit hugs every muscle, the way he casually stands with his sinful hands in his pockets, the way he leans against the doorframe. Such dominance, such power. *Delicious.*

I force my eyes back to my computer. "I did."

I feel his scorching gaze on me. Why do I always feel like I can't breathe when he looks at me?

"Thank you."

My brows furrow and my eyes snap to his. "For?"

"She's having trouble…adjusting."

I tilt my head. "To?"

He clears his throat. *He's feeling…vulnerable?* "She's only been topside for a couple of months."

I lift my chin. "Topside?"

He seems to consider me, seeming to search my face for an answer to a question he's not asked. "She was born in the Underworld."

My eyes go wide. "How?"

"The Underworld is a living thing. Even I don't know the extent of what lives there." He frowns. I get the impression this makes him uneasy, that he needs control.

I swallow at the thought, thinking about him controlling my pleasure—

I blink at him, pushing that thought from my mind. "Oh…"

Silence.

"I-I invited her out this Friday."

He slides one of his hands from his pocket and presses it against the doorframe. My mouth goes dry at how even that small movement makes his muscles shift. My gaze locks on those large hands, and I try to push away thoughts about how they would feel exploring my body.

"I'm sure she would like that."

I blush and pull my gaze away from him. *Stop being horny for your boss, P.*

"I-I appreciate that."

Did he stumble with his words?

I look back up at him. "I like her."

His lips pull into a soft smile, a tender smile. He cares about her. "So do I. She's…not had it easy."

My stomach lurches. *Am I…jealous? No. Surely not.* Such tenderness, a side I've never seen of him. Although, I don't imagine he lets many people see any of his sides apart from "arrogant boss." I nod, not trusting my words or tone.

He clears his throat again. "You don't have to work overtime. Most people go home at 5:00."

I force my face into a smile. "I'm good. I have things to finish up."

He nods once, frowning before pushing off the doorway and going back to his office. I immediately miss his intoxicating presence. *Uh oh. Let's repress the shit out of that thought.*

It strikes me then. The feeling when I'm in the room with Hades is similar to how it feels with Mellie. Not quite the same, but it's definitely there. Maybe because they are both tied to the Underworld? While, with Mellie, it's just a comfortable awareness. With Hades, it's an overwhelming…rightness?

Around an hour later, I finish up with my task. I pack up my things and head to the elevator.

Hades's office is unmisted for the first time in over a week. I feel that undeniable pull to go to him, to be around him. My feet move on their own accord, and before I know it, I'm knocking on the glass of his office.

He glances up at me, and I once again feel the ever-present weight of *him* when our eyes meet. His tie is loosened, the top two buttons of his shirt undone, allowing a peek of that perfect chest. His hair is tousled, like he's run his fingers through it many times today. *Should have been my fingers.*

I open the door slightly. "I'm heading home."

He nods. "Goodnight."

I hesitate. *Leave, P. What is wrong with you?*

Hades notices my hesitation and tilts his head at me, obvious intrigue on his face. "Yes?"

I pull my bottom lip between my teeth, trying to work out why I'm reluctant to leave.

Lie. You know why you don't want to leave.

"Night." I turn and leave, every step feeling like walking through tar. My aching body screaming to return to him. To slam my lips to his and—

NO, P.

I barely register my commute home, lost in a blur of fantasies, imagining the alternative endings of our farewell. Mindlessly dreaming of how tonight could have been better…*different. Not better.*

So distracted on my way home, I go to my apartment instead of Helios's. Remembering the second I open the door and my awareness of my lack of funds crashes down on me again. I pray for sleep to take me as I crawl into bed. My stomach growls angrily after missing lunch and dinner.

I lay in my bed, restless, but it's not the hunger keeping me awake. It's the unrelenting thoughts of my boss. I realize it's futile to think of Hades like this. He's not interested. There is no way. Why would the God of the Underworld care about the Goddess of Spring? One dark, one light. His power, terrifying, consuming, alluring. My power, pretty, lovely and…benign.

I open my palm, a daisy blooming right in the center, so unconcerning. Why would someone like him ever be interested in someone like me? I consider the flower, frowning down at the perfectly formed petals. And more than that, why would someone as powerful as him be… intimidated by me?

The guilt once again intrudes upon my thoughts when I remember Jackson. Kind and honest Jackson, who also knows there's something not right with our relationship. We enjoy each other's company, but that can also be said for Helios and I. And the sex…infrequent and satisfactory. It's never been *mind-blowing*, but it's good, I guess.

I sit up in bed, a thought striking me. I haven't had sex in a while. These thoughts about Hades are just channeled sexual frustration!

Lie.

I just need sex, and I'll stop thinking about Hades.

Lie.

I don't even want Hades.

Lie lie lie.

I lay on my back, looking up at the ceiling, basking in my lies, trying to find comfort in them. I finally fall asleep, thinking about Jackson and the blissful future we'll have together.

Lie.

Chapter Thirteen
Hades

THE NEXT MORNING, I LIFT MY HEAD UP FROM MY DESK, licking my lips, trying to get rid of the dry mouth. I rub my face, pulling off the report that is stuck to the side of it. I lick my lips trying to clear out the strange taste. I'm a wreck. Standing, I run a hand through my hair, trying to shake off the lingering sleepiness, before leaving my office, heading for my own floor.

"Morning," a familiar throaty voice calls. *Persephone.*

Chaos save me, does she have a never-ending closet full of clothes to torture me with? Today it's a wrap dress that cuts tight under her breasts, leaving a daring glimpse of cleavage. Her hair is down for the first time, and my eyelids lower, imagining the fiery dark mass wrapped around my fist. Would the red interlaced in the brown sparkle when it was spread across my pillow? Or when it was stuck to her back from the sweat of our bodies, after I brought her to the edge repeatedly, before pushing her over?

Even her lips are that same bright shade of red. Since the first moment I saw her, I thought it was the color of battle. A wordless call to arms. How right I was. Each day I see that color, I know that it's a taunt by fate. Telling me what I'll never have. That I'll never feel that red staining my skin, my lips, and my cock. She's breath-taking, even this early in the morning.

And I'm in the same clothes from the day before, looking rumpled and in disarray. Yet she looks like she just stepped out of my nightly fantasies.

"Morning," I grumble back, heading for the stairs to my floor, rather than walking through the entire floor to the elevator. If Persephone's here, there's a good chance it's later in the morning than I prefer. I've already have a reputation for being a complete taskmaster and worka-holic. I don't need to prove it right.

Even though it was.

"You look rough. Long night?" she remarks.

Even though her voice is factual, it's laced with a huskiness that always makes me respond. I can imag-ine that voice whispering to me, begging me to pleasure her, to fuck her. Even after last night, when I thought I'd reached the depth of exhaustion that I simply didn't have it in me to respond to her, my body proves me wrong. What had she asked me? Oh, right. About my long night.

It's always a long night. There's no end. Each day is the same as the next. If I'm not in this office, I'm in the Underworld, weighing the souls placed in front of me. Souls whose lives were too close to neutral, not defined as good or bad, are brought to me to judge during the six months of the year I'm bound to the Underworld. And the other six months of the year, I'm on the mortal plane. By the time I'm completely at ease on either plane, I'm forced to prepare for the move.

In my absence, the souls are judged by the three for-mer kings who established the laws of the Underworld, which I enforce. Minos, Rhadamanthus and Aecus, all fulfill their jobs admirably, but they often bicker over each soul, taking longer than they should for each one. By the time I'm back in the Underworld, there is always a backlog of souls they didn't get to in time. I've tried to work remotely while in the Underworld, with the advancements in mortal technology allowing me to duplicate it downstairs, but I'm not physically able to work both jobs at the same time. I can't be King of the Underworld and give enough time to my business on the surface. I had to learn to balance them. It takes a while for the company to adjust to my yearly absence. During which they believe I live in Greece, and become *unreachable.* When I come back to the surface, there's a backlog of things that need my immediate attention. It's months before I'm caught up.

Then it's back to the Underworld.

Not to mention, both jobs are interrupted constantly by my calls to mediate my brothers. Even worse when either of them is fighting with their respective wives and end up staying with me. I'm constantly caught in the middle of something.

"Fell asleep in my office again," I grunt.

Her gaze roams over me, likely taking in my disheveled appearance with a critical eye. She nods before continuing past me into her own office. Her hair ruffles as she passes by me, and I clear my throat to stop myself from groaning at it. Is it as silky as it looks? How would it feel sliding along my skin as she dragged it down me, her mouth on its way south.

Okay, should probably stop that train of thought until I'm alone in my shower. I head to my flat on the floor above the office, taking a long shower, clearing the cobwebs from my mind, and taking care of the lust boiling in my loins.

Hades, God of HR Complaints.

I'm a nightmare for human resources at this point, since I'm fantasizing about the ways to fuck one of my employees in my shower. Not to mention that *incident* with the same employee's cardigan. Fuck, I can't even imagine how I could ever spin that. How would I make that sound not stalkerish?

I shake my head clear of those thoughts, forcing myself out of the shower and into a clean suit, looking far more put together than I feel at the moment.

I smell Persephone before I see her in her office, unable to stop myself from glancing at her as I pass. My gaze goes to her unerringly, like a magnet searching from my mate. Was I always looking for her? Not just today or since I met her, but always? Have I always been searching? Looking? Aching for *something*? Something always out of reach?

Aching for my fated queen.

Chapter Fourteen

Persephone

I'M PULLED FROM MY WORK BY A SOFT KNOCK AT MY DOOR. I smile brightly when I see Mellie through the glass. She pushes open the door with her hip, balancing two trays full of food.

"Um, hi. I got extra food."

It smells exquisite, and my stomach rumbles loudly, having not eaten since yesterday morning. I close my laptop and gesture for her to take a seat in the chair facing me.

"Mellie! Come on in!"

She smiles softly and holds a tray out for me. "Hope you're hungry!"

I nod, accepting the tray, and eye her suspiciously. "You don't have to buy me lunch, though."

She blushes. "Oh, I just thought…it would be nice…I can leave though." She starts to stand.

I stand from my desk. "Mellie, please stay. I'd love to have lunch with you. My finances are…just a bit tight at the moment."

Her face relaxes before pulling into a frown. She sits down again. "Tight? I thought you were with Plutus Bank?"

My brows furrow. "What do you mean?"

"I mean, doesn't Hades do your finances?"

My fists clench slightly. It's so easy to dislike him

when I'm reminded about my current poverty. *Until he's in sight and you melt.* "We're still…working out money at the moment…"

Her eyes flash, and she practically throws her tray down on my desk. She stands suddenly and stomps to my office door, her space buns twitching with her erratic movements. "Hades! Come here!"

I lift my eyebrows, trying to ignore the warm curl of heat igniting in my belly in anticipation of seeing him. Will he still look deliciously sleep rumpled like he had this morning? He *definitely* caught me looking…

A moment later, Hades strolls into my office. His scowl immediately softens when he looks at Mellie. "Hello, sweetheart."

Wait…what?

Sweetheart?

Mellie crosses her arms over her chest, her face twisted in anger, her eyes flashing. "Don't sweetheart me. Why are Persephone's finances *'tight at the moment'?*"

He mirrors her, also crossing his arms, his suit jacket seeming to struggle under the strain of his thick biceps. A conflict rages within me. Desire and jealousy waging war within me. The battlefield: my heart.

"That's not your concern." His tone is unrelenting, but gentler than most are afforded.

"It is when she's not eating." Her voice is practically a growl, her stare hard, refusing to back down.

The desire to be swallowed up by the ground is made worse when Hades's gaze finally meets mine.

"You're not eating?" An array of emotions flash over his face before settling on his usual scowl.

I tilt my head and give him a sweet smile. "Buying food is pretty tricky when one has no money."

He scoffs, and a wave of fury cascades through me. My ears burn with anger.

"You have money. You got your wages from your

old job back."

I pull my phone from my desk drawer. As if using muscle memory, I open and sign into my online banking app. I don't even look at the balance, wanting to avoid the nausea that always follows. I walk over to him and hold my phone up. "I did not."

He frowns. His large hand covers mine as he looks at my phone. My skin tingles at even that small touch.

"Hm." He keeps his hand over mine, his fingers still. "Fixed."

I lift an eyebrow and turn my phone, pulling my hand away from his touch. I'm surprised and relieved to see that I now have a balance again.

How did he do that?

I immediately mourn the feel of his warm hand around my cooler one. I take a step back from him, needing to either be farther away from him, or a lot closer and…more naked, hating this in between.

"Perfect."

"My apologies. Your original funds should have been returned to you."

I blink, looking away from him. His heavy gaze too much in this small room.

"I'll leave you two to your lunch."

Mellie immediately starts pushing him out, closing the door behind him. My lips twitch as the usually timid girl bosses around the great and powerful Hades. *Are they together?*

"Men!" she exclaims. "Even worse, gods!"

My stomach twists, dreading the answer, but I need to know. "Are you and Hades…?"

She blinks, and I prepare for her answer, knowing it's going to feel like I've been kicked in the chest.

"WHAT?!?!" She makes an exaggerated retching noise. "He's, like, my dad!"

Oh? Oh! That makes sense. You're a crazy, stalker psy-

cho, P.

My eyes widen. "Oh! I'm sorry!"

Mellie snorts and spears a piece of chicken with her fork. "He found me wandering around Tartarus a couple of months ago. He took me in and brought me topside."

I look down at my salad, trying to hide my smile. The knowledge that Hades has this side to him makes me feel warm, content, intrigued. "Are you happy up here?"

Mellie pauses, her fork hovering halfway to her mouth, and she bursts out laughing. "You've never been have you?"

I chuckle. "I've never been anywhere."

She snorts. "I mean downstairs."

I lift an eyebrow. "To the basement or the Underworld?"

Mellie snorts and eats another piece of chicken. "Yeah, happier is an understatement. Aren't you happier here? I don't imagine Olympus being all that wonderful."

"I am." Even two years on, I still can't pinpoint exactly *why* I'm happier here. Yes, I have screeds more freedom, but it's far from paradise, and the trials and tribulations of mortal life don't occur on Olympus. Or maybe they do…I was always so sheltered, how would I know?

Mellie smiles. "Good, I'll kick Hades's ass if you need me to. I'm the only person besides Hekate he seems to listen to."

My lips twitch. "I can handle him. I think he's scared of me."

"Oh?"

I lean in, lowering my voice. "He completely freaked out at me the other day." It strikes me that I maybe shouldn't be divulging this to Mellie, but it's been eating at me, and she's the only person I know that might be able to provide some insight into his bizarre reaction to me.

"Hades? Spill the tea, sis."

I sigh. "I made a comment about the God of the Underworld being afraid of the Goddess of Spring, and he…ran away from me."

She bursts out laughing, and I don't know why I'm surprised by her reactions. She never does what I expect. The more I get to know Mellie, the more unhinged she seems, and the more I like her.

"That's probably because of the curse." She continues to eat, as if she'd just told me nothing of consequence.

My brows furrow. "Curse?"

"You know." She speaks around a mouthful of lettuce. "That his fated queen will be a goddess of life and renewal."

I blink.

Mellie sighs, exasperated that I'm not grasping her meaning. "AKA Spring. Goddess of Spring. And what is spring if not 'life and renewal'??" She shrugs and continues to eat.

I laugh nervously, trying to shrug off this revelation. Can't think about this now. Not now.

Time to minimize and repress.

"You're way off. He hates me." I hesitate. "Anyway, are you coming on Friday?"

She shrugs again. "What do I know? I'm just the Goddess of Nightmares."

Did that ease me at all? Mellie has to be mistaken… there is undeniably a pull on my end, but he *hates* me. There is no way…no way.

"Are you sure you still want me to?" she asks, hesitantly.

I'm grateful to be pulled from my thoughts, unease clear on her face, and my heart aches for her.

I nod. "My friends will love you, and Jackson will be there!"

She blinks. "Jackson?"

"The guy I'm seeing."

She chokes on her chicken. "You have a boyfriend?"

I lift an eyebrow at her. "No. We're just casually dating. I'm going to try to not be offended by your shock that someone would actually want to be in a relationship with me."

"No, I mean…wait, where was he when you were struggling with money?"

"I didn't tell him. He was away on business. And we're not official or anything." I stab a slice of cucumber, looking away from her.

"Oh, hm…" She frowns. "Is that…uh, normal?"

I shrug. "It is what it is." I silently beg for her to change the subject, desperate to avoid having to explain to her why I won't fully commit to Jackson. I can't bear to see that look of bewilderment that always follows when I utter the words, *Something just…isn't right."*

"Who else is going with us Friday?"

I sigh heavily, thanking every deity I can think of for this small allowance.

I smile at her, sensing her unease. "Some friends of mine, mostly mortal. One god."

She swallows nervously. "Another god?"

"Yes, Helios."

She shrinks into the chair. "Maybe I shouldn't go… he's a mountainer."

I sit forward. "Please come? He's the most down-to-earth god I know. I mean…not that I know many…"

Mellie flushes. "I'll try." She stands, throwing the rest of her food in the trash can.

"What's wrong?"

"Nothing, just nervous. Better get back to the pit."

I nod. "Mellie?"

When she turns to face me, the dark hair from one of her buns starts to come loose, the white hair in her other bun, still perfect. "Hm?"

"Thanks for having lunch with me."

She visibly relaxes. "You're welcome."

The second I'm alone in my office again, I lean back in my chair, only one question in my head, repeating over and over.

Is Mellie right?

Chapter Fifteen
Hades

SHE WAS STARVING HERSELF? I pace repeatedly outside of her office, wanting to storm in and demand answers. But she's in there with Mellie. And with the door shut and glass misted, the least I can do is give them privacy. I know how much Mellie wants a friend. I shouldn't intrude. I shouldn't slam into the office and shout.

Finally, the door swings open, the walls unmisting. Mellie gives me an annoyed look as she glides past me, stepping on one of my feet with her heavy boots. I cover a wince, focusing on Persephone, looming in her doorway.

My voice snaps out, "You were seriously starving yourself?"

She rolls her eyes at me, opening her laptop.

I move forward, forcing the laptop closed. "Answer me."

She sighs, her eyes slowly raising to mine. I suddenly realize how close we are. I hadn't meant to get this close, only to get answers. "Only at work. I stayed with a friend."

I've been starving her? Could I be any more of an unfeeling asshole?

"You didn't think to talk to me?" I growl at her.

She tilts her head, her dark hair falling over one shoulder, sending me a wave of her scent. "Why do you care?"

My hand tightens on her closed laptop, close to breaking the fragile electronic. "I didn't intend to starve you."

Just intended to punish you for hiding from me. For thinking to outwit and outmaneuver my protocols. Not to mention the fact that you're also my fated queen. Yeah, I wanted to punish you for that too.

I'm. A. Fucking. Asshole.

Her eyes drop to my lips. "No? What did you *intend*?"

I frown at her, moving closer, till I'm hovering over her. "You should have told me."

What are we arguing about again? Cause now all I can imagine is those lips of hers sheathed around my cock.

She leans closer to me, her dress giving me a view of those curves I dream about. "Why?"

I lick my lips slowly, satisfied when it draws her eyes. "So I could have…fed you."

I'm pretty sure we're not talking about food anymore. Or at least a different form of meat.

Her lips part slightly, her back arching. "Why do I doubt you would have *fed* me?"

Oh, little spring, I'd feed you so good.

I step closer, a predator lured by prey. "You doubt my…feeding abilities?"

Her breath hitches almost imperceptibly. "I doubt you'd offer to do anything to help me."

I'm around her desk in the next breath, turning her chair to face me, my hands going to its arms, caging her in. "Anything?"

She stares up at me, her breathing shaking, her breasts heaving. She pulls that maddening bottom lip between her teeth and nods slowly.

I lean closer, my lips hovering over hers before

whispering. "Are you...*starving?*"

She throws up that defiant chin, even as she arches toward me. "I just ate."

My breath brushes against her lips, not brushing it with mine like we both seem to want. "Too bad."

She sits back in her chair, away from me, and I can see the muscles in her legs flex as she squeezes them together. I straighten completely, not even bothering to hide my own reaction to her. "If you need...feeding, you know where to come, *little spring*."

She crosses one leg over the other. "You'll hunger before I do."

Does she know how breathless she sounds?

I lean my head back, making sure she takes in full view of my throat and jaw, laughing deeply. The sound is full of the promises of pleasures I can give her, things she's never known, things that only exist in the dark of the mind. "Would you like to place a bet on that?"

She stands from her chair, stepping closer to me, walking her fingers up my chest. "What's the bet?"

The first touch goes to her. I wonder if she knows it's the first time she's touched me.

"That you'll be on your knees before I will be," I growl huskily, my voice raw at the things running through my mind. All the fantasies that have fed me for millennia, fantasies I plan to take out on this goddess before me.

Her eyes glow, staring up at me, smirking. "Deal."

My shadows, my mindless servants, extensions of me, tickle around her ankles. "You should know, I always win."

I don't enter into any game without knowing the outcome.

She twists her hands, and I look down at my feet, seeing vines growing and wrapping around my ankle, rising up my calves. "Only because you've never faced me."

Fuck, her arrogance should not be so fucking alluring. The shadows creep up, slipping under her dress. I barely have the presence of mind to click the button to mist her office windows and door, leaving us alone.

"We'll just see about that, little spring."

Her vines continue up my legs, the leaves caressing my skin. "We will, demon."

Demon? She has no idea how fitting that name is, because I am ready to do things absolutely *demonic* to her body. The shadows make it to her panties, and I can feel what they do, like a ghost of a touch. I let out a groan. "You're wet."

The vines move under my slacks, wrapping around my cock, a verdant hand. "You're hard."

I arch into the feeling. "Every time I smell you, you have me like stone. Impossible to focus on work."

Or anything but you.

The vines move on my cock, stroking me. She purrs, "Oh?"

The shadows move past her panties, the feeling of intangible fingers pressing in. I growl at her, all animalistic need. "You smell like a garden of the freshest roses, so fucking distracting."

She moans softly, twisting her hips as my shadows move. "Please. I see the way you look at me. Pure hatred."

"Pure desire," I correct. "I wonder if your cunt tastes as delicious as you smell. I can't wait to find out."

Chapter Sixteen

Persephone

THE GHOST OF THE FEELING OF HIS TOUCH MAKES MY SKIN TINGLE. Goosebumps break out all over my body. I touched him, the briefest feeling of the pads of my fingertips against his hard chest, and it was enough to make me crazed.

Then, when I felt the softest of touches sliding up my legs, when I saw those tendrils of his smoke-like shadows, when I felt my panties being moved to the side and felt a finger pushed inside of me, I was lost to him, completely at this mercy.

This bet is dangerous, and I have no idea why I agreed to it, except for the fact that when Hades is close to me, when his warmth and scent is surrounding me, all rational thought ebbs from my brain. The need to press my body against his, to feel his hard muscles against my soft curves, almost makes me beg for him. The shadows feel incredible, but I'm willing to bet they pale in comparison to how those perfect, calloused hands would feel exploring my skin. My vines curl around him. They're sensitive and everything they feel I feel. But I want my bare skin against his.

I feel his hard length under my vines. His size makes my mouth water. I want to open his pants, to wrap my hand around him, to feel the weight of his cock. I moan as he works his shadows inside me.

I start to move into him when a shrill ring comes from my desk. My hooded gaze remains locked on his as I reach for my phone, my trembling fingers fumbling as they search for the aggravating disturbance.

I answer before checking the caller ID, my voice curt. "Prosperina."

"Hi, darling!" Jackson's cheerful voice is like a bucket of ice water being dropped on me.

I turn from Hades, my hand gripping the back of my chair. I feel Hades moving closer behind me, recommencing his shadow ministrations. I bite my lip to stop my moan.

"Look at you, big time, working for Plutus!"

I tighten my vines on Hades, a warning for him to stop. "Jackson. Hi, darling!" It takes an enormous amount of effort to hide my struggle. Even then, my voice comes out breathy.

Hades moves my hair over my shoulder and licks my neck. He bites it, the shadow fingers still slowly moving inside me, my pussy clenching around them. I tilt my head for Hades, my eyes rolling closed. *Fight this, P...*

"Are you alright? You sound out of breath."

My eyes snap open, and I once again twist my hand. More vines appear and pull Hades against the back window, holding him there. "Yes, sorry. Just ran up the stairs. Are we still on for tonight?"

Hades keeps those maddening shadows moving inside me, moving them faster. I try to stop the growl traveling up my throat.

"Yeah, I can't wait to see you."

I keep my vines moving on his cock, stroking him, caressing him. I stifle a moan, pleasure suppressing the guilt I should be feeling. "Me either, darling. I have to get back to work."

Hades starts thrusting his shadows into me harder,

86

my nails dig into my chair.

"I'll see you...tonight..."

I barely hear his response as I end the call, dropping my phone to the floor.

The second my phone lands, I'm pushed down on the desk, my forehead against the wood. I feel his shadows pushing my dress up, feeling the cool of the air-conditioner against my dripping wet cunt. I should feel self-conscious; I'm completely bare to him. He can see his shadows sliding in and out of me, can see every inch of the slick skin between my legs, can see the evidence of my desire for him running down my thighs.

I moan loudly, my fingers pressed against the hard desk beneath me. I work my vines faster, wishing I could see him, too, wishing I could see how I'm affecting him. "Fuck!"

More of his shadows wrap around my wrists, my ankles, and he pulls them, opening me up fully for his viewing pleasure. "Look at that cunt of yours." My stomach twists deliciously at his dirty mouth. "I can see how much you want me, how much you need me."

Part of me wants to protest, but...he's right. I do need him, right now.

I try to look over my shoulder at him, but his hold on me is restraining me completely. I grate out, "Stop. Talking." Needing him to not know how much his words affect me as much as his actions. Needing him to not know that his dirty talk is spurring me on even more, getting me ever closer.

I can practically hear his smirk. *He knows.* His shadow fingers move faster inside me. "Take it, little spring. Beg for it."

I push my hips back as much as I can. The tight coil of my orgasm, ready to spring at any moment. "So close..."

Immediately, the shadow fingers vanish. I growl, my

pussy throbbing with need.

"Beg." His voice is dominating, hard.

I still my vines on his cock. "You first, demon."

I feel him trying to thrust into my vines. He must be close too. I move them with his hips, not allowing him any friction. His shadows lightly rub my clit. "Do it, and I'll make you come."

I clench my jaw, unwilling to submit to him. "You. First. Demon."

He snarls. I hear him panting against the vines, feeling his cock throbbing. "I won't submit."

I pull against his shadow restraints. "I guess we're at an impasse then."

Hades releases his shadows. I hear the frustration in his voice. "I suppose we are."

I stand and correct my panties. I wave my hands, and my vines immediately disappear. I don't turn to face him, but I hear him fix himself in his pants.

"You should have submitted," he says, his voice, tense, unsated.

I clip my hold-ups to my garter belt. *When did he unfasten these?* "Do you deserve my submission?" I fix my dress, smoothing it over my thighs.

I hear his angry footsteps and turn to face him, surprised to see him approaching me. He towers over me, his face inches from mine. If I stood on my tiptoes, my lips would brush against his.

"I demand it, Persephone."

I refuse to shrink under his intense, furious gaze. "Then, you're going to be disappointed, Hades."

He growls, his eyes flashing, before turning from me and storming out of my office.

Chapter Seventeen
Hades

I DROP INTO MY OWN DESK, FISTING MY ACHING COCK, my head dropping back. The tight coil of unfulfilled desire is only escalated by the fact that she refused to beg me. Her stubbornness should not be as arousing as it is. But her scent is still in my nose, the sight of her bent over her desk, pinned by my shadows. Helpless for me. How am I ever going to be able to stand in her office again? Even look in her direction? Without remembering the sight? And she *dared* to refuse. Game on, little spring. Game fucking on.

Even though my walls are frosted at the moment, my hand on my cock, I can hear the sound of someone making their way to the restroom, and I take a deep inhale, smirking. I know exactly who it is. Thinking of making her own retreat to take care of what she *refused* to let me finish her. I don't think so.

With my free hand, I pull out my phone, texting her,

HADES

I know what you're doing.

Her response is immediate, and I can hear her tart tone in my head.

PERSEPHONE

What am I doing, Hades?

I smother a knowing smirk that she doesn't have to ask who it is. Even though I've never texted her before. I'm not normally a *texting* person. I would much rather do everything face-to-face. But, since she refuses to submit…I'll use any means necessary in our little game.

HADES

You've got your fingers in your dripping cunt.

Because she refused to beg me and let me finish her, she's fingering herself in the bathroom, wishing it was me.

I wish it was me too.

PERSEPHONE

Is that what you're imagining while you stroke your cock?

That's exactly what I'm imagining.

HADES

I'm imagining you riding my cock as I snap those little garters of yours till they break.

I caught sight of the maddening little lingerie and couldn't stop wondering how often she's been wearing those. How many times had I looked over her mouth-watering pencil skirts, not knowing that she hid those beneath them? My hand moves faster on my cock as I imagine what would have happened if we hadn't stopped in her office.

PERSEPHONE
How did you get my number?

By violating some crucial tenets of human resources. I can almost feel the eyes of Kelsey, head of HR, glowering at me. There is a very short list of individuals who make me *pause. Hekate. The Primordials. Kelsey.* She might be the only human to ever be on that list. And with good reason. Her disappointed emails were…the stuff of nightmares.

HADES
Does it really matter?

Plausible deniability. I'm sticking to that. And avoiding the question.

PERSEPHONE
What do you want from me?

I thought I was pretty clear what I wanted. *I want her to beg.*

HADES
Send me a picture of you, right now. Show me what you're doing to yourself.

I hold my breath and freeze my hand on my cock, waiting for a response. My phone dings with a response. She's set her phone on something, showing her flipping me off in the foreground. But in the background, I can see her hand between her legs. *Knew it.*

I send her a picture back, my middle finger trailing along the piercing on my cock's slit. I don't know how things keeps escalating between us. The idea of her touching herself, remembering not only what we almost did, but at the sight of my cock...*fuck.*

She rewards me with a photo of her finger circling her clit. I can't stop myself from responding with a video clip of me working my hand along my cock. I moan as I take it. "Fucking spring."

Escalating and escalating our little exchange.

It takes a minute before she sends me a video back. I fist my cock faster as I watch her push a finger inside herself, then followed by a second. Her thumb circling her clit, her moans breathy and loud. Her fingers make sounds as they thrust, telling me how soaked she is.

HADES

Fuck, I'm going to come.

PERSEPHONE

Me too. Fuck.

I can't focus enough to hold my phone as I come, only enough to cover my mouth to keep the roar quiet as my back arches. I pant at the mess, coming down from the force of my orgasm, using tissues to clean up the mess on my desk.

HADES

What are we going to do about this?

Tell me you'll see me tonight, Persephone. Tell me you want me like I want you. I can rearrange my night to spend it with her.

PERSEPHONE

Well, I'm going back to work.

She might as well have kneed me in the balls. She wants to pretend like nothing is between us? Like this didn't just happen?

HADES

But...

I want more. I want everything.

PERSEPHONE

What?

Fuck. Am I truly that oblivious? That wrong about what is between us? I know that we are fated. But she... doesn't. As far as she knows, I'm her boss. She's my employee. I want her and...
She doesn't want me.

HADES

Get back to work.

I can't clear my head of what just happened for the rest of the day, the way she just brushed this off like it meant nothing. Was this just a normal occurrence for her? I mean goddesses were not exactly known for their chastity, but she must *sense* that we're more. We're fucking fated after all. Yet, she couldn't care less. Even that moment of relief and pleasure with her are forgotten, replaced with a knot of tension that refuses to dissipate. Only growing worse and worse as the day continues. I bark at my assistants, and my staff, sending everyone into a deluge of work, hoping to lose myself in work and forget about the moment I shared with the Goddess of Spring.

The Goddess of Spring, who wants nothing to do with me.

Chapter Eighteen
Persephone

WHAT THE FUCK WAS THAT? I stumble back to my office from the bathroom, my steps surprisingly steady considering how unstable and boneless I feel. My orgasm, while good, still didn't sate me.

It's absolutely *not* because the whole time I was thinking about Hades, wishing it was him, considering storming back to his office, getting on my knees and begging for him to touch me, taste me, fuck me.

Lie.

My cheeks burn as I walk back down the corridor, concern flaring inside me that someone heard me. But no one reacts to me, no one is paying any attention to me, actually. I clench my fists as I walk past Hades's office, the glass still misted. *You know what he's just done in there. While thinking about you. While wanting you, needing you.*

My pussy throbs at my thoughts. My knees shaking slightly. I quicken my steps and practically collapse in my chair when I arrive back in my safe space with zero confrontation.

I glance at my phone and open my text messages with Hades. It is absolutely not smart to save his number, and yet…my fingers move over the screen, type in his name, and click that damning "save" button. My gaze snags on our text chain, and I start scrolling. *Bad idea, P.*

HADES

I'm imagining you riding my cock as I snap
those little garters of yours till they break.

My stomach flutters, and I squeeze my thighs together again. The lace of my panties uncomfortably damp. *Fucking Hades.*

I lock my phone and practically throw it across the desk. *Work time. Head in the game and off your hot boss.*

I can't believe my luck, it's been almost three full days and I've only seen Hades twice. Of course, I've only accomplished this by arriving early and leaving late, plus making it my life's mission to only leave my office when Hades's office windows are clouded in the thick white mist. But once again, the power of throwing myself into my work has done wonders, in fact, I've barely thought of Hades all week.

Lie.

I glance up from my computer and see Mellie walking along the corridor. I estimate I have around fifteen seconds to school my face and find something complimentary about her outfit. It doesn't look *bad,* just very… out there. Very Mellie.

My face pulls into a genuine smile when I realize I love it for all the reasons I love her, not that I could ever pull off her grungy look. Her hair is pulled into space buns, one the darkest black, the other the lightest white. Her psychedelic crop top is a craze of blue and purple. She wears black short shorts with fishnet tights that peek out of the top of them. And of course, her trademark black Doc Martens.

We've gone for very different vibes with tonight's outfit. I glance at my dress bag, hanging on the coat rack.

Mellie enters my office, not bothering to knock anymore. The thought that she's already more comfortable around me makes my heart swell. *I finally have a friend at work.*

"Yo!" She snaps her fingers at me, pulling me from my thoughts.

I'm also noticing, the more comfortable she gets with me, the more unhinged she becomes in my presence. *How about the fact that this is the longest you've gone without thinking about railing your boss for almost a week?*

"Hi, Mellie! You're early!"

She frowns at me. "It's 8:00 p.m.…"

My eyes go wide, and I glance at the time on my laptop. Fuck. "I completely lost track of time! I need to change."

I stand from my desk and grab the dress bag. I dig through my bag and find my pair of heeled pumps, that some would consider stilts.

I smile at her. "You look nice."

She eyes the dress and shoes I'm holding and frowns looking down at her outfit. "Is this not right?"

I tilt my head. "You look amazing, Mel. A trendsetter. I'm going to look boring next to you."

She smiles, blushing slightly. "I wasn't sure what to wear"

"I'll be right back." I disappear down the hall to change in the bathroom, taking care to not let my eyes linger on Hades's office, the walls still misted.

The bathroom is another version of fresh hell.

Memories from earlier seem to stick to every wall. My body responds, a whisper of the desire I felt before pooling in my tummy.

I return to Mellie wearing a short black cocktail dress and my heels. My hair is left down in loose waves, and I decide on basic makeup but a bold red lip.

"How do I look?"

She grins at me. "Stunning, like a rose with a bite."

A rose with a bite.

I've never *felt* like the embodiment of spring. Never felt like I truly knew who I was. My mother didn't either. I met Mellie less than a week ago, and yet, hearing that... it fits me. Spring with an edge, a darkness that I've never been able to explain, but have always been aware of, clawing to get out.

I grin at her and grab my phone. I blush when I notice the texts from Hades are still open. I quickly close them and open my text chain with Jackson.

PERSEPHONE

We're on our way to the club now!

JACKSON

We're here.

I grab Mellie's hand and pull her to the elevator, happily chatting about the night ahead. I'm relieved when we're able to immediately find a cab to take us there, sensing Jackson's annoyance at our tardiness through text

The cab ride is short, and Mellie's leg bounces the whole way. I can feel her nerves, her excitement. I take her hand and squeeze it in reassurance.

When the taxi pulls up to the club, I immediately spot Jackson, waiting for me. Once again, that near-constant feeling of guilt settles in, ready to torment me the second I realize that…I have never reacted to seeing him the way I react to seeing H—

No. Not tonight, P. Tonight is about Jackson.

The way I react to seeing *a certain god.*

I force my face into a grin, and I wrap my arms around his neck. "I missed you."

He squeezes me tightly. "Helios is inside, waiting for you."

I pull back and kiss the corner of his lips. "Oh sorry. This is Mellie, a friend from work."

Mellie flushes at the attention. "Hi."

"Nice to meet you. I'm Persephone's boyfriend, Jackson."

I grimace at his introduction. It's not the first time he's prematurely introduced me as his girlfriend, and it sets me on edge every time. We've never had that discussion, but I have told him, repeatedly, that I'm not ready to label it.

Mellie smiles, glancing at me uneasily, obviously sensing the tension radiating off me. She looks back at Jackson. "Nice to meet you. I promise to stay out of your head."

Jackson's easy smile turns uncertain. "What does that mean?"

I take his hand in mine and kiss his lips gently, trying to push down my annoyance at him. We can discuss it later. "I'm glad you're back."

I feel him smile into my lips. "You need to tell me about your new job! I hear Plutus is a hard ass."

I pull back slightly, my traitor brain presenting a memory of his perfect ass. "We can talk about it later. Let's go see everyone."

It's not the only thing we'll be talking about later.

He nods and pulls his hand from mine to wrap his arm around my back, guiding me into the club. The second we step through the doors, the pounding music envelopes me, practically making my bones rattle. Jackson directs me to a booth. I chuckle when I see Helios, half naked in the center of the dance floor, completely surrounded by people. Helios loves attention and will use his innate sex appeal and good looks to draw people to him. I roll my eyes. *Moron.*

Jackson gestures for me to sit in the booth before leaving to get drinks. Mellie jumps in beside me, her eyes glued on Helios.

She leans into me, her face close so I can hear her over the music. "Is that your god friend?"

My gaze follows hers to Helios. "Mr. Subtlety over there? Yeah, that's him."

She frowns, her gaze locked on Helios, taking in every movement. "He seems to be enjoying himself."

Jackson returns, hearing the tail end of our conversation. "Helios is always enjoying himself. Guy thinks he's the center of the universe."

I place my hand on Jackson's thigh, squeezing lightly. "He's a good guy."

One thundering beat melts into another as Helios graces us with his presence, leaving a trail of disappointed mortals in his wake, all of whom want to know him, speak to him, fuck him. It's always the case, whenever we go anywhere with him. He draws the eye.

"Petal!"

He slides into the booth, forcing Mellie to move over slightly, completely invading her personal space.

He grins at her, holding his hand out to her. "Helios."

She glances at his hand and looks away, bored. "Not interested."

Jackson snickers, and I bite the inside of my cheek to stop from laughing. Mellie is quickly becoming my hero.

I expect Helios to have some absurdly flirty and arrogant comeback, but he simply blinks in shock at her. Mellie grabs my hand and starts to pull me out of the booth, shoving Helios out of the way.

"Let's go dance, Persephone."

I follow her and look at Jackson and Helios. "Keep a look out for Freya, Lucy, and Justin!" is all I manage to get out before I'm dragged to the dance floor.

Mellie starts dancing, chaotically and wonderfully. I stay swaying my body to the music, letting it wave through me. Giving into the vibrations coursing through me. I grab two shots from a passing waitress and hand one to Mellie.

"To new friends."

She grins and lifts her glass. "To new friends!"

We both down the liquid, and I grimace at the burn as it slides down my throat.

The liquor immediately loosens me up, and my hips sway and grind to the music. My skin heats as I feel eyes on me. But I push away the feeling, passing it off as the tequila.

I feel my dress inching up my thighs as I lift my arms, but I don't care. I've not felt this at ease all week.

"Yikes." I blink my eyes open and see Mellie, tense, looking up at the balcony.

I follow her gaze. "What is—"

Those dark blue eyes lock with mine. His intense gaze trained on me, eyeing me like a predator would watch prey. It...arouses me. My skin tingles, and I feel the hair stand on the back of my neck. I see his perfect dark brow raise as he looks at me. I imagine that's the look he'll get before he punishes me. My eyes travel down his chest, halting on his hands, his knuckles white as he grips the railing. *He's thinking about me too...*

"Guess he had the same idea," Mellie says.

I grab another shot from a tray and down it quickly. When I look back up at Hades, his gaze is no longer on me. Free from his scrutiny, I start dancing again. But I'm hyperaware that the second I turn my back, his eyes are roaming over me once again.

Chapter Nineteen

Hades

SO SHE BLOWS ME OFF TO SPEND TIME WITH A MORTAL? I grind my teeth as I look down at Persephone and Melinoë on the dance floor, trying to not bend the metal of the railing beneath my hand, feigning nonchalance as I raise a glass to her, before downing it. She's wearing a short black dress and high heels, Mellie dressed in something between goth and a raver. But I can't pull my eyes from my fated queen. Or what my shadow spies have learned since she arrived. I watch the dance floor below, pretending to be surveying the cloying group of mortals, not focusing on her as she takes another shot and beckons Jackson to dance with her.

Jackson. What a stupid name.

Is it a last name? Is it a first name? Either way, it's fucking stupid. And she's *dating* him? Yet it didn't stop her from using her vines on my cock, or sending me pictures of herself fingering her cunt to thoughts of me.

The metal bends in my grip.

She wraps her arms around his neck, swaying to the music. My eye twitches as he wraps his arms around her.

Mine. She's mine. And I'll prove to her that the mortal will never be enough to satisfy.

My shadows move, sightlessly, gripping her hips as

she dances with him. She doesn't try to pull away from my shadow hold, instead moving her hips away from Jackson and grinding against my shadow form. A replacement body, which only she can perceive, only she can enjoy. She leans forward to kiss the mortal's jaw, and I might as well hear the bells of war being declared in the club.

My shadows move to her abdomen, down to the edge of her dress, sliding up her inner thighs. The mortal dances with her, oblivious, not knowing that the body she truly wants is mine. She brushes against the mortal, but I can see the flash of her face as she bites her lip. To stop herself from moaning at my touch?

My smile turns wicked as I watch her from above, holding the railing in one hand and a handful of empty glass in the other. Yet, my shadows do what I cannot. They grip her ass hard, likely leaving bruises. Bruises which will look like my fingerprints. I wonder how she'll explain that to the mortal?

Her hips buck, and the mortal frowns at her, their words lost in the deafening sound of the club. She pulls away from him, her cheeks flushed. She nods at him, leaving the dance floor and my sight. But my shadows see her. They follow her to the corner where she's hidden from the rest of the club. Her back hits the wall, and her chest heaves. My shadows continue, pressing her dress up, pulling her panties down, vanishing them until I feel them inside my pocket. My trophy.

My phone vibrates in my pocket. When I pull it out and read the message, my cock throbs.

PERSEPHONE

Come do it yourself, coward.

In a swirl of darkness, uncaring if the mortals notice, I'm in front of her, slamming my lips to hers, yanking her legs up and around me. Her mouth is a haven, even more mouthwatering than I thought, and I'm an addict the moment our lips touch.

Her arms wrap around my neck, locking me to her. As if I was going anywhere at that moment. I bite her lip hard in punishment, my fingers moving between our bodies, pressing inside her, groaning into her mouth at the feel of her wet cunt.

She slides her hand down my chest, cupping my cock. I buck into her hand, pressing another finger inside her, forcing her mouth open for me. Forcing her surrender. Forcing her submission.

She moans into my mouth, her tongue sliding over mine.

I rock my hips into her hand, the maddening rub of her palm, growling at her, "You're going back to him with the memory of how I made you come."

You're going back to him to realize that I'm the one you need.

She ignores me, pulling my mouth back, her hand slipping inside my slacks. I rock my fingers inside her, curling them, as I rub my aching cock against her palm. She wraps her hand around me, stroking me, breaking from my kiss to moan, "Fuck, you're so hard."

"All for you," I growl back.

All things for you. Everything for you.

Her hand tangles in my hair, gripping it tightly. My hand moves to the back of her neck, forcing her glowing gaze to lock on mine, as I move my fingers inside her, as I make her come. So she knows it's me who makes her feel like this. Me and no other.

Her moans are drowned out by the thumping music, the club oblivious to us. She rolls her hips, leaning in to whisper in my ear, "I wish it was your cock…"

I hiss, "When you're mine," *you will be,* "I'll give it to

you. Let you suck me off beneath the desk during conference calls, but until then—"

She pulls her hands from my slacks, tearing at my fly, making it easier to stroke me. Her hand, wrapping around my cock, fucking me with her fist. "When I'm yours?"

I bite her earlobe. "When you don't have a boyfriend waiting for you to come back."

I won't share you, Persephone. When you're mine, you'll be only *mine. I won't accept half of you.*

She kisses down my neck, moaning, "Fuck…I'm so close…"

I curl my fingers inside her, finding the spot she needs. "Scream who makes you come."

Scream so he knows you're mine.

She screams my name, but the loud music drowns her out, her cunt squeezing my fingers. Her hand moves faster on me, until I can't help but follow her, coming with a shout.

She clings to me as we both come down from the force, both of us looking for something secure, when the world seems to spin around us.

Chapter Twenty

Persephone

I CLING TO HIM, MY BODY QUAKING FROM THE RELEASE I've been waiting for since I first laid eyes on him. My first and only thought: *I was right about the shadows.*

Every place our skin touches is like electricity. Like my skin is desperate to be touched by his. Like it yearns for him like I do. Even now, with his hand gripping the back of my thigh, his tongue sliding over my neck, I'm so hyperaware of the contact. It's never felt like this before. Yes, it's always felt good being touched, but never as though I needed it, as much as I needed water or air.

He drags his lips up my sensitive neck, his voice a low growl. "To think...you could have had all of this earlier, if you weren't so stubborn."

Bastard.

I unwrap myself from him, my legs feeling like those of a newborn deer. I lean against the wall, trying to hide any weakness. My gaze meets his, and I lift my hand to my lips, licking his release from my skin. A tactic to try and regain control. Unexpectedly, I'm completely overwhelmed by his taste. My eyes practically roll back in my head, and I moan the second it touches my tongue. I glance back at him, greedy for his reaction.

"I wasn't the only stubborn one."

His heated gaze locks on mine, and his eyes sparkle

with mischief as he bring his own hand to his mouth. He groans as he sucks on his finger. "Fuck, you taste like pomegranate."

My cheeks heat.

"And, yes, you were." He smirks.

I wrap my hand around his wrist, stopping him from licking any more of his fingers. I bring his hand to my lips, I close my lips around the pad and slowly suck it into my mouth. I moan at the taste of my own arousal.

"That's mine," he snarls.

I lightly bite down on his finger before releasing it. I let go of his wrist and hold my hand out, palm up. "My panties?"

He smirks. "Consider them a…souvenir."

My eyes flash, and I carefully school my face into a glare, attempting to hide how aroused that makes me. *He's keeping my panties. That's creepy, P. Not hot.*

Lie.

I smooth out my dress, and turn to leave, only to be stopped by his large hand wrapping around my upper arm. My body immediately responds to him, and my breath catches in my throat.

"Break up with him."

I slowly drag my gaze away from his grasp on me to his piercing deep blue eyes. "Excuse me?"

He growls, jaw clenched. "Break up with him."

I lift an eyebrow. "Why?"

He lets his gaze slowly crawl over my body, practically setting me alight. It wouldn't surprise me if my panties spontaneously dropped because of this particular look, *a theory I'm unable to test given the current location of them.*

His eyes trail back up, snagging on my lips. "So I can give you what you need, Persephone."

Smooth bastard.

I instinctively step toward him. I look up at him, my

gaze hooded. "And what is it I need, Hades?"

He leans in, my breaths come out as short pants as his tickle my ear. "You need me to fill that greedy cunt of yours, to bend you over my desk and fuck you to within an inch of your life."

I stand on my tiptoes, my hand pressed against his chest to help me balance. I bite down on his earlobe. "What makes you think I want that?" I dig my nails into his chest.

His groan sends a wave of desire though me. "How fucking dripping you were just a moment ago."

I slide my tongue along the shell of his ear. "I think you mean, 'how wet you are again right now.' "

He groans again, his hands fly to my waist, squeezing me. For a second, I wonder if I'll bruise, and I'm vaguely horrified that the thought makes me even wetter. I feel it slowly sliding down my thighs, making the bare skin there slick.

"Break up with him, and I'll give you more."

I kiss along his jaw before pressing a kiss to the corner of his mouth. "Goodbye, Hades."

He clenches his jaw and steps back from me. An emotion flashes over his face, but it is quickly masked. *Was that hurt?* Black smoke surrounds him, and in the blink of an eye, he disappears.

I lean my back against the wall again.

What are you doing, Persephone?

I feel my phone vibrate in my bra, and I pull it out seeing a text from…

My eyes go wide. *Fuck, Jackson!*

I make my way back to him, legs still feeling like jelly.

He smiles at me warmly. "You okay, babe?"

I nod, my old friend, guilt, digging his unrelenting claws into me.

He stands from the booth and kisses me softly. "Are

you ready to head home?"

I nod, feeling slightly dazed.

He takes my hand and waves to Helios and Mellie, who are arguing with each other. I briefly wonder if I should go and check on Mellie, but there's something about her demeanor that warns me off doing so. She can definitely handle herself, especially with Helios.

I glance back as Jackson leads me out of the bar, deciding to check on Mellie one more time.

Lie.

The cool evening New York air washes over me the second we exit the club, and reality comes crashing back down. I glance at Jackson, watching him futilely trying to hail a cab. Every vibrant yellow car disregards him in favor of other customers. There he stands, his arm raised uselessly as he tries to hail us a ride.

Irritation flits beneath my skin, and I walk past him, moving to stand in the street. Locking eyes with a coming driver, I raise my arm, feeling the hem of my dress lifting slightly. I smirk as the driver slams on his brakes, earning honks from the drivers around him. I don't even look back to check if Jackson follows me, but his hand on my ass, "supporting" me as I climb into the car, alerts me to his presence.

He climbs in behind me and gives the driver my address. I bristle at how he takes charge of the situation, given he wasn't even able to source a ride in the first place. The second the door closes, he pulls his phone out, checking for work messages. Some would mind, but I sit back in the seat, grateful for the peace, the cheap leather uncomfortable against the backs of my bare thighs barely bothering me.

I look out the window, as we cruise through the city. The high-rises blend together, until we pass one in particular. The cab stops at a traffic light in perfect view of Hades's building. I look up, my gaze focusing on the top two floors, both in darkness, but I see a single light on, the third floor down. *Hades.*

The car lurches into motion, and I blush, feeling like I've been caught doing something I shouldn't be. I glance at Jackson. but he's still engrossed in his phone. *Stop thinking about Hades.*

The taxi pulls up outside my apartment building, and while I collect my bag, Jackson pays the driver and climbs out his side. He comes around to my side to open my door for me. I smile up at him. He really is a gentleman.

He holds out his hand for me, and I place mine in his as he helps me out of the car. "I missed you, babe."

I smile at him. "I missed you too."

Lie.

I *would* have missed Jackson was it not for…*him.*

I gasp as Jackson pulls me against him, kissing me deeply. I pull back in shock. Jackson has never been one for PDA. My body seems to reject him, though. It doesn't thrum for him the way it does for Hades. If I'm honest with myself, it never has. His lips are not firm like Hades's, but soft. His kiss isn't demanding in the same way. Hades's kiss completely overwhelms me, makes me want to submit to him completely. When his lips are on mine, I would do anything he asked, demanded, needed. When Jackson kisses me, it feels…nice?

He presses his lips to mine again, moaning into them, his words breathless. "Are you going to invite me up?"

After doing the bare minimum to class it as a mutual kiss, I pull back again. "I don't know, I'm not feeling too good…"

He frowns, obviously not buying my excuse. "But I just got back…didn't you miss me?"

Really, dude, you're guilting me? I have enough guilt without you piling it on.

I hesitate, trying to weigh the pros and cons of inviting him inside. We're not going to be intimate. Not after what I did with Hades tonight. But I don't suppose I can say no when I've not seen him in over a week…*well, fuck.*

"One drink."

He grins and starts guiding me inside. He takes my keys from my hand and unlocks the apartment.

Needing space, I head straight to the bar to pour drinks, making mine a double.

Jackson follows behind me, his hand sliding over my hip. Again, I find myself comparing his touch to Hades's. It's too soft, too gentle. My cheeks heat as I remember *his* grip on me, and I almost moan at the thought of Hades's handprint-shaped bruises on my body.

Jackson presses his lips to my neck and groans. "Fuck, you smell so good."

I tense slightly. "Jackson…"

He stills behind me. "What?"

I turn and hand him a glass. I take a deep drink of mine, the golden brown liquid leaving a comforting burn in its wake as it slides down my throat.

He takes the drink, frowning down at the tumbler. "You're seriously giving me a drink?"

I lift an eyebrow at him. "A key part in the act of *drinking.*"

"Is something wrong?"

I take another sip of scotch, trying to buy myself time to come up with a convincing reason for why I'm being so distant, for why I just want to be alone right now. "I told you, I'm not feeling well."

Jackson moves closer. He lifts his hand to my forehead. "You're not running a temperature…do you want me to make you some soup?"

I shake my head, the coil of tension in my stomach finally loosening. "No, I think I just need to sleep."

I hear my phone buzzing in my bag. "Sorry, I need to

check that, it might be Mellie."

Jackson nods and sips his drink while I check my phone. My heart races the second I see his name on the screen.

HADES
I'm waiting.

I curse the thrill I feel when I read his message.

PERSEPHONE
For?

HADES
Him to leave.

I blink down at my phone. How does he even know Jackson is here? I glance at Jackson, nervous that he's suddenly received some super power, which allows him to read text messages from across the room, but he's looking at his own phone, cradling the whiskey tumbler in his other hand.

PERSEPHONE
And why do you want that?

My heart races as I wait for his response. *What am I even hoping for here?*

HADES
So I can finish what I started.

I swallow loudly, the traitorous low curl of heat

warming my stomach, making my toes want to curl in anticipation.

I lock my phone and look at Jackson. "I think I'm just going to go to bed. But why don't we have lunch tomorrow?"

His face drops, but he quickly corrects it. "Oh, alright." He leans in for a kiss. I quickly divert his lips to my cheek and press my hand to his chest.

"Don't want to get you sick."

He smiles softly. "Goodnight, babe, see you tomorrow."

I release a breath I didn't know I'd been holding the second the door closes. I press my back against it and my eyes roll shut. "What the fuck am I doing?"

Chapter Twenty-One

Hades

THE SECOND SHE STORMS BACK TO HER *MORTAL*, I stomp back up to my balcony in the club. I snarl with annoyance when I see she's already left. I should go home. What the fuck was even my intention in coming here tonight? I certainly had not expected to see her. I thought I might find someone who could help me get my mind off how Persephone utterly blew me off earlier. But fate clearly had other ideas. And fate was also a fucking bitch. Because my fated queen not only wants nothing to do with me, even after making her come on my fingers, but also after our office…power play.

What the fuck am I missing here? Why doesn't she want me? What does this mortal have? I should have just gone home. I should definitely not be sitting across the street, watching her apartment. I should definitely not be doing that. Yet…I watched them arrive and her inviting him upstairs. She must want a private location in order to break up with him.

What could he possibly be doing here? How long does a breakup take exactly? From across the street, I remain hidden in a shadow cover, but I watch her apartment. Trying to give her a modicum of privacy, though I'm practically frothing at the mouth to storm into her apartment and kick her soon-to-be *ex* out on the sidewalk, so I can have her all to myself. She's mine. She needs to understand that. We were fated.

I roll my shoulders, trying to control my thoughts and my shadows, both of which are torn between thoughts of killing her mortal and the things I'm going to do to her when she's mine. I'm going to punish her for this. For making me wait. For having a mortal boyfriend. She could have sent him home before, the fact that she let him up to her apartment. My hands fist at the idea. That he didn't immediately leave after a short terse fight between them. He must be fighting to remain with her. What man wouldn't fight to remain connected to Persephone? I am desperate for even the smallest glimmer of connection to her.

My jaw ticks. I glance down at my watch. It's been almost twenty minutes since they went inside. How long does it possibly take to break up with someone?

HADES

I'm waiting.

PERSEPHONE

For?

Gods, she's stubborn.

HADES

For him to leave.

For you to be *mine.*

116

And why do you want that?

I barely hold my scoff in.

So I can finish what I started.

It's agonizing waiting after that. Finally, I see him walking down the steps from her apartment, his hands tucked in his pockets. I expected tears or some shouting, something more from the mortal when he realizes that Persephone will no longer be his, but that she's always been *mine.*

I suppose that doesn't matter now.

I shadow directly to her door, knocking on it firmly, insistently.

When she swings the door open to answer, I'm on her. I slam my lips to hers, wrapping my arms around her waist, yanking her up my body. Feeding my addiction to her. Soothing the ache that persists in me when she's not around.

She moans into my mouth, her tongue greeting mine, pressing her body to mine. I walk into her apartment as her legs wrap around my waist, closing her door behind me. Our bodies belong joined, as a union of limbs. To keep us apart for even this short time, was a strain.

"You kept me waiting," I growl against her lips. She tastes like strawberries and pomegranate, cherries and raspberries. *Sweet.* Addicting. Just like her scent, but the raw hunger that she responds to my kiss with. That's what I need. The darkness she hides inside. The dark-

117

ness that meets mine in a flurry of lust and desire.

She tangles her fingers in my hair, tugging. "Shut up."

She kisses me fiercely, forcing her tongue into my mouth. I bite her lip, stumbling back until we enter her bedroom, landing on her bed. "Drove me mad knowing he was in here with you."

Her hand moves down my chest, fiddling with my shirt buttons, ripping them with her urgency. She feels this. She has to. This coil of desperation. Of the idea that we weren't complete without the other. That we *need* each other.

I moan, kissing down her chest, my teeth finding the edge of the dress that drove me mad, ripping it. "How'd he take it?"

Did he realize that he lost a prize so much more valuable than gold? That he barely escaped with his life?

She tenses slightly, even as I kiss her skin. "Take what? Me telling him to leave?"

I pull back, frowning up at her. "The breakup."

She pushes up to her elbows. "I didn't break up with him."

I snarl, jumping to my feet, away from her, my shirt hanging open. "You're joking."

She lifts an eyebrow at me. "Why would I joke about that?"

To be cruel?

I pace back and forth at the foot of the bed, trying to figure out what I'm missing here. I pleasure her more than the mortal does. Her body practically weeps for mine, needing mine. I could give her more comfort, more material things than he ever could. What could I possibly not do better than the mortal? I'm a fucking god!

"Why not?"

She stands from the bed, her ruined dress falling

from her body. I'm too embroiled in my own thoughts and emotions to appreciate the sight before she puts on a robe. "Why would I not joke about it? I don't think it would be very funny."

You're not enough for me, Hades. I want the mortal, not you. The fated bond...it must not affect her like it does me. I'm...I'm craving her, desperate for her. And she couldn't care less.

I vanish in a swirl of shadow without another word to her.

Chapter Twenty-Two
Persephone

DID YOU BREAK UP WITH HIM?"

His question repeats in my head, over and over, and my blood boils. He thinks he can *demand* that I do something, and I'll do it without thought or question?

Ridiculous.

Not that I'd even have to break up with Jackson, but the fact that Hades feels he can make such demands of me…

I pour myself another drink. My heart races in rage *and unmet desire*. The fact that I'm still this turned on when I'm this furious with him does not bode well for me.

Need to control yourself around him, P.

Indeed, if he had stayed here and fought it out with me, I have no doubt we'd resolve our frustrations through hot, primal, desperate sex.

Wishful thinking?

I can practically see the scene.

I push him down on the bed, ripping open my robe and push it off, along with the scraps of dress that remain, before straddling his hips. My lips slam to his, and I grind against him, his hard shaft pressing against me. His growls of frustration at the clothes separating us send waves of desire through me. I drag my nails down his chest, leaving angry red marks in their wake. I open his pants and push them down and wrap my hand around his cock, pulling it free. My hand immediately starts stroking his perfect, heavy length.

"Panties, now." His voice is guttural.

I moan into his lips. "Rip them."

The sharp bite of the lace as it tears against my skin makes me even wetter. I line his cock up with my dripping pussy and—

I'm pulled from my fantasy when my phone alerts twice, as two messages come in at once. I silently curse.

MELLIE

I did something stupid.

HELIOS

Have you heard from Mellie?

Uh oh, maybe I shouldn't have left them alone...
I open Mellie's message first.

PERSEPHONE TO MELLIE
What happened?

I roll my eyes. *This should just be a group text.*

PERSEPHONE TO HELIOS
What happened?

I click out of my chain with Helios and see them both typing, both of them stopping and restarting. *What the fuck has happened?*

MELLIE

I...fucked Helios in the bathroom at the club?

I gape at my phone. Of all the things I expected to receive back…that was not one of them. Had I missed something? They glared at each other most of the night and seemed to constantly clash. But, then again, if someone were to observe Hades and I, they would probably make similar observations, and yet, there is an unmistakable magnetism between us.

Plus, you were too busy hand-fucking Hades to notice much of anything.

My phone alerts again, a text from Helios.

> HELIOS
> She vanished from the club.

I lift my eyebrows at his reply. *Somewhat out of character for Helios. He's* definitely *one to kiss and tell.*

> PERSEPHONE TO MELLIE
> What the fuck, you guys hated each other?????

> PERSEPHONE TO HELIOS
> What did you do to her?

Besides fuck her brains out in the club bathroom.

Not that I could judge. Not long prior to that, I was getting fingered in a secluded hallway in that very club. *More pleasure than I've ever felt…*

I sigh in relief as a text from Mellie pulls me from that diverting train of thought.

> MELLIE
> You've never hate fucked someone?

No, but you did interrupt a particularly steamy fantasy when you decided to text me about your own hate fucking en-

counter, Mellie.

> **HELIOS**
>
> Me?!

> **PERSEPHONE TO MELLIE**
>
> I just didn't know it was your style. I love that for you! How was it?

> **PERSEPHONE TO HELIOS**
>
> I'm rolling my eyes so hard right now.

> **MELLIE**
>
> Fantastic...but I kind of panicked and knocked him out afterwards.

I blink down at my phone before bursting out laughing. The thought of Helios rocking her world and then her knocking him out and leaving him in the bathroom is one that I'm going to cherish forever.

> **HELIOS**
>
> I didn't!

> **PERSEPHONE TO MELLIE**
>
> You knocked him out????

> **PERSEPHONE TO HELIOS**
>
> Well what happened then?

> **MELLIE**
>
> I PANICKED!

> **HELIOS**
>
> You know what, I'm not going to tell you.

My brows furrow in thought. Why was Helios being so evasive unless...*Oh, my fucking god. He* likes *her.* Not once in our two years of friendship has Helios spoken to me about romantic feelings. I've not so much as heard a name mentioned, and yet, with Mellie, he's all flustered and *needing my advice.*

PERSEPHONE TO HELIOS

Fine. Deal with Mellie on your own.

PERSEPHONE TO MELLIE

Oh Mellie, we're going to be real good friends.

MELLIE

Because I'm painfully awkward?

PERSEPHONE TO MELLIE

Because you're an icon.

I see Helios typing, then deleting, over and over. Finally, the message comes through.

HELIOS

So you have heard from her?

What's my duty here as a friend? I've alluded to Mellie being alright, and clearly she doesn't want to speak with him.

PERSEPHONE TO HELIOS

Goodnight, H.

MELLIE

Okay, I'm going to ghost him and you won't hate me, right?

HELIOS

...If you hear from her, will you text me?

I sigh, wishing they would just talk to each other

about this.

I lift my eyebrow at the message preview for Helios's most recent message. My heart starts to race.

HELIOS

Don't make me play dirty, petal.

I stare at his message, my head tilting. *What?*

I watch as the three little dots bob up and down on the screen as he types. My stomach twists. I know what he's going to say before he even says it. I feel it.

HELIOS

How long have you been fucking Hades?

I blink down at my phone and let out a shaky breath. *Deny deny deny.*

PERSEPHONE

I don't know what you're talking about.

Lie.

> **HELIOS**
>
> So you just bailed on Jackson for no reason?
> Not to get lucky in the hallway of the club
> with the God of the Underworld?

My jaw clenches.

> **PERSEPHONE**
>
> I wasn't getting anything!

> **HELIOS**
>
> I saw you with your legs wrapped around
> him, petal.

The hallway had seemed secluded enough, but I remember feeling the risk of someone catching us. It excited me...turned me on. But someone *had* caught us, and now the moment was over, my stomach turned.

> **PERSEPHONE**
>
> How are you so sure it was me?

He has no proof...

The next text I receive from him makes me gasp. A picture flashes onto my screen. It's dark and grainy, but you can clearly see me, and you can *clearly* identify who I'm wrapped around. *And what we're doing.*

The photo is so intimate, so erotic. You can see how hard his fingers are digging into my thigh, my head thrown back in ecstasy, his face moving toward my neck, peppering it with searing kisses, my fingers tangled in his hair. I remember that moment so well, and so does my body.

I snap myself back to reality. We'd been caught and there was evidence.

> **PERSEPHONE**
>
> YOU TOOK A PHOTO? PERVERT.
>
> **HELIOS**
>
> I didn't know it was you. I was planning to
> send it as a joke but then looked closer...

I narrow my eyes at the screen, my jaw clenched.

> **PERSEPHONE**
>
> So you're blackmailing me?
>
> **HELIOS**
>
> What? No! Just tell me if you spoke to Mellie!

I consider for a moment. Surely, there would be nothing wrong with divulging that I *had* spoken with her since their tryst.

> **PERSEPHONE**
>
> Fine. I spoke to her. Delete that photo. Now.
>
> **HELIOS**
>
> I deleted it. What did she say?

I sigh in relief.

PERSEPHONE

I know you fucked her and that she knocked you out. Unrelated: She's now my favorite person in the whole world.

HELIOS

Shit, she told you that?

HELIOS

WHY DIDN'T YOU TELL ME SHE WAS A GODDESS?

PERSEPHONE

I'm not discussing this any further with you, Helios. It's nothing to do with me. You tell no one what you saw tonight, understand?

HELIOS

Hades is not a good idea, P.

PERSEPHONE

No? Why not?

HELIOS

Your mother will kill you.

PERSEPHONE

She'll kill me anyway. Besides, Hades and I aren't anything.

Wow, P. That might be your biggest lie yet.

PERSEPHONE

I'm still with Jackson.

HELIOS

YOU DIDN'T BREAK UP WITH HIM?!

PERSEPHONE

Not you as well. We're not exclusive.

HELIOS

Who, you and Hades or you and Jackson?

Ouch...

PERSEPHONE

Goodnight, Helios.

I watch as Helios starts and stops typing, before the three bobbing dots stop completely. While waiting, I find myself scrolling back through my conversation with Helios, swearing to myself that it's not to see that incriminating photo again, that damning photo, that... incredibly sensual photo.

My breaths shallow as I gaze at it. My skin seems to tingle where he'd touched me, kissed me, grabbed me. Before I know what I'm doing, I find myself saving the picture, not even trying to justify the reasons to myself anymore. I lock my phone and sigh, leaning back on the couch.

I don't know why people are acting outraged about the situation with Jackson. At no point have we defined relationship terms, or labeled our situation. Deep down, I *know* that he and I aren't right. I have always known. Being around Jackson is nice, but I don't crave him the way I should. It feels easy being around him, but not natural. Some would argue that the reason for that is my secret divine status, but I've never felt compelled to share that with him, quite happy to keep that side of me tucked away, unlike with Hades.

I'm also acutely aware that while Jackson and I aren't *together,* it is a much-needed buffer between Hades and I. I know that, when Jackson and I go our separate ways, Hades and I can move forward with whatever it is we're doing, and that terrifies me. I've not even known him a fortnight yet, and he has completely consumed my mind. Every thought, every decision, every second is laced with him. Having Jackson around dilutes it, forces me to push Hades to the recesses of my mind, giving me a moment without him consuming me, a moment of clarity.

Since the first day I saw him, it's felt as though there is a part of me that is screaming to get out, a part that was completely dormant until our eyes locked for the first time. And now it claws at me, yearning to be free. He awakened it, and I have absolutely no idea what it means.

I gaze up at the ceiling, realization crashing down on me like a ton weight.

The end is already in play…

Chapter Twenty-Three
Hades

ITRY TO FOCUS MY GAZE ON THE REPORTS IN FRONT OF ME, trying to make sense of what I'm seeing. There's something I'm missing. Not just in the numbers and meticulous notes and evaluations. *Focus.* The countdown is ticking down and down, I need to be present and focus. But it's impossible. I'm not here. I'm still in Persephone's apartment, trying to understand why she won't break up with that mortal. What does he give her that I don't? Does he pleasure her as much as I do? He can't, or she wouldn't be so on edge around me. Does he provide for her like I could? No, or she wouldn't have gone hungry. He can't protect her like I can, not a mortal. What if…she loves him? We may be fated, but there's nothing about love in the prophecy. Love and fate didn't always go hand in hand. She could be in love with him. And I'm pushing her for something she doesn't want. Forcing my obsession on her.

I place my elbows on the desk, digging my hands in my hair. Is it just physical for her? I'm just an itch to be scratched? Nothing more?

A desire she's unable to deny, despite her heart belonging to another? I'm forcing her to be disloyal to the man she loves?

I tighten my hands in my hair, practically tearing at the strands. Before I can think better of it, my hand is out, dialing the number from memory.

"The Bolt," Zeus answers, in lieu of hello.

I stop myself from rolling my eyes. "It's me."

I hear Zeus sitting up, leather creaking under him. He's probably hiding in his top-of-the-line man cave, because he pissed off Hera again. My little brother never seems to learn.

"Well, well, this is a surprise," Zeus says, the sound of a sports game being muted in the background. I can see him in my head, wearing a bright Hawaiian shirt, cargo shorts, and sandals. No doubt, he has some crumbs in his white beard.

"I called to ask…for advice," I grind out, the words unfamiliar to me. People come to *me* for advice, not the other way around.

"Hit me." Zeus snickers, no doubt enjoying this unprecedented phone call.

"I met someone," I whisper.

"Awww, is Hades in love? Is she *the* one?" Zeus asks.

"Why did I call you again?"

"Wait! Wait, I'm just kidding, tell me." Zeus laughs.

I run a hand down my face, filling him in on hiring Persephone, and the current situation. To his credit, Zeus only interrupts thirteen times, with unnecessary commentary. I threaten to hang up on him twice, finally getting through the entire story.

"So you hired the person who you're fated to make your queen…as a social media manager?" Zeus muses, reveling in my discomfort.

I rub my hand down the back of my neck. "Yes."

"And you basically can't keep your hands or dick away from her, despite the fact that she has a boyfriend whom she refuses to break up with," Zeus adds.

My neck heats with embarrassment, hating how easily Zeus has summed up the situation between us. Why did I call him again?

"Well, there were some other things," I murmur.

"Yeah, yeah, not important." Zeus snorts. "I hate to break it to you, H. But it sounds like…she's just not that into you."

I drop my head back on the chair, sighing. "I was worried you were going to say that."

Zeus snickers through the phone. "Take it from someone with a long, colorful history with the fairer sex, sometimes you got to learn when it's time to move on."

I laugh sadly into the phone. "You know, if historians could hear this conversation…"

"I know. They'd be insisting I can't keep my dick in my pants," Zeus jibes. "In fairness to them, did I have trouble with monogamy? Sure. But I've grown in my old age."

I roll my eyes. "You're younger than me."

"But you also got swallowed by dear old Dad, along with the guppy, and grew up in a pocket dimension, so, technically, I'm older and, therefore, wiser," Zeus pontificates. True, our father swallowed Poseidon and I in fear of a prophecy that his son would overthrow him. Our mother intervened before he could swallow Zeus as well. Zeus was able to free Poseidon and I when he fought our father. Together, my brothers and I presented a terrifying force on the battlefield. *From the skies. From the seas. From below.* There was nowhere to run from us.

"So, you think I should…move on?" I whisper. "Even if she's the one who's supposed to rule beside me?"

"I think she's sending some clear signals that she doesn't want you," Zeus says. "Outside the physical, do you actually *know* anything about her?"

I run a hand down my face. *Fuck, he's right. I don't know anything about her outside of how much I want to fuck her.* "Fuck."

"Yeah, that's what I thought," Zeus crows.

"I'm hanging up on you," I snap, before slamming

the phone back into the receiver.

Am I really considering taking advice from *Zeus?* I mean, he is prolific with lovers. Though he finally cut down the amount of extra-marital affairs after the second time Hera released the titans. Maybe Persephone really doesn't want anything to do with me. Outside of the passion that ignites whenever we are together. But that could just be fate trying to intervene. I…I don't really know anything about her.

I'm her boss. She's in a relationship. All reasons for me to leave her alone.

In the handful of stolen moments with her, she hasn't indicated wanting absolutely anything with me. At all. Outside of the explosive chemistry with each other, she doesn't even seem to *like* me.

I close my eyes, dropping my head on the back of my chair, staring at the ceiling, inhaling. What do I know about her? *She tastes like strawberries and pomegranates.* What else? *She smells like roses during a misty morning.* Fuck. I look to where her desk sits empty. She's incredibly dedicated to her job, taking pride in her work and her thoroughness. She took the time to befriend Mellie, despite most of Olympus giving the goddess a wide berth. She refuses to cower before me. She's everything I could want in a queen.

And she wants nothing to do with me.

I need to move on from her. Be just her boss, and nothing else.

Chapter Twenty-four

Persephone

I WAKE WITH A START, MY BODY SLICK WITH SWEAT, CHEST HEAVING.

But...it felt so real...

I look at my hands, and I slide my thumbs over my fingertips. I can practically still feel his skin under them. I wipe my damp forehead and moan softly as I shift in the bed. My thighs press together, and my swollen clit throbs. Memories of my dream flash in my mind. Hades above me, his powerful thrusts shaking the bed, Hades's perfect face between my legs, his sinful tongue drawing pleasure from me, licking as if I taste like the sweetest of nectars. My lips wrapped around his thick, throbbing length, the feeling of fullness in my mouth as I swallow down his shaft. I woke just before I found release and I feel...on edge.

I clench my fists, my clit practically begging to be touched, but no. I won't give Hades the satisfaction. He owns too many of my orgasms already.

Cold shower it is.

Every step I take toward my bathroom makes my pussy ache more. Every time my thighs brush together, the small amount of friction sends a jolt of pleasure through me.

Under the nearly ice-cold water, I get some much-needed clarity, and my desire-addled brain clears enough to push my thoughts from H— *Don't even think it P.*

I decide that the best course of action is to keep myself busy, so I turn my coffee maker on and start sifting through my mail. *Bill. Bill. Bill. Bank statement. Bill.*

I pour my coffee as I look over my bank statement. Since *someone* decided to take control of my finances, I've made a conscious decision to be more aware of my incomings and outgoings, ensuring I can account for every transaction.

Dropping the envelope on the counter, I cradle my mug, the rich, earthy smell bringing me comfort. I check the time, 6.15 a.m. *Fuck, how have I almost been awake for the better part of an hour?*

I take another sip. Already dread going into the office. The way Hades left yesterday made it easy to guess how his mood will be, especially if he's anywhere near as sexually frustrated as I am. It occurs to me that he might not have gone home after being here. Maybe he has a whole harem of women, ready and waiting for his call.

The thought sits heavily at the center of my mind, making my stomach churn. The thought of him with another makes me nauseous.

He's mine.

I blink, where did that thought come from? He absolutely is not *mine.*

Grabbing my phone, I open my work email.

I stare at my phone long after the email has been
delivered. I hate calling out of work, but I just don't feel
ready to see him. Plus I have lunch with Jackson later,
and he deserves my full attention.

I open my laptop and jump into work. Time seems
to speed up as I pin all of my concentration on Photoshop and socials.

I sit back in my chair. As the hours progress, so does
my horrible mood. The tense feeling low in my stomach
aches and throbs. I know that, if I check right now, my
panties will be soaked through. They always are these
days. The second Hades enters my mind, the lace between my thighs becomes damp, my body constantly
anticipating him.

Luckily for me, I barely think of him.

Lie.

I quickly dress for lunch, choose to wear a short lavender sundress, sandals, and *new* panties.

Someone knocks on the door promptly at noon. I
open it to see Jackson's smiling face. I smile back at him,
keenly aware of my lack of reaction to him. I wish I felt

like this about Hades.

"Hi!" I lean in, kissing his cheek.

"Hey, babe." His hand goes to my hip and squeezes it softly.

"Let me just grab my purse." I turn from him and shove my phone, keys, and wallet in my vintage Chanel purse and intertwine my fingers with his outstretched hand.

"Feeling better?" he asks as I lock the front door.

"Much, thank you." I turn to face him

He leans in and kisses me. "Anything I can do?"

I can't help the smile from blooming on my lips. He really is a sweet man. "Take me to lunch."

He winks at me and starts guiding me down the stairs and out of the building. "Feeling bossy today, hm?"

I nod. "So where are you taking me?"

"A little café down the street."

We walk in companionable silence. It's one of the things I enjoy most about being with Jackson. He's comfortable. We don't need to be talking or touching. It's just nice being around him.

No passion though, P. Not like with...him.

There is no denying Jackson is the *safe* option. Nothing wrong with the safe option, right? He is also the option that doesn't completely overwhelm me, threatening to take every part of me and leave nothing behind. The option that doesn't threaten to completely destroy me when he changes his mind about me.

We arrive at the café, and the waitress takes us to an open table. She hands us menus on wooden clipboards.

I lift my eyebrows as I look around. *This place is hipster as shit.*

I start looking through the menu, considering whether or not carbohydrates will cure my near-painful lust or my new crippling anxiety.

"I wanted to talk to you about something," Jackson

138

says, his voice shaky.

I continue looking at the menu, browsing the salads. *Please, no one ever* wants *a salad, P.*

Jackson draws my attention to him by clearing his throat loudly. As I drag my eyes from the clipboard, my gaze snags on a small white box now sitting in front of me on the table. My lips part and my eyes widen as I gape at it.

"Jackson…" I breathe.

He clears his throat again, steeling himself, obviously about to ask something very important. *Please not* that.

"I know it's soon, but…I kept thinking about the other day, how I don't ever want to leave you again. And if we were married, you could come with me on trips, and you wouldn't have to work anymore."

I bristle slightly at the insinuation that I *want* to be a kept woman. *Not the time, P.*

We're not even exclusive. How could he have gone from casually dating me to a proposal of marriage?

My gaze finally meets his. I stare at him, slack-jawed. "I—"

"So…you will?"

I look back down at the box. My heart races, and I seem to have forgotten the steps to successfully take a breath. I need to get out of here. I push my chair back from the table and stand, not looking at Jackson.

"I forgot I have something to do at work. I have to go. I'm sorry."

He frowns. "Wait, what?"

I kiss his cheek quickly. "It's not…I need to…I have some time-sensitive work." I grab my bag and leave the restaurant, feeling much less claustrophobic in the busy streets of Manhattan than I did in that spacious restaurant.

Chapter Twenty-Five

Hades

FOR THE REST OF THE WEEK, I'M THE PERFECT BOSS. I'm standoffish...and hard. I'm far too busy getting ready for the fall to even notice much else. Everything is a blur. A complete blur. Throwing myself into work to act like I'm too busy to notice the way Persephone's pencil skirts mold to her hips. Or how, when she bends over slightly, the stitching tightens to the point of breaking. I'm not noticing. Far too busy. I am absolutely not imagining in my head various ways to take advantage of my employee. In my head, I can imagine keeping her bent over like that, ripping those stitches wide, kicking her feet apart, and forcing her to take every frustration and muted lust inside me. To punish her for being mine but not. For flaunting a body I have no right to. Yes, for this week, I was the perfect boss.

At least at work.

When I'm home alone, I'm forced to work out as if training to compete against Heracles in order to keep myself restrained. Each day, I push my body to the limits, blasting music in my gym, as I try to purge the need to fuck Persephone within an inch of her life. I've never been in such good shape, or so sore the next day. I suppose part of me should be grateful for that. But I'm not.

Not until I find a way to purge this *obsession*. Exercise hasn't worked yet, but I have to believe there is a way to get her out of my head.

My muscles burn with the exertion, sweat dripping. I've moved from just cardio and weight lifting to complete Krav Maga and Muay Thai, using a heavy bag to batter my limbs against. I pummel it, my mind already supplying that mortal's face a little too easily. Each hit of my fist excels in power and speed. Till I feel my knuckles split, my golden ichor spilling.

I pull my hand back, looking down at my bleeding knuckles. Each of my fingers move, and my wounds heal slowly with my eyes locked on them. I exhale, watching. I need to move on. I need to stop thinking about her. Stop obsessing.

Move on.

My music is interrupted by the office alarm, making me tear my gaze away from my healing knuckles, going downstairs to inspect the alert. I only turned on the alarm for the weekend. I don't like people in the office without me there to look over things. It's hard enough to be away from it for six months. Every neurotic and obsessive part of me balks at not being present to oversee every aspect. Even though I receive a weekly summary from my COO when I'm downstairs, I can't help but itch to be present.

I use the stairs to head down to the office, not bothering to change out of my sweat-soaked workout clothes. Distracted. *I'm always fucking distracted these days.* I would have a completely clear head if it weren't for a single goddess. Everything would be clear if she hadn't shown up.

"Hello?" I call in the empty office, trying to find the source of the alarm.

I hold back a curse when I inhale the flowery scent, alerting me to who exactly has decided to come into the office on a Saturday. *Roses in a dense fog.* A mysterious and hauntingly sweet scent. One part is the Goddess of Spring, the flower. The other…the mist. *The Underworld.*

I hiss in realization. *She smells like home.* Like the mists that linger around the palace.

I take a steadying breath, pausing in the doorway of her office, where she's working diligently on a laptop. She's dressed in a pair of black shorts, and a loose-fitting cropped top. Clearly, she wasn't planning on being at work in any formal capacity dressed like this.

I snap at her, "What are you doing here?"

Her head jerks up, her eyes trailing over me, and I try to stop myself from responding. "I—"

I frown at her, crossing my arms over my chest. "It's a Saturday."

Her gaze hardens, her vibrant eyes darkening. "I didn't realize I wasn't allowed to be here on a Saturday."

"Usually we lock the door," I throw back.

She tilts her head, lifting a dark eyebrow. "Are you telling me I have to leave?" Her face falls slightly, and I step forward almost instinctively. "You won't notice I'm here. I promise."

She doesn't want to go home. Am I such a monster as to throw her out?

I can't stop myself from closing the distance, touching her cheek, wanting to erase that look from her face. "Is everything alright?"

She releases a deep exhale, almost relieved? "I just…I need a distraction, and work…helps."

I rub her cheek with my thumb. "Would you like… company?"

She turns her head, her lip brushing against my palm, before nodding. My heart catches in my throat at the soft and intimate moment between us. She nods, looking up at me.

I smile at her softly. "Why don't you come work in

my office? I have work to do too." I pull my hand from her cheek as she stands and collects her laptop, following me to my office. "I'm going to shower and I'll be back. Make yourself comfortable."

She pauses at the doorway of my office, both of our bodies hovering in the small entryway. She looks up at me, going to her tiptoes, kissing the corner of my mouth, her voice low. "Enjoy your shower, Hades."

My breath catches in my throat, and I force myself to leave and shower. I'm her boss. I'm reading into things. She has a boyfriend. Yet, I'm taking my cock in my fist under the water of my shower, picturing it if she decided to follow me to the shower, and I could fuck her mercilessly under the spray. I would wrap those maddening legs of hers around my waist, until she begged for me to let her come.

I can't stop myself from coming to the idea. I shake under the hot water, forcing my thoughts to clear, drying myself off. Dressing in comfortable sweats, I go back downstairs, walk back to my office, and sit across from her, engrossing myself in work, rolling my shoulders, pretending the object of my obsession is not sitting across from me. A mere handful of feet away.

After an hour of silent work between us, she stands from the desk, stretching. "Coffee?"

I look up at her, trying not to follow the way her limbs stretch and move. "I can order some."

She nods, stretching again, before sitting back down. "Soy vanilla latte, please."

I pick up the phone at my desk, calling the bakery at the corner, ordering her latte, adding muffins, croissants, and three espressos for myself. She glances at me over her laptop, smiling.

"What?" I ask. "I'm hungry."

She shrugs, smiling, going back to work again.

When the food is delivered, I hold out her soy vanil-

la latte, and our fingers brush each other's, our eyes locking. It takes longer than it should for me to pull away
from her, going back to my own work.

Chapter Twenty-Six

Persephone

THE WEEK SPEEDS BY IN A HAZE OF RE-PRESSION AND AVOIDANCE. I've been dodging Jackson since our lunch, and the guilt sits heavily on my shoulders, every excuse I throw at him adding another small weight to the pile. They're getting worse too. My last one being that I couldn't see him last night because I needed to "sort my stockings into pairs."

This morning I caught myself pacing in my own apartment.

Maybe work will distract me.

I glanced at my laptop and immediately knew there was no way I'd be able to focus on my tasks enough to complete them to my high standard in this environment. So I grabbed my computer and headed into the office, hoping the change of environment would distract me. It had been a smart plan…until Hades appeared. I was expecting him to be an asshole, to tell me to leave. I could tell he thought about it, but instead…he cupped my cheek, so tenderly, his gentle touch igniting that fire in me that I'm growing so used to now. I'm still unclear how that interaction brought me to where I am now, sitting opposite Hades in his spacious, luxurious office.

The space is much the same as mine, but larger, and more populated with plush furnishings. The black desk in the center of his room is both wider and longer than mine, and his swivel chair is black with a taller back than the others in the office, like he is the king, and this is his throne.

I look up at Hades, his work ethic like a tangible object in the room with us. There is absolutely nothing sexier than a man who takes pride in his career.

Stop drooling, P.

"Are you alright?"

He releases a heavy sigh. "Fine."

My lips twitch. "You're a terrible liar."

He glances at me, his gaze missing that usual sparkle of primal hunger. "What?"

I sit back in my chair, crossing one of my legs over the other, and I wait for his reply.

He rolls his eyes at me. *I wonder, if I did that to* him, *would he spank me?*

"Those de-mountained are burning through their accounts."

I lift an eyebrow playfully, trying to get back to the flirty banter I'm so used to, the flirty banter I crave. "Want me to beat them up for you?"

He lets out a short laugh, his face relaxing. "I'm sure they wouldn't see that coming."

Goddess of Spring can throw hands.

Lie.

I look back at my computer. "Barely anyone knows I exist. They definitely wouldn't see me coming."

I feel that intense gaze on me. "Why is that?"

My eyes flick to his. "My mother kept me like the most precious of secrets."

He frowns. "That's unusual."

I shrug, my smile not reaching my eyes as my resentment surges. "Even the great Hades, God of the Underworld, King of the Dead, didn't know about Persephone, the Goddess of Spring." I hesitate, my voice turning sharp. "Demeter's best kept secret."

His hand slides over the table toward me, such a tender action. My heart leaps. It takes everything in me to not reach out to touch his.

"So you left?"

I continue to stare at his outstretched hand, but it doesn't feel like enough. Being in this room with him, alone, his scent surrounding me, his deep blue eyes staring into my very soul. I stand from my chair and move around the desk, perching on it next to him, close enough that I can feel his delicious warmth radiating from him, but no part of our bodies touch.

"So I left. It took me centuries to convince her, but I did it."

"Surprising that she would let you."

I tilt my head, my eyes roaming over his perfect face, taking in his cheekbones, his strong jaw, his exquisite eyes, before finally snagging on his lips, those perfect, full lips. I try to convince myself it was so much easier to overlook them before I'd experienced them pressed against mine. But even before I'd experienced his firm but soft lips urgently slanting over mine, they had overrun my dreams. Now I know exactly how it feels…my desire to repeat the act is almost unbearable. "I can be very…convincing." I pause. "Plus, there are rules."

He lifts his hand, bringing it to my thigh. He strokes the back of his fingers along the fabric of my shorts. Even that small touch forces me to bite back a moan. I feel as if my skin is on fire.

"Rules?"

I shiver as my skin breaks out in goosebumps, and I nod. "Rules."

His fingers continue stroking me, never touching my bare thigh. "Which are?"

I let out a shaky laugh. "No men…" I tilt my head at him, glancing at his lips. "No fraternizing with gods…"

My lips curl into a half smile. "And I get checked up on every six months to ensure the rules are being followed."

His mouth pulls into that maddening smirk that makes me want to slap him and sit on his face. "How's that going?"

My eyebrow quirks. "I've never been one to follow rules."

His fingers slide off the denim, the pads of his fingertips touching my skin. My breath hitches as his hand glides down my thigh. "I've noticed."

I lean into him. "Oh? How so?"

"I'm a god...and a male." He smirks again. "You're... fraternizing."

I roll my eyes. "Those aren't *your* rules."

He growls and pulls away from me, my skin already missing his touch. "I expect obedience when I demand it, Persephone."

My eyebrows lift and I smirk. "Oh, hit a nerve, did I?"

He clenches his jaw and looks away from me dismissively. "I should get back to work."

I purse my lips, frustrated at his reaction, then sigh heavily. "Fine." I stand from the table and move back to my seat, the feeling of his hand burned into my skin, my thigh tingling as my flesh clings to the memory of his scorching touch.

Chapter Twenty-Seven

Hades

I GRIND MY TEETH AS I FOCUS ON MY WORK, trying to figure out what exactly Persephone is thinking. I feel like she wants me, and I can still feel the side of her thigh under the back of my fingers. The soft feel of her shorts, the heat from her skin barely kept from me. Her scent became even more intoxicating that close to me. Even more so than when I had her under me in her apartment, or in the club. Was it because I wasn't already lost in the throes of lust when it happened?

What do you know about her besides the physical? Zeus's words ring in my ears, and even though I shouldn't, I've been noticing more and more about her, even when I'm pretending to be the perfect boss. She has a weakness for sweets. I've seen her pillaging the free food in the community breakroom, always picking the sweet over the savory options. She wears heels every day, despite massaging her sore feet under her desk at work. She must think them worth the pain. From the way her ass moves when she wears them, I might have to agree with her. Her favorite food is sushi, or at least it's the food she's ordered three times this week. Always from the same place. Though maybe that's just the place she's interested in this week. Next week, it might be burgers. I think she does yoga at least three times a week. She's left work with a yoga mat before. I've heard her discuss books, movies, and plays in passing with some other employees, making mental notes of each. Just little scraps of information I've gathered from my borderline stalker behavior.

And now she's in front of me. Every breath she makes feels like a brush against my skin. Even across my desk, without touching her.

She rolls her neck and shoulders, tension clear in her brows.

"Do you want me to call a masseuse?"

She shakes her head. "No, I'm just tense."

Join the club. I can barely remember a time when I wasn't tense. Where I wasn't on the verge of launching across the desk and yanking her to me, finally putting myself out of my misery. When I didn't both dread and long for each workday. For the chance to see her. Even when I have no right to have her. Besides the one fate keeps trying to force upon us.

I crack my jaw, using my shadows to press into her shoulders, massaging. Even if I'm annoyed at her, even angry, I can't let her be uncomfortable. I won't touch her. My shadows don't count. At least, that's what I tell myself. *Doesn't count if it's not actually my touch. My shadows are not technically me.*

Though I feel what they feel, see what they see. *Semantics.*

She brushes off my shadows, glancing at me, but only for a moment. "I'm fine."

I shoot her a look, my shadows vanishing. "Fine."

She glares at me before burying herself in work again. I try to do the same, but as each minute passes, I feel the anger boil in my blood, surging forth. She lets me pleasure her, then blows me off. She wants me. Then she hates me. I'm losing my mind trying to figure out her thoughts and feelings. Every time she touches me, I lose it a little more. I'm a pot about to boil over. Heating more and more in her presence.

The corner of my lips still burns from that kiss she gave me earlier.

My hand flexes on the laptop, remembering her hand in mine. The slide of her skin against me, the heat mingling between us. Pulsating.

Yet she dares to act as if there is nothing between us?

She grabs a muffin from the table and picks at it. And something about the casual movement makes my temper unleash. The pot *explodes.*

I slam my laptop shut, the screen cracking with the force, as I whip out, "What's wrong with you?"

She lifts an eyebrow at me, and my eye begins to twitch. "What?"

What? WHAT?! She knows exactly what I'm talking about. This thing between us. The palpable chemistry that seems to vibrate whenever we're together. We can't keep our hands off each other. Yet she acts like that's nothing? When it is *everything.*

"One second, you can't get enough of me. Next you're blowing me off," I snarl at her.

"Me?!" she demands. "You're the one who's hot and cold!"

ME?! Is she actually insane? If there is anyone who's hot and cold, it's her!

I scoff. "You're the one with the boyfriend! Who you refuse to break up with!" My teeth grind. "Does he know how you screamed for me in that club?"

Her eyes flint. "That's none of your business."

I snarl, shoving back from my desk. "Until you do, I'm just your boss."

Her fists clench. "Why do you have this need to possess me?"

BECAUSE FATE SAYS YOU'RE THE ONE FOR ME!

151

"Why do you have this need to provoke me?" *The need to turn me inside out with your thoughts and words.* And why does she succeed at it? Why is she so deep inside my skin that I feel the need to claw at my skin until she's out?

She stands from the desk, her chest heaving. I can't hear whatever scathing words she's about to unleash upon me. I don't know how I'll react.

I slam my hand on the desk, hissing. "Get out."

She slams her laptop shut and storms out. I watch her through the glass walls as she goes to her own office, grabbing her phone. Even as she moves to the elevator, pushing the button multiple times, tension clear in her shoulders.

Don't run after her. Don't run after her.

Our eyes connect when she turns back, stepping on the elevator. The door closing between us.

Fuck you, fate.

Chapter Twenty-Eight

Persephone

DON'T GO BACK TO HIM. DON'T GO BACK TO HIM.

My breath catches in my throat when I turn and see him staring at me. My gaze locks with his. I lift my chin defiantly, a silent "fuck you."

The doors close, slowly, too slowly, and every second, my body wills me to go to him. To grab his face and kiss him, to straddle his hips and grind against him.

The doors finally close, and almost on cue, my phone alerts.

JACKSON

We should talk. No more excuses, please, Persephone.

Fuck.

PERSEPHONE

We should. I'm really sorry about this week. Wanted to impress the new boss.

Lie. You wanted to fuck the new boss. Still do.

JACKSON

I understand if you're not ready.

PERSEPHONE

Dinner, tonight?

JACKSON

I can pick up takeout?

PERSEPHONE

7:30?

JACKSON

See you then.

I move to the back of the elevator and lean against it, lightly hitting my head against the metal wall.

Oh what a tangled web we weave. Luckily, I'm extremely well-adjusted and able to unravel my messes painlessly.

Lie.

I lean against the wall, looking at the front door, waiting for Jackson to arrive. My commute and time at home weren't spent thinking of Hades.

Lie.

Weren't *fully* spent thinking of Hades. I thought at length about what I was going to say to Jackson. There was absolutely no way I could say "yes" to his proposal, but did I want to end it with him fully?

Yes.

Hades is so hot and cold all the time, it confuses me. Acknowledging my reasons for keeping Jackson around is *not* something I want to delve into too deeply right

154

now. I can try and convince myself that I wouldn't *have* to start anything with Hades when Jackson and I amicably part, but that is too big a lie to swallow, and I'm not sure if I'm ready to knock down that barrier quite yet.

Jackson and I may not be official, but that doesn't seem to matter to Hades. He won't be happy until I'm completely unattached.

I sigh, once again settling in with my old friend, guilt. I know that I'm being unfair, and yet…there is something stopping me from ending things, something other than the shield it provides between me and my boss.

At 7:30 on the dot, Jackson knocks on the door. I stop anxiously pulling on my fingers and open the door. He smiles at me, but I can tell he's just as anxious as I am.

He holds up a bulging bag of food, the air thick with awkwardness. "Hi, babe."

I lean in to kiss him, pressing my lips softly to his, pulling back after a moment.

Don't think about Hades. Don't think about Hades.

He brushes past me, heading straight to the kitchen, and starts pulling out various cardboard containers. I watch him.

"How was work?" His voice is gentle. He genuinely cares about my day.

"Productive." My thigh still tingles where Hades's hand caressed me. I clench my fist, trying to push the thoughts from my mind.

I walk to him, nudging him over with my hip as I help him open containers. "How was your day?"

He glances at me. "It's been a tough couple of days."

I tense. *Of course it has. Stupid fucking question, P.*

Jackson nudges me with his shoulder. "I'm okay, P."

I nod, looking away from him. "Good, I'm glad."

He places a hand on my lower back. "I get that you're not ready."

I still. "We're not even officially dating, Jackson. We've never labeled—"

Jackson sighs, cutting me off. "Persephone…am I wasting my time? Cause I thought this was where we were heading."

I turn to face him. "You're not wasting your time—"

"I'm just moving too fast?" He tucks a stray strand of hair behind my ear.

"Way, way too fast." My words come out sharper than I intend.

He visibly recoils. "Sorry."

Silence.

I sigh heavily. "You really bought a ring?"

His eyes roam over my face before he pulls the familiar box out of his jacket pocket and opens it, setting it down on the counter.

My eyes widen, and I tilt my head at the large sparkling rock staring back up at me. The ring is comprised of a main cushion-cut diamond and smaller diamonds surrounding it. Obviously extortionate. *Not to my taste, but I can appreciate the beauty.*

"Oh, Jackson…"

"Biggest and best for you."

I slide my thumb over the edge of the box, unable to tear my eyes away from the diamond.

"Do you like it?" I can hear the nerves in his voice.

I reluctantly pull my gaze from the ring, frustration rising at Jackson as he pulls my attention away. The anger dies the second I'm out of the stone's thrall. "It's beautiful, Jackson."

He leans in, kissing me sweetly. My body has zero reaction to him, still.

What is wrong with me?

"You deserve it."

I smile at him before looking back at the ring. Almost instinctively, I pull the ring out of the box, the gold band catching the light from the lamp. My eyes widen as it glitters and sparkles.

Would marrying him really be so bad?

"It was several months' of salary. You deserve every penny."

My cheeks flush, but I don't look up from the ring. An overwhelming urge to slide it onto my finger overtakes all rational thought. "May I...?"

He nods. "Sure."

I slide it on, my skin tingling under the cool metal. I gaze down at it. The second the ring is situated, it is as if the fog clears, and I stare down in horror at the gold hoop hugging my finger tightly.

NOT RIGHT NOT RIGHT NOT RIGHT.

It feels as though my skin is trying to repel the gold, push it off.

NOT HIM NOT HIM NOT HIM.

Jackson leans in, tenderly kissing my cheek. My eyes remain glued to the ring, no longer in wonder, but dread. I slowly try to take it off, trying to not alarm Jackson with my distress. The gold easily slides to my first knuckle and...stops.

I furrow my brows. It felt a little loose when I first put it on. I tighten my grip on it and pull it harder, making my finger swell even more.

"Fuck."

Jackson laughs. "Hm, that's a sign you're not supposed to take it off."

I look up at him, laughing nervously.

Fuck fuck fuck.

NOT RIGHT NOT RIGHT NOT RIGHT

TAKE IT OFF TAKE IT OFF TAKE IT OFF

I swallow down my panic and glance at Jackson, praying that I'm doing a satisfactory job of hiding it.

"I'll try again later. Let's eat."

He nods and grabs a few of the cartons before settling on the couch. I grab one, too, and follow him. I take care to sit close enough for things to appear normal but far enough away that we barely touch.

I push my noodles around with my chopsticks. I'm so strangely aware of the heavy weight on my ring finger. Almost as if the gold is scorching me, and not in the consuming way Hades's touch sears me. This feels like my whole being is rejecting, not only the proposal, but Jackson as well.

As a hopeless romantic, there is no explanation for why I wouldn't want this. Marriage has always been something I fantasized over. I spent my lonely childhood dressing up and styling linen as a wedding dress and veil, imagining my handsome prince at the end of the altar, waiting for me, ready to bind his life to mine.

Jackson is not your handsome prince.

There was the issue, Jackson was never who I pictured standing at the end. The man I always imagined never had Jackson's dirty blond hair or brown eyes. He wasn't gentle and quiet.

No, the man I imagined was tall, dark, and handsome. A good man, but…with an inner darkness. Powerful. Passionate.

Jackson shifts on the couch, pulling me from my thoughts. He places his food on the coffee table and plucks mine out of my hand, discarding it too. I smile at him, slightly dazed. He leans in and kisses me softly, his fingers threading into my hair, pulling me closer.

I clench my fists as my body fails me once again. Refusing to respond to Jackson with even a quarter of the desire I feel when I'm with Hades.

Stop thinking about Hades when you're making out with someone else, P.

He shifts again, deepening the kiss and pulling me closer.

I pull away slightly, parting my lips from his. "Jackson…"

He kisses me harder, his lips insistent on mine. His hands roam over my curves as he pushes me back.

Not the right hands. Not the right mouth. Not the right ring. Not the right man.

I push against his chest, trying to pull away again. I feel his hard length pressed against me. I feel nothing, no desire, no lust. It may as well be a metal rod pressing into me.

Jackson pulls back, looking down at me. "What is it?"

I swallow, looking up at him. I cup his cheek. "I can't tonight. I'm all in my head about everything."

He sits up, his body tense. "How many more excuses are you going to give me, P?"

I pull myself up, sitting so my back is against the arm of the couch. I can't get any further from Jackson and remain on the couch. "Excuse me?"

He glances at me. "You're not feeling well, too in your head."

I blink at him. "You proposed to me out of thin air!"

"Out of thin air?" Jackson scoffs. "Please, we were heading there."

"Maybe eventually, but—"

Jackson stands. "I want to take care of you. If you married me, you'd want for nothing. I'd give you everything."

My gaze hardens. "Jackson."

His jaw clenches. "What could you possibly need to think about?"

Is he fucking joking?

I lift my eyebrows. "First of all, we aren't even boyfriend and girlfriend yet, and second of all, even if we were in that place, it's a decision that will affect the rest of my life, Jackson."

"Do you love me?"

Fuck...I can lie to myself, but can I lie to him? Do I love him? Did I ever?

"Jackson, I—"

"Is there someone else?"

Fuck fuck fuck.

I blink. "You have two choices here, Jackson."

His eyes narrow. "That's not a no."

I sigh, trying to control my face, my body, my tone. "It's none of your business."

He takes a step back, his face twisted in anger. "You know, most women would *kill* for what I'm offering you here, and you...you can't decide."

"I am not *most women*, Jackson."

He looks as if he's about to say something, but he just turns and storms out, slamming the front door as he goes.

Good one, P.

Chapter Twenty-Nine

Hades

MAYBE FATE WAS WRONG, maybe the Fates themselves were trying to fuck with me. I knew fate to be cruel, but this? I texted Zeus for his advice again. Unsurprisingly, he was of little help. He kept insisting that, if she wanted me, she would have been with me. When I give up on Zeus, I call Poseidon for advice, who is shockingly less helpful than Zeus.

Which is why I'm currently sitting at a bar waiting for a date from one of those mortal apps to show up. I can't believe I downloaded that app again. I even resorted to doing research online about creating a successful profile. I was overwhelmed with the amount of information on how to have a successful online dating experience. So much of the information I discovered was completely contradictory. Some claim people want you to be honest; others encourage you to lie. I eventually went with *Hoping to forget someone who's not interested.*

I held my breath when I confirmed the account, surprised when I didn't get immediate suspension of my account. Was it because I was more honest? Or because I took some candid photos of myself that couldn't be found when you googled Plutus? Either way, it worked, and I am meeting up with a girl named Amanda at a bar that is close to her apartment.

I glance up, standing slightly away from the bar, trying to call her attention.

She smiles awkwardly at me before darting between the bodies pressing in on each other, coming to my side. "You must be Hades. Great name, by the way."

I shake her hand when she offers it. She's several inches shorter than Persephone, who already barely comes to my chest. I would need to break my neck to kiss her. She moves to sit next to me on the bar stool, turning to look at me. I catch a whiff of her scent, as her dark hair—not as silky or shiny as Persephone's—cascades over her shoulder. *At least it's floral. I can pretend it's the overwhelming and desire-fulfilling scent of a Goddess of Spring, who shall not be named.*

I take a sip of my drink, trying to buy time to think of the first thing to say to her. She orders her drink, and we wait in awkward silence for a moment.

"First date?" Amanda adds, glancing at me.

I clear my throat, rubbing my hand down my slacks. "That obvious?"

She laughs softly, and I try not to wince visibly at the sound. Nothing like the dulcet tones of the Voldemort in my head. "You look uncomfortable in your own skin."

I wince, sighing. "I've…there's a woman."

Amanda laughs again. I cover my wince this time by finishing my drink. "I figured there was, based on your bio. Listen, I'm getting out of a really bad relationship. I don't want to be holed up in my apartment, afraid to go outside. So let's make a deal? Yeah?"

I turn to face her fully, intrigued. "A deal?"

Amanda raises a dark brow, and her makeup cakes slightly at the movement. *Persephone never needs makeup.* Damn it. I'm not so shallow, am I? Women can wear makeup, it's their prerogative. They don't do it for leering men like me, who keep comparing them to someone else I can't stop thinking about.

"I tell you my story, you tell me yours. End of the night, we call it a day and lose each other's numbers," Amanda asserts, making me blink repeatedly at her.

"I thought you—"

"I'm not interested in a man who is so completely in love with someone else, they're trying to use Tinder as a way to escape." I can't cover my wince at that observation. "Sorry, but yeah."

I let out an exhale, relaxing in my seat for the first time. "I just…can't get her out of my head. And she's not interested."

Amanda pats my hand softly. Again I try to stop myself from pulling away at the overly soft feel of her hand. "My ex was abusive. I didn't realize it till years into it. He cut me off from all my friends and family, to the point where I have no one left to talk to but a date from Tinder."

For a moment, I'm tempted to hug her, comfort her. But I know if I do, I'm just going to compare her to *you-know-who*. Which isn't fair.

I really should not have gone on this date.

"But you got out. Many in your situation don't," I add softly, wishing I could offer more.

She takes a steady drink. "There was a moment where I could tell that the only way our relationship was going to end was in a body bag. His or mine, I couldn't tell."

I palm my second drink, looking down at it. "She has a boyfriend, and she's not broken up with him, despite…" I can't bring myself to say it.

"Despite you two being more than friends?" Amanda provides, saving me.

I nod, taking a long drink.

"They often talk about how hard it is on the wife when the husband cheats. It's hard on the person he cheats with too. I mean, so long as they're not an absolute asshole," Amanda adds.

"We haven't…gone all the way. I'm sorry this sounds like such a fucking shallow and petty thing to be upset about compared to you." I groan. *Gods, I'm the worst.*

Amanda shakes her head. "You can't compare trauma to trauma. We all deal with it differently. One trauma is not worse than someone else's."

I take a swig, glancing at her. "You sound…incredibly well-adjusted."

"I wasn't for a long time, but my shrink is actually… she's helped a lot." She shrugs, finishing her drink. "She actually picked out your profile for a date. She could tell you weren't looking for anything but someone to talk to."

My brows knit in surprise at that. "What's your therapist's name?"

Amanda snorts. "Why? Hoping to make an appointment?"

I shake my head. "Call it morbid curiosity."

Amanda shrugs. "Her name is Athena Parthenos."

I barely stop myself from cursing a blue streak. Is there no escape from the ever-present eyes of the divine?

I finish my drink, tossing it back. "Thank you for listening, Amanda."

She stands from her seat, touching my shoulder softly. "Just be patient, Hades. If it's meant to be, it's meant to be."

I nod, looking back at my drink, a crack forming in the glass from my grip.

It is *meant to be. That's the fucking problem.*

Chapter Thirty
Persephone

NOT RIGHT NOT RIGHT NOT RIGHT
TAKE IT OFF TAKE IT OFF TAKE IT OFF
I groan and pull a pillow over my head, trying to drown out the yelling, but the pillow doesn't help because no one is screaming. The turmoil is completely internal and has been unrelenting. *All fucking night.*

I'm ready to cut my finger off to rid myself of this piece of metal.

I push the pillow off and roll onto my back, thinking of the nearest jeweler that would be able to remove it.

I hear my phone alert, and happy for the distraction, I check my messages. A decision I immediately regret.

> MELLIE
> So I have like 10 missed calls from Helios.
>
> JACKSON
> Mail me the ring.

I sigh. Not knowing what to say to Mellie, I decide to ignore that one for now. But Jackson's message…

I'll talk to you when you're not being a
dickhead.

I lock my phone and climb out of bed, more than
ready to get this fucking ring off.

I get off the subway the next day, stressed, tense,
frustrated. I tried five jewelers yesterday, all of which
were closed. Which meant another sleepless night of my
body loudly repelling the stupid piece of gold that sits
seemingly harmlessly on my finger. I'll need to get this
fixed at lunch.

Every miserable moment I lay in bed, my ring finger throbbed, and my mind chanted, begging for me
to remove the ring. I tried over and over to pull it free,
to end my torment, but, with every try, my finger got
more swollen, until the band was stuck at the very base,
completely unmoving. The large diamond seemed to
get heavier with every minute that passed, increasing
my awareness of it. Throughout the night, I could have
sworn the ring was beckoning me, trying to enthrall me
again like it did when I first gazed upon it, but now my
instincts raged within me, beating out the urge to be en-
ticed by the valuable jewel.

As I walk to work, the smell of coffee from one of
the cafés draws me in and I have to stop. The small café
is bustling, and the baristas look overstretched as they
line to-go cups along the counter, trying to keep on top
of the endless orders streaming in from white-collar
workers needing their early morning caffeine fix.

I order and pull my phone out, scrolling through the
news as I wait.

I smile at the burnt-out looking barista as I accept
my coffee. I'm bringing it to my lips for that perfect first
sip, when my attention is stolen by what I can only de-

scribe as a banshee screech.

Within the blink of an eye, I'm being tackled. Long, slim arms wrap around me, completely encasing me, both the reason I nearly crashed to the ground and the reason I didn't. I turn my head to see bright eyes excitedly staring at me, one black, one gray. *Mellie.*

"You've been avoiding me!"

Mellie begins jumping up and down, jostling me. I hold my coffee out, trying to not spill it, needing this life-giving liquid more than ever today. "Sorry, Mel. Rough weekend."

She turns to the barista, completely oblivious to the queue. "Four lattes please."

I blink in surprise when no one calls her out for skipping the line.

Her gaze briefly returns to me, but like a magpie, her eyes are drawn to the shiny object tightly wrapped around my finger. "O-M-G!" She grabs my hand and lets out another screech, her eyes wide.

I quickly pull my hand away, shoving it in the pocket of my blazer. "It's not what it looks like."

She blinks. "How is it? Because it looks like you're engaged."

She accepts her order, barely pulling her gaze away from the ring, and we start the short walk to the office building, dodging fellow commuters barging past us down Wall Street.

"He...he did propose. But I didn't say yes. The ring is stuck. I'm getting it taken care of at lunch." My gaze hardens. "Do not tell anyone."

She blinks again. "Who would I tell?"

Hades.

"This just stays...between us, alright?"

She nods. "Though...I would like to know why you didn't say yes."

I hesitate, not because I don't trust Mellie, but because even *I* can't fully comprehend why I'm not over the moon about this. I refuse to believe it's because of some childhood fantasy.

"It's just…something isn't right, Mel. And it's far too soon."

Mellie frowns as we talk into the building. "Something isn't right? Like he's only into anal?"

My eyes widen. I glance around to see if anyone heard. Luckily, the concourse is buzzing with people all having their own conversations. I shoot her a glare.

"What? It's a thing!" She smiles sheepishly.

I shake my head, chuckling, and take a sip of my coffee, frustrated when the movement of bringing my cup to my lips intensifies the strange ache under the gold.

Mellie nudges me. "Something's just not right."

I smile at her and press the button for the elevator. "See you later?"

Mellie nods, but her attention is drawn when the receptionist calls out her name. I don't miss the glare the receptionist shoots me. She still doesn't like me from my first time here. The receptionist places a stunning bouquet of red roses on the desk, smiling wistfully at them. Mellie stills mid-step when she sees them. Tension seems to radiate from her body. She suddenly lunges over the desk and grabs the receptionist's phone. I stand watching the scene with wide eyes, as I see Mellie's face, animated with rage as she speaks on the phone. I only catch some of the conversation.

"…the fuck are you doing…"

"…roses? Really?"

She slams the phone down, smashing it against the receiver again and again. I'm relieved when the elevator arrives, and I slide inside. The last thing I see before the door closes is Mellie taking a pair of scissors to the vibrant red petals and the receptionist's face contorted in shock and fear.

Chapter Thirty-One

Hades

BY THE TIME MONDAY COMES ALONG, the slight relief which came from my disastrous date with Amanda has evaporated. I'm shouting at my staff, unable to stop the unending frustration and rage that seems coiled inside me. I thought the moment of explosion would have eased me. As if expelling my anger would soothe me. Instead, it only begins to build again. Another pot is simmering, and it keeps heating more and more, as I think about her. If I'm not thinking about Persephone, I'm trying to figure out what's going on.

I called Athena three times. She is avoiding my calls. Athena, Goddess of Wisdom and War, de-mountained less than a month ago, and suddenly she's a therapist.

A therapist who seems to be sourcing patients by walking straight up to them without preamble and saying she can solve all their problems. I tried to corral her, because she is risking exposure, not to mention her highhandedness with my date. I shout at someone, who scurries out of my office. First Persephone, now Athena.

Gods actually getting *jobs*. Gods were *worshipped*, or at least we used to be. Most didn't have the work or drive to actually work. So what the fuck?

My head snaps up at the sound of the voices in the hall. I should have closed my door. I usually did. But my absolutely pathetic self left it open so I could catch a whiff of her scent.

I catch Minthe's pinched voice, exclaiming, "Oh, congratulations on your engagement, Persephone!"

I'm on my feet in the hallway before I register it. *Engagement?* That has to mean something else. It can't mean what I think. It has to mean something else.

"Wow, this ring is huge! You lucky duck!" Minthe continues.

I make it to the doorway of her office, and my eyes dart inside, seeing the ring on her hand. My eyes trail from the blazing diamond on her finger, to her eyes. Her eyes dart away, looking at the computer screen.

I crack my jaw. "Get back to work, both of you."

I storm back to my office, not looking back to see her face again. Or that ring on her finger. *His ring.*

Back in my office, I glare at the reports on my desk, but the numbers swim in front of me. But my fingers don't shake as I type out a message on my phone.

HADES

Please keep your personal matters outside of office hours.

Gods, I'm a petty asshole. But I'm lashing out. Fuck, maybe I should schedule a therapy session with Athena.

PERSEPHONE

Please stop using my personal number for work-related matters. And keep your damn secretary in check.

What does that mean? And if she wants to keep me out of her phone, I have other means.

To: Propserina@Plutusindustries.com

Subject: Work Matters

What do you mean keep her In check?
Hades Plutus
CEO
plutus@plutusindustries.com

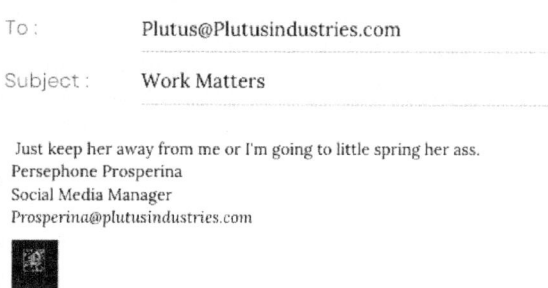

I know Minthe isn't the friendliest, but the nymph is efficient at her job. Damn efficient. The only person on this floor who has more work ethic is me...and Persephone.

To: Plutus@Plutusindustries.com

Subject: Work Matters

Just keep her away from me or I'm going to little spring her ass.
Persephone Prosperina
Social Media Manager
Prosperina@plutusindustries.com

I have to smother a smile at the thought of the nymph and goddess going toe to toe. I could sell tickets. Even though I can tell who the victor would be. There was a primal fierceness that lurked beneath Persephone's skin, something that called to the same inside me. *She's engaged.*

To : Propserina@Plutusindustries.com

Subject : Work Matters

Why? She was congratulating you.
Hades Plutus
CEO
plutus@plutusindustries.com

I glance up from my computer, forcing myself to look at her office, through the clear glass. But I see nothing but her closed computer. Did she leave? Leave me?

She didn't leave me. She was never mine, ever. Isn't that what I keep forgetting? I close out of my emails, picking up the phone without looking at the name as it rings.

"Plutus," I snap into the phone.

"My, my, is that any way to talk to your favorite niece?" Athena remarks into the phone, amusement clear.

I let out an exhausted sigh. "You've been avoiding me."

I hear the sound of a chair creaking as she leans back against it. "Avoiding? No, I would call it a strategy."

"Athena, I really don't have time for this," I hiss into the phone, my patience worn thin.

"Let me guess, too busy thinking about the girl you're obsessed with?" She hums.

I growl. "You know there's something called therapist-client privilege."

"Probably helps that I'm only a therapist in name."

I rub my hand down my face. "Athena—"

"Oh no, sounds like a lecture in coming. Should I

172

put on some tea?" Athena jibes.

"This is not the old times. Humans are not for us to mess with! The rules have changed!" I half shout into the phone.

The Goddess of Wisdom goes quiet for a moment. "I don't want… I seek to help them. To make amends for the past."

I flinch, hearing the pain in her voice. She has much to atone for, if that's her goal. *Medusa, Arachne, Tiresias.* Athena may have been the patron of heroes, but her punishment was just as legendary.

"If you wanted to help, there are other ways," I say.

"They are just…so lost, Hades," Athena murmurs.

So are we, Athena. We're as lost as they are. We're no different. Bumbling our way through the world for thousands of years, only we make bigger mistakes, bigger messes.

"When are you coming in for an appointment?" Athena asks, breaking me from my thoughts.

"How about never?" I snap back.

"You don't think therapy works?"

"I have no issue with therapy. I might even be open to it. But not with my niece as my therapist. No way," I state.

"So if I were to send a recommendation, would you see them?" Athena probes.

"Will it end this incredibly frustrating call?"

"Actually, yes."

I growl into the phone. "Fine, send me your recommendation."

She starts speaking again, but I hang up. Taking deep breaths to control my own annoyance.

Chapter Thirty-Two

Persephone

JACKSON

I'm sorry about the other day.

I **CLOSE MY EYES, TAKING A DEEP BREATH.**
Between Jackson's message, Hades, and *Minthe,*
I am already done with today, and it's 9:15 a.m.
Perfect.

I drop my phone into my purse and decide to take an extremely early lunch. I need this thing off me. Right now.

The nearest shop is only a block away, and the walk proves to be helpful. The tension headache eases as I inhale the fresh air. *Well, outdoor air. I mean, it is New York.*

"Machines broke," the gruff middle-aged man barks at my query.

I look down at the ring, my fists clenching. "When will it be fixed?"

He shrugs, continuing polishing a thick gold chain necklace. "Probably tomorrow. Maybe Wednesday."

I curse under my breath. I am *not* wearing the right shoes to be traipsing around Manhattan. And my feet are already screaming in protest.

I have similar luck at the second store I try, although my encounter is much more pleasant.

174

I enter the third store, almost ready to give up and go along with my plan to amputate the digit, ring and all.

"Oh, sure. I can do it right now." A young man, obviously fairly new to the job, enthusiastically responds to my request. I could kiss him.

You have enough men on your plate, P.

I wait patiently as he readies the machine, idly looking around the store. The mahogany cases scream luxury, and looking at some of the jewels within the fine glass cases, I can guess the targeted demographic. It looks like the sort of place Hades would shop if he was seeking jewelry for a girlfriend. Even from that simple, passive thought, jealousy prickles my skin, and my cheeks heat.

The young man clears his throat, I sigh in relief at the distraction.

"This way, miss."

The second the ring is cut from my finger, my body relaxes, finally free from being shackled. My brain ceases its chant, no longer screaming about the parasitic jewelry. I look down at it, glaring. It looks so harmless now, and yet there is still an eerie pull coming from it. The temptation would be overwhelming if it hadn't just welded itself to my finger and become an unwanted lodger for the past two days. I shove it in my pocket, where it sits like a ton weight, but at least it's not wrapped around my skin anymore. At least when I can't see it, I don't feel that sickly sweet wrongness that covers me like a mist, clinging to my skin.

I sigh and make my way back to the office, glaring at Minthe as I pass her. Her heavily made-up face pulls into a maddeningly smug look.

Oh, how I'd love to smack that look off your damn face.

I kick off my heels when I get to my office, relaxing into the expensive leather, my toes curling in the plush carpet of the cream rug.

My computer pings, the sound alerting me to an office-wide memo.

I roll my eyes. *Petty fucker.*

It's difficult to be annoyed at anyone or anything when waves of relief are still surging through me at my newfound freedom. *Why is everyone always trying to chain me up?*

I open Photoshop, finally feeling clear-minded enough to begin working.

DungeonMaster6969 12:08
The fuck is this memo about?

I roll my eyes but also chuckle at Mellie's choice of intercompany instant message name.

Sprung4Spring 12:08
I went for an early lunch.

DungeonMaster6969 12:08
And that pissed off the boss?

Someone needs to peg him.

Sprung4Spring 12:08
Everything I do pisses him off. It's a great source of pride.

Talk to me about an*I one more time, istg.

DungeonMaster6969 12:09
Listen, pegging is a gift, why do you think Helios is simping for me so hard?

176

I sigh at my computer, shaking my head. This is not a conversation I want to be having at work. No, this is not a conversation I want to be having anywhere. Ever.

Sprung4Spring 12:09
I am SO close to blocking you.

DungeonMaster6969 12:10
You know what's great for being blocked up?

Pegging.

I close the IM window, that sense of calm I was feeling now quickly evaporating. Almost the second I open Photoshop again, another IM pings onto the screen. I groan as I see Minthe's name pop up.

I'd rather talk pegging with Mellie...

MintyFresh 12:10
There is a guy with flowers here to see you, your fiancé perhaps?

Fuck.

I hurry out of the office, and my eyes immediately go to Jackson, standing next to Minthe, holding a bouquet of roses.

Historically, roses don't have a *great* shelf life in this building.

Rose with a bite...

I try to walk to him calmly, but everything in me wants to get him out of the building as soon as possible. "Jackson, what a surprise. What are you doing here?"

My stomach drops as the air changes, and I feel Hades leaving his office. My skin prickles in awareness of him as his scent washes over me.

Sandalwood and citrus.

"I wanted to bring you these, an apology, a peace offering, I suppose."

I smile, but I know it doesn't reach my eyes. I'm barely listening to my "fiancé." As I feel Hades approaching
slowly, I once again feel like an antelope being stalked
by a lion.

Please, can they not interact? Fuck.

"Uh… Thank you. I'm actually really busy today—"

"You must be the lucky man! I'm Hades Plutus."

I have to suppress a shiver at his low, commanding
voice just over my shoulder. His arm brushes against
mine as he reaches to shake Jackson's. The small contact makes the knots in my stomach start to wriggle deliciously.

I glance at Jackson, trying to gauge his reaction. He
blinks at Hades, having to raise his head slightly to meet
his eyes. He reaches out and clasps his hand. Is that…awe
in his eyes?

"Jackson. It's an honor!" His brows furrow. "What
do you mean lucky?"

Hades smiles easily at him, but I can see his eyes are
tight with tension. "Your engagement. The news is all
over the office." To someone who didn't know him, his
voice probably sounded as if he was just stating a fact.
But I hear the sharper edge to it.

Is he jealous?

My eyes dart between them, my words stuck in my
throat.

Jackson blinks repeatedly. "We're not engaged."

Hades frowns, but there's something else in his expression. "You're not?"

I glare at Hades and hold up my *very* ringless left
hand. "No, we're not."

Our eyes meet, and there's a palpable electricity. My
skin tingles, desperate to touch him.

Jackson's eyes slide between Hades and I, and when I finally drag my gaze back to him, I feel like I've been caught in the act, and I feel my cheeks heat.

"It was a pleasure to meet you, sir. Walk me out, babe?"

I look away, nodding. I walk to the elevator, not checking to see if Jackson is following.

Need to get out of this office.

When the doors finally close, I let out a breath.

Jackson eyes me. "Your boss is nice…"

Great, small talk.

I stare ahead, my jaw clenched. "Mhm."

Jackson doesn't say anything again until the doors start to slide open. "I'm sorry."

I nod. "I know." I reach into my pocket and pull the ring out. "Also, this is yours."

He blinks at the ring, almost as if he doesn't even recognize it. "You should keep it, until you decide."

I nod again, reluctantly shoving it back in my pocket. "I should get back to work."

Jackson hesitates, pushing the elevator door open as it tries to close.

He leans in and kisses my cheek. "Text me?"

I nod and smile. "I'll text you tonight."

Jackson backs up, letting the doors close. I lean against the wall, squeezing my eyes closed, praying to a more powerful god than me, that Hades is not there waiting, ready to pounce.

Chapter Thirty-Three
Hades

EVEN SEEING HER MORTAL UP CLOSE DOES NOTHING TO SOOTHE ME. He looks friendly, *nice*, even. He appeared genuinely excited to meet me, which means she hasn't told him anything about us. *Cause it doesn't mean anything?* But at least, she isn't engaged, though if she isn't, why the fuck was she wearing his ring? The item didn't suit her at all. It was huge and gaudy, a trophy ring. Is that what the mortal thought of her? A trophy? And she's allowing this? Someone treating her as a prize? She's no one's prize. She's a queen.

My queen.

She was made to rule, not sit idly by as a battle rages. No. Persephone would never sit on the sidelines. So why is she not breaking up with him? Why is she using him as a barrier between us?

I make it less than ten minutes before I'm pulling out my phone, opening up a text. My fingers hover over the keys, trying to figure out what to type. I run a hand through my hair over and over again. Should I demand answers? An explanation? *Why are you resisting this, Persephone? You feel it, too, I know you do.* But she's fighting it. Now using this mortal as a shield. Why?

I put my phone down immediately, pulling up some work on my computer, glancing down every couple of seconds at it. She walked the mortal out, so it might take a minute for her to respond. I'm sure I'll have a complete story from her when she answers. A perfect, tidy explanation, maybe even her telling me how she was so wrong to deny me and that she broke up with the mortal the second she left.

When it pings with a response, I lunge for it.

PERSEPHONE
I don't owe you an explanation.

Fuck. I don't know why I got my hopes up. Has Persephone done absolutely anything I've expected? No. Instead, she delights in fighting with me, defying me. I can't help it, but my hackles immediately rise, typing out and sending out a response without thinking it through.

HADES
Fine. Stubbornly stay with someone, even when it doesn't feel right, just to spite me.

I close my eyes, hissing, hoping she doesn't catch my slip. *Shit.* I made a promise, and a moment later I broke it. She provokes me in a way even my brothers can't. She won't catch my error. It's innocuous enough. I could be assuming that things didn't feel right between them, not because someone told me Persephone felt that way. But her response immediately dissuades me of that notion.

181

I curse to myself. Fuck, fuck. Why can't I stop myself? Restrain myself? Act even somewhat normal? Yet, since that day Persephone appeared in my penthouse, I've lost all semblance of control. Unraveling at the very seams. Mellie told me something in complete confidence, while I was moping about Persephone. She made me swear on my crown to not say anything. *And what do I do the second Persephone riles me up?*

She's fated to be your other half.

My phone rings, and I curse immediately upon seeing the number, even as I answer. "Hello, sweetheart."

"You're a fucking asshole, you know that?" Mellie snarls into the phone.

I wince. "I'm sorry—"

Mellie doesn't pause, continuing like I hadn't even spoken. "I told you something in confidence! Because you looked absolutely pathetic! Like someone kicked your balls and was showing them off to you as a necklace!"

"Mellie—" I try to interrupt again, though I don't even know what I would have said.

"So I took pity on you! You big stupid ass! And what do you do? You immediately go and open that big mouth to the one person you're not supposed to tell! Gods!" Mellie berates me, turning my ears hot.

I can't remember the last time anyone laid into me like this. My mother certainly never did. No, Rhea only cared about using us in her battle against our father. She would never have cared enough to lecture me.

"Mel—"

There's nothing but the slamming down of a phone

182

and a dial tone. I let out an exhale, putting my own phone back into its place on my desk. I wince, running another hand through my hair. Can I do anything right?

Hades, God of Colossally Fucking Up.

Hades, God of Alienating Women.

In one fell swoop, I alienated Melinoë and Persephone. The only women I actually care about. *Fuck, care about? Do I...care about Persephone? Outside of our fated bond?* And I just colossally fucked it up with her...again. With them both. Not that I have an actual relationship with Persephone.

When it's approaching five o'clock, my entire day has been a complete waste. I just stared at my screen, not even hearing the conference calls I was in. Some repeated the information, like, ten times, and it still didn't sink in. Too many of the meetings should have been an email instead. My drive and determination for work, for putting things in order for the winter, is *gone.* I can't focus on anything, trying to think of a way to make amends to both Persephone and Melinoë.

Nothing.

The sound of teetering heels and a trilling voice with a thick accent calls, finally drawing my attention. "Hades! Darling! You're going to make me wait forever?"

I come out of my office, surprised to see Gisele, her statuesque form, her olive complexion glowing, her midnight hair perfectly coiffed. She's been a friend since I worked on an acquisition for her years ago, and she likes to stay in touch. Though she enjoys being overly friendly with me in public, she knows it makes me uncomfortable. I've come to be charmed by it. "I didn't know you were in town."

Gisele flies at me, jumping to wrap her legs around my waist, giving me a loud kiss. "A good surprise, no?"

I place the model down onto her feet, smiling at her. "You've got to stop jumping me. People think we're an item already."

Gisele wiggles her eyebrows. "And fun to let them imagine."

I nod. "I'll meet you downstairs. I need to get something from my office."

Gisele kisses my cheek, heading to the elevator. I dart into my office to grab my phone before following.

Chapter Thirty-Four
Persephone

M Y GAZE IS LOCKED ON THE TALL PICTURESQUE WOMAN CURRENTLY WRAPPED AROUND HADES. On his genuine warm smile for her. On their easiness with one another.

My blood surges with jealousy. Her eyes sparkle as she talks to him, her animated face bright, glowing, stunning. Hades smiles brightly back at her, his whole demeanor more relaxed than I've ever seen him. She squeezes his arm, and my stomach clenches in response. *She touched him...and he let her?* I watch as she walks to the elevator...alone. My brows furrow, why isn't Hades joining her?

Before I know it, I'm on my feet and following her. I briefly almost swerve into Hades's office, but my eyes remain on Ms. Perfect, currently waiting on the elevator. The short walk is filled with trying to comprehend what I'm doing. Trying to justify why I'm ambushing this stranger in the elevator. Why I continue to feel this possessive over someone I don't even like.

The door opens just as I approach. Her long easy strides in her heels are elegant and graceful, and I try to find one flaw in this woman. I flush slightly, inwardly apologizing to my feminism for that thought. I'll just add "making me a bad ally to women" to the growing pile of reasons to dislike the God of the Underworld.

She looks at me expectantly when she turns around to press the button, her head slightly tilted, her silky dark mane sliding over her shoulder. "Going down?" Even her voice is musical and light, perfection.

I hate her.

I nod once, trying to hold myself taller in my sky-high stilettos. She still stands at least a head taller than me, and her perfect legs seem to go on forever. I enter the elevator, briefly glancing at my office. I notice my purse laying on my desk. I sigh, knowing I'll eventually have to come back up to retrieve it.

She snaps her fingers, drawing my attention as she has a moment of recognition. "You're the new social media manager! Oh, your work is *fantastic!* I lectured him over and over about social media, but he doesn't listen." She chuckles. "Which, I'm sure, you're more than aware of."

Ugh, gorgeous and nice. Fuck. I actually like her.

"Thanks, sorry. I don't think I caught your name…"

"Gisele." She smiles warmly at me.

I nod, considering my next move. I can feel the question burning my throat, dying to be asked. The fear of her answer holding me back, but…I need to know. "Are you and Hades together?" The words come out fast, mumbled, forced.

I hold my breath. *This shouldn't matter. This doesn't matter.*

She laughs, the sound is just as musical as her voice. "No, no. Work is his first and only love."

I lift an eyebrow. "Huh…"

She smiles at me, her eyes sparkling with understanding. "He would never give me the attention I require. We're only good friends."

I nod slowly, discomfort settling heavy in my stomach. How could she have known what I was about to ask? We just met, and already, she knew what I needed to hear at that moment to ease my anxiety.

"Not like you and him," she adds, glancing at me knowingly.

My head snaps back to her. "Excuse me?"

"I feel the tension from you two. It's like…fire."

I tilt my head. She hadn't even been in the room with Hades and I and yet she sensed it.

"Like walking into a minefield," she continues before the elevator door slowly opens.

My brows furrow, a minefield? Uncertain, treacherous, dangerous. Not something I'd want my relationship with *anyone* to be compared to, and yet, somehow, it fit. There is a feeling of danger whenever I'm around Hades, adrenaline coursing through my veins at even the thought of being in a room alone with him. And what are Hades and I, if not a mess of uncertainties?

There is no Hades and I…

Lie.

"There's no tension," I mumble, more to myself than to her.

Lie.

She steps out of the chamber and turns to face me, her head tilted. She laughs again, obviously having heard my blatant lie. The doors start to close. I remain frozen in place.

"Aren't you getting off?"

I start moving to the doors, but they close, and the elevator starts ascending.

Like walking into a minefield. One misstep and it's all over.

I furrow my brows. What if I misstep? Have I already? There is no denying the pull I feel to Hades. The way I ache for him, the way I pine for him. Is there any stopping it?

Ding.

The doors crawl open, and I know he's going to be there. I'm so aware of him, always so aware of him. My breath hitches at the sight of him, standing, waiting. My gaze trails from the floor, up his powerful, hard body, finally locking on his own intense gaze. His eyes, dark, hungry.

I curse under my breath, pinned under his stare. My breaths become shallow, his presence stealing the oxygen from the room. I should get out. I should go retrieve my purse and leave for the day.

Gisele's words echo in my mind, *"Like walking into a minefield,"* and I see exactly what she meant. There is absolutely no good outcome from staying in the elevator, being in the same enclosed space as him, his scent enveloping me, caressing me, but…the idea of giving up the chance to be alone with him, however briefly, feels painful. Feels like I'm going against something bigger than I by preventing it.

"Forget how an elevator works?" His words are arrogant, but there's an undertone, a huskiness, a dark promise.

I find myself once again frozen in place. I don't move to get out of the elevator. I can't. I feel blood rushing to my cheeks. My lips part on a shaky inhale. I lean back against the wall and will my body to stop reacting to him. Willing myself to be strong.

Well, you weren't strong enough to get off this fucking elevator, P.

Chapter Thirty-Five

Hades

JUST HER BOSS. JUST HER BOSS. But the mantra is becoming quieter and quieter with each repetition. Until it's white noise in my head. My body doesn't care. And neither will my mind.

The door to the elevators close, locking us in. Our shoulders brush against each other. Something inside me...snaps. Like an echo in the small conveyance.

I grab her by the back of the neck, slamming my lips to hers. She doesn't pause, kissing me back immediately, her delicate fingers grasping at my lapels. She felt it. The way our souls were tied together. The way...we crave each other.

My palm hits the emergency stop button of the elevator, making the car jolt to a halt. My hands go to her ass, yanking her up, falling with her to the side of the elevator, pressing her against the wall, between the cool metal and my heated body. A body which needs to possess her in every way. To fuck her in every way.

Her arms wrap around my neck, keeping me from moving away. As if I am going anywhere at this moment. Or any moment when she is against me.

My hands drop frantically to her skirt, attempting to push it higher up, only to rip the fragile stitches in my haste. My hands land on her ass again, gripping tight enough to leave my fingerprint-shaped bruises on her.

Marking her in some small way.

I should gentle myself. I should—

My buttons fly as she tears open my shirt, dragging her nails down my chest, till my skin is red and marked by her. But I need more. My mouth drops to her neck, sucking her skin, biting her, marking her more.

She's mine. She knows it. Her body knows it. Yet she pretends. I pretend. Two liars unable to deny themselves when trapped in a tiny elevator. Her hand goes to my belt, tugging at it, her mouth biting my ear.

I tear her shirt in response, her buttons flying to join mine. My mouth drops down to her chest, frantic, sucking one of those luscious nipples, then the other. She's even more mouthwatering than I thought, her skin more addicting. I crave her like I crave food, water, fresh air.

Like she's essential. *Necessary.*

She arches into my mouth, moaning softly, her hand going from attempting to undo my belt to gripping it. Holding it for some anchor as I worship her breasts. I bite one nipple hard, sucking it again. She cries out in response, her other hand tangling in my hair.

"Hades..." she cries out.

The elevator phone rings shrilly, and I growl in frustration at the intrusion. I'm sure they're calling about the suddenly stopped elevator and the shadows cloaking the cameras in the corner.

I keep her pinned to me, picking up the emergency phone. "Hm, I see. I must have accidentally hit the stops. Let me check."

I have zero intention of moving from this spot. Persephone's chest heaves, watching me with lowered lids, trying to pull her shirt back together. I frown at her, shoving them apart again.

Despite the interruption, I'm very much not finished. I lean down to suck one of those nipples into my mouth, my other hand covering her lips, the other still holding the emergency phone. My finger covers the receiver, so they can't hear my mouth on her. The way I'm worshipping her. As only I can.

As I'm fated to.

"Nope, still not moving," I murmur in response to the question. I pretend to press another button, sucking her nipple again, rolling it over my tongue. "Yeah, nothing. Try restarting the system."

I hang the phone up as her palm goes to my pants. Rubbing against my cock, aching and hard for her. She bites her lower lip, moaning at me. I bite her nipple softly, before closing her ruined shirt. "Wrong place, wrong time, little spring."

Her hand pulls away from me, and my cock protests. "W-What?"

I frown as the system reboots, the elevator descending again. "As much as I want to finish this…"

She pants as I slowly lower her to her feet. She waves her hands, causing large leaves to cover her body, enough to pass as an elegant wrap dress. She moves to the other side of the elevator.

I blink at her, trying to understand why she's putting distance between us now. "What are you doing?"

She takes a deep audible breath, looking at me. "Hm?"

I hold my hand out for her. "Come here."

Let me hold you. Be mine.

She looks at my hand, her brows furrowed in suspicion. "What are you doing?"

What am I doing? She's not mine. She'll never be mine. My hand drops slowly. "Oh. I…I thought…" *things would be different.* "Nothing."

My hands go into my pockets to keep from reaching for her again.

She clears her throat, but I don't look at her, staring straight ahead. "I-I can't touch you right now, Hades."

Because you belong to someone else. She's not yours. Fate be damned.

"I understand." I reply coldly, looking directly in front of me. "We can forget about it." My hands grip the inside of my pockets.

Her breaths are still shallow. "You don't understand."

I close my eyes, grating out, "It's fine."

Mercifully, the elevator stops and the doors open, and I paste on a fake smile for Gisele. I can't look back at her. Even as Gisele fills the silence on the way to the restaurant, my mind is full of Persephone.

HADES

I'll leave you alone from now on.

It's what she wants right? Or she'd be with me.

PERSEPHONE

You're an idiot.

I blink down in surprise at my phone, barely registering that we're now at the restaurant and being escorted to a table.

HADES

It's what you want.

Isn't it?

PERSEPHONE

Idiot.

I notice Gisele watching me text out of the corner of my eye, but I ignore her, too focused on Persephone.

HADES

You're the one who isn't...

Mine. She isn't mine; she's someone else's.

PERSEPHONE

Aching for you? Out of my mind with need?
Unable to be attracted to other people? No. I
am all those things.

She is?

HADES

Available.

That's so lame.

PERSEPHONE

I'm going to try and alleviate the ache now.
Alone. Enjoy your date.

I groan, noticing that Gisele is typing away on her own phone, not even really minding that I'm not paying attention.

HADES

It's not a date. Will you think of me?

I shouldn't have added that. But I can't help it. I keep replaying the elevator over and over again.

PERSEPHONE

If you were here, I wouldn't have to just think
of you.

I want to be there, little spring. But…

HADES

I don't want part of you. I want all or nothing.

I pick up some bread, absentmindedly, from the table. Gisele is shamelessly flirting with the waiter.

PERSEPHONE

Even if I told you how wet I am? How
desperately I need you?

My next bite of bread is tasteless in my mouth.

HADES

Even then. All or nothing, Persephone. I want
you badly enough not to settle for less.

I swallow down my tasteless bread, waiting for her
response.

PERSEPHONE

Goodnight then, Hades.

HADES

Goodnight, Persephone.

Chapter Thirty-Six

Persephone

THE MORNING SUN STREAMS INTO MY BEDROOM. I stretch, moaning as my muscles loosen. The all-too-familiar ache between my legs draws attention to my need.

I brought myself to release twice last night. It didn't even take the edge off.

My lips still tingle from the memory of his kiss yesterday. Every inch of my body he touched, grabbed, and kneaded burns with the ghost of his heat.

My eyes flutter open as a text comes through. I frown. *It's early...*

But my lips pull into a smile when I see the sender.

> **HADES**
> Good morning, my spring.

My? I flush at the show of possession. I have always steered clear of possessive males, and yet, Hades being possessive over me makes me feel...crazed.

> **PERSEPHONE**
> Good morning, demon.

I bite my lip, smiling at my phone.

HADES

How did you sleep?

And I'm not a demon.

I mean, I have horns, but that doesn't make me a demon.

A triple text? Hm...

My smile widens as he chastises me for using that particular term of endearment. *As suspected...*

PERSEPHONE

I have horns, too, you know.

HADES

You do?

What do they look like?

I lift an eyebrow, looking at my phone. Like last night, my pussy is in full control right now.

PERSEPHONE

Come see for yourself.

HADES

Are you available?

PERSEPHONE

At 6 a.m. on a Tuesday?

I'm such a brat.

HADES

You know what I mean.

I sigh at my phone, pouting that he's not playing with me. Wanting him to flirt with me. To tell me how badly he needs to touch me, to kiss me, to fuck me. Literally anything.

PERSEPHONE

Hades...

HADES

I'll take that as a "not available" then.

My smile fades, and I glare up at my phone. He's not being unreasonable, but my desire doesn't care about reason. It cares about getting my hands on his smooth, hard body. Besides, it's not as though I'm locked down in

PERSEPHONE

What do you want from me?

HADES

I thought I made it clear what I wanted.

PERSEPHONE

And when I end things with Jackson?

HADES

When?

any sort of commitment.

Fuck fuck fuck. Genuine slip or Freudian slip?

PERSEPHONE

If.

HADES

IF you break up with Jackson, I'd ask you out on a proper date.

My heart flutters. *A proper date?*

PERSEPHONE

Tell me about the date?

HADES

It's a surprise.

PERSEPHONE

Alright...tell me about...after the date.

HADES

After the date, I'd take you home, walk you straight to your door, and kiss you softly on the lips before going home alone.

I lift an eyebrow at him. *Is this all in my head? Does he not burn for me?*

PERSEPHONE

And if I invited you in?

HADES

I'd make up an excuse about how I have to work early the next day.

PERSEPHONE

You'd make an excuse to not be alone with me?

HADES

Only because...I know I wouldn't be able to keep my hands off you if I was.

Oh...

PERSEPHONE

I don't want you to keep your hands off me...

My free hand creeps under the covers and down over my stomach.

HADES

Right now, little spring?

PERSEPHONE

Right now. And let me tell you, my fingers
don't feel anywhere as good as yours.

I slowly circle my clit with my middle finger, moaning softly as the small touch sends a jolt of intense pleasure through me. I gasp as I feel his hands trailing up my calves, my thighs.

Shadows.

HADES

This is the best I can do until you're single,
fully single.

My breath hitches.

PERSEPHONE

I want to touch you too.

HADES

No. This is for you.

His shadows push my legs open roughly, caressing higher and higher up my thighs, almost to the apex. I moan loudly as two shadow fingers push inside me. I arch my back, giving in to the feeling.

Another shadow climbs up my leg, this one focuses on my clit. It feels exactly how I've imagined Hades's tongue would feel.

I grab my phone, my hands shaking.

PERSEPHONE

But I want to play with you.

His shadow tongue is as sinful as my fantasies. I grasp the sheet with my other hand.

HADES

I want the next time you touch me for it to be you. I will accept no substitutes. No vines. Your skin against mine.

Another shadow travels up my body, pinching and rolling my nipple. My body writhes.

PERSEPHONE

I want you to watch.

HADES

I can see you perfectly. The shadows are me, an extension...

PERSEPHONE

I need to feel your eyes on me.

INCOMING FACETIME CALL FROM HADES

I quickly accept the call, glancing at my own image in the corner. Noticing how dark my eyes are, how swollen and red my lips are.

"Couldn't face me in person?" I ask, breathlessly.

His laugh is throaty. "I wouldn't be able to stop touching you."

I moan, my breaths shallow and uneven under his ministrations, his hungry gaze. "I never want you to stop touching me."

His groan sends waves of feral desire through me. "I won't, once you're available."

I pull my bottom lip between my teeth, my gaze locked on his. "Are you...are you touching yourself?"

My breath hitches as he shifts the camera, showing his hand wrapped around his perfect cock. My eyes shutter at the sight, my lips parting. "Fuck, I want to suck on you so bad."

He groans again. That sound is maddening. I want to own it. Every groan. Every growl. Every roar.

"When you're mine, I'm going to make you choke on it."

I moan again, that possessiveness making my belly flood with heat. "Yours..." An admission? A question? Who knows.

A third shadow finger pushes inside my dripping pussy, edging me closer, closer, his tongue flattening against my clit, driving me insane.

"This cunt is going to be all mine."

I roll my hips with his shadows, needing more. Needing *him.*

My cunt clenches. I feel myself nearing release. "All...yours...Hades!"

I watch as his hand moves faster on his cock, filthy sounds escaping his lips. *He's getting close too...*

"Yes, my spring?"

"Let me see you."

He shifts the camera so that our eyes lock.

"I'm yours... Fuck... Don't stop..."

His growl is guttural, perfect, desperate. "Come for me, Persephone."

The coil, so tightly wound, finally releases, and I scream as my orgasm shatters through me. My body arches, and my toes curl at the force, his shadows unrelenting.

Fuck...

I pant, my body quaking from the force of my release. I watch as his orgasm follows mine, his release covering his chest.

Fuck me. Is there anything more erotic?

His shadows leave me. I feel…empty, and I already miss the ghost of his touch.

I look at him, seeing his intense gaze trained on me. I flush under it.

"I guess I'll…um…see you at work."

He laughs, his lips pulled into a teasing smirk. "No kiss goodbye?"

I quirk an eyebrow. "You want a kiss goodbye?" I glance at his lips. "Come get it, demon."

I quickly end the call and relax back on my bed.

Fuck…did I…did I tell him I was his?

My chest aches, and once again, my body screams at me, but not in the way it did when I wore Jackson's ring. It screams in recognition. The darkness inside sighs in relief as my brain catches up with my heart.

Hades belongs to you. You belong to Hades.

It's time. My lips twitch, and I grab my phone again, opening my message with Jackson.

PERSEPHONE

We need to talk.

Feeling lighter than I have in weeks, I drop my phone on the bed, staring up at the ceiling.

Hades belongs to you. You belong to Hades.
Hades belongs to you. You belong to Hades.
Don't fight it.

Hades and I are inevitable. There is no fighting it.

I climb out of bed and take my time in the shower. The guilt, the resentment, the uncertainty dissipates as the revelation seeps into me, soaking into every muscle, every fiber.

202

Hades belongs to you. You belong to Hades.

After my shower, I glance at my phone, frowning when I see the message pop up from Jackson.

JACKSON

Just got on a plane, work emergency. I'll be back in a week or two. We'll talk then?

There may be no fighting it, but it looks like I will have to delay it.

I sink down onto my bed, dropping my phone next to me. Once again, my mind drifts to little Persephone and her fantasy wedding. I sit up straighter, my head tilts, and my eyebrows furrow. Was it...was it Hades I always imagined standing at the end of the aisle? But I had no idea who he was...and yet...the more I think about it, the more I remember his intense stare, his strong jaw, those lips, his piercing eyes...

My eyes go wide and my lips part.

It's fate. We are fated.

Hades and I are inevitable. There is no fighting it.

Chapter Thirty-Seven

Hades

COME GET IT, DEMON. Does she think I don't want to? That I don't ache to? Feeling and tasting what my shadows did isn't enough. Seeing her come, hearing her scream for me. Beg for me. She said she was *mine.* For a moment, I thought it was a fantasy, another one featuring Persephone. It wouldn't have been a surprise. Yet it was reality.

It isn't enough.

I want more.

I *need* more.

PERSEPHONE

Looks like you're going to have to wait longer
if we're following your ridiculous terms.

My ridiculous terms? Oh right. Her lack of singleness.

HADES

Oh? There go my plans for working today
with you on my lap.

I dress for work, and sit at my desk at precisely eight in the morning. Though my eyes keep looking up at the elevators, waiting for her to arrive.

When she finally steps off the elevator, she's dressed to kill. And she's dealt a fatal strike to my resistance to her. She's in a tight black pencil skirt, which emphasizes her ass. Every step she takes in those heels makes my heart pound. Her dark red shirt is low, but professional. The color might as well be a flag waved in front of my nose.

Come and get it, demon.

HADES

I know what you're doing.

She settles into her office, but my eyes don't leave her. Especially when those wicked lips of hers curve as she reads my message. She looks up, blowing a kiss at me through the walls before responding.

PERSEPHONE

What am I doing, sir?

My eyes spark at her from across the space, barely glancing at my phone as I type out a reply.

HADES

You're trying to make me forget that you're not single.

That you're not mine yet.

She bites her lip, and I watch her fingers fly over the screen.

PERSEPHONE

Well, my opportunity to be single has just been delayed by at least a week. Probably two.

My heart slams against my ribs.

HADES

...and you will be single then?

She's hinted at it, but this is the first time she's said it so point blank. Giving me a time limit. Fourteen days until she's mine. I've waited this long. I can wait longer.

PERSEPHONE

Looking forward to the company-wide meeting today.

Why? I turn to catch her watching me. Her eyes pinning me to my seat. She locks her phone, placing it down on the desk. She looks away from me, starting to work. I groan, diving into my own work, avoiding looking at her.

By the time the meeting starts, I'm in my typical seat at the black marble conference table at the front. Persephone arrives in a cloud of her mouthwatering scent, sitting in the seat next to mine, her notepad and pen on the table next to me.

I nod at her, trying to figure out her games, and look up as the speaker begins, the meeting all wrapped to the presentation.

"We've just finished the absorption of the new mining colony in Africa and are beginning the transition from the use of diamonds to the synthetic alternative.

Of course, we are getting to the beginning of fall, which means we will lose our CEO for several months, but it is my belief it will only grow under the structure he's put in place."

I nod, watching him, smiling roughly. I feel every shift of Persephone next to me, every breath. She drops her pen, and places a casual hand on my thigh, bending to pick it up. It's a light electric shock to my body, and I muffle a curse when her position gives me a view down her top. Thankfully, the speaker and the meeting continue on obliviously.

She keeps her hand on my thigh, and leans forward, listening to the presentation. Or so it appears. But her hand slides slowly up my thigh. My hand slams over hers, gripping it tightly, not letting it go any higher. She digs her nails into my thigh, nodding at the speaker, before scribbling onto the writing pad in front of me. Moving it so I can see it.

Imagine I was under the desk, sucking your cock.

I bite my lip, tightening my hand on hers, writing back.

You're a menace.

A menace to my sanity and the ability to focus during this meeting. She digs her nails into my thigh harder, coming close to tearing my pants. Even as she writes back,

I want to gag on you.

I want that too. I gulp, scanning the rest of the room, seeing no one noticing our little exchange.

I'm about to tie you up so I can focus on

work.

She glances at me, her fingers flexing under mine. *Or you could tie me up for more fun activities.*

My mind supplies all the ways I could have her bound for me. My cock hardens to the point of pain, almost reaching for her hand.

I growl softly, turning back to the presentation, trying to focus. She wiggles her hand free, and slips it over my cock, squeezing roughly. I jolt in her grip. I bite my lip hard enough to draw blood. I yank her hand off me, putting it into her own lap, slipping my fingers into hers to keep it there. *You're a disobedient little brat who I'm going to throw over my knee.*

She bites her lip, picking up the pen. *Do it.*

I stand up the second the meeting ends, shifting the coat of my suit to cover the outline of my aching cock. "Excellent meeting. Back to work everyone."

My many employees file out of the conference room, allowing me to reach down and grab Persephone's arm, dragging her with me to my office. Each of my words is short and clipped. "You. Are. A. Menace."

She keeps pace with me at my side, until we're in my office. I put her into the seat across my desk, moving to my own chair. "Text him. Now."

My tone brokers for no disagreement. Yet she leans back in her chair, her eyes rolling over me, promising more. "He's away on business."

I narrow my eyes at her, still shifting in my seat

208

from the ache in my cock. "You can't call him?"

She leans forward, leaning her elbows on my desk. "For two weeks. I am not ending things with him via text."

I run a weary hand down my face. "Why not?"

She stands from her seat, rounding the desk. I can't stop her. I'm still helpless against her. She opens my laptop, trying to throw off the prying eyes of people peering through the glass at us. She leans over me, her tits beside my face. "It's disrespectful. He deserves better."

I move my chair slightly away from her, trying to clear her maddening scent from my nose. "I'm not touching you while you're still in a relationship."

She opens up the company website, pretending to point to it. "I'm not in a relationship, but fine, let me touch you."

I growl. "No."

She straightens, walking to my office door. "Then I suppose we have nothing further to discuss."

My eyes narrow on her, trailing over her form. "The second you're available…all bets are off."

Chapter Thirty-Eight

Persephone

I FEEL HIS EYES ON ME THE WHOLE WAY BACK TO MY OFFICE. I take my time, swaying my hips as I go.

Good, stare at my ass. Look at what you're missing.

I still feel his eyes on me as I open my laptop. I look down at the screen, trying to ignore the feeling of my skin igniting under his gaze.

> HADES
>
> You say he deserves more than a phone call. You deserve to have all of me. Like I deserve all of you.

> PERSEPHONE
>
> And the promise of all of me isn't enough?

> HADES
>
> I won't share you. I'd hope you wouldn't share me.

My fingers tighten on my phone at the thought. My skin prickles with jealousy. How many times have I had judgmental thoughts about his shows of possession? And yet, I appear to be no better.

> **PERSEPHONE**
> I don't share.

> **HADES**
> Then why are you insisting that I have to?

> **PERSEPHONE**
> I'm not insisting you share me. I am yours.

How easily I say that now. How casually it rolls off the tongue—or finger tips. I stare down at the message, waiting for the panic to hit, but it never does.

I belong to Hades.

> **HADES**
> Not yet. But you will be.

I sigh and lock my phone, leaning my head back against the chair.

> **HADES**
> I'll make it worth the wait.

I look at his message, considering for a moment. The thought of being in the office for a whole two weeks, being able to see him and smell him but not touch him, feels like the cruelest torture, especially given my recent revelations.

> **PERSEPHONE**
> I think I'm going to work from home for the couple of weeks.

> **HADES**
> Persephone...

I lean forward, looking at him through the glass. His brows are furrowed as he looks down at his phone. I smile at how unboss-like he looks. Leaning back in his chair, legs splayed in a way that makes me want to crawl under the desk, open his pants, and wrap my lips around him. Sucking on him until he gives me what I need, what I crave.

I bite my lip, imagining swallowing him down, memories of being in that hidden corner of the club rush into my mind, until I can practically taste his salty release on my tongue.

As if he can hear my thoughts, he glances up. His eyes, just as dark, as hooded as I imagine mine are.

He keeps looking at me, his thumbs flying over his phone.

Ping.

I reluctantly tear my eyes from him to read his message.

> HADES
>
> You can't be around me at all?
>
> PERSEPHONE
>
> I ache for you, Hades. I don't have the restraint you do.

He frowns down at his phone. It looks so small in his big, strong hands.

> HADES
>
> I'm trying to respect the man you bound yourself to. It's near impossible for me.
>
> PERSEPHONE
>
> Bound? We're casually dating...

I glance up at him, seeing him rub an impatient hand over his face.

HADES

You said he deserves better. I...I crave you, Persephone. With everything I am or ever will be. It's been impossible to see you dating another. To know that someone else has a claim to you.

I sigh, he's right. I hate it, but he's right.

PERSEPHONE

I understand.

HADES

Do not ever doubt how much I want you. I'd give my entire kingdom and crown to have you.

Well, fuck. I read his message over and over. That relentless low heat curls in my stomach.
Can't think. Can't breathe.

PERSEPHONE

Alright.

I blink down at the message. *What the shit, P?!*

HADES

Not the response I was expecting.

PERSEPHONE

What were you expecting?

HADES

Just...not that. You might as well have texted me "K."

I glance up at him, my eyes greedily roaming over him. I read that message again, *"I'd give my entire kingdom and crown to have you."*

PERSEPHONE

Hades, I'm really struggling...

HADES

With?

I look up at him again. When I don't immediately respond, his gaze meets mine. The second it does, I see his Adam's apple bob as he swallows. My lips part. I can only imagine that my pupils are so big, my eyes look black. My breaths come out in short pants. My cheeks feel hot, a flush I can feel spreading down my neck and chest.

HADES

Fuck.

PERSEPHONE

I think I should go home for the rest of the day.

HADES

How about a compromise?

I lift my eyebrow, reading his text. I see the little dots bounce up and down as he continues typing. What is he planning? I try to consider the possibilities of this "compromise" but come up empty. Surely, there is no way for us to get through these two weeks while following his rules and also working in such close proximity.

HADES

I won't touch you like...we both want. But I wouldn't mind...holding you while you sleep.

I snort.

PERSEPHONE

"Wouldn't mind"?

HADES

I desperately want to sleep in the same bed
with you. Is that better?

I glance up at him, that hungry gaze already trained on me. I throw him a flirty smile. I briefly wonder if he can be nudged, not to break the rules, but bending them a little, so we aren't completely miserable for the next two weeks. I smirk down at my phone as I type out my reply.

PERSEPHONE

Kissing?

HADES

No tongue and only above the chest.

PERSEPHONE

Your place or mine?

HADES

Mine.

His bossiness gives me a thrill. This is going to be difficult.

PERSEPHONE

I can't wait.

Truth.

Chapter Thirty-Nine
Hades

THE REST OF THE DAY CONTINUES ON IN HALTING FLASHES OF SPEED, some meetings flying by me and some conference calls dragging. Like the world knows I get to hold her in my arms as I sleep. That I'll soon take in a deep inhale of her scent as I doze. Will she still haunt my dreams if I'm holding her? Or tonight will I have some sort of reprieve?

When we're finally the only two left on the floor, my eyes find her in her own office. Not that they had strayed much at all during the day. I could close my eyes and see every minuscule stitch of her entire outfit, each strand of her hair. If I had ever been able to develop an artistic skill, I have no doubt I'd be able to sketch her with perfect detail, down to the scrunch of her nose when she's focusing. The way her pupils consume her irises with desire or when her eyes spark with rage. I should have spent time mastering the skill. But I was always the scholar and never the artist. Though my brothers were never artistic either. Sometimes I doubted that Poseidon could actually *read*.

I look up when she knocks on my door. My lips curl in a welcoming smile. "Hi."

She smiles back at me, warm and inviting. So different from the barbs we usually exchange, the barely contained, coiled desire. Is this a shadow of the future we might one day share?

"I'm heading off."

My heart slams immediately, and dreams of the future die in my mind. A quick, wordless death. But I still ask, "Wait, what?"

She's not staying? I thought we'd come to an agreement. Was I wrong? Is she still clinging to the mortal as a defense between us? Had all the progress I thought we'd made only been in my mind? A frantic illusion?

She walks over to me slowly, her hips moving side to side, maddeningly. Every stray thought and internal spiral flies from my head. "I need to go home and pack a bag."

I exhale audibly, unable to contain my relief. She's coming back. "Oh."

She bends down, that dark skirt tugging over her hips, kissing the corner of my mouth. "I'll see you soon."

She can't help herself. She loves to tempt me. To torture me. Such a brat. I growl, my hand landing on her ass, spanking her hard. "Hurry."

I've dreamed far too much about spanking that ass of hers. *Far too much.*

She squeals and hurries away, but bites her lip as she does. Oh, I'll be turning that ass of hers red, *soon*. Once she's mine. There's many things I've been fantasizing about doing to her. *So. Many. Things.* I'd need an eternity to do them all. Good thing I'm fated to have one with her. I'll need it.

Time passes slowly without her, and I keep glancing at the elevator, waiting for her to return. Every tick of the clock makes me more impatient, and I try not to twitch or allow my leg to bounce. It takes forty-five minutes for her to return, and she leans against the door-frame, drawing my attention to her curves again. "Still working, demon?"

I glance up at her, my lips twitching into a smile. I don't think I've ever smiled as much as I have today. Not in the past millennia. "Work needs doing."

She tilts her head, her hair falling over her shoulder. In the low light, her hair is more brown than red. "Well, I'm finished working for the day, so I'm going to head upstairs."

I nod, glancing at the stack of things I still have left to do today. Then, I say to my fated queen, "Are you hungry?"

Her eyebrows quirk, but the way her lips curve is sinful. "Starving."

I have so much to do, but I turn to my computer, powering it down, standing slowly from my desk, rolling my shoulders absently. "I'll cook."

She picks up her overnight bag, turning from my office, walking toward the elevator. I follow her, delaying my steps a bit longer to watch the sway of her hips, before threading my fingers into hers. "In a hurry?"

She looks up at me, her eyes practically black. "No."

Her word is practically a purr, dragging along my skin in a caress. I fight the shiver.

I lift her hand to my mouth, biting the back of it. "Your expression says otherwise."

She pulls her hand away and hands me her bag. I frown, stepping into the elevator with her, taking it from her. She immediately presses her hand against my chest, slowly backing me into the wall. I feel the cool surface against my back, looking down at the ravenous goddess about to swallow me whole.

I blink at her, not letting go of her bag. "What are you doing?"

She leans in and kisses my neck.

I groan. "I thought you were hungry."

She kisses up my neck and along my jaw. "I didn't say what I was hungry for."

I moan, my hands going to her hips, dropping the bag. "We had a deal."

She nibbles my jaw. "It was left…open-ended."

I groan, pushing her away when the elevator pings on my floor. "It was not."

She shrugs. "Fine. I won't touch you."

"Food." Anything to distract from the way she's looking at me.

I pick up her bag, moving off the elevator, striding to the massive kitchen. I start pulling things out of the fridge. "Pad thai?"

She nods, wandering through my penthouse, looking around. I notice her linger over my collection of paperbacks, smiling at the signed editions of *Lord of the Rings* and *A Song of Ice and Fire.* I love high fantasy, and the more complex and political the story is, the more invested I am. I even have a signed copy of *Throne of Glass.* Though this collection is only a small part of my dragon's trove. The majority is in the huge library in the Underworld.

I unbutton my shirt at the wrists, rolling my sleeves to the elbows to start cooking.

She wanders over to my record player and plucks out a record. "The Ratpack?"

I smile at her over my shoulder. "Frank was a friend, once upon a time."

She laughs and plays the record, closing her eyes as crooning fills the apartment.

Chapter Forty
Persephone

I TAKE A DEEP BREATH, TRYING TO CALM THE BUTTERFLIES. I don't know why I'm nervous.

Hades and I are inevitable.

But maybe that's the problem. Before now, being around him has felt as easy as breathing, but being in his apartment like this feels so much more intimate somehow. Knowing that he and I are meant to be should ease my concerns, but I feel more nervous than ever. I could chalk it up to having no confirmation, but how would I confirm it? The only evidence I have is a gut feeling...no, it's more than that. It's like my very soul recognizes his. From the very beginning, there was the slightest tremor in my body, an awareness, a dormant part of me awakening, but the second I *allowed* myself to feel for him, that tremor became an earthshaking, life-altering, realization.

Hades belongs to me. I belong to Hades.

Of course, the knowledge that we're fated doesn't necessarily mean that he'll *want* me. Just that we have the potential to be good together, that we're *meant* to be together. I wish I knew the statistics of fated mates' success rates. I wish I knew if there were any cases where mates rejected one another.

Are fated mates common with the divine?

I wander around his apartment. The comforting sounds of Sinatra crooning in the background and the gentle hissing of the vegetables as Hades throws them into a hot pan doing their best to ease my knotted stomach. I am keenly aware that, while I'm feeling nervous, I like being in Hades's apartment. There is something comforting about being in his space, whether it be the decor, the muted colors, or the fact you could tell that Hades lives here.

Feels like home.

I walk to his bookshelves, trailing my fingers over the leather-bound spines. Everything is so classy in his apartment. So perfectly decorated. Not too minimalist, not too cluttered. Not dissimilar to him.

The space is open, light, homey. I smile as I realize why the apartment is so comforting.

"Wine?" His voice hits me like the smoothest of honey, making a shiver run down my spine.

I turn to look at him, the corners of my lips pulling into a smile as I watch him plate the food. I marvel at his large hands as they wrap around the serving spoon.

My domestic god.

He looks up expectantly when I don't reply.

"Of course."

He smirks at me, having caught me perving on him. He turns, letting me see that perfect ass of his, and plucks two wine glasses from the shelf.

I walk to the kitchen island, drumming my fingers on the cool marble as Hades pours two glasses of red wine and places them on the table, beside each of our plates.

He looks up at me, his usual arrogant easy smile replaced by something a little less sure. He pulls my chair out for me before taking his own seat.

"I hope you like it spicy."

I smile at him, nodding before taking a sip of my

wine. The smooth, full-bodied flavor slides down my throat, instantly easing some of my irrational nerves. My gaze stays locked on his the whole time.

He spears a piece of chicken with his fork. "What?"

I smile at him. "You're full of surprises, demon."

He snickers. "I could say the same about you, my spring."

My *spring. My demon...*

My heart squeezes at the thought.

I take another sip of wine. "What surprises you about me?"

"Besides everything?"

I chuckle and put my glass down, taking a bite of the pad thai. My eyes roll back, and I moan at the taste of the perfectly balanced spices.

My eyes flutter open and go straight to Hades, his cheeks slightly flushed with anticipation. "Good?"

"Incredible." I take another bite.

"I..." He hesitates. "I could teach you."

I tilt my head at him. "I'd love that."

We finish our meal in companionable silence. Every so often our eyes meet, and it feels as though an electrical charge passes between us. When we finish eating, he slides his hand over the table, reaching for mine. I lean forward, placing my much smaller hand in his.

My skin tingles at the small contact.

"Have you picked a movie for tonight?" My shaky voice gives away my inner turmoil.

"Should I have?"

I lift a shoulder in a shrug. "Not necessarily, but now you have to deal with my pick."

He stands from his seat, pulling me up, too, my body so close to his I can feel his body heat, his scent surrounding me.

"Oh?" His eyes are bright.

I crane my neck, staring up at him.

He smiles, drawing my gaze to his lips. "What would be your pick?"

I press my hands against his chest and slide them up over his shoulders, moving in closer, so my body is flush with his. I reach up on my tiptoes and press a kiss to his chin. "Pride and Prejudice."

He clears his throat, and I feel his hardening cock against my stomach. "The five-hour one?"

I kiss along his jaw. "No, the movie. It's only two and a half hours."

The glint of menace in his eye is the only warning I get before he scoops me up into his arms, carrying me to the couch. He gently places me down and grabs the remote for the television and turns it on. The second he sits down next to me, I spring up, grabbing my overnight bag.

"I'm going to change into something more comfortable."

He lifts an eyebrow at me. "What's wrong with what you're wearing?"

I look down at my work clothes and roll my eyes. How could anyone relax in a pencil skirt and tight shirt? "Get the movie ready. I'll be two minutes."

He shrugs, turning away from me.

My smile turns wicked and I hurry off to change.

Chapter Forty-One

Hades

I NEVER THOUGHT TO BE SO DOMESTIC. To spend moments of the day not thinking about work, or the things that would need to be done the next day. On the clock ticking down until I head downstairs. I'm lost in the future looming, instead of the present. Yet here I am, sitting on the couch, waiting for my fated queen to return so we can watch a movie after I've made dinner for us both.

Her scent clouds my nose as she glides back to me. I turn to look at her, smiling, but every thought flies from my mind when I see her. *Chaos save me.*

Her curvy, hauntingly luscious body is encased in nothing but the smallest scrap of pink silk. Every movement is seduction, the silk teasing along her skin, and thought is a distant memory. My brain doesn't come back online, even as she sits on the couch next to me, her negligee riding up her thighs.

She nuzzles my neck and purrs. "Much better."

I blink at her, my mouth utterly dry, barely managing to demand, "What is that?!"

She narrows her eyes, those luscious lips of hers forming a knowing smirk. "What?"

I point to her outfit. She stands and turns slowly for me, showing the whole, *minuscule* outfit. Her curves are *barely* contained. It looks like a deep breath will reveal her ass and pussy to me. My eyes almost roll back in my head imagining that.

She asks coyly, "Don't you like it?"

The way she purrs the words, full of feminine satisfaction, forces me to jump and put the couch between us, shaking my head to clear the lust clogging all rational thought. "Of course, I do. That's why you wore it."

She blinks at me, her satisfaction dimming. "What are you doing?"

I narrow my eyes at her, trying to not focus on the way those tits of hers are stretching the silk, leaving nothing to the imagination. To *my* imagination. It was already torture having her here and not touching her. Now this? Does she sense how close I am to breaking? Her here in my home, well, *one* of my homes. How easy it is to forget I need to resist her, that she's not completely mine. Not yet.

"You're trying to break our bargain," I hiss, forcing myself not to rub my aching cock against the back of the couch in front of me. To not search for some kind of release. *Any* kind of release.

She holds her hands up, palms facing me. "I won't touch you."

Sincerity shines in those lovely eyes, but my eyes drop to her tits again, even as I growl, "Swear it?"

She nods. "I swear. I'll sit at the other end of the couch if you want."

I don't want that. I wanted a nice night with her.

I shake my head, moving back to the couch, holding out my arms. "No. I want you here next to me," *on this couch and on the throne*, "but no wandering hands."

She nods, sitting next to me, her hands obediently on her thighs. I wrap my arm around her side, trying to focus as I press play on the movie. She shifts in her seat and her lingerie rides up, displaying more of those

225

thighs that I want so desperately wrapped around my head. To smother me as she sits on my face. Her head moves to rest on my shoulder, and I cover one of her hands on her thighs.

She slides her hand up her thigh, taking mine with it. *Menace.*

I growl at her warningly. She stills her hand. I should reward her for her obedience. I need to be a good host.

I readjust my hand on hers, guiding her hand up to where she needs it. Where I need it. She touches her cunt with my fingers guiding hers. She moans softly from her own touch, dragging her elegant fingers along her clit. I press one of her fingers inside, trying to stop myself from replacing it with my own. I'm towing a dangerous line, pushing myself, and her, to the edge of this bargain.

Her breath hitches, and I look at her, snapping when I see her eyes flutter closed, "Eyes open. Watch the movie."

Her eyes open, though her breaths are short. I keep my own eyes on the movie, though I'm not really paying attention. Instead, I'm using her finger to thrust in and out of her slowly, maddeningly. She moans louder, and moves her fingers under mine, rubbing against my palm. Letting me feel how soaked her cunt is for me.

I hiss, smacking her hand on her pussy. "You are my puppet. My little doll."

She nods. "Your little doll."

I smirk at her, pressing another finger inside her, my hand moving to her wrist, thrusting her fingers in and out of her faster, in time with the rising crescendo of the music in the movie.

She rolls her hips wantonly. "Hades…"

I hush her, before adding a third of her fingers inside her, moving them faster. She cries out, writhing. I can tell how close she is, even without looking at her. I release my hold on her wrist, allowing her to continue thrusting them in and out of herself. I grab her other hand, using it to pull her nightgown down. I cover her fingers, using them to pinch and roll her nipples.

She arches into her own hands. "I'm going to come, baby."

I use her hand to smack her breasts. "Come."

She suppresses her scream as she obeys me, shaking and shuddering with the force of it.

I smirk, listening to her, not looking at her. I move to fix her negligee, focusing on the movie. "Good girl."

She pulls her fingers from herself, standing from the couch, walking to the bathroom. I pause the movie. waiting for her to return, ignoring the continuing ache in my cock. There will be time for that later, time for everything later.

Once she's completely mine.

Chapter Forty-Two

Persephone

I SIT ON THE EDGE OF HADES'S LARGE CLAWFOOT BATHTUB, needing a moment to collect myself after…whatever *that* was. *How his hand controlled mine, how he demanded I keep watching the movie, how he called me his little doll…*

I stand and walk to the sink. I wash my hands, my lips twitching when I notice that, even the hand soap he owns is expensive. When my eyes drift up, I meet my own reflection, the same face I've had for over 200 years and yet…somehow different.

I tilt my head, observing my slightly brighter skin, my flushed cheeks, swollen lips. All of which are probably post-orgasm hue, but ever since the moment I accepted that Hades and I are fated, there has been something different.

I take a moment when I enter the living room again, a moment to just look at him. He's obviously been running his fingers through his hair. I briefly wonder if he's feeling as sexually frustrated as I am, usually…still. His legs are crossed, his ankle anchored at his knee, and he's cradling a tumbler of a golden brown liquid, probably scotch. There is something so innately masculine about him, it makes me ache.

My bare feet are nearly silent as I pad back over to him, taking my place on the couch, careful not to touch him. I don't want to push him more than I already have, and if he's anywhere near as aroused as I am, it wouldn't be fair to continue teasing him. *But I do so love teasing him.*

I tuck my legs underneath me and wait for him to play the movie again, but he frowns at me.

"Come here."

I glance at him. "Can I touch you?"

He blinks. "What do you mean?"

I pivot to face him fully. "You want to cuddle? Let me touch you."

He scans my eyes. "I just want to hold you."

Lie. I see that bulge in your pants, demon.

"We have a bargain."

Don't tease, don't tease, don't tease.

I lean into him and hover my hand over his chest. I slide my hand down over his stomach, no part of my hand touching him. "You *just* want to hold me?"

The answering growl makes my breath hitch as a thrill shoots through my core. "For now."

I move my weight onto my knees, bringing my lips to his ear. "Let me touch you," I whisper.

In a flash, I feel his fingers at my hips, and he pulls me onto his lap, his hard length pressed against my ass. "I told you it would be worth the wait, didn't I?"

I roll my hips slightly, grinding my ass against his shaft.

"The original rule was that I could kiss you. Is that still in play?" I ask, my lips pulled into a faux coy smile.

His eyes narrow, his pupils so big the piercing blue is barely visible. "Above the chest and no tongue."

I shift so that I straddle him. My bare pussy against his hard cock. Only his pants between us.

"I can't put my hands on you, right?"

He shakes his head. I feel his fists clenched at his sides.

My tense demon.

I lift my hands and slowly move them behind my back, clasping my fingers to keep them there. I lean forward and trail kisses from his ear, along his jaw, to his chin, my hips gently rocking against him.

"Aren't you glad I decided to not wear panties?"

He drops his head back against the leather. I glance down, seeing his knuckles, white with the effort. Struggling to not touch me, knowing that, even if he touches me modestly, he may not be able to stop himself.

"I feel the heat from your cunt on my lap." He lifts his head and looks down. I pull back, letting him see the dark patch on his pants, my arousal covering his slacks. He groans, low and deep.

I press my lips to his neck and start pressing open-mouthed, hot kisses along his skin. "If you opened your pants…you could feel it on your cock."

Almost without hesitation, his hands fly to his pants. He unbuttons and unzips them, his shaky hands barely fumbling. I shift my weight, allowing him to push his pants down slightly.

My mouth waters as I look down at his perfect length. So big and thick and…pierced. *Fuck.* Seeing the tiny glint of metal in person. It takes everything in me to not hover my cunt over the tip and sheath it fully inside me.

"Mark it with that dripping pussy." His voice is guttural, husky, delicious.

I shuffle forward and use my hips to press the underside of his shaft flat against my cunt. His swollen, pierced crown slides against my greedy clit. "Fuck. You have a perfect cock."

His hands return to his sides, clenching hard. He groans the second I settle on top of him. "And you're going to take every inch when you belong to me."

My pussy aches, clenches, throbs for him. "It'll be a

230

tight squeeze."

"You will take every inch, Persephone," he pants.

His domineering voice makes me even wilder. I start rocking my hips faster, my arousal coating him, making his cock slide easily through my soft folds. My clit aches with every touch. I feel it building already.

"Fuck, Hades…"

"You're going to make me come like this…" he hisses, and finally relents. His fists unclench, and he grabs my thighs, his fingers digging in hard. The bittersweet feeling of pain only adds to my pleasure.

Fuck, please, bruise me…

I lean forward, pressing my lips to his, but keeping it close-mouthed, as per his rules. I tighten my grip on my own hands, the need to touch him overwhelming. "Good. I'm so close…" I pull his bottom lip between my teeth, sucking on him.

That maddening growl escapes him again, spurring me on, and I roll my hips faster still, getting closer, closer, closer. His fingers, still clench my thighs, as if he's anchoring himself to me.

He rocks his hip in time with me, and with one last brush of the tip of his cock over my clit, I come, hard.

My back arches, and I scream his name, every muscle contracting at the force.

His roar follows, and I feel him arching as his release spills from him, covering his stomach.

I slow my hips, panting, and slump forward, my head resting against his shoulder.

I smile as he nuzzles into my neck. "Good?"

I shiver, and nod against his neck.

He presses a tender kiss to my shoulder. "You like bending my rules."

I pull back, an eyebrow raised. "I followed all of your rules." I make a show of unclasping my hands and bringing them back in front of me, still not touching him.

He raises a brow. I can tell he disagrees. He waves a hand, and my brows furrow, wondering what he's doing. A moment later, it becomes clear, when a shadow forms around my waist, forming some kind of belt, but it doesn't just circle my waist, part of it extends underneath me, between my legs.

"So you'll behave."

I look down at it. My head tilted. "What is it?" I touch it, my eyebrows raising when I notice it appears like shadows, but it is solid under my fingers. I slide my hand down between my legs, and it strikes me, I can't touch myself. "You have got to be joking."

He smirks. "You can't seem to help yourself, and I have two weeks until I can fuck you."

I lean back, inspecting the device. "Hades…"

He groans. I don't miss his cock twitching again. "Fuck, you look gorgeous bound for me. Only I get to release you."

Bound for him? Fuck, that is hot. But…he's not the only one with the power to bind…and I'm pissed, so…

I tilt my head at him, my lips pulling into a mischievous smile. I twist my hands, and vibrant green vines protrude from the back of the couch. They curl slowly around his arms, caressing as they go, restraining him. I slide off his lap and kneel between his legs.

"You wanted me on my knees for you, I guess you won." More vines wrap around his legs, holding him open for me. His hungry gaze roams over me, watching my every move. I sit up on my knees and lick his release from his stomach, careful to not touch his cock. Careful to not place my hands on him. The only parts of me that touch him are my tongue and my hair, which has fallen over my shoulder.

He pulls on the vines as my tongue drags over him, and his cock begins to harden again.

"Release me, Persephone," he snarls.

My gaze locks on his as I slowly lick every drop from him, taking my time. Savoring every second, every drop, every grunt and moan as Hades watches me, his eyes glowing.

I stand from the floor and finally release him from my hold. His eyes glow as he looks up at me. He rubs his wrist, and before I know it, he grabs my hips and throws me over his lap. I look over my shoulder at him, his breaths shallow.

I feel him slide my negligee up, exposing my ass. He rubs it, kneads it, before lifting his hand. I'm about to protest, when he brings his palm down on me hard, the snap of his hand against my skin loud in the otherwise silent room.

I moan, my body lurches, but I push my hips back, greedy for more. I vaguely notice the shadow belt disappears and reforms around his touch.

"Disobedient little slut, aren't we?" he growls.

I push my hips back into his hand in answer as he caresses the stinging skin.

He lifts his hand again and brings it down harder this time, making me cry out.

"Say it. Say you're a disobedient little slut who's hungry for my cock."

Slap.

"I-I'm a disobedient little slut…"

Slap.

Every time his hand comes down on me, it stings more, makes my pussy even wetter. I feel my arousal slide down my thighs.

"Finish."

My fingers dig into the couch, the leather groaning under my grasp. "I'm hungry for…your cock."

Suddenly, I feel those maddening shadows fill me, but this time…they don't feel like fingers. They're big and hard and perfect. "This will have to do for now."

My pussy clenches around his shadows. "Fuck, Hades!"

He growls. The shadow stops moving inside of me. It just sits there. I try to rock my hips but gain no friction. "You're going to walk around with this inside you, because you need to be filled. And only when you give me what I want will I replace it with the real thing."

Wait, what? He expects me to have this inside of me for two weeks?

I panic, my body desperate for him. I can't take this for a moment longer, let alone two weeks.

"I-I'll do it tomorrow…"

I hear the smugness in his voice. "Oh?" The shadows vanish from inside me. Leaving me empty and. once again. unsated.

Did I really give up so easily? Weak, Persephone.

You win this round. Hades.

Chapter Forty-Three
Hades

I S THIS REALLY A CONFIRMATION? That she's not just going to end things completely with the mortal, but that she'll be mine? I can already imagine it wasn't her grinding against my cock, but it firmly inside her. That I own that pussy of hers. That I *own* her. As I fear...*she already owns me.* It's only fair I have the same from her.

She shivers, still sprawled over my lap. The shadows that formed her belt are still in place, though the ones that mimicked my cock are gone.

She whispers shakily, "I'll...I'll need the day off work."

I frown down at her, my hand trailing along her back for a moment. "For a text?"

The emotional recoil? How attached is she to this mortal? Why does she need the day off? Why does she need to think twice? After what just happened, how can she want anything but...more? She has to feel this pull. It's fate. It's wrapped around her as tightly as it is around me. I stopped fighting it. Hasn't she? *Don't fight it anymore, my spring.*

She glares at me, looking over her shoulder. "I'm doing it in person. I told you."

I sit up fully, forcing her to do the same, her knees pressed into the couch and her heels digging into her red

235

ass. The shadows only keep her from touching herself, and make me grit my teeth, my cock already hardening. "How?"

Her face turns stony, none of that softness from a moment ago. I feel a pang at the loss.

"I'll go to him."

Leave me, to talk to him?

"I'll go with you."

She shakes her head at me, her voice firm and unyielding. "No. I need to do this alone."

You're not needed.

I growl, insisting. "No. I'll go with you."

She growls back, and my cock twitches in response. "I am able to be by myself, you know?"

"Why can't I come?" What if she changes her mind? Decides to stay with him? She picked him over me once already, why not again? She clings to the barrier he provides between us. If she goes, she'll just rebuild the wall between us. Till I'm, once again, sitting on the opposite side, longing for my fated queen alone. *Alone, always alone.* The lonely god.

She blinks at me, surprise softening her voice. "Why do you want to? I'm going to end things. Then I'm returning to you."

But will you return? To me? And the future that I can't warn her about?

I cup her cheek, rubbing my thumb along her soft skin. "But…"

Do I dare give voice to my fears?

"But what?"

I sigh heavily. "What if you don't come back?"

Her hands curl into fists on her thighs. "I will come back."

I slowly drop my hand. "I guess we'll see."

Her eyes flare, her hands tighten, like she needs to restrain herself. "Fuck, Hades. Let me touch you."

It's so tempting. To let her soothe me, to touch me and make me forget. I scan her eyes, looking for something, not finding whatever it was. "When you're mine."

She pulls back from me even more, no part of us touching. "Fine. But I need you to know that, if you were being reasonable, I would kiss you. Hard. Until all your worries went away."

I smile sadly at her. "I don't know if they'll ever go away."

She leans over, kissing my jaw. "I'll take that challenge. Let me just book my flights, and we can get back to our evening?"

I nod, shifting for her to cuddle into my side as she grabs her phone, searching for flights. Trying to cover the unease gnawing at my stomach. The feeling of dread that insists this is the last time I'll hold her like this.

She leans into me, swiping through different flights. "I can get the red-eye back."

I kiss her head, trying to inhale her scent and take it into me. "You can upgrade to first class."

She selects economy. *Stubborn thing.* I focus my power on her phone, watching as it switches to first class without me having to touch it. Being the God of Riches did come with benefits, especially in the electronic age.

She rolls her eyes but confirms the details, locking her phone, and tossing it back onto the coffee table. "I'll be gone for approximately twenty hours."

I kiss her head. "Will you miss me?"

She lifts her face to mine. "Every second."

I lean down to kiss her softly, wishing I could extend this moment, freeze it, capture it. "Will you give me updates?"

She presses her lips more instantly to mine. "Yes."

I nibble her plump bottom lip. "How many?"

"How many do you want?"

I laugh, trying to cover my unease. "I suppose it's

obscene to ask for things during the breakup. A recording? Live stream?"

She snorts. "Why would you want that?"

I kiss her hard again. "So he knows that he lost you."

So I know that you're truly mine.

She shakes her head at me, smiling ruefully. "Take me to bed, demon."

I lift her into my arms, kissing her head. I carry her to my bed, tucking her into the covers before changing into a pair of sweats and crawling into bed with her.

She lays next to me, whispering, "Let me touch your chest? No lower, I promise."

I nod. I'm too weak to deny her right now.

She moves closer to me, laying her head on my chest. A tentative hand presses against my chest. "Hades?"

I wrap my arms around her. "Yes?"

She nuzzles her face into my chest. "Thank you for tonight."

I kiss the top of her head again. "It wasn't too much?"

She shakes her head, a soft yawn coming from her throat. "You're perfect."

Liar. I wrap the covers tightly around us. "I'll keep you warm tonight."

She kisses my chest softly, biting a piece of my skin. "Goodnight, demon."

"Goodnight, my spring."

Chapter Forty-Four

Persephone

I GROAN AS A SHRILL SIREN NOISE PULLS ME FROM MY BLISSFUL SLEEP, my blissful dream. I stretch, my brows drawing as I realize my head is not on a soft pillow, but something hard. I nuzzle into it, moaning softly as the smell of sandalwood and citrus surrounds me. *Hades.*

I slide my hand up his chest. His soft skin beneath my fingertips feels better than the most expensive silk. Reluctantly, I roll over and turn my alarm off. I look back at Hades, so peaceful in his sleep, the lines of his face, usually pulled into a hard scowl, relaxed. He looks so young, so unburdened, my heart aches as I consider his worries, wishing I could ease them for him. The urge to slide back into his arms and bury my face in his chest is almost impossible to resist.

Carefully, I slide out of bed trying to not disturb him. He stirs slightly. When I'm confident he's still sleeping, I head for a shower. Under the hot spray, I consider what I'm going to say to Jackson, how he will react, what he will say…and also my return to Hades. My Hades.

I leave the bathroom and see Hades starting to awaken. My heart flutters at the sight of him. The sheet hanging low on his hips makes something else flutter. I tighten the towel around my chest and smile softly. Walking to the bed, I press a gentle kiss against his cheek. "Shh, good morning, baby."

He frowns, blinking his eyes open. "Why are you up so early?"

Glancing at the clock, I sigh and move away from him to collect my overnight bag. I drop the towel and pull on my underwear. I hear the bed creak as Hades shifts, and I feel his eyes on me. "My flight is in an hour and a half."

He sighs. "Right."

His voice sounds so defeated, so sad. I clasp my bra and pause dressing. I climb onto the bed, crawling up his body until he's beneath me. I lean down, brushing my lips over his. "In less than twenty-four hours, demon…" Another brush of my lips. "In less than twenty-four hours, I will be back in this bed, and you can bury yourself inside me over and over…and over."

He pulls my bottom lip between his teeth, sucking on it. "Hm?"

I moan, nodding. "And it's going to be all I'm able to think about."

He growls, a low, primal sound that oozes with the promise of all the wicked things he wants to do to me. I feel the lace of my panties becoming damp.

"What if I want to take it slow?"

I chuckle into his lips and place one of my hands against his chest. I drag my nails down his chest, down his stomach, stopping where the sheet covers him. It's maddeningly low. I slide my thumb over the trail of hair that leads to his perfect cock. I lower my hips a little, grinding against the tented sheet, giving us both the smallest amount of friction, barely perceptible through the shadows still around me.

"You want to take it slow?" My eyes sparkle with mischief.

"You better get going, Persephone, before I convince you that I should come with you."

240

I smile into his lips and kiss down his jaw, down his neck. I let my lips trail over his stomach, over that small patch of hair. I press one kiss over the sheet against the swollen crown of his cock.

"Menace," he hisses.

I wink at him before climbing off the bed and continue getting dressed.

Smoothing out my cream sweater, I glance at him, hesitating. His eyes remained trained on me. He watches every movement as I get dressed, groaning when I bend down to pull on my jeans. His gaze still makes me feel as if I will burst into flames. As if I need to be naked that very second.

"Should I...should I come here when I get back?" I avert my gaze, still expecting rejection from him.

After a moment, when he's not replied, I look at him. His brows are furrowed, and he's looking at me like he's never heard a more ridiculous statement. "Do you want to come home to me?"

I nod.

He smiles and his face relaxes. "Then do so."

I grin at him, and before I know what I'm doing, I run to him, jumping on top of him. I slam my lips to his, my arms wrapping around his neck. I slide my tongue over the seam of his lips.

He growls. "Bad girl." I feel his cock twitch under the sheet.

His words make me shiver and I reluctantly pull away from him.

"I'll see you later," I say, breathlessly.

His hand goes to my ass, and he squeezes it hard. "Go, before I drag you back to bed and keep you here." He groans.

I try to push down the deep thrill that sends through me, and I climb off the bed. I grab my purse and my phone. I pause at the door, looking over my shoulder.

"Less than twenty-four hours…" I wink at him and blow him a kiss before leaving him there. My heart aches the second I leave the bedroom.

I grab onto the armrests of the seat as the plane lands, finally releasing the breath I've been holding since we started our descent. It's foolish to be afraid of flying. If the plane went down, I would walk away relatively unscathed, and yet there is still something that makes me feel uneasy.

The second the plane stops, I turn my phone off flight mode and open my text messages with Jackson.

PERSEPHONE

Hey, I'm in DC. Do you have time to meet?

I close out of those messages and open my messages with Hades, the tension in my face instantly easing.

PERSEPHONE

Just landed.

HADES

I miss you. I was smelling the sheets…

PERSEPHONE

Smelling the sheets?

No reply from Jackson…he might be in meetings. I try to call him, but it goes to voicemail.

HADES

Don't judge me. I'm a needy god.

I roll my eyes at his message, but my lips twitch. *My needy god.*

I try Jackson again, voicemail.

PERSEPHONE

I can't get hold of Jackson.

HADES

Do you know where he's staying?

It occurs to me that I know very little about Jackson. It never even crossed my mind to ask him where he was staying.

I scroll through my contacts, vaguely remembering that I have his PA's number in my phone. I call her, but it goes straight to voicemail too.

I finally manage to get off the plane and frown down at my phone.

PERSEPHONE

No and I can't get through to his assistant.

HADES

Do you want me to come?

PERSEPHONE

What would that do?

I try calling Jackson once more.

HADES

I would be there to hold your hand.

I smile down at my phone, desperate to turn, get back on the plane, and demand they fly me back to Hades.

I decide to call the main building for Jackson's work. Surely, they would have his information.

"Norton Construction, this is Moira."

I think back, trying to remember if I have met Moira at one of the business dinners Jackson took me to.

"Hey, Moira, it's Persephone, Jackson Lawrence's... friend. I'm trying to get a hold of him, but I can't seem to reach him. Do you have a note of which hotel he's staying at in DC?"

"Oh, Persephone! How lovely to hear from you! Give me two seconds."

I hear her acrylic nails tapping against the keyboard.

"Looks like he's staying at the W Hotel downtown. Oh, even got a room number. It's 1128."

I pull the phone from my ear, quickly typing the details into the notes app.

"Thank you, Moira!"

"No problem, Persephone! Speak soon."

I hang up and flag a cab, thinking that, if I head for his hotel, I can possibly intercept him before my flight back. One thing I am sure of, I need to be on the plane back to Hades tonight. My whole body thrums for him.

For the whole drive, my stomach is in knots. I chalk it up to anticipation for the difficult conversation I'm going to have. I reread Hades's last message over and over on the drive to calm myself.

Hand holding would be just the beginning,
my spring.

The second the taxi stops outside the W, I pay the driver and quickly slide out of the cab. Knowing the room number, I stroll right past reception to the elevator.

Everything about the small chamber feels wrong. It's not the elevator that took me to Hades that first day, not the one we kissed in, not the walls he pushed me up against.

Finding Jackson's room is relatively easy, but I silently curse myself when I realize I don't have a key. Would reception give me one?

I tilt my head at the door, seeing it slightly ajar, a stray item of clothing wedging it. My ears twitch when I hear noises coming from inside. I furrow my brows and push on the door. My steps are nearly silent as I walk down the small hallway, the moans of pleasure become louder. Items of clothing are strewn all over the floor, giving the impression they had been removed in haste.

"Oh, Jackson!"

My eyes go wide and I follow the noise, blinking at the scene in front of me. Jackson is on top of his assistant, his face buried in her neck, fingers digging into her long blond hair.

"Hello, Jackson."

His body tenses, and he stills completely. His assistant's eyes go wide. I hear his colorful curse as he pulls his cock from her. Snatching a pillow from under her head, he covers himself modestly. Completely disregarding her.

His eyes go wide when I burst out laughing at how utterly ridiculous this situation is. I laugh so hard, I need

245

to grip the wall to stay upright.

"Babe, this isn't what it looks like..." Jackson lifts his free hand, his palm facing me.

I wipe my eyes, tears spilling from them from laughter. "Really? It looks like you were balls deep in your assistant."

Jackson flushes. His assistant looks like she'd rather be swallowed into the ground than have to endure this confrontation.

"It was a one-time thing! A mistake! I was just upset!"

My laughter eventually dies down enough for me to form sentences. "No, this is perfect, actually." I pull his ring from my pocket and place it on the dresser. "Goodbye, Jackson." I turn and leave his room. I hear him chasing after me.

"Babe! Wait!"

I glance over my shoulder as I walk back to the elevator. "And Jackson, don't recycle that ring. Get her something classier."

The elevator closes as Jackson hurries down the corridor, fighting with his pants as he tries to yank them up while chasing me.

Almost as if he can feel my emotions, I get a text from Hades the second I leave the hotel.

HADES
Did you find him?

PERSEPHONE
Changing my flight, I'll be home soon.

I roll my eyes as a text from Jackson comes through.

246

JACKSON

Please, babe! It was a mistake! I love you.

I delete the messages from Jackson and open the unread one from Hades.

HADES

I can come get you.

PERSEPHONE

From the airport?

HADES

I can be in front of you in a moment, my spring. Do you want that? You can fly express.

I furrow my brows, looking at my phone. I'm desperate to see him. To touch him.

PERSEPHONE

Yes.

Within the blink of an eye, he's in front of me, towering over me. I nervously look around, worried that someone saw him materializing, but the humans seem blissfully unaware. *Must have a cloaking power.*

I grab his face. Pulling him down to me, I press my lips to his and wrap my arms around his neck, needing him closer. The second he opens his lips, allowing me entry, I slide my tongue over his, moaning at his taste.

"Take me home. Now."

Chapter Forty-Five

Hades

SHE SLAMS INTO ME WITH SUCH FORCE, her lips on mine, and those worries that have haunted me since she left slip away. Water against stone. Her hauntingly sweet scent soothes me, in a way only she can. Her hands are in my hair, locking me to her, kissing me. Lips sealed against mine.

Before I can lose myself in it, I pull back. I frown at her, shadowing her with me until we're back in my penthouse in my bedroom. "What happened?"

She grabs my face tighter, kissing me hard, her hands dropping to my shirt, ripping it with an audible tear. Her hands move along me, every inch of my skin, urgency clear in every touch. "Too much time wasted. I am yours. Officially."

Words from a dream. From every dream of mine. Yet I can't succumb, not yet. I need to understand. I once leapt with her, assuming she had broken up with him. I need to hear her say the words this time.

I take a step back. She reluctantly relinquishes her hold on me, a predator with claws sunk into her long-awaited prey. "Wait. Tell me what happened?"

Her eyes flash with anger and barely leashed desire. "He was fucking his assistant."

I blink several times, before I feel the power coursing into my veins, needing to punish. He was fucking someone else? When he could fuck *her?* My body coils with darkness, a deep well inside me that just cracks, ready to spill into the world. My voice is unrecognizable, even to me. "His life is forfeit."

She steps closer to me. "Hades. The only thing I'm angry about is time lost with you."

I take another step back, afraid to grab the future in front of me. "But…"

She frowns, a flash of something I don't catch clouding her face. "What?"

I scan her eyes, murmuring., "How can he take for granted what I am so willing to kill for?"

Her eyes soften. "It doesn't matter, Hades. I am yours."

I am yours. The stirring of fate seems to wrap around us, even as I use my shadows to wrap around her waist, pulling her to me. Her feet lift from the floor, gliding. as my shadows close the distance between us. "All mine?"

She shoves the tattered shirt off my shoulders, locking eyes with me. "All. Yours."

All the permission I need. I smirk, grabbing her by the waist and throwing her onto the bed. The shadow chastity belt vanishes as an afterthought. Though I wouldn't mind belting her again, controlling when she can touch herself. Her pleasure is *mine.* Every moan and whisper of ecstasy. But now, I need to free her, to devour her, to finally do all the things I've dreamed of doing. I lunge to pin her beneath me, barely coherent as we begin. Too many fantasies and too many close calls have made it so I can barely think straight now that the time has come. Her skin is heated under my lips as I drag them along her skin, starting with her chest, licking those nipples of hers, so fucking distracting. Down her stomach and settling between her legs. The new center of my universe.

I wrap her knees around my head, burying myself

between them. Hoping to never breathe again, to only inhale the cunt glistening before me. The perfect pink flesh, waiting for me. I've only tasted the briefest bit of it. I need more. Face-to-face with the pussy that I've spent so much time fantasizing about. "I can't tell you how I've dreamed of devouring this cunt."

She gazes down at me, her bottom lip between her teeth, her eyes molten.

I keep my eyes locked on hers, as I take the first lick, immediately groaning, "Fuck, you're addicting, so fucking sweet."

I need more. I need to taste her as I've dreamed. To devour her. Her hips buck, her head thrown back. I grind her cunt against my face, my tongue vibrating on her clit, pushing her toward the climax. The first of many I'll need her to experience before I'm satisfied.

She moans again, her hips writhing. My arms wrap around her waist, keeping her against me. I bite her clit, shifting, using my fingers to curl inside her at the same time. I should take my time. Slow down. Be less *savage.* But any kind of restraint in me shattered when she claimed she was *all mine.* She cries out, her pussy tightening on my fingers. So tight, and all fucking *mine.*

"Hades...fuck!" she screams.

I growl into her clit at my name, ordering her, "Come."

She screams my name, her body arching off the bed. Her legs squeeze around my ears, and I take every last drop she has. Every last lick. I slowly pull back from her, letting her legs slide bonelessly from my shoulders.

I smirk wickedly at how thoroughly sated she looks right now. Glowing from within. But this is just the beginning. I grab her hips, tossing her onto her front. My hands on her hips, yanking them up. Spanking her ass as I line my cock up with her. I spank her again, watching that life-changing ass of hers ripple from the strike before I slam inside her. I should have dragged it out, like I dreamed, but she's too fucking tempting. I need to be inside her.

"I want to see you helpless for me," I growl. The feeling of finally being inside her is indescribable. She fists the sheets as I seat myself inside her.

Her flesh resists my size, even as she moans at me stretching her. "Gods."

I smack her ass hard, leaving a red handprint, correcting her. "One god."

She pushes her hips back into me, trying to get more. As if I won't give her everything. "One god." She whimpers. "You. Only you."

I grip her ass hard, my fingers digging in. My shadows move around us as I thrust. Every part of her is touched by me or my shadows as I fuck her. I rotate my hips, my shadows rolling her nipples at the same time. Each inch of her body is being explored by me, exposed and touched, even as I thrust inside her, over and over, piercing her. Needing to hit her deeper, fuck her better.

I have to bite my lip to stop myself from coming immediately at the feel of her. Too much time waiting to be inside her, to fuck her, and I'm already on the verge. It shouldn't be this fucking good. I shouldn't be so lost already. But each thrust of my cock into her is even better than my fantasies. I couldn't have ever fantasized about this, because I didn't know such a state of pleasure existed. That it was waiting for me out there, inside this goddess. Inside my fated queen.

Her body writhes under my shadows and me. Her cunt squeezes me, throbbing around me. She's so close, I know it, even before she speaks. "Hades..."

I rotate my hips again. Needing more. It can't be over, not yet. There's so much I still want to do to her, need to do to her. "Not yet, spring, not yet."

She arches her back, pressing her face into the bed,

her body quivering as she fights her own orgasm. "Yes, sir."

Such a good fucking slut for me. An unspoken truce, that when she's in this bedroom, she's going to obey, but outside it…

Her cunt squeezes me and her body shoots tighter with tension. I can barely think enough to yank my cock out of her, before dooming us both. My cum shoots from me, a never-ending torrent, marking her back instead of her cunt, as she screams her own release. It drips over her, marking her as mine. I fill her with my fingers to draw out her climax. She shoves her hips back into me, burying her face. My cum slips and slides down her back as she writhes and quakes from her orgasm, so lost. A part of me is so fucking satisfied to see her covered in my release, but yet I'm already wishing I was seeing it drip out of her. Our combined releases leaking from her over the day, constantly marked by me. She'd sit at her desk at work, knowing that a part of me is still inside her. Marking that fucking cunt of hers for hours after I fucked her.

I shake as she finishes, her body twitching from the force. I pull my fingers out, licking them, collapsing on the bed next to her, sated. At least for now. Need more. *Need everything.* Just the beginning.

I'm going to fuck you like my life depends on it, Persephone. So you never think of another again.

Chapter Forty-Six

Persephone

ECSTASY.

That's how it felt when Hades was inside me, pure, unadulterated ecstasy. Every thrust, every movement made my body writhe in pleasure.

I collapse on the bed, lying on my front as my body quivers from the earth-shattering orgasms I just had. A shiver runs down my spine as I remember how his sinful mouth felt between my legs, how his tongue lapped at me, how it flicked my sensitive bud, pulling my orgasm from the small bundle of nerves. How perfectly his cock filled me, stretched me, so big and thick. The feeling of overwhelming, pleasurable fullness, quickly overtaking the initial discomfort of his size. I start to ease my death grip on the sheets, no longer needing anchoring.

Hades collapses beside me, spent. He leans over and presses a soft kiss to my lips, the small act already making my pussy flutter with need.

"Still with me?" His voice, so husky, makes my toes curl at the sound.

I moan in acknowledgment, not able to talk yet. Basking in the post-orgasm void.

I shift slightly and feel his release trailing over my hip. I lean on my elbows and glance over my shoulder, seeing my skin covered in his spend. Seeing my skin marked like this makes that low curl of heat in my stomach reignite. *As if it ever dies when in the presence of the God of the Underworld.*

Hades laughs, waving his hand, magically cleaning my skin of him.

I roll onto my side, pushing down the disappointment that I'm no longer covered in his release.

I slide closer to him and kiss him deeply. "Was I worth the wait?" I whisper into his lips.

He cups my cheek. "Even if I had to wait a thousand more years."

I smile into his lips, sliding my hand up his muscular chest.

He playfully bites my lip, making me moan. "You sure I shouldn't send Thanatos to collect his soul?" His voice is teasing, but with an edge. I can tell he's seriously considering it.

I push him onto his back and straddle him, my lips pressing against his. *His lips are so addictive.* I slide my tongue over his, caressing it, and murmur into his lips, "I don't give a fuck about him."

"So you made me wait for no reason?"

I pull back, lifting my eyebrow when I see his frown. "If I remember correctly, demon," I tilt my head at him, "*you* made *me* wait."

He shoots me a look of annoyance. "I did not. I was single the whole time."

I roll my eyes before leaning down to kiss his neck. I press hot, open-mouthed kisses to his skin, biting him occasionally. My lips move to his collarbone and down his chest. I look up at him. "Stop talking." I continue to kiss down his body, stopping when I'm kneeling in between his thighs. His divine resilience is already making him hard again for me. *Addicting.*

He growls at my command. "Don't order me, little girl. Your ass is still red from the last time."

My lips twitch, but I try to suppress my smile. I keep

my gaze locked on his as I wrap my hand around his cock. I slowly bend and lick the tip, lapping at the small bead of moisture there. I close my lips around the swollen crown and suck on him. "Hm?"

My eyes roll back as I taste myself on him, taste the last few drops of his previous spend.

His eyes darken, and I immediately feel something like a hand spanking my ass. Hard.

Shadows...

My loud moans send vibrations down his hard length, my ass stings from the hit, and I feel my arousal track down my thighs. I suck his cock deeper into my mouth, as his shadow hand comes down on my ass again, making my eyes water.

His groan is the most erotic noise I've ever heard, and it drives me wild with need.

"You taste that delicious cunt on my cock?"

I nod slowly, taking even more of his length into my mouth. When his cock hits my throat, I gag hard on him.

I feel his fingers tangle in my hair as he guides my head. More of his shadows appear to tease me. One feels like a finger sliding over my clit, another pinching one nipple, then the other.

I swirl my tongue around his shaft as I suck on him, gagging each time his cock invades my throat. Craving the feeling of my throat struggling around his size.

He growls, pushing my head down on his cock over and over. Hades summons yet another shadow. This one feels like his cock, which he mercilessly pushes inside my waiting cunt. I push my hips back into him.

I was right. The shadows don't compare to the real thing. But right now...I'm desperate to worship him with my mouth. Needing to taste him. I cup his balls, massaging them, appreciating their heavy weight in my hand.

"You're going to make me come again," he groans.

I hollow my cheeks as I suck on him harder, faster.

With a powerful thrust, he comes, his release filling my mouth. I moan at the taste, moan at how it feels sliding down my throat. I keep lightly sucking, robbing him of every drop.

I watch him, his chest heaving, his grip on my hair easing. I lick him clean, not wanting to waste a drop, before pulling back.

He looks down at me, his eyes bright. He crooks his finger, beckoning me. I crawl up his body, lying on top of him.

"You're such a good girl."

I shiver, my pussy still throbbing. He presses his lips to mine and rolls us so we're both lying on our sides, and those perfect hands begin to wander…

Chapter Forty-Seven

Hades

I CAN'T KEEP MY HANDS OFF HER. My cock out of her. I need to claim her in every way I possibly can. Even if I can't come inside her without activating the curse. I barely remember each time I'm inside her, so lost in the union of our bodies it's nearly impossible. But I can't. I won't curse her to half the year in the Underworld. Not after she fought to leave Olympus. I won't put her in another prison. Even if I'll be there too. I need to make every moment count with her. We have less than two months left. Now, I need to take advantage. I've had her physically, now I need her heart. Because, with every moment, I'm losing mine more and more to her.

I pant, brushing her hair back from her damp face. My chest aches as I look at her, at her flushed cheeks, her swollen lips, her eyes which are still close to black. "You know, we should go on an actual date." I kiss her brow, licking some of the salty sweat there. "Flowers and chocolates."

That's something we can do in the limited time we have. The ticking clock that began the second we slept together. How am I to leave her here? When she's finally mine?

She smirks wickedly, purring. "Sex?"

I laugh. She's insatiable. *So am I.* "I could be persuaded."

She rolls her eyes at me, climbing off. I frown at how her face has changed. The glow of a moment before has vanished. Though her skin is still slick with sweat and her hair matted from my fingers and the bed. She picks up one of my shirts from the floor, pulling it on, leaving me alone in the bedroom. She didn't look back at me. Not once.

Did I do something wrong?

I grab a pair of sweats from the floor, pulling them on. My gut twists as I follow her, finding her with her head in the fridge. I wrap my arms around her stomach, putting my head on her shoulder, seeing her hands are full with fresh strawberries. Is that why she tastes like the red fruit?

I open my mouth, asking, "One for me?"

She picks out one, pressing it to my lips, allowing me to take a bite. I lick at the juice on my chin before taking another bite, enjoying the sweetness of the fruit, but I'm still thinking about the other sweetness I want more. "Are you going to tell me why you're out here? Instead of being in bed with me?"

She turns in my arms, looking up at me, taking a sharp bite out of the strawberry. Her eyes are hard, with none of the softness or pleasure that was there a moment before. I have the strange urge to cover my cock for protection. I lean down to lick at the juice on her lip, but she turns away, giving me her cheek.

I must have really fucked up. Shit.

I scan my memories, trying to pinpoint what I could have done or said to upset her. We were fine, then she talked about dates and…I come up blank. "What did I say? Did I do something wrong?"

I must have for her to be so tense. She shrugs, but her eyes are harsh. "Maybe I'm done having to *persuade* you to be intimate with me."

My arms drop from her, my eyes blinking repeatedly, trying to understand what she just said. Nope, still doesn't make sense. "You can't be serious."

She looks away from me, wrapping her arms around her middle. Leaving me reeling. "You really think you have to persuade me? You have only to breathe for me to be aching for you." I scan her face, trying to understand. "You knew I only resisted because you were involved with someone else."

She doesn't look at me but nods. She might as well have slapped me. I let out a sad chuckle. "You don't believe me."

It's not a question. It's written all over her face. She turns away, stepping away from me. I put a hand onto the fridge door to keep from staggering at the emotional blow.

"I don't know...I just...keep waiting for you to realize I'm not what you want."

You're the only thing I've ever wanted. There's something else. There has to be. Some reason that the confident, sexy, intelligent woman I know is acting like this. Is she trying to shelter me from the truth? Was...Was I wrong?

"Is this because he cheated on you? I would never do that." Some gods don't take vows of commitment seriously. I'm not one of them.

She sighs, still not looking at me. "No...it's because you're...King of the Dead, and I'm...just the Goddess of Spring."

You don't even know what you are yet. What you could be. You're half life and half death, the duality that exists in all mortals personified. My Queen of the Dead. My Goddess of Life. But the words of fate have bound me. So I can't say anything. Those who know their fate are helpless to do anything to change it.

I cross my arms. "What does that have to do with

259

anything?"

She turns to face me, but her eyes won't meet mine. "You're so impressive. I'm nobody."

"Bullshit," I snap. She never cared who I was before, it never presented a divide. I've always been the God of the Dead and Ruler of the Underworld. I haven't changed. So this... A treacherous thought slithers through my mind, making its way to my lips. "Do you... regret it? Regret being with me?"

Her brows furrow. "Hades..."

The way her voice softens, as if about to deliver words of truth. A truth she hoped to spare me from. The first word wasn't *no*. And that's all that matters to me. She didn't say *no*. She keeps talking, but I can't hear her, the ringing in my ears drowning it out. She regrets it. Regrets me.

I take a step back from her, touching my stomach. "That wasn't a no."

I look away from her before shadowing out of the penthouse.

Chapter Forty-Eight

Persephone

I STARE AT THE SPOT HADES HAD JUST OC-CUPIED. The last few wisps of his shadows dissipate into nothing. My brows draw as I think about our conversation. In what world does "you are the best thing that has ever happened to me" mean "I regret fucking you and wish it had never happened"?

My chest aches. *How easily he can leave me...*

I pull out my phone and open my conversation with Hades.

PERSEPHONE

> You are the best thing that has ever happened to me = I regret nothing.

> You have shown me what it is to live, Hades.

I look down at my phone, waiting for him to reply, waiting for those three little dots to appear on my screen, indicating that he's typing.

Is it so ridiculous to need a little reassurance? He is the great and powerful Hades, widely known and feared, and I am...some silly little goddess who was hidden away for centuries by her mother.

I'll be considered a joke next to him.

Hades rules the Underworld, and I...conjure flowers. I lift my hand, palm up, and watch as a daisy grows there. I stroke the delicate petals and tilt my head. My stomach clenches.

No idea who you are, Persephone...

Under my touch, black lines start flowing through the petals, like the veins were infected, dying. I lift my hand closer to my face to inspect the flower, but in the blink of an eye, all evidence of darkness has disappeared, and the daisy, once again, sits unconcerned on my palm. I slide the pad of my finger over the petal again, but nothing happens.

My phone alerts, pulling me from my thoughts, and I close my hand before checking my phone.

HADES

I feel like I'm trying to catch smoke with you.
One wrong move and I'm left without you.

PERSEPHONE

You left me, in a literal puff of smoke.

HADES

Fine. I'm pretty sure I'm falling in love with you and you said you were tired of persuading me.

I blink down at my phone, reading the same eight words over and over. *Pretty sure I'm falling in love with you.* My breath catches in my throat and my eyes sting.

Hades and I are inevitable.

PERSEPHONE

Come home.

I wait for him, seconds, minutes, nothing. No sign of him even replying to me. I read his message again. *Pretty sure I'm falling in love with you.* My heart pounds in my chest, and I stare at my phone, as if I can will him here by wanting him hard enough. By needing him hard enough.

A shiver runs down my spine, and a moment later, he appears in front of me. He's the picture of casual calm, his hand in his pockets, leaning against the doorframe, but I can see the concern in his eyes, the way his shoulders seem tense.

I don't move from my spot, my gaze locked on his.

"You..." I swallow, trying to calm my racing heart, knowing he can hear it. "You're falling in love with me?"

His cheeks flush, and he pulls his hand from his pocket to rub the back of his neck. Is he...nervous? "I've never acted like this—"

The eight feet of distance feels like too much, and I run at him, jumping into his arms. My lips slam to his. The second my body collides with his, he catches me. I know I can trust Hades with my heart, my life, my soul. He kisses me back near instantly. I slide my tongue along the seam of his lips as I tangle my fingers into his hair.

I pull back, looking at him, my eyes roaming over his perfect face. "I'm falling for you too."

He blinks repeatedly. "Y-You are?"

I nod and slam my lips to his again, deepening the kiss immediately.

"You never have to persuade me," he whispers into my lips, between desperate kisses.

I trail my lips over his cheek and along his jaw. "I'm sorry. I just felt a little uncertain..."

"Uncertain? You?" He groans as I press open-mouthed kisses to his neck, biting and sucking as I go. I take his earlobe between my teeth and bite down.

"I have my moments."

He cups my ass with his large hands, squeezing possessively. "I don't like that. You must tell me when you're having them."

I pull back. "Hades...I did. And you left."

He tenses. "I—" He frowns, considering. "I shouldn't

have left. I won't do it again." He squeezes my ass again.

I moan as his fingers dig into the ample flesh, desperately hoping I bruise from his grasp. "Deal."

I kiss him again as he carries me to the kitchen counter. His thin shirt provides no protection from the feeling of the cool marble beneath my ass. I shiver but keep my lips against his, my tongue tangling with his.

Hades removes his hands from my body. I'm about to protest when I feel him shift in front of me, the sound of the elastic groaning as he pushes his sweats down. Within moments, his greedy hands are on me again, sliding up my thighs, pushing his shirt with them.

He groans as he slides the swollen crown of his cock through my slick folds, already so wet for him. In one quick motion, he thrusts inside me, the tight walls of my cunt struggling to stretch for him, to accommodate him. The tight fit makes me feel so full, waves of pleasure ripple through me.

I dig my nails into his shoulders as my body starts to accept his, the intense pleasure making me cry out for more, for him, for everything.

His hand slides up my body and cups the back of my head. He presses his face into my neck, his thrusts becoming brutal, jarring.

The only noise in the apartment is our skin slapping together, our frantic breaths, our desperate moans. His cock fits so well in my pussy, it's as if we truly are meant to be. Every thrust makes me wetter, every moan against my neck sends a shiver down my spine.

I bite down on his shoulder and drag my nails down his back. I feel the sticky warmth of his gold ichor under my nails. His primal growl immediately quells my concern that I've hurt him, and he rewards me by starting to drop his glamour.

I pull back, my eyes going wide at the sight in front of me. Proud large black horns protrude from either side of his head. They are…magnificent. They gracefully curl behind his ear and then away from his head.

The perfect handlebars...

I see his fangs elongating in his mouth, and before I can consider how badly I need him to sink them into me, to mark me as his, he does. His bite is claiming, the bittersweet pain bringing me ever closer to release, his hips still pistoning into me.

The second his fangs pierce me, I feel the urge to lower my own glamour, and I make my horns visible for the first time in decades. I bring my hands to one of his horns and lightly trace my finger over it. His answering shudder gives me a thrill.

He licks my neck, caressing the two small holes his fangs made. His tongue slides over the sensitive skin there, making me arch into him, tilting my head even more for him.

I wrap my hand around his horn and stroke him slowly, like I would his cock. His moan is guttural, desperate, and he quickly pulls out of me as his roar fills the room.

Confused, I lean in and bite down on his earlobe, my voice a sensual whisper. "Don't stop. So close…"

He immediately replaces his cock with his fingers, his hot mouth on my neck, sucking hard on the sensitive flesh there.

His thumb brushes over my clit, and my orgasm barrels through me. I scream his name, needing him to hear me, needing him to know how badly I need him.

He hisses and presses a gentle kiss to my throat. I tangle my fingers in his hair and pull his face to mine, kissing him deeply, moaning into his lips.

Completely addicted to the God of the Underworld...

He presses his forehead to mine as we both try and catch our breath.

"I'm sorry I left."

I am so fucking done for.

I manage a smirk. "You will be, demon."

I open my eyes and my gaze snags on the floor, *is that...?*

He pulled out...again. *Does he...does he not want to come inside of me?*

My brows furrow, and I finally bring my gaze back to him. His face is flushed, not from his orgasm, though, but embarrassment. He waves his hand and within a moment, his release has been cleaned from the floor.

Should I ask him about it?

He kisses me again, sweet and quick. "Hungry?"

I nod and file the thought away for later.

Chapter Forty-Nine

Hades

I SAID IT. The truth that had been festering inside me—how I felt about her—and she didn't run. *Because she doesn't know the whole truth.* How much longer will fate allow me to pull out of her? To prevent the curse from activating? Many, many people have fought against their fate, raged against it. All have fallen to it, gods and mortals alike. I'm attempting to do the same. Somewhere distantly, I can hear the sands of a midnight hourglass clinking down to the glass beneath. Each ping of the glass feels like a hit to the balls.

She moans into my lips, and I pull back, pressing my forehead to hers. "I'm sorry I left."

She's falling in love with me. She smirks. "You will be, demon."

My chest tightens at her smirk. And I have no doubt she'll find a terribly creative way to even the score with me. She'll never be a meek queen, no. She'll bend all to her iron will. Even me. *All hail the Iron Queen.* Not queen. Not yet. Not ever. I won't imprison her. If I put her in another cage…she'll never forgive me.

Her eyes slowly open, focusing on my release on the floor. I flush at the mess I made, using my shadows to clean it up. Wishing I could erase the thought in my head that whispers, *Imagine how much better that cum would look dripping out of her cunt.* I don't know if it's fate or my own inner desires that plant that thought.

She looks up at me, her dark brows furrowed. But I can't explain. I knew, when I first spoke to the Fates centuries ago, the price to be paid. If you speak to the Fates, if you know the future. You are helpless to change it. But I was so arrogant. Now I can see Persephone's eyes light with questions, but I can't confess. *Don't ask. Don't ask. I can't answer. I can't give you what you want.*

I kiss her again. "Hungry?" She nods, though her eyes are still distant, trying to figure me out. "What would you like?"

She wiggles away from me, jumping down from the counter. Even after just being together, I can feel her pulling away. And there's nothing I can do to stop it. "Anything. I'm going to take a shower."

I raise a brow, looking at the food, then at her. "And I'm not allowed to join?"

Gods, we just fucked, but I'm already thinking about taking her again. Is it always like this with a fated match? Insatiable. I need to bring us closer when I feel her retreating from me. Even though I know it's my fault. She's drawing back because I'm hiding things.

She shrugs. "You're making breakfast."

I glance at the kitchen again. "I can't do both?"

She turns from me, slowly pulling my shirt off her body, walking to the bathroom. I groan loudly, watching her vanish into the bedroom. I stand there, frozen, until I hear the shower turn on.

I shadow into the shower stall with her. "Breakfast can wait."

She presses her back into my chest, raising the loofa with her hand, scrubbing her body. I take the loofa from her, using it on her. She reaches behind, wrapping her hand around my already-hard cock. I jolt into her hand. "Not exhausted after earlier?"

Is she as desperate for me as I am for her?

She strokes my cock slowly, my eyes rolling back. "Are you?"

Never. For you, my queen, I'm always ready. I growl into her ear, pushing her forward to the wall of the shower, biting her shoulder. "Show me your horns."

She glances over her shoulder at me, her eyes sparkling. "Say please."

I caught only a glimpse of the horns earlier, but I want to see them now. To truly look at them. Only the gods of the Underworld have horns, which is why the modern world thought us to be demons. I wasn't born with horns, I also wasn't destined to be an Underworld god. I was *given* the Underworld, and always felt on the outside. Until my horns grew in, and my body became more in tune with the Underworld.

I let the glamour around my own horns drop, seeing the reflection of the obsidian horns, jutting from the side of my head and curling back.

"Now," I order.

Her own glamour drops slowly around her hair, and small white horns curl up and point to the sky. My breath catches at them, leaning forward to rub mine against hers. I shudder at the feeling, the horns sensitive to the touch, like someone raking their nails along my balls. I pull her hand from my cock, putting it on the shower wall.

I hook one of her knees around my arm, raising it enough for me to thrust inside her. Will I ever get enough? Ever feel a day, a breath, without this ache? I bite her neck as I thrust, her own moans lost in the shower. She pushes back, meeting every thrust. Feeling the same kind of desperation?

The demand in the low base of the spine to combine ourselves into one. To bind our fate. *Is that what this is? Fate trying to make me seal the bond?* The second the

269

thought forms, I discard it. No this…this is all us. No fate interferences. The way I crave her, it is far more than just fate.

I rub my horns against hers, moving faster. "Mine."

She shivers. "Hades…"

I growl, thrusting faster. Vines start sprouting beneath her hands against the shower wall. "Fuck…"

I hiss, "You going to come, my spring?"

She shoves back against me. "Yes. So close. Please…"

"You're mine."

Her tight cunt squeezes me, and she lets out a scream as she comes. I pull out at the last second, coming on the shower floor. I pant at the force, pressing my face into her shoulder.

Chapter Fifty

Persephone

I SHIVER AS HE SLIDES HIS NOSE ALONG ONE OF MY HORNS, the feeling similar to someone lightly trailing their fingers down my spine.

His deep, sensual voice in my ear makes me shiver. "I *love* these…"

I want to tell him that I love his horns, too, that I want to lick them, that I want to grab them as I straddle his face, steering his head, but he continues with his maddening ministrations, nuzzling my horns, stealing my words from me.

I've never particularly liked my horns. I'll always remember my mother's reaction when they grew. She was horrified, disgusted. I had just turned four when I started getting headaches, and after a matter of weeks, two small pearl spikes protruded from the top of my head, obvious against my dark hair. The first time I saw them, my eyes went wide with wonder, and I ran to tell my mother about them, excitement making my tiny legs carry me faster. My elation was quickly quashed the second I saw her thunderous expression. The following weeks were filled with a slew of visits with healers, some light, some dark. They all told my mother the same thing—nothing could be done.

"Mama, why don't you like my horns?" I ask her as she

drags me along a dark street. In response, she pulls my hood further over my head, concealing them more. The street lights cast an orangey glow, the light and the dark battling it out, but the street is barely luminated, the shadows swallowing as much light as possible, feeding on it.

She pulls me into a damp-smelling, derelict building. My stomach rolls in the atmosphere. There is something eerie about this place, and that small voice in my head begs me to run.

"Clotho? Lachesis? Atropos?" My mother's voice shakes.

I've never seen her afraid before. I look up at her, her pale face stricken. The silence is deafening until, moments later, a chilling voice replies. The hair stands on the back of my neck, my mother's hand tightens on mine.

"Ah...Demeter..."

I turn but cannot see the source of the voice.

"We wondered when you would contact us again." Another voice from elsewhere in the room. My head whips around.

"I see the change has begun, just as we predicted," says a third voice from behind us.

"There must be a way to change this. I will not have her tied to—" My mother's voice turns sharp.

I look up at her, worried she is angry at me.

"Careful, Demeter."

"It is done."

"It has been written since before even you were born."

"I do not accept this. There must be a way." Mama starts to push me behind her, but I'm acutely aware that the three voices surround us.

"Do not hide the light within Persephone. It will anger the darkness that also resides."

"There is no darkness in her," my mother spits.

"Even now, I hear it calling. It is angry."

"Dark just as much as light, entangled within her."

"To suppress one is to destroy both."

"You're wrong. You're all wrong." My mother grabs my

272

hand and pulls me from the building. I hear the three voices cackling from behind, the sound ominous.

"I like her horns," the first voice says, her voice dripping with smugness.

The next day, my mother and I started working on my glamouring power, and I was told, in no uncertain terms, the punishment for dropping said glamour would be brutal.

Hades pulls me from my memories as he begins massaging my scalp, rubbing the shampoo into my hair.

Instinctively, I start to replace my glamour, never feeling fully comfortable having any part of my true self showing, after decades of discipline whenever I let the facade fade even slightly. Having my glamour off feels like taking my bra off at the end of the day, so freeing and comfortable. Or at least it would, were I not so self-conscious about the delicate pearl horns.

"Why did you do that?" he asks, still rubbing the shampoo into my hair.

"What?" I tilt my head back, allowing him to start rinsing the soap.

He gestures to my head. "The glamour."

I feel my cheeks heat, and I shrug, trying to play it off as no big deal. "Habit, I guess."

He shifts me slightly so that my hair is directly under the spray before asking, "Anything else you're hiding under that glamour?"

I smirk, enjoying how easy it is with him, how quickly he can pull me from being contemplative to being playful. "Maybe..."

He bends and selects another bottle of product. It smells similar to the shampoo, like pomegranate and strawberries. He rubs it into my hair, lathering. "Maybe?"

His fingers working my scalp makes me moan. Later I'm going to let him massage me all over, those hands

273

both delightfully gentle and sinfully firm.

My answer to his question is another moan. I'm not sure why he expects anything different when he's touching me like this.

I feel his lips brush against my shoulder, pulled into a smile. "What if I have things hidden?"

I blink my eyes open and turn to face him, my head tilted. *Never fails to intrigue me.* "Show me."

His cocky smile falters, and once again, I am given a glimpse at his vulnerable side. He blinks. "Are you sure? It's…a bit…demonic."

I rinse the conditioner out of my hair, my gaze locked on his. "Show me."

He takes a steadying breath, and my heart aches seeing him this self-conscious.

He slowly drops his glamour, and my jaw slackens. His horns, proudly curling from his head, large black wings tucked in close to his back, black as onyx, with a hook at the top of each one and a thin forked tail twitching side to side behind him.

My lips part as I take him in, inch by incredible inch. It should embarrass me how freely I'm ogling him, but he is Hades. *My* Hades and he is magnificent.

I step forward, closing the small distance between us, my fingers itching to touch his wings. I reach out, hesitating before I make contact. He may not want to be touched here.

I glance at him, his assessing gaze watching me carefully. "May I?"

He nods once, opening his wings slightly for me. "You may."

I gently graze the inside of his wing with the tips of my fingers, tilting my head at the feel. They feel like the most expensive of leathers, soft and buttery, delicate and yet hardy. His wings shudder at the contact, and Hades shivers. I walk around him, my fingers trailing over

274

his sensitive wings as I go, not wanting to stop touching them, wanting to know what feels good to him. My goal is always to please Hades.

When I'm behind him, my gaze snags on his tail, still darting back and forth. I run my knuckles over the base. "Incredible…"

I'm rewarded with another shiver from my god, and I gasp when I feel something wrap around my ankle, rubbing the inside. I glance down and see his tail is wrapped around me. There is something so deliciously possessive about it.

I smirk as I have an idea. Leaning in, I slide my tongue over his wing.

He immediately tenses. "Persephone…"

Success. How about this?

I drag a nail down the main body of his wing, feigning ignorance. "Yes?"

He shudders. "They…ah, they're sensitive."

I lick them again, smiling into the leathery membrane. "You want me to stop?"

"No," he says, releasing a shaky breath. His tail slowly starts to rub my calf, and I bite back a groan.

Unable to help myself, I drag another nail down his wing, greedy for his reactions, for his pleasure.

His head drops back. "Shit…"

I follow the trail of my nails with my tongue. "Tell me what to do."

He pushes back into my touch, groaning. "Just your touch, it makes me come undone."

I start walking around him again, once again trailing my nails over his other wing as I walk. Standing in front of him, I lean in and kiss his neck, my body nearly flush with his. "I can't drop my glamour here."

"Why not?" I can practically hear his frown.

I slide my hands over his hips and caress his wings again, chuckling. "Not everyone's wings are as happy in water."

Within the blink of an eye, he snaps his glamour back into place, and I pout. He pulls back from my touch and looks down at me. "What?"

I move into him again, kissing his jaw. "You want to see me without my glamour?"

He nods.

I graze his jaw with my teeth. "I'm not showing you in the shower."

Without another thought, he turns off the water and grabs a towel.

I smile, feeling lighter than I ever have. He is excited to see the Persephone I have spent centuries trying to conceal.

Chapter Fifty-One

Hades

T**O YOU, HADES, GOES THE UNDERWORLD,"** *Gaia murmured, my two brothers on either side of me before the primordial. All three of us were bleeding ichor all over the white marble of Olympus's throne room. I had a gaping injury to my stomach, my hand pressed to it, forcing my innards to remain inside. Poseidon was missing a hand, his still-intact one holding his wrist, attempting to stem the bleeding. Zeus was the worst of us. He was missing half his face from our father crushing his skull. But we weren't able to tend to our wounds before we were summoned by Gaia.*

The Earth Mother didn't seem to notice or care about our various injuries, instead dividing the world between the three of us. Gaia looked over us all, but her eyes were worlds away. I barely felt her put the bident into my hands, the instrument that marked my new dominion. But when my fingers curled around the gold, my power exploded. As did my brothers', as they tightened their own hands. Zeus's on the bolt, Poseidon's on the trident. Our wounds healed as our powers buffered against the others.

Lightning meeting seas meeting darkness. A torrent of power lashing. Yet Gaia just stared at us. Her words echoed over the marble. "You're tied to your domain. You draw your power and strength from it. It dies....so do you."

She's pulling away from me. Even as our bodies become one, over and over. Even as she says she's falling in love with me. *She's putting up walls.* Fate is keeping my tongue tied, and a wedge is forming between us. Or maybe it's just me. I can't continue to blame fate for the way I'm ruining things. The only blame belongs on my shoulders. And I'm clinging to her more tightly, trying to stop her from retreating. Is this what it's usually like? I've never been in an actual relationship. How could I ever commit to someone, knowing that fate has already tied me to another? Tied me to *her?* To the goddess who's just stepped out of the shower behind me. Maybe I should have tried to prepare myself better for this. For *her.* Yet, I didn't. And now…I'm constantly feeling like I'm missing something.

She's pulling away from me.

She grabs the towel from my hand, wrapping it around her waist.

I frown, looking at the rack of fluffy towels that are right next to Persephone. Instead, she took the one I held. Why?

"That was mine," I point out. That is clearly the wrong thing to say, even if the towel was in my hand when she took it from me. When there are plenty of other towels waiting for her. Is this part of the relationship I don't yet understand? Is my lack of emotional experience damaging us? More the secrets I'm forced to keep? More than the looming hammer of fate about to make her a prisoner. A curse. *My curse.* One that, if I'm not careful, will spread to her. What if she's tied to Gaia's orders? What if…something happens to the Underworld

278

and she dies?

She glares at me, dropping the towel at my feet, before grabbing another and leaving the bathroom. I wrap it around my waist, trying to figure out why she's mad at me...*again*. Is this going to be our future? I click my tongue at her back. "Persephone."

I follow her, wrapping the towel around my waist. I narrow my eyes on her back. "Are you seriously pouting over a *towel*?"

She pulls on a pink thong with a bow on the back, my mouth drying at the sight of it. "I'm annoyed that you snapped at me. Over a *towel*."

I blink. "You took my towel. I didn't snap at you."

Had my tone been harsh? I hadn't meant it so. But she clearly took it that way. I needed to be more careful. Sometimes, it's too easy to forget that she can't read my thoughts and feelings. Unless I speak them aloud. I'm not used to explaining myself to anyone.

She tightens the towel around her body. "Fine."

I move across the room, grabbing her hips. "My spring. It's a towel."

She quirks an eyebrow at me. "Exactly."

I kiss her shoulder. "Forgive me?" She nods, tilting her head to the side, allowing me to kiss her neck. I can't resist adding, "Though...it was my towel."

She jabs me in the ribs.

I hiss, "Ouch."

She turns and kisses my collarbone. I drop my hand from her hips, and spank her bare ass. "Wings?"

She smirks. "You want to see?"

I nod.

She grabs her bag, pulling out a corset, thigh-highs, and a garter belt. "Well, it's only fair you should see me at my best."

Is she trying to kill me? I'm already stiffening at the idea of the lingerie. Add that onto her true form? I'm a fucking goner. I groan. "Persephone."

She smiles up at me, her eyes flickering with mischief. "Hm?"

"You're testing me." I growl, imagining her luscious body tied up in the lingerie she holds.

She tilts her head to the side. "How?"

I look her up and down, my mind already seeing her incredible curves in the corset and thigh-highs. "I'm having trouble focusing on anything but your body."

On focusing on anything but the fact that you're pulling away from me. How much longer did we have? How soon would this peaceful—somewhat turbulent—bubble last?

She kisses my cheek, before disappearing to go change, leaving me behind. I sigh, pulling on some sweatpants, lying on the bed, waiting for her to return. A thought intrudes as I wait for her.

Will she wait for me to return when it's time?

Chapter Fifty-Two
Persephone

HIS DEEP GROAN SENDS A THRILL THROUGH ME. It makes me want to run to the bathroom to change. I stop myself, wanting to feel his hungry gaze on me the whole way there. Craving the feeling of his eyes on me.

I lean against the closed bathroom door, the confidence ebbing from me. When Hades looks at me, I feel unstoppable, like I can face anything. That we will face it together. Panic starts to set in, the walls of the large room feel as though they are closing in on me.

"Never show your true form, Persephone."

My mother's shrill voice invades my mind.

"There is no place for an ugly Goddess of Spring."

I close my eyes, trying to push her from my head.

"Horns are repulsive. We spent thousands of hours on strengthening your glamour for a reason, Persephone."

But then, Hades flashes into my mind's eye. He didn't seem repulsed by them. I shiver as I recall him rubbing his own horns against them. Recall his eyes heating at the sight. I drop my glamour just enough to show them and tilt my head, looking in the mirror. They're not big and daunting like Hades's, rather, small and dainty. Where Hades's are the blackest black and seem to swallow light, the light reflects off of the pearlescent white of mine, almost making them glow.

Hideous.

I look away, snapping my glamour back into place. Turning from the mirror, I sigh, looking at the lingerie.

Can't back out.

Hades trusted me with showing his glamour-less form, even though I could tell he was extremely nervous about it. I try to take comfort in the fact that he seemed to like my horns.

Hades and I are inevitable.

I unwrap the towel, letting it fall to the floor, and pick up the white and gold corset. I hold it to my torso and use my vines to assist me with the ribbons on the back, pulling it tight. The thong and the garter belt match, and I chuckle as I clip the straps to my thigh-high stockings.

Why did you bring this outfit, P?

I reluctantly turn and look in the mirror again, sliding my hand over the silk of the corset.

I fluff up my hair and take a deep breath before leaving the bathroom. I lean against the doorframe, trying to at least give the impression that I'm feeling confident and sexy.

"Ready, demon?"

My lips twitch when he sees me. His eyes seem to glow, and he shoots up into a sitting position.

My demon has zero chill.

I swallow, pushing off the doorframe.

I can do this. I can do this. I can do this.

I take one step forward, drawing this out as long as possible. Trying to push down my fears that he will take one look at me and run, thinking me a monster.

Hades and I are inevitable.

I take another steadying breath and slowly start to drop my glamour. I shiver slightly as I feel the cool AC blow over my pearl horns.

Hades growls, and I force myself to open my eyes. I

need to see his reaction to me. I need to be strong.

The feeling of letting my glamour drop is like I've been wearing jeans two sizes too small, and I've finally opened them at the fastening. It occurs to me that the last time I was fully out of my glamour was at least 200 years ago, that I've been shackled to my "beautiful" form.

Hades's eyes go wide, and I know what he's seeing. My eyes turning lavender, my cheeks growing pink and my lips red, my skin glowing, the faintest pattern of leaves and old Greek symbols covering me. My hair, changing from dark brown to...whatever color correlates to the emotion I'm feeling at the time. I look down at my chest, seeing the long locks are pastel pink now, but I know it won't stay that way for long. Finally, I want to moan in relief as the glamour drops from my back, allowing my large, feathered, white wings free. I roll my shoulders and stretch my wings. Slowly my gaze trails back to Hades.

He is now on his knees, moving to the bottom of the bed, toward me. His deep blue eyes seem to glow even brighter, and there's something else in his expression...

Is that...awe?

"Fuck." Hades pauses. "I could barely resist you before. How will I ever do it now?"

My lips part and I stare at him. "You...like it?" Out of the corner of my eye, I see my hair starting to change color, now pastel purple.

He groans. "Fuck..." His eyes roam over me. "Was the corset just to torture me?"

My lips twitch and I hold up my palm, the perfect daisy sprouting. "For the full spring effect."

He looks down at the daisy, tilting his head before he, once again, begins hungrily looking over my body.

He...likes it? He doesn't think I'm a monster?

"I don't know where I want to touch first."

I close my hand around the daisy, and with my other

283

hand, I take his hand, placing it on my hip. "Here?"

He frowns. "There?"

I bite the inside of my cheek, stopping myself from smiling. I guide his hand over my hip to my ass. "Here?"

He moves in, towering over me. I crane my neck to look up at him. He grasps the soft flesh hard, making me gasp.

"I love your ass. I love watching it while I'm fucking you."

I guide his hand away from my ass, and he starts to protest before he realizes where the destination will be. I glide his large hand over the silk of my corset and place it just under one of my breasts.

"What about here, demon?"

He squeezes, making me moan, his eyes locking on mine. "I have plans for these."

I move his hand again, this time removing it from my body and placing it on my wing. I shiver at the contact. My precious wings, so much more delicate than his. and yet, I trust him completely.

I remove my grip on him and allow him to explore them, to feel them, to caress them.

He smirks when I shiver again, his fingers so gentle, maddening. "Sensitive, little spring?"

You have no idea...

I force myself to glare at him.

He tilts his head and pulls his hand away from my wings. "Tell me, Persephone, if I were to...touch you between your legs, would I find you wet for me?"

I swallow, looking up at him, unable to speak.

He moves his hands, his fingers gliding over the damp silk covering my pussy. He groans. I bite my lip as he pushes my panties to the side and slowly pushes one finger inside me.

"Are you my good girl?" His low, husky voice says at my ear.

284

I moan, rolling my hips. "Yes…"

He rewards me by pushing a second finger inside. He curls them, hitting the spot I desperately need him to. "This is *my* cunt. I *own* it. Just like I own *you.*"

I tangle my fingers in his thick hair and pull his face to mine. I brush my lips over his. "You…you like me in this form?"

His laugh is dark, full of the promise of pleasure, desire. "Persephone, I like you in every form." He spears his fingers inside of me, making me moan. "Though…I'm partial to this one. You are stunning."

Stunning? In my true form?

Surely he can't mean it…although…

I feel his hard cock pressing against my hip, and there is a wild look in his eyes, like he is as desperate for me as I am for him.

I press my lips to his again, sliding my tongue over his bottom one. "Hades…I-I need you."

He pulls back slightly, looking out the window, his lips curl into a mischievous smile. "How about…in the air?"

My eyes darken, and I see my hair turning red with need.

Hades curls a lock around his finger, staring intently at the thick mane. "With your mood?"

I nod, blushing.

He presses his lips to mine, and I am immediately lost.

Chapter Fifty-Three
Hades

I GRAB HER, WRAPPING HER LEGS AROUND MY WAIST, walking to the balcony. With an easy jump, I balance us on the railing, until I fall backward, heading face-first toward the ground. A comet about to land. Her feathers aren't made for sudden descents like mine. I wonder if the fragile appendages would tear if she tried to stop us from plummeting to the ground below.

My shadows cloak us, keeping us invisible to any who look up, but we feel the thrill of the descent. I love flying, but with my ability to shadow, it's something I never take the time to do. Shadowing, I can be across the world in a moment. Flying would take me hours to do the same. I've never had the opportunity to fuck someone in the air. The only time I ever show my full form is in the Underworld, and I have to be truly enraged to do so. There's only been a handful of times that's occurred since Gaia placed the control of the realm in my hands.

Persephone doesn't look frightened, though, or even concerned, keeping her feathered wings tucked into her back. Her eyes are focused on me, even as we fall. We wouldn't die if we hit, but it would hurt, bad. Yet she doesn't look away, those stunning eyes staying on me. Not on the ground below. *Trusting me.* Her trust humbles me more than anything.

We spin slowly in the air, heading for the ground, our eyes locked. Stunning lilacs of the freshest blooms and the unspoken black flame clash as we look at each other. The wind is secondary. There is only this. Only her. There was always only her. The wind catches us as I snap my wings out, jolting our descent. My tail curls around one of her ankles, rubbing the skin. My tail tightens, as if I need to keep her even tighter to me.

Her lips move to my neck, biting down on my collarbone, breaking the skin. She doesn't have fangs in this form, but she bites down hard enough to spill my golden ichor. For some reason, I wish she did. I groan at her savagery, moving to tear at my sweatpants as we fly.

My voice is almost lost on the wind, a gravelly demand, "Need inside you."

I thought it was a frenzy before, but now I know, with the sky above us, the ground below us. I can finally understand this fervor I've had since I first fucked her. Like a clarity is finally apparent to me, which was shrouded in our glamours.

Time is running out.

I'm racing against the ever-falling sands in the midnight hourglass I can't see. As sure as I know that Persephone is my fated queen, I know that I'm on a path of losing her. An ever-present sense of doom which hovers above us, since the moment I finally fucked her. And the desperation begins, a coil in the base of my spine, heating my blood with a need to bond us together physically. As if, each time we're together, it slows the black sand of the hourglass.

She slides her panties to the side, wrapping her arms around my neck. She moans, uncaring of us hovering above the ground. "Please…"

I flap my wings harder, putting us higher in the sky. I rip her panties instead of being satisfied with them only pushed to the side, the silk fluttering to the ground below us. We need each other. To become one, over and over. As if that can suspend us. I adjust my hold on her, allowing me to thrust myself inside her. *Running out of time.*

"Who owns you?" I growl.

Her nails dig into my shoulders, crying out, even as we continue to fly and fuck. "You. You do!"

I yank her garters until the elastic snaps, shoving her thigh-highs off her legs, until they fall to the world below. She never needed to wear the outfit. Just her true form was enough to have me desperate for her. I rotate my hips as we fly, hitting deeper. Needing to imprint myself on her, as if I can reach a level of physical intimacy that will prevent the future.

Running out of time.

She rolls her hips as much as she can, riding me in the air, even as she growls, "You're mine."

I groan, struggling to focus on flying and fucking at the same time. Persephone consumes my thoughts so completely. It's impossible to do both. I head out of the city, closer to the mountains, away from the densely populated area, just to be safe, keeping my cloaking, flying, and fucking at the same time. I may be a god, but I do have limits. "Yours."

I've always been hers. I always will be. I start thrusting faster, lost, until I realize we're falling. We hit the ground hard, forming a crater with our bodies with the impact, but I can't stop needing everything from her.

She drags her nails down my throat and bites my neck hard enough to draw more blood. My back arches at her nails. My claws shine as I cut down her corset, shredding it. My claws go to her hips, embedding into her skin.

She arches her back, moaning. "Harder. Please… mark me…"

I growl, my claws pulling out of her skin, to carve onto her hip. A single H. "Mine."

Marked. I'm almost disappointed it will heal soon, and that she won't bear the permanent scar from my claws.

She lifts her hips, her body writhing beneath me. I growl, moving faster, more of the darkness inside me taking control. Her cunt clenches around me. "Hades...I'm going to come..."

I snarl, "Come for me."

She screams, vines and flowers exploding from her, her pussy clenching me like a vice. I yank from her at the last possible moment, groaning as I come on the ground. She pants below me. I collapse on the ground next to her, wrapping her in my wings. Keeping her close to me.

Chapter Fifty-Four
Persephone

I GAZE UP AT THE SKY, PANTING, already missing the fullness of his cock inside me. Something gnaws at me, a feeling of trepidation. I felt him growing close inside me, felt him about to spend inside my awaiting pussy and yet, once again, he pulled out at the last second, choosing to come on the ground instead.

Granted, Hades and I never had a discussion regarding contraception, but he has also never initiated it. Aren't men usually desperate to come inside their partner?

My hand absentmindedly goes to the small tattoo behind my left ear, my fingers brushing over it. Small and discreet...and the most effective birth control you can get in any of the realms.

I glance at him, his face relaxed in post-coital bliss. "Hades…?"

He buries his face into my neck and presses a gentle kiss there. He nuzzles into me.

Reluctantly, I pull away slightly. "Hades?"

He frowns. "What?"

I look up at him, my brows furrowing at his sharp tone, is he avoiding this subject?

"You know…I-I'm on birth control."

He snorts, and brushes his lips against my shoulder. "I didn't, but that's good to know."

I nod, hesitating. "Is that why you won't come inside me? Concerned about babies?"

He blinks. His mouth opens and closes a few times, obviously trying to think of an answer. He settles on, "No. It's not that."

"Oh?" My brows furrow.

His eyes appear to scan mine. "I don't think the God of the Dead can bring life."

No kids? Ever? I'd never really thought about having children, but to say never, especially as an immortal... *and I'm the Goddess of Spring...new beginnings, new life...*

"Oh...so you just don't want to?"

He frowns at me, making me feel like I shouldn't have asked. "Why does it matter?"

Why is he being evasive?

I wince slightly at his dismissal. "I-I was just wondering."

He nuzzles into my neck. "Don't worry about it."

My body remains tense. "Is it because you don't want to? Because that is totally fine."

He shakes his head. "It's not that."

I frown, trying to work out what else it could be.

He leans in and kisses my neck. "Is that really what you want to talk about? Not this crater we just made in the mountain?"

I try to laugh, but it's a pathetic effort.

He continues trying to distract me, dragging his fingers over my skin, making me shiver. "I like you comfortable and in my arms." He wraps his wing around me. "Inside my wings."

I press my lips against his jaw, kissing him lightly.

He moves his hand to my feathered wings and strokes them. "Would it hurt if I pulled one?"

My lips twitch. "Well it wouldn't *not* hurt."

He tugs gently at a feather, and I moan, goosebumps breaking out over my skin.

He kisses me deeply, making my head spin before pulling back. "I should take us home."

I nod, looking around at the new crater Hades and I have created, vibrant flowers strewn everywhere.

His shadows surround us, and suddenly we're back in Hades's apartment, in his bed. I climb off the white sheets and shake my wings, trying to rid them of some of the dirt.

I still when I notice Hades staring at me intensely, as if seeing me for the first time. How can a look make me want to hide, burst into flames, and also be naked and beneath him all at once?

"You're...everything," he says, his gaze locked on me, roaming over me as his glamour slowly falls back into place.

I reglamour myself at the same time, tilting my head at him. "Oh?"

He continues to look at me in such a way that I need to go to him. I climb on the bed and kneel beside him. Disappointment sinks heavy in my stomach when my troubling thoughts continue to weigh on me, despite my proximity to Hades. I sigh at the realization that the concerns are getting more and more difficult to push aside. I look at Hades, feeling the question on the tip of my tongue before it rushes out of me, needing to be answered. Needing one truth to hold on to.

"Hades...why did you freak out when I told you that I am the Goddess of Spring?"

He immediately tenses, the awed expression on his face long gone. "Why are you asking me that?"

My brows furrow. "I've been...remembering something I overheard my mother saying...about you. It was centuries ago, but I just can't...put it together." I pause. "And when you reacted like that I—"

"What did she say?" he growls.

I turn, sitting on the edge of the bed as I try to remember.

I sit on my bed, hearing my mother's raised voice outside my room.

"She will not marry...him. I will die before I let that happen." *My mothers' voice is a low hiss.*

"I'm not sure you will have much say, my dear Demeter," *a vaguely familiar voice replies.*

"I will lock her in her damn room if I must."

A melodic chuckle follows. "You think that will stop fate?"

"I will do whatever it takes. It will not happen," *my mother snaps.*

"Hades is aware."

"Of her existence?" *I can hear the terror in my mother's voice. Is she afraid of this person?*

"Of the prophecy. It is only a matter of time," *the stranger replies, voice ominous.* "He is seeking his goddess of life."

My heart squeezes at the thought of a man seeking a woman out, wanting her, needing her. Why would my mother be trying to prevent the match?

Who is the Goddess of Life anyway?

I think back to my earlier musings about childbearing, about how I am the Goddess of Spring, and what represents spring if not new life?

Why would my mother be so keen to keep us apart?

"Something about keeping me away from you."

"That's...odd."

I turn and look over my shoulder at him. "Hm?"

His brows are drawn. Clearly lost in thought, he clears his throat when he notices me looking at him. "Never mind."

I turn to face him. "Tell me."

"Just strange that she would say that."

"Why?"

He shrugs. "I don't remember meeting her before."

I chuckle. "Some people have all the luck."

Chapter Fifty-Five

Hades

IT'S STRANGE TO SEE PERSEPHONE'S DE-MEANOR CHANGE AS SHE TALKS ABOUT HER MOTHER. I've heard of Demeter, of course, the Goddess of Harvest and Fall. She was instrumental in us overthrowing Kronos, my father. But her motives after, her life after, I know nothing about. Not that my own mother is perfect. She did nothing as Poseidon and I were swallowed whole by our father, only interfering when Zeus was born. Until my youngest brother reached his majority, freeing us from the realm outside of time, to fight at his side against our father.

In the end, our mother aided us. So different from being spirited away and hidden for years. Kept in the dark about the rest of the world.

I cling to this topic, even though the knot of tension is still sitting between my shoulders. *Why did you freak out when you found out I was the Goddess of Spring?* One part of me hopes she'll have enough information to piece together the truth without me saying anything, the other half dreads it. *There's another prison fated for you, Persephone. You escaped one, only to be fated to fall into another.*

I nuzzle her head, keeping my focus on the present, away from the future. "Tell me about her."

She shrugs. "She is ruthless, strong, powerful, willful."

"As are you," I point out, cradling her in my arms, pulling her closer.

She rubs her nose along my jaw, whispering, "I know you're hiding something from me, demon."

My entire body tenses, muscles locking on bone. How? Does she know about the curse? About why I pull out of her each time? No. She can't. She would have run from me. She just told me about her oppressive mother, who kept things from her.

"I am?" my voice croaks out.

She sighs, full of resignation. Is she not going to push the issue? Demand to know what I'm hiding? That is…surprising.

"You are," she states.

I should have expected that she would sense this. Persephone won't be content with me keeping her in the dark. No matter the reason. Especially with what she just told me about her childhood, her mother.

I gulp audibly, scrambling. "Can't some things be a mystery?"

She pulls back, her eyes locked on mine. "I'll leave it for now."

My breath whooshes out of my chest in relief.

"But, Hades…"

"Yes?" I whisper hoarsely. *She's really not going to demand answers?*

She leans in, kissing me softly. "I will find out."

Time is running out. That pressure of foreboding is weighing down my shoulders. My knowledge of the incoming doom coils inside me, eating me from the inside out.

I groan, attempting to play off my unease. "You're relentless."

Don't push for more. I can't tell you.

She pulls back from me, climbing out of bed. I

295

watch her carefully, trying to anticipate her mood, but my stomach roils when she starts getting dressed. She's pulling away from me again, reestablishing the careful barriers she clung to before.

I pull her back onto the bed, demanding a little too roughly, "Where are you going?"

Time is running out. With the ticking clock, I want to spend every moment with her. As if I can pack an eternity in less than two months. I can't ask her to wait for me to come back after six months, can I? We just started dating. It's too soon. Too soon to ask her to wait. To ask for a commitment of that magnitude, this early? Despite having expressed our…deepening feelings for each other, a commitment was something *more*.

She glances at me, wearing only her cropped sweater and thong. "I need to go back to my apartment."

I frown. *She's leaving?* She just got here. "No."

She turns to face me fully, her eyes flashing with that sort of deceptive serenity. It sets my teeth on edge, every nerve in my body going on alert. "What do you mean 'no'?"

Tread carefully. She knows I'm hiding something from her, Maybe being a commanding and controlling ass is *not* the play here.

I clear my throat, revising my approach. "Why can't you stay here?"

She softens, kissing my cheek. "I'm out of clothes, baby."

My frown deepens, though I can see her own irritation with me fade slightly. Though it doesn't vanish completely. "You can wear mine."

She chuckles, smiling at me. "What do you expect me to wear to work tomorrow?"

Strange to think how short a period of time we've had together. Yet I've tried to fill it with everything I could. We'll have to act normal when tomorrow comes;

work is on the other side of today. We'll have to pretend that nothing has changed for us. That we're not...*whatever* we are. *Boyfriend and girlfriend?* The terms make me cringe internally. Too *mortal.* Despite being fated, I can't think of a term that fits our current situation. When I look at Persephone, the only term that fits is *mine.* Well, there is the other one, but I dare not speak it aloud. *Queen.*

I groan. "Work."

She frowns at me. "What?"

I sigh. "Things have to be done."

The fall is coming. Time is running out. More midnight sand slipping.

Some of my thoughts must leak into my expression as she climbs on top of me. Did she forget her decision to gather more clothes in favor of me? She pushes me back onto the bed. "Right now?"

I press my lips to hers, losing myself in the softness. "I suppose it can wait."

She slides her tongue over my lips. "Feed me?"

I bite her lip. "What would you like?"

She wraps her arms around my neck, pressing her chest into me. "Waffles."

I pull back. "What do you want in it?"

She hums. "Pomegranates seeds and strawberries and whipped cream."

I snicker. "Anything else?"

She kisses me again. "Save some of the whipped cream for later."

I growl at her, imagining licking the cream from her body. I clamber out of bed, grabbing some sweatpants, pulling them on.

Chapter Fifty-Six
Persephone

I STRETCH IN THE BED, TRYING TO FOCUS ON THE FEELING OF HIS EGYPTIAN COTTON SHEETS AGAINST MY SKIN, but that little voice in my head chants, *"He's hiding something, he's hiding something, he's hiding something."*

Part of me longs to leave his apartment, knowing that I don't think clearly when I'm around him. The other part begs me to never leave his side.

I hear him in the kitchen, my lips twitching at the sound of him whisking, cracking eggs, the quiet sizzle of the non-stick spray against the hot waffle iron. Even now it surprises me how domesticated my God of the Underworld is.

He's hiding something, he's hiding something, he's hiding something.

I stare up at the ceiling, my mind racing with possibilities. Jealousy surges through me as I consider the possibility that he could potentially have someone else. Just because Hades and I are inevitable, doesn't mean he is happy about it. But if it was someone else, surely my attachment with Jackson would have made things easier for him, would have provided him with an excuse to deny fate.

Could he be looking for a way out of this?

While he appears to enjoy spending time with me,

the prospect of eternity is a daunting one. Even many mortal males find commitment difficult to stomach, and they're lucky if they're talking sixty years, not *eternity*. I consider my own feelings about spending the rest of my immortal life with him. The only fear I feel is when I think about what he could be hiding. The idea of waking up with Hades for the rest of my life, of spending our days together, of traveling with him and…building a life with him, makes me feel…warm.

Maybe he doesn't think you'll be a good queen.

My heart skips a beat when he walks back into the bedroom, holding two plates of steaming waffles. I push the errant thoughts out of my head and focus on him. He hands me a plate before sliding into bed with me.

The beige stack is presented perfectly and smothered in strawberries and pomegranate seeds. I smile when I look at the whipped cream on top in a shrewd attempt at a heart.

Hades blushes when I look up at him, and my heart squeezes.

"You want to watch something?" he asks, turning on the TV.

I nod, taking a bite of my breakfast. The fluffy, light waffles are completely divine, and I can't help but moan at the taste of them.

He pauses scrolling through Netflix and glances at me. "Good?"

Again, it surprises me how nervous he gets about his cooking skills. It's easy to tell that he does it because he loves it, and yet, it's also obvious that it's important to him that his creations are enjoyed.

I grab his face and kiss him. "Is there anything you can't do?"

Except be open and honest with me.

My smile falters, and I try to repress the thought. Desperate to enjoy my time with him. I'm acutely aware that it's becoming harder to ignore the feeling.

His laugh pulls me from my worry, such a joyful sound, laced with filthy promises. "Well…"

I cut a bit of my waffle and spear it with my fork, offering it to him, even though he has his own plate. I love the intimacy of feeding him.

He leans forward slowly and bites down on it, making me grin. I love playful Hades. *I love every Hades.*

Oh, look, another feeling to repress.

As if he's heard my thoughts, he smiles at me. "What?"

I immediately avert my gaze, looking down at my plate. "Nothing."

He tenderly kisses my cheek. "Pick a show."

I grab the remote from him and start scrolling. My eyes light when I see what I want to watch. "Oh! I love *Charmed*!"

"*Charmed*?" He blinks.

Ignoring him, I press play, and am immediately engrossed. I still remember the first time I watched it. I had just arrived in this realm, and I was settling into my new place. Completely awestruck by just how *human* everything was. I sat on my green, crushed-velvet, second-hand couch, and pulled a pink pillow against my chest. I remember looking at the black screen of the powerless television and feeling…homesick. It was the first and only time I felt like that. I switched on the flat screen and *Charmed* was the first thing that came on. I instantly felt better. Seeing the actors portraying witches and using powers just made me feel so much more at home, so much less of an outsider. Since that day, it has been a comfort show of mine. But, since finding a job I enjoy, I'd started using work as an escape instead, probably not as healthy, but definitely more productive.

"These women need more supportive bras."

I turn to him, an eyebrow raised. "So that's where

your attention is?"

"Look at them. They're fighting and don't have ample chest support."

I bristle at his ogling other women. I've never been a jealous person, apart from with Hades. I know I am being unreasonable, but I cannot stop. I pause the show and cancel out of it to the main Netflix page again, glaring at the TV. Well, I guess I'll never be watching my comfort show with Hades again. Will I even be able to watch it at all now, knowing *my* Hades is attracted to the power of three? I try to shake the irrational thoughts, the jealousy. I need to be level-headed, to be the bigger person.

My lips curl slightly as I have an idea. Who cares about being the bigger person?

Let's see how jealous you get, Hades.

Chapter Fifty-Seven
Hades

ANOTHER DOMESTIC MOMENT WITH MY FATED QUEEN. Strange to have more than a handful of moments like this with her. Or to want more and more of them, to not only want to fuck her into oblivion and beyond, but to cook for her, watch television with her. Discuss my favorite books and plays with her, show her more of the world she's barely explored. The other worlds that are out of view from our own, but accessible if you've studied all the ways, like I have. Which will be her favorite? The realm where every color is ever brighter? The realm with stunning men and women with pointed ears?

She changes the program from the women with very unsupportive clothing, and I smile to myself. Sitting and arguing over what to watch. As if we're two mortals, completely at ease. We've satisfied our craving for each other's bodies, I've fed her waffles. And now we're arguing over what to watch. Though I do have to admit the show she wanted to watch looked interesting, the clothes were distracting. How did one fight demons without proper support? I imagine they flew everywhere while combating evil. Yet I felt Persephone's annoyance escalate when I pointed that out. She changed the channel almost immediately.

I look back to the screen, and my brows furrow at the movie she stopped on. "Is this about...strippers?"

Mostly naked men are gyrating, even stripping off the very few clothes they have on. She doesn't look at me, nodding, her eyes locked on the television. I frown at the screen, commenting at the intense dancing the strippers are performing. "They must dislocate their hips."

She bites her lip, watching the men. I tilt my head, studying her. Her eyes are turning dark, watching the naked men, and her breath is coming in shallow pants.

I look at the screen, then at her, my eyes narrow. "Change it."

She lifts a dark brow, her voice full of satisfaction. "Why?" She did this on purpose, to get back at my comment about the unsupportive clothing of the last show. Didn't like me looking at another woman's breasts? Even if it was a television show?

Her eyes scan my face, the desire vanishing. No doubt, just for show. "Oh, you don't like me looking at other men dancing provocatively?"

I growl at her, looking at the way her cheeks are flushed. Though that could be from what we've done repeatedly today.

She rolls her eyes at me before turning off the movie.

I smirk, kissing her ear, whispering, "You want me to dance provocatively?"

If she likes seeing them do it, I imagine she'll enjoy it far more if I do it.

She looks at me, her eyes heating. "You want to dance for me?"

Oh, you'd love that wouldn't you, my spring? If only I had the actual skill to perform any of the dances we'd just seen on screen.

I raise a brow at that. "I'd prefer if you danced for me instead."

She leans closer, teasing me with a brush of her lips against mine. "I could dance for you."

I yawn softly, even though my body hardens. "Tomorrow. We have to work."

Time is running out. Soon I'll be leaving for downstairs. For the Underworld. My chest aches at the thought of leaving her behind. Of this new small bubble of intimacy and laughter shattering. *She can't come with me, not unless I make her my queen.* But then, she'll be trapped there. For six months of the year.

"Are you working today?" She smiles.

I would love to take the day off, but I have so much to do. *Time is running out.*

I sigh before nodding at her. It's unavoidable. I have to work. Have to get ready to go downstairs, but I stifle a groan at the idea of all the work waiting for me at home. And I won't have Persephone with me.

She sighs, climbing off me.

I frown at that heavily.

"Okay. I'll need to go back to my apartment then."

"I'll go with you," I offer immediately.

She glances at me, pulling her jeans over her ass, and my eyes lock on the material. The material stretching over that life-changing ass of hers. I could watch her get dressed all day, though I much prefer to strip her out of them. "You can get to work. I'll be an hour."

I groan as I relent. "You'll come work on my lap?"

A compromise. Work will distract me while she goes back to her own apartment. Maybe I won't even notice she's gone.

Hades, God of Lying to Himself.

She leans over, fully dressed, kissing me, and asks, "What if we're not the only ones in the office?"

I shrug. I don't want her out of my sight, or out of my touch for long. Fuck everyone else. Though the chances that the office will empty on a Wednesday are

304

slim to none.

She rolls her eyes at me. "I'll see you in an hour."

I get out of bed when she straightens, making a little hip movement for her, mimicking the one from the movie that we barely watched. "How was that?"

She presses her lips into a hard line, practically shaking with mirth. Though she demands, "Do it again."

I make another small hip movement, grinding against the imaginary pole. She winks at me, heading to the elevator. "I'll see you later, demon."

I groan and move to get ready for work.

Chapter Fifty-Eight

Persephone

I CHUCKLE AS I LEAVE HIS APARTMENT, BUT THE SECOND THE DOOR CLOSES MY SMILE DROPS. The gentle hum of the elevator creates a backing track for my inner thoughts. *He's hiding something, he's hiding something, he's hiding something.*

Over and over it repeats, and by the end of the short elevator ride, my mood is low.

My whole journey home I think about him, about what he could possibly be hiding from me. I try to take comfort in the fact that his feelings seem to be true, at least. Although, even that thought morphs into a dark one.

How could one as powerful as him love me?

My brows furrow, and I stop suddenly in the street, earning tuts from fellow commuters. Before Hades, my power felt like a kernel. Small and insignificant and yet a comforting presence within me. Since I met him, my power seems…deeper, more entwined with me, and much bigger.

The closer I get to Hades, the more my power grows, like he's unlocking a part of me that has been imprisoned for years.

An hour later, I arrive back at the office wearing another pencil skirt, tight shirt, and heels combo. I knock on Hades's office door, needing to see him, to be in the

306

same room with him for just a moment.

He glances up from his laptop, obviously having been engrossed in work. "Yes?"

The hard, impatient glare of his quickly melts into his heartbreaking smile when he sees me, the sight making my heart skip a beat.

"Can I borrow the key to your apartment? I brought some spare clothes." I hesitate for a second. "I hope that wasn't too forward of me."

He crooks a finger, beckoning me to him. My gaze glued to his, I start to gravitate toward him, my feet moving of their own accord. As if we are magnets.

As I move to him, my stomach flutters and my fingers itch to touch him, to drag my nails over his strong arms. I glance behind me, hyperaware that the office is all windows. I walk over to him, dropping the overnight bag in front of his desk.

Hades reaches into his top desk drawer and pulls out a keycard. He holds it out to me. "Yours."

I take the keycard, my head tilting as I look down at the nondescript rectangle of cool metal, the small bronze chip dull against the platinum. My brows furrow. "Mine?"

He nods. "So you can come and go as you please."

Oh. *Oh.*

He's *giving* me a key to his apartment. He wants me to drop in whenever I want. He wants to take this next step with me.

The near-constant chorus of *"He's hiding something"* is muffled by another inner chant, my favorite inner chant. *"Hades and I are inevitable."*

There is absolutely nothing sexier than a man who makes the first move, who takes control, who knows what he wants. Well, that's not strictly true. There's no man sexier than Hades. He could make vacuuming sexy.

My voice drops as my eyes meet his. "I'm going to

show you exactly how much I appreciate this later."

"Hurry," he growls in response. His eyes are just as dark as mine probably are. My silk panties dampen every moment.

I lift an eyebrow. "Hurry?"

He tilts his head. "You have…work to do."

I incline my head before grabbing my bag and taking it up to his apartment.

Sliding my fingers over the keycard, I wait for the elevator to take me to his apartment. I consider how different this feels from wearing Jackson's ring. This commitment feels the complete opposite of the last. Instead of the weighing sense of foreboding, the heaviness of an incorrect decision, it feels light, easy, right.

Pushing the card into the slot, I feel a thrill as the button for his penthouse lights up.

When I return downstairs, I don't look at him as I walk past again, heading to my office. I open my laptop and jump into work, needing something, *anything,* to distract me from going to Hades.

Not even thirty minutes later, my phone chirps from my bag.

HADES

Did the key surprise you?

PERSEPHONE

I love it.

HADES

It's not too fast?

PERSEPHONE

We're not exactly conventional.

HADES

So it is too fast?

PERSEPHONE

I love it. Like…really love it. As in…I'm going
to thoroughly show you my appreciation
later…

HADES

Promises, promises.

PERSEPHONE

Oh my sweet, sweet demon…

I smirk down at my phone, thinking of all the sinful ways I can appreciate this man. I lift my eyebrow as I have an idea. There's nothing I love better than torturing him. And I know how much he loves a photo.

I sit back in my chair, sliding my skirt up a little. The lace frill of my thigh-high wraps around my leg. I hitch my skirt up a little more, giving a hint of bare thigh also, and snap a photo for him.

His response is almost immediate and it makes my stomach twist deliciously.

HADES

A. Menace.

PERSEPHONE

Your menace…

HADES

All mine. Now get to work.

I roll my eyes before putting my phone to the side, sighing as my head and my heart continue to battle it out. My head screaming that he's hiding something, that something isn't right. My heart, aching for him, soothing me with the feeling that Hades and I are fated, meant to be...inevitable.

Chapter Fifty Nine

Hades

THE REST OF THE DAY PASSES IN A BLUR. Between work and Persephone, I think of little else. The dance thankfully never happened, mine or hers. I don't know how I would have been able to leave my penthouse if I saw her dressed in only scarves. An inch of her skin revealed, then hidden. A tempting display, taunting me. Torturing me.

I was too focused on giving her a keycard to my penthouse and how I might be moving too fast. What if I scare her off? She'd been afraid of committing to me before, and I can feel her pulling away more with each day. Even though I'm the one leaving, the one with a deadline looming over my head. I'm clinging to her, smothering her, giving her sex as much as possible. As if I can keep her from pulling away from me emotionally by satisfying her sexually.

Even now, at my desk on Thursday, listening to a report droning on in my ear, I'm thinking about her under my desk, distracting me with that mouth of hers.

As if I conjure her from my fantasy, she strolls into my office, my mouth watering at another one of her pencil skirts. She must have a never-ending supply of them. Does she pick them each time wondering how to torture me?

The droning continues in my ear, and she moves to perch on the desk next to me. Her scent is covering me, enveloping me, her voice low and husky, "Take your lunch."

The word is laced with promise of more. I don't even make up an excuse as I hang up. I'll pretend I lost signal.

My phone rings again immediately, and I switch off the ringer.

I look at Persephone, my eyes trailing over her slowly. "It's ten in the morning."

She licks her lips slowly, as always painted a bold color. My eyes follow the small flash of pink along the dark red. She repeats, "Take your lunch."

I look over her face, her eyes so dark and heated. I feel scorched even standing this close to her, like she's generating a flame. I slowly move to my feet, turning off my computer, not touching her. If I touch her, I won't be able to stop touching her. I'll end up taking her on my desk like all those fantasies I've had.

I growl at her, "Fine."

I have the distant memory of an interoffice memo about lunch hours, but it's too hazy to focus on when my fated queen is in front of me. Those rules don't apply to me, right? I'm the boss. The rules my employees follow shouldn't apply to me as well. Though a nagging voice in the back of my head is saying I should lead by example, that voice is easily smothered under Persephone's luscious scent.

She beams at me, straightening from where she is perched on my desk. I can feel eyes on us through the glass walls of the office, and for the first time, I wish there were actual walls to prevent us from being watched.

I tuck my hands into my pockets, curling my hands into fists, walking at her side. Each step makes that twisting mass of fire and darkness slip over her shoulders, sending another wave of her mouthwatering scent. *Roses in the early morning fog.* I adjust my hands inside my pockets, making it look like I don't have the achingly hard cock in my slacks.

Finally, we make it to the elevator, and I don't move my hands from my pockets, the image of restraint. We look like we are about to head to discuss something. Something of clear importance. Which we are. Though the important matter is that my mouth is not buried between her thighs.

It seems like the wait is interminable before it dings and opens. Each step inside is focused, concentrated. A testament to my will power. Which is already almost non-existent where Persephone is concerned. But I can't touch her yet; I still feel the eyes on us from the office.

Persephone scans her new keycard, lighting up the button for the penthouse, and the doors slowly close. It makes my heart ache how easily she uses that new card, the one I offered her. So she can come and go from the penthouse as she pleases.

Finally, the metal doors meet in the middle.

Then I lunge for her. Her fingers already grasp at my shirt, prepared for the assault. Yanking me to her, her lips seal over mine. She knows how much I need her, how much she needs me. The desperation that gnaws at us both. Her fingers rip at my shirt, sending the buttons flying, even as I still wear my suit coat, to sink her nails into my chest. I lift her feet from the ground, my arms wrapping around her, her legs going around my waist to keep me locked to her.

I distantly hear the elevator ding for the penthouse, and I stumble out of the conveyance with her. My hands are frantic on her clothes, my own, tearing them from us. Needing skin-to-skin, needing to deepen the connection between us.

Her tongue pushes into my mouth, feeding me her

addicting taste. My hands fist the material of her maddening skirt, yanking it up. I want to tear it from her, but stop myself, reminding myself that, if we come back to work in different clothes than we left in, we might as well have fucked in my office in front of everyone.

The skirt reveals those garters she so adores, and I snap them against her skin. I pull off my suit coat, tearing at my tie.

Her fingers cover mine on the tie, throwing it off, before fumbling down to shove off the remains of my shirt. I rip her buttons, too impatient, I forget that I should be tempering myself. Blindly walking to my bedroom, I toss her onto the bed, lunging to pin her beneath me. Underneath me, about to be fucked.

She brings her knees to cradle my hips, dragging her nails down my chest. I bite back a moan. I drop my hand to her panties, ripping them off, tearing off my belt. I shove off my pants down only enough to thrust inside her. She cries out as her body slowly accommodates me. She's so fucking wet already. Had she been grinding against her chair to thoughts of me?

I pull her ankles around my waist, thrusting harder, brutally, inside her. I growl at her, "Driving me insane."

Chapter Sixty
Persephone

ILIFT MY HIPS, NEEDING MORE, NEEDING EVERYTHING. His deep voice against my skin makes me break out in goosebumps. It would be embarrassing how crazed he makes me if he did not also appear to be in such a fervor.

"Needed this all day. Fuck…" Even I don't recognize my own husky voice, the desperation so clear.

He rolls his hips, hitting even deeper inside me, his cock fitting me so fully, so perfectly. I moan as his hand snakes its way up my body and he wraps it around my throat.

He squeezes, and the thrill is like nothing I've ever felt. My pussy throbs as he tightens his fist, trusting him so implicitly with my airway.

I drag my nails down his chest, raking them through the small patch of perfect dark hair there.

He hisses at the bite of my nails against his skin and pushes his chest into my hands, spurring me on. Angry red lines are left in their wake, and I long for them to be permanent, proof of this, of us. Proof that he is mine and I am his. Proof that I'm not dreaming.

The only noises that fill the large room are our breathy moans and the sound of his hips slamming into me, our skin slapping together, the soft, wet sound of his cock pushing inside me over and over.

I thread my fingers into his hair and pull his face to mine, kissing him hard, my tongue playing with his. His taste intoxicates me, making my eyes roll back in pleasure.

His hand tightens on my throat, and I gasp into his lips, moving one of my hands to wrap around his wrist. Not to remove his grip on my throat, but to hold him there. Already feeling that tight coil of pleasure low in my stomach, ready to spring.

"So. Close," I whisper.

His answering growl sends a jolt of pleasure through me. "Shit."

My hands slam onto the bed, and I desperately grasp at the sheets as I come hard, my body arching to him. I am vaguely aware of his own release coming, but mine overtakes me so fully that my head swims in post-orgasmic bliss.

The feel of his body on top of mine, his intoxicating scent enveloping me, is complete perfection. I shift slightly in the bed, shivering as my skin meets something cool and…wet. I frown and slide my hand down my body to feel the sheet, tensing when my fingers meet the culprit. He pulled out at the last moment again.

I glance over at him, trying to decide how to best approach this, to understand him better. It's not that the sex isn't mind-blowing without it, because it is. I crave him, even now. After I've just had an earth-shattering orgasm. It's that I feel like he's holding back from me and I don't know why.

An impenetrable barrier is in place to only let me get so close. To never let me see…something.

Frustration builds as I look at him, trying to telepathically pull the secrets from his head.

He kisses my neck and a shiver slides down my spine, bitterness sliding away, as if never there. I moan softly as his lips graze along my jaw before pressing against my cheeks.

I wrap my arms around his neck, needing him to stay close to me forever, holding him tight, knowing that he'll leave me. But maybe, just maybe, if I hold on tight enough, he'll remain.

He nuzzles into my neck, his voice throaty. "You needed me?"

I draw shapes on his back, feeling the relaxed muscles tensing under my teasing touch. "So badly."

He chuckles. "You demanding I take my lunch was a bit of a hint."

I shake my head giggling. "How much longer would you have held out then?"

"You beat me by less than a minute. I was dreaming of you sucking me off during my call."

I lean in, biting his shoulder. "How do we make that a reality?"

He laughs, such a rich, perfect sound. "I'd need a different office."

I move my lips up his neck to his ear, biting on the lobe. "But imagine it, baby… You're on a super serious work call. And I'm under the desk, gagging on your cock."

He turns his head and covers my mouth with his hand, his expression looks like a mixture of pain and… arousal. It makes my toes curl. Playing with him always eases my anxieties about our future. It's easy and exciting, leaving no room for doubt.

"You are too tempting, my spring."

I trail my nails down his back, thrilled that I'm rewarded with a shiver.

"You're terrible."

I pull his hand from my mouth, kissing his jaw. "Or maybe…" I continue, letting my imagination go wild, "I'm sitting in the chair opposite you, and I start touching myself while you're on a call." My skin tingles as I watch his eyes darken. "And you can see how wet my cunt is for you, but you can't do anything about it."

He covers my mouth again, his gaze roaming over my face. "Stop it. You're a menace."

I protest, but his hand across my mouth, muffling my reply.

Chapter Sixty One
Hades

APERFECT LUNCH BREAK WITH MY FATED QUEEN, yet still I can feel the knot of tension in my shoulders tightening. Growing. *She's pulling away from me.* There's nothing I can do about it, because if I ask her why she's doing it, she'll demand answers for my own secrets. Secrets I can't answer. Even if I wanted to.

Fate squeezes my throat shut. *Enjoy the time you have now. Don't want more.* Time flies ever forward, more and more sand slipping, not just through the glass, but now I feel it against my fingers. As if I were trying to stop it from falling, but it has no effect. If anything, the sand falls even faster. Time moves quicker. The more I will the grains to stop.

The powerful God of the Underworld...*powerless.*

No doubt Nemesis is smirking somewhere at the idea. The Goddess of Revenge's voice rings clearly in my head: *Karma will always choose to be a bigger bitch than I could ever be.*

Lowering my hand from her mouth, I kiss her hard, breathing against her lips. Our breaths become one. Our hearts twined, our *souls.* "I have to get back to work."

She pouts at that. My eyes go to that lush lower lip with a moan.

But she admits, with a long exhale, drawing out the word, "Fine."

I kiss her again, unable to help myself. I ask, "Behave?"

Her lips twitch when I pull back, her stunning eyes alight with mischief, her scent becoming stronger. For a moment, I feel my own power rising, as if in response to hers. "What answer will make you stay?"

I sigh heavily. "My spring…"

If I had unlimited time, I'd spend it with her. I would cook for her, read to her, bicker over what to watch. So many things to do with her, always with her. But I don't have the time. *Time is running out.* All the things I want to do with her, I won't have the time. I need to pack everything I can into these few moments.

She kisses along my neck, tempting me to forget about the impending deadline. The work that still needs to be done. She purrs at me, "Yes?"

I lean down, biting the point between her neck and shoulder. The point that I want to mark permanently. The point which makes her come undone. "I wish I could laze in bed and fuck you for hours, but…I have to get ready for the winter."

So much to do. So much work to be done, before the time runs out. Less than two months until the Underworld will yank me to it. Six months as king, unable to leave the entire time. Six months away from her, unable to touch her, kiss her, fuck her. Be *with* her.

She pulls back from me, her brows drawn, her voice losing its huskiness immediately. "What do you mean?"

I furrow my own brows at her. She was there. She knows the answer. "The winter. You know, they talked about it in the meeting?"

The meeting where she was so incredibly distracting. They'd mentioned I was leaving for the winter, saving me from having to tell Persephone myself.

320

She just stares at me, waiting for me to explain.

I blink at her in surprise. "Do you not remember?"

"Remember what?" she asks. "I was fairly...distracted at that meeting."

I flush. I had hoped that the meeting prevented me from having to explain it to her. From having to break this to her when we're here alone. I thought she knew this was what she was getting into when we...started.

"I...I go downstairs. In the winter."

She lifts an eyebrow. "To the basement?"

I shake my head. "Lower."

"Oh." She lifts her eyebrows. "For how long?"

I tense, clearing my throat. "Six months."

She blinks, and I see the understanding leach into her eyes. Almost as if preparing for a blow. "Six months? What about...me?"

"You..." I brace myself this time. "You can't come with me."

"Why not?" She frowns.

"The Underworld," I whisper softly, "only accepts gods who live there, or are tied to it."

You're not the queen yet. If she was, she'd be able to come and go from the Underworld, just as I can. Outside the six months of the year, where I can *only* be in the Underworld.

Her eyes flicker and die. "Oh."

I try to remedy her broken eyes, though I can only offer a pitiful scrap. The little bit of reassurance of the impending deadline. As if I can soften the blow. "I'll still be able to talk to you, FaceTime and text."

I just won't be able to touch you, taste you, kiss you. Things I haven't gotten to do nearly enough during this short time together.

She nods. "I should get back to work."

"Persephone..."

She's avoiding talking about it, despite how clear-

321

ly upset she is. She climbs out of bed, dressing in new clothes.

I grab her hand even as she pulls on a shirt. "It's not for another month and a half."

She nods, smiling sadly at me, pulling her hand away to fasten her thigh-highs again.

I stand up slowly, fixing my own clothes. I keep glancing at her.

She smiles at me, but it's brittle and forced. "I'll be down in a minute."

I kiss her softly, wrapping her arms around my neck. I lift her off her feet. "The best lunch break I've ever had."

She smothers my face in kisses.

I laugh, but I can still feel her withdrawing from me. "How am I going to go back to work after this?"

She bites my jaw. "You're going to think about tonight…when we get home…and I dress up in nothing but scarves…and I dance for you."

I shudder, already imagining it. "A menace."

She trails kisses down my neck. "You want me to stop?"

I drop my hand to her ass, spanking her. "Never."

She yelps. "Put me down and go back to work, demon."

I put her down, kissing her hard before leaving.

Chapter Sixty-Two
Persephone

THE SECOND HADES IS OUT OF SIGHT, MY SMILE DROPS, and I feel my eyes sting with the threat of tears. I never seem to get a smooth run at things with him. It's always one thing after another, and once again, I find myself sitting on the edge of a bed with that sinking feeling in my stomach.

Six months without him...

Was this why I felt like he was hiding something? The anticipation of us being apart?

No. There is something else...

I frown at the thought. What could be worse than him leaving this realm for six months? I think back to what he said.

"The Underworld only accepts gods who live there, or are tied to it."

What does that even mean? "Live there, or are tied to it." Would I ever fit into one of those categories? Technically, Hades lives there. If we eventually marry, would I be considered "tied to it"? Or is my fate to only ever see him six months of the year?

My head spins with questions, scenarios, and "what ifs". My stomach rolls with nausea, how did I end up in a situation where I don't have my own answers? In a situation where someone else holds the information I need to know my own fate?

Time to visit my old friend, denial, and repress the hell out of this until I can speak to Hades.

I begin to steel myself to go back to the office, not sure I'm ready to face anyone, knowing I'm just one accidental nudge away from having a full-on breakdown. My phone chirps, dragging my attention away from my thoughts.

> HADES
>
> Your ex is here. He's refusing to leave until he talks to you.

Fuck.

I rub my hands over my face. If I thought I couldn't handle being in the office already, going head to head with my ex after my current...whatever Hades is... dropped that bomb on me, now it will be even worse.

I check my outfit in the mirror and touch up my hair and makeup. I may be a mess on the inside, but I'm sure as hell going to look like a boss-ass bitch on the outside. I sigh, looking at myself once more before going straight down to the main reception to meet Jackson.

The whole elevator ride I fidget with my fingers, trying to find some semblance of calm before the storm I can feel coming. If not from Jackson, from Hades.

My stomach knots when I see Jackson pacing in the busy foyer. The second he sees me, he closes the distance, his feet echoing in the near-empty lobby, every step against the marble making me feel more uncertain than the last.

"Persephone."

I give him a tight smile. "Jackson."

"You weren't answering my calls."

I nod slowly, trying to comprehend what he can possibly want to talk to me about. "Yes, because...Jackson, we have nothing to talk about."

"It was one time, Persephone. A mistake!"

I soften slightly. "Jackson, I'm not mad at you. I'm just...not with you anymore."

"Because of one little thing?"

I sigh. "Because of a number of thi—"

"You were going to marry me," he interrupts.

I shake my head, my palms raised to him, needing him to understand that he and I were never meant to be. "No, I wasn't."

Jackson grabs my hand. "You were. I know it."

I gently pry my hand away from his. "Jackson. Stop."

He grabs me again, more insistently, and slams his lips to mine. His hard lips trying to pry mine open. My whole body recoils at the contact.

Yanking my head away, my palm connects with his cheek hard, the sound echoing, bouncing off the marble pillars and walls. The quiet lobby turns dead silent, as the few bystanders gawk at us, desperate for a glimpse into the reason for the assault.

He pulls back, looking aghast, his face dropping, his expression conveying the betrayal and hurt. "You said you loved me, Persephone."

"No. I didn't. Ever."

"Please." He looks at me with pleading eyes, desperation plastered over his face.

I take a step back. "Goodbye, Jackson."

Jackson pauses, his eyes seeming to harden as they scan my face. "There's someone else. Isn't there?"

A chill runs down my spine, and my stomach turns. My brows furrow at the edge to his voice, one that I've never noticed before. In an almost disembodied tone, his words do not seem to be merely a question, but a warning, a threat.

Fuck.

Chapter Sixty-Three
Hades

THE COMPUTER SCREEN FRACTURES UNDER MY GRIP, leaving the glass embedded in my fingers, the security feed going dark. I curse at myself, turning to the other screen, thankfully still in operation, but I immediately tense at the scent of orchids and fresh-baked cookies filling my nose.

I jump slightly in my seat in surprise, seeing someone standing behind me in the office. Leaning against the wall at my back, her eyes flash in the now-black screen in front of me, reflecting her. How long has she been there watching me? Long enough to see me lingering over the security feed?

I grind my teeth so hard they almost turn to dust. My voice hisses out from behind them, "You know I hate when you do that."

A charming laugh echoes, but its charm fades too fast, leaving behind only the feeling of the wails of the lost. The screams of despair that I know she loves to listen to as she drifts off to sleep in her own home.

Her voice echoes, a young voice, a middle-aged one, and an elder one at the same time. Unlike the Moirai, it's not three different voices harmonizing. But the same voice at three different moments of life. "I know, that's why I do it."

I force myself to turn off the still-intact monitor, but it's too late. I know she saw. Nothing is ever missed by her. Nothing. It's impossible to avoid a goddess with three faces, even when she's only wearing one at the moment. She still has three sets of eyes, even if I can only perceive one.

"Why are you here?" I turn to face her, unsurprised to see her dressed in a long pilgrim dress, her long, dark hair in two plaits. *Wednesday Addams as a goddess.*

To mortals, she would seem odd, out of place. Maybe considered a form of *elder goth.* But her eyes. A form of swirling black, her pupil lost in the darkness.

Hekate holds out her long black nails, each filed to a sharp point. Absently, I notice the letters in blood red on each spell out *WITCH BITCH.* "Oh, you know, I thought I'd come see the sights. I heard they finally finished that absolutely hideous building they were constructing when I was last here."

My brows furrow. "It's called the Empire State Building now. You'd like it."

Hekate scoffs, strolling to the windows of my office, looking down at the city sprawled beneath it. She rests her forehead against the glass, and the reflection gives me a view of her eyes. Fathomless depths. There are a few gods of the Underworld that hate to leave it—the Primes, like Hekate, are among them. Everything about her warns against crossing her. Those who worship her, who beg for her aid, are *lucky* when she doesn't answer. And for those she does...

Her black eyes move back and forth frantically, watching those below. I know she's counting the number of mortals walking on the street. There's too many for her to count. *She hates being outnumbered.* Her voice is more cutting than I remember it ever being. "Why haven't you activated the curse? Why is our world still

327

without a queen?"

I glance at the door, exhaling when I see that Persephone hasn't suddenly appeared to hear that. "You make that sound like I'm choosing to keep her away."

"Aren't you?" Hekate snaps back, turning to face me.

I grind my teeth harder. "She's…not ready."

Hekate laughs, the sound of a flock of crows taking flight. "Not ready? The future Queen of the Dead? Destroyer of Worlds? Definitely sounds like she needs protection from you."

I glance to the door again, stopping myself from exhaling again in relief. I growl back, my shoulders still tight with tension. "She doesn't know."

Hekate hisses, and it sounds more like a pit of snakes this time. I'm half surprised she doesn't conjure one just to bite me in the ass. It wouldn't be the first time, or the last, I'm sure. Too many times, I've found a scorpion in my shoes, or a beetle in my coffee, when she's been pissed off with me.

"You're keeping *my* queen in the dark about her destiny," she snarls.

I have no illusions about where Hekate's loyalties will lie when Persephone takes the throne. She's made it very clear since I took the throne from the Primes, with the declaration from Gaia, that she would *never* bow to me. She'd never bow to any man. She'd make an exception for the legendary Destroyer of Worlds. My fated queen…there is so much more to her destiny than just ruling at my side.

She is the queen even Hekate will bend a knee for.

"You are not allowed to interfere, *witch*," I snarl back.

Her entire body shifts, her head tilting, and I wish I could immediately call the words back. Hekate is not an enemy I ever want to have.

I whisper, "I shouldn't have said that." I usually do *not* apologize. But this was a blunder. And the Primordi-

328

al of Witchcraft takes payment in *blood.* All the old gods did.

Hekate slowly moves away from the window, closing in on me. Every step is predatory, laced with lethal intent. She's too fast for me to even block before she grabs my jaw in a vice grip, those black eyes locked on me.

Her nails dig into my cheek but don't break the skin. "Claim my queen, and I'll forget about your momentary loss of sanity."

I try to hiss or yank my face out of her grip, but she's gone in a flash of black smoke, leaving a single tarot card behind. I look down, sighing at the Empress card. Hekate was never subtle. She wants the queen she was promised. *The Iron Queen. Destroyer of Worlds.*

Persephone, Goddess of Spring.

Chapter Sixty-Four

Persephone

I BLINK AT JACKSON. *WHAT'S THE POINT IN LYING TO HIM NOW?*

I sigh, resigning myself. He may as well know. While I never considered us to be officially in a relationship, I did care about Jackson, and he obviously cared about me. I'd also love for him to move on with his life and don't want him to continue being eaten up by guilt because he fucked someone else when he was perfectly within his rights to do so. Besides, while Hades and I weren't actively having sex, we were…doing things. And I did something much worse than Jackson. I fell in love.

How could I not? We're inevitable.

I soften my gaze and take a step closer to him. "I did…"

Jackson narrows his cold eyes. "You were fucking him when we were engaged."

I lift my chin, my own gaze hardening, not willing to accept all of the blame for the downfall of Jacsephone. "First of all, we were never engaged. Second of all, I didn't *fuck* anyone while I was seeing you. Third of all, you have a nerve, considering what was happening with your little secretary."

Jackson scoffs. "*Wanting* to fuck someone is just as bad."

I blink. "In what world?"

"It is."

I laugh humorlessly. "Jackson, we obviously weren't right for each other. Both of us ended up looking for more."

"I slept with her once, and I don't care about her. I care about you," Jackson says, stepping forward. The edge in his voice is back, but I can tell he's working hard to hide it, making his words sound hollow, empty.

I take a step back, my gut telling me to put some distance between us. "It's over, Jackson."

"You never wanted me," he hisses.

I blink at him, unsure where he's been hiding this side of himself. *I hid more than a* side *of myself.*

"Jackson, that's not true."

He growls, "It's Plutus isn't it? Ever since you got this job…"

I lift an eyebrow. "Ever since I got this job, what, Jackson?"

"You changed!"

I scoff. "How?"

"You don't have time for me."

I shake my head in disbelief, had it not been his job, too, that had stopped us from spending time together? "What are you talking about?"

His eyes narrow. "Where did you go when we went to the club? I saw your boss there."

I take another step back. "I have to get back to work, Jackson." I turn and walk back to the elevator.

"I knew it. You're a slut."

I stop in my tracks. Slowly, I turn to face him, my gaze murderous. "Excuse me?"

His hateful gaze roams over me, his mouth pulled into a sneer.

I turn again and press the button for the elevator.

"I'm sure your mother will love to hear about you slutting it up with your boss."

331

My head snaps to look at him, my stomach clenching. "What?"

His lips pull into a wicked smile, his eyes flashing. "She called me."

"You're lying…"

He's not lying.

He raises a brow, making him look even more menacing. "Call my bluff then."

I swallow, my stomach churning, waves of nausea rolling through me. "What did she say to you?"

He laughs ominously. "What do you really know about Hades, Persephone?"

My brows furrow. *He's hiding something, he's hiding something, he's hiding something.*

But why would my mother tell Jackson? She despises mortals. How does she even know about him? Surely, she would not have confided in him about the divine would she? And even if she did, would the thing that Hades is keeping from me be something widely known?

Never have I been more frustrated about my lack of knowledge, feeling again like I've been failed. It seems everyone knows so much about my destiny. Everyone but me.

"What are you talking about?" The words fall from my mouth before I've considered them. I stumble a step forward, needing the information being kept from me.

Jackson smirks. "You have a week to decide, me or Plutus."

"You don't even want me."

His eyes narrow, and when he smiles, a shiver runs down my spine. "But I don't want him to have you."

"So you admit it then?"

He tilts his head at me, making it clear he won't be saying any more on the subject until I forsake him or myself.

I try to school my face into a look of bored indiffer-

332

ence, never being more glad that he's mortal and can't hear my heart pounding in my chest or smell my fear. "I'll let you know."

Smirking smugly, obviously thinking he's won, he turns and leaves.

The elevator pings and I hastily walk in, pressing my back against the wall, not trusting my legs to carry me any longer. I squeeze my eyes closed, willing the nausea to subside, the dizziness.

I look up at the ceiling, trying to take deep breaths to calm my racing heart.

Fuck fuck fuck.

Chapter Sixty-Five

Hades

WHEN I TURN THE SECURITY CAM-
ERA SCREEN BACK ON, Persephone's
gone. There's no sign of her or Jackson,
the lobby empty except for our receptionist. No trace of
my fated queen and the mortal who once claimed to be
her paramour.

I dig my hands into my hair, hissing. Of course, she's
already gone. I shouldn't have snapped at Hekate. That
was a fucking stupid move. I can't even imagine how
much she's going to make me pay for it when I get home.

I click through the other security cameras, demist-
ing my office glass, frowning when I don't see Persephone anywhere. Did she go with him? To a secondary
location? *Hasn't she seen* Investigation Discovery? *NEV-
ER GO TO A SECOND LOCATION.* Calm down. Don't
jump to conclusions.

I find my phone, thankfully not shattered like my
monitor. I type out a message, my fingers a blur.

HADES

My spring?

Where did she go? She couldn't…she wouldn't have
left me right? Gone off with that mortal? No. Not after

what she saw, what…what we shared. No. She wouldn't. But I keep holding my phone, frozen, waiting for her reply. My muscles are locking on my bones, my entire body strung tight.

PERSEPHONE
I need to go home. I'm not feeling well.

I focus on her office again, seeing her purse is gone. How did I not notice before? Is she already home? I try not to feel the ache in my chest when I realize that she's gone to her apartment. Not the penthouse. *Not to our home. Her home.*

HADES
I'm coming with you.

I stand, preparing to shadow to her apartment. She needs me, she's not feeling well. She needs her…*boyfriend.* The title sounds foreign, even in my head. Too temporary. My mind jumps to the next title, and my heart races in my chest. *She needs her king, her husband.*

Her response comes through jolting me out of my thoughts, and I frantically read it.

PERSEPHONE
No, I'm okay, baby. Just need to rest.

I exhale, falling back into the chair. *Baby.* Her feelings haven't changed. But we haven't had the chance to discuss the deadline. The winter. I didn't have the chance to tell her I've been working on a way for her to visit the Underworld, even for a day or two, during the six months. It's been unbearable to imagine spending six long months without holding her, touching her.

335

I didn't get the chance to explain fully, I thought I'd have more time. I counted too much on her remembering the meeting, on allowing that to do the explaining for me. *Coward.*

PERSEPHONE

No. I'll call you later.

She'll call me later. That's good. She's not leaving. Well, just to her apartment. That's fine. She'll call me later. She's not coming to *our home*. At least the home we've shared up here. *Not the home we will share.* Fuck, when did I start thinking about that? Acting like I'm entertaining activating the curse?

Time is running out.

HADES

Alright.

I can't smother her. I'd be no better than her mother. Imprisoning her. I grind my teeth, reminding myself that fate was shoving us down this path. Are my feelings even really mine? Are hers? Or are we only fate's toys, dancing for a tune?

My office phone rings, scaring me. I don't look at the number as I answer.

"Persephone—" I begin.

A dryly amused voice stops me. "Now, I have many nicknames, but that's a new one."

I freeze, before pulling my head away from the phone, staring at it in disbelief, before pressing it back to my ear. "Eros?"

Eros, God of Love and Desire, *never* calls me. The irreverent god is often frolicking and creating mischief on the West Coast. I am far too *serious* for his taste. As he has delighted in telling me. On more than one occasion.

"You're wondering why I'm calling you," Eros says.

I look at the phone again.

"Call it an old favor for a friend," the other god continues, without waiting for my response. "I had a feeling that you needed to ask me something."

Fuck, the God of Love.

"How could you possibly know that?" I demand. Eros doesn't have any kind of oracular power.

Eros snickers into the phone. "You have thirty seconds left. Sure that's the question you want to ask me?"

Eros didn't mention a time limit! *Fucking trickster.*

I glance at my watch, before blurting, "Is it possible for fated couples…" I can't form the question, my words seeming jumbled even in my own head. "Are my feelings…her feelings…are they *ours?*"

Eros pauses for only a second before smoothly answering, "Fate cannot create love. Why do you think the Moirai hate me so much?"

I open my mouth to ask more questions, but Eros hangs up. I blink in surprise, pressing the redial button, only to get the busy tone. I try a third time, and get: *This number is no longer in service.*

What the actual fuck just happened? I run a hand down my face, then throw myself into work to distract myself as the hours go by. Though I keep texting her throughout the day, unable to help myself.

HADES

I miss you.

Her response is immediate, soothing some of the

lingering doubt in my mind.

PERSEPHONE

I miss you, too. How's work?

I look around the office, everyone continuing on as if nothing has changed.

HADES

Terrible. Are you coming home to me?

It takes a lot for me to not demand she come home to me. *Don't smother.*

PERSEPHONE

I think I'm going to stay here tonight, still feeling unwell. Why is it terrible?

My shoulders slump at that. She's not coming home to me.

HADES

Did I do something wrong?

You're not here.

I must have done something wrong. I must have or she'd be back with me. Sending me pictures of her discarded lingerie to get me to hurry through work and home to her.

PERSEPHONE

You didn't do anything wrong. I hope your day improves.

I force myself back to work and off Persephone's strange behavior. I stop myself a dozen times from picking up the phone and calling her. Even more times, I'm tempted to shadow to her just to see her for myself. But I can't overwhelm her.

Even though...*time is running out.*

Finally, after the work day is over, I pick up the phone to FaceTime her. Unable to resist when I'm lying in bed and smelling her pillow.

She answers on the second ring, and I bolt up in bed when I see how puffy and red her eyes are. *She's been crying?*

"I'm coming over," I state plainly.

She plasters a smile on her face, but she can barely manage it. "I'm fine, demon!"

I ignore that, shadowing directly into bed with her, looking her over.

Love is immune to fate.

Chapter Sixty-Six

Persephone

I'M COMING OVER. Three words, but the impact is so great that I almost burst into tears again, knowing that this male cares for me so deeply, he would drop everything to be here, to comfort me.

He's hiding something, he's hiding something, he's hiding something.

I school my face into a smile, willing my voice to not break. "I'm fine, demon!"

His skeptical look is the last thing I see before the bed shifts as he shadows beside me. The second his shadows dissipate, I burst into tears again, his sandalwood and citrus scent wrapping around me like the softest of blankets.

"My spring?" He looks down at me, and I climb into his lap, nuzzling into his neck, inhaling him. Half because I need to be comforted by him, half to shield him from my ugly crying face.

His arms immediately wrap around me. The second I'm surrounded by him, my chest stops aching and my breathing seems easier.

"Why didn't you tell me you were upset?"

I press my face into his neck, tears still streaming from my eyes. Not wanting to think about anything other than the fact that *my* Hades is here. Holding me, comforting me. And yet, I can't stop crying.

I cling to Hades as the emotions from the last few weeks spill out of me. The anger at Jackson, the frustration that the love of my life is hiding something from me, something big enough that I can feel his anxiety about it, something that has as much to do with me as it does him.

He kisses my head, nuzzling into my hair. "I'm here, my spring." He presses another kiss to my forehead, squeezing me again. "I'm here."

Around twenty minutes later, the tears start to dry up. I pull back, silently cursing the fact that I know my face is puffy and my eyes are red.

"I'm fine now. I'm sorry."

He lifts my chin gently and softly presses his lips to mine. I kiss him back, my hand against his chest, over his heart.

He smooths my hair, tucking it behind one of my ears. "I'm here."

His deep blue eyes search my face. I can tell he's aching to know what happened. Trying not to push me but trying to draw the answers from my micro expressions.

I look away from him, my voice barely a whisper. "She's going to…take me back."

He cups my cheek with his hand, soft but firm, gently turning my head, coaxing me to look at him. His brows are furrowed. "Talk to me."

I swallow, my gaze hardening at the memory of my encounter with Jackson. "Jackson, he–"

Hades growls at the mention of his name, but I continue.

"—threatened to…" I hesitate. "He's going to call my mother, if you and I don't…" I pause again, my stomach twisting, unable to even speak the words. "She knew about him the whole time."

Hades's eyes narrow. "How?"

I lift a shoulder in a shrug. "She must have been watching me closer than I thought."

His eyes glow bright blue, looking into the distance, looking every bit the God of the Underworld. The most fearsome god. My fearsome god, my protector. "I'll take care of it."

I move my hand to his arm, squeezing. "Hades."

He looks at me, the promise of death is his gaze settling as his eyes roam over my face. "What?"

I cup his cheek, shaking my head. "This is my problem."

He leans his head into my hand. "You're my problem. Your problems are mine."

My lips twitch. "I'm a problem, huh?"

His eyes return to that deep blue, more captivating than the rarest of sapphires. He laughs softly. It warms my heart how easily I can bring him back to me. "A bit, sometimes."

I roll my eyes but reach for my phone. I watch the cursor flash on the screen as I try to formulate a plan. I need to be smart about this. I need to glean as much information as I can from him without giving up any information myself. The last thing my mother needs is even more ammunition.

My previous messages to Jackson sits there, staring at me, taunting me.

Hades kisses my ear, his hand lazily stroking my back, comforting me. "We'll figure it out."

I look up at Hades, knowing that he's going to hate what I say next. Trying to figure out the best way to convince him that it's the smartest move. A small part of me considers that I should just do my investigation solo, keeping him in the dark.

No... Bad plan, P.

But if he can keep secrets from me...

I sigh, resigned. I'm obviously going to tell him. "I need to see what he knows."

342

Chapter Sixty-Seven

Hades

HE'S BLACKMAILING HER. *I will kill him.* His body will serve as a warning for all who dare to come at my queen. I tilt my head, trying to analyze her words, understand what she's not saying.

"What do you mean?"

I'll find out what he knows. Torture it out of him if I must.

I smother the thought that whispers my darkest and most savage nature. *I'll enjoy listening to him scream.* I keep the voice down. I've been the God of the Underworld for thousands of years, ruler of Tartarus, and the pit of festering evil which were imprisoned inside. The Underworld was built around the heart of a dying primordial named Tartarus, who sacrificed himself to create the great prison. But, over the millennia, it's rumored that what remains of the primordial has become twisted and evil, just like the gods and monsters he imprisoned within his body. Sometimes a voice whispers in my mind, and I worry that, soon, I'll be like the prime. *Consumed by the pain and darkness, until I become as evil as the spirits that reside within.* Need to be careful. Persephone can bring out the best and worst in me.

She sits on the edge of the bed, her back to me. The way her entire body tenses, makes my entire body tighten. "I need to meet up with him."

My fists clench at my sides. The continued coil of tension that seems to persist since Persephone and I finally sealed our relationship grows. I roll my shoulders, as if I could dispel the knot with the movement.

"Never," I snarl.

If her ex is in contact with her mother, she could take her from me. I'd never be able to touch her again. Completely out of my reach. A vein ticks under my eye. It wouldn't be for only six months, it would be *permanent.* If Demeter took her back to Olympus, or to wherever she raised her, I don't doubt that the goddess will find ways to keep us apart. *A mother's love can be suffocating.*

She still doesn't look at me, her hands pressing into the mattress. That vein ticks even faster, my vision wavering with it.

Her voice was steady, but cautious. "I need to feel him out."

I narrow my eyes on her back, suspicion growing. My own voice turns soft and deadly. *Dangerous.* "What aren't you telling me?"

She sighs. "So, you can withhold information, but I can't?"

I can't stop my flinch at that. "Direct hit."

She's right. I am hiding so much from her, yet demand that she reveal all. *Fate is holding my words captive!* It's more than that. I'm not an open person by nature. Most assume me cold and unfeeling, but not Persephone. With her, *everything is different.*

She turns finally, crawling into my lap, even as I remain stiff, her soft curves against my body. Something that normally makes me happy only makes me tense more.

She kisses me softly, whispering, "I'm sorry, I need you to trust me."

So you're the only one who can withhold information?

344

Her words still ring in my ears. The secrets I hold are building a wall between us, and I can do nothing but watch it build and build. Even as I press my forehead to hers, longing for the intimacy we usually shared. "So I blindly follow your lead?"

It's not something I do. I issue orders. I *lead*. But when it comes to Persephone? *I will always follow.*

She straddles my lap, kissing me again. Her soft hands frame my face, keeping me trapped in her gaze. *The golden sun in a clear spring sky.* "Yes."

I growl, "For how long?" I don't know how long I can promise to not interfere in this. To not take matters into my own hands.

She kisses down my neck, her voice turning deep and husky. "For as long as I need."

So you're the only one who can withhold information? "But the deadline."

A little under two months remain before I am sequestered away. To some, it's a lifetime, a world packed into it. For me? It will never be enough. *Time is running out.*

She leans away from me, grabbing her phone, typing out a message she doesn't show me.

Don't snatch it from her fingers, don't snatch it.

She sighs. "It's done." She tosses her phone away, focusing back on me. "We need to...talk about it."

About the deadline. About me going downstairs. About us being apart. She looks over my face, kissing me deeply again. Is she avoiding the subject? I want to, as well. But I can't.

I pull back, looking down at her. "Persephone..."

She winces at my withdrawal. I stop myself from yanking her back to me, to erase the look in her eyes. "Yes?"

"I'm trying to find a loophole...for the deadline," I whisper. "I want you...to be able to come visit me."

It's a long shot, a *very* long one, but I can't go the six months without touching her. It's not enough. Not for me, and I sense not for her either.

She frowns, but hope flickers in her eyes. "You think that's possible?"

I shrug slightly, not wanting to get either of our hopes up. "I don't know. Would you want to? Come visit me?"

She kisses me hard, trying to imprint herself on my mouth. "Of course. The idea of six months without you…"

I exhale, our breaths mingling. "You might only be able to visit for a day or two."

She pulls at my shirt, her tongue pushing into my mouth. "I'll take anything."

I cup her face. "I would give you everything."

My throne. My kingdom. My heart. My life. It's all hers anyway.

She finds the edge of my shirt, tossing it off. "What do you want?"

I grab her jaw. "Your heart."

She glances at my lips, licking her own. "It's yours."

I shake my head. "Not yet. But it will be."

Her dark brows furrow. "What do you mean?"

I smile softly. "When…When you commit to me. Completely."

"Like…marry you?"

I hate how my heart leaps at that, at the idea of her calling me *husband,* of her wearing *my* ring. But mortals take years or *months* to come to these kinds of decisions. Even if we're fated, even if, when I come into this world, I am destined to be with her. To rule the realm given to me with her.

I clear my throat. "It's too soon to talk like this… right?"

She blushes. "Maybe. It's definitely the future I want

though."

Chapter Sixty-Eight
Persephone

MY HEART FLUTTERS AS HE PRESSES HIS LIPS TO MINE. Will I ever grow tired of the feeling of his lips? *Fuck, I hope not.*

He pulls back, and instinctively, I move with him, not willing to part from him, especially now that I know we have a time limit.

"Tell me about your plan." His words come out soft, like a caress, everything about him coaxing me to bend to him.

I sigh as the weight of his request comes crashing down on me. I grimace, thinking of how to word my answer, knowing that the gentleness will leave him instantly. "You're not going to like it," I admit.

He frowns. "Why not?"

I sigh, lifting my shoulders in a shrug. "I'm going to have to charm him."

His body immediately tenses. I can practically feel every muscle stiffening beneath me. "What does that mean?"

I need to soften him, relax him. I brush my lips over his, my hand stroking his arm. "Flirt with him a little."

His chest vibrates with a low growl, I almost shiver at the sound. "How much is a little?"

I kiss along his jaw, trying to ease the tension that's

radiating off him. "A touch of the arm, a suggestive look. That's all." I slide my hands over his bare chest, his skin like silk under my fingers. "Enough talking."

He growls again. This time I don't stop my shiver as a pleasure pools low in my tummy.

"But…"

I push him back on the bed, slowly dragging my nails over his stomach. "But what?"

He grabs my hips, digging his fingers into my flesh. "How will he know you're mine?"

I slowly slide my own shirt up my body, over my stomach and over my breasts. I lift it over my head and throw it to the side, leaving me only in a pair of lace panties. "He won't. At first."

His gaze roams over my body. I can see the hunger there, but his brows are still tensed in a frown. "At first?"

I lean down, digging my nails into his chest. I kiss down his neck, slowly working my lips down his strong, perfect chest. "Do you trust me, demon?"

He shudders. The reaction makes me smile as I continue to kiss him, slowly moving down, down, down.

"I have to."

I pause, my lips at his stomach, glancing up at him. "So you don't then?"

He groans when our eyes lock. "I do."

I nuzzle into his happy trail, open his pants, and curl my fingers into his boxers. I start to slowly tug his pants and underwear down, smirking when he lifts his hips to allow me to pull them down easier. My mouth waters when his cock springs free, and I wrap my hand around his heavy length.

"Good. Because, I am yours."

He shivers as my hand closes around him. I squeeze his shaft, rewarded when he lifts his hips, desperate for my touch. "Fuck. I don't want to let you go."

I lick the tip of his cock. "You're not letting me go."

His hand flies to my head and he tunnels his fingers into my hair. "Why can't I just…fuck…kill him?"

I close my lips around the tip, my tongue sliding through the small slit of the swollen crown before pulling back. "Then we wouldn't know what my mother knows."

His grip on my hair tightens. "But I'd feel better."

I chuckle, closing my lips around his cock again, sucking him in deep, my cheeks hollowing. I pull back again. There's nothing I love more than teasing Hades. "Better than when I'm on my knees for you?"

He groans, his gaze locking with mine. "You're not finished being on your knees for me."

I slide my tongue from the base of his cock to the tip and start sucking on him again.

His moans fill the room. He starts guiding my head, his fingers still tightly gripping my hair, his hips thrusting into me.

I take his full, hard length, my eyes watering as I gag on him. Desperate for more. I suck harder, my tongue swirling around him as he pulls his length from me before thrusting it back in.

"I'm-I'm going to come, Persephone," he hisses, his voice thick, guttural, barely recognizable.

I stare up at him, my gaze hooded, letting him control my head completely. My low moans send vibrations up his rock-hard shaft. As I move, I feel the damp lace of my panties rubbing against me, making me moan louder.

I shiver as I feel his shadows caressing up the backs of my thighs, inching closer and closer to my aching cunt. Hades yells as he comes inside me, filling my mouth with his thick release. I swallow it down, needing every single drop.

I feel his shadows kiss along my panty line, but…I don't want his shadows. I want him. I need him. Like a starving man needs food, like a flower needs the rain.

A darkness waiting to grow.

Chapter Sixty-Nine

Hades

THE WAY SHE WORSHIPS ME WITH THAT MOUTH OF HERS, I can barely process. My shadows move without my conscious order, but they must know I need to touch her. Even when the very distant voice in my head is trying to remind me that she's using sex to…*something.* I can't remember. Something she didn't want to talk about. It's hard to think when she's got her mouth on my cock.

My shadows dance around her panties, focused on pleasuring. As always, I need to make her feel more than she ever has. To be the best. And to do that, I need my shadows to work with me to make her feel better. What I can't do with my hands, my shadows will provide.

She swallows every drop, licking me clean. Her eyes looking up at me, practically black. "Hades. No shadows."

No shadows? They're a part of me, as much as my hands and feet. Is she denying me? I tense. "What? Why?"

She slides her panties off and climbs up my body, until she straddles my face. *I'd much rather her sit on my face than use my shadows to tend to her.* There are certain things I would rather do completely myself, and sucking that soaking pussy will *always* be one of them.

I groan, grabbing her hips, sticking my tongue out.

Rocking her over my face, making her ride me. Her body arches, slowly rolling her hips against my mouth, letting me drink her addicting cunt. I flick my tongue over her clit, stiffening my tongue, fucking her with it. Her sweet taste slides down my mouth, the perfect elixir. More potent and addicting than ambrosia.

She moans loudly, her voice huskier than I've ever heard it. "Drop your glamour."

I hesitate a moment before obeying. She bends slightly, wrapping her hands around my horns, using them as handlebars. My toes curl from her grip on them, even more as I see her own glamour drop. "So close…"

I lick her faster, my tail smacking her ass, likely leaving a fork-shaped imprint. She screams my name as she comes, her thighs squeezing my head. I groan at her grip, panting. She rolls off me, collapsing.

I pant shakily, licking her off my lips. She rolls onto her side, kissing me and moaning softly. I bite her lip. "I want to keep you here."

I'm tempted to wrap my wings around her and never let her go. To shelter her inside them and never release her. As if I could keep her inside them. Persephone would rip my wings to shreds if I even attempted to control her.

She tangles her fingers in my hair, tugging at me as if to keep me in the present. Away from the future that looms. "I'm here."

I pull her leg over my hip, needing her close. *Needing her.* I should tell her. I need to tell her. *You're my fated queen,* but what comes out instead is, "But you will leave me."

Then, I'll leave you.

She pulls me on top of her, until my weight pins her to the mattress. I use my hands to keep from crushing her. "I'll be gone for two hours. Max."

"Swear to me?" I whisper. I don't even care how

desperate I sound. Every little wall I should be building between us, to prepare for our separation, has only the briefest moment of solidity before it's torn down by the way she looks at me. With those eyes that promise everlasting spring and flowers I've never seen bloom. Not since the division of the realms.

She reaches down between us, wrapping her hand around my cock, which hardens at her touch. It obeys her. *I am yours to conquer. A queen worthy of the Underworld, who will never break under its demands.*

She slides the crown along her pussy. "That I'll only be two hours?"

I hiss, "Yes."

That you're not leaving me for him. That, if I tell you the truth, you won't run. That you'll want to be my queen. So many words that will not leave my lips. That *can't* leave them. She deserves so much better than half-truths, and lies of omission.

She positions my cock at her entrance, distracting me even as she reassures me. "I will return to you."

I thrust hard, until I'm impaled to the hilt inside her, our bodies joined now, even as she readies to leave me. She'll still feel me, even when she sits across from him. "You're mine."

She rolls her hips. "Yours."

The words should really reassure me. But they're not what I should be saying. *Stay.* It's not really about her going to meet her ex, not completely. It's just the beginning. The first of so many goodbyes.

She digs her nails into my shoulders, crying out.

I kiss her hard, biting her lips. "I'm yours."

She wraps her legs around me. "Mine."

I rock inside her, but it's slow and languid, not urgent and frantic. A deeper intimacy sparks between us. Her eyes lock on mine, cupping my face as I thrust. I move faster, my chest aching, feeling more than just our

354

bodies becoming one. She kisses me, moaning into my lips, sharing breath.

I groan, whispering, "I need you."

I'm in love with you. And I can't tell you, because there's so much more to it. Fuck, I'm utterly in love with the Goddess of Spring, my fated queen, and I can't tell her.

She flicks her tongue against mine, her eyes sparkling with emotion. "Mine."

Does she feel it too? That we're meant to be together? That there's so much more?

I roll onto my back, hissing, "I'm going to come, my love."

She arches into me. "Me too... Fuck. So close..."

I hiss, pulling out of her before I come, my fingers replacing my cock for her.

She looks at me. "No! Inside me! Please..."

I groan, about to come, my cock pearling with pre-cum. Pushing her to her own orgasm.

"No," I say, even as I make her come.

Chapter Seventy

Persephone

I TENSE, MY BODY ACHING WITH NEED, BUT MY HEAD A MESS.

Why doesn't he want this with me?

My heart pounds in my chest and the room starts to spin. Nothing ever seems to be easy with Hades. Can I spend my life like this? Never knowing where I stand? Only ever getting half a story?

My impending orgasm is a faraway dream.

He frowns at my change in demeanor, obviously sensing my unease. He presses his finger on my clit. While it throbs under his touch, the mood is gone, uncertainty setting up camp deep within me, ousting my burning desire for him. My traitorous mind floods with intrusive thoughts.

No. Not like this. No more.

He's hiding something, he's hiding something, he's hiding something.

Repress and distract. If he won't let me in, he cannot expect me to let him in.

I reach down and wrap my hand around his wrist, stilling him.

His frown deepens, and he looks down at me, panting, obviously still feeling the strain from his unmet desire, but there's something else flickering in the background. Something is eating him up, destroying him as much as it is me.

"What are you doing?"

I brush his hand away from my pussy and push him onto his back, leaning over him. I wrap my hand around his cock and start stroking him. My need may be a faraway thought, but that doesn't mean I don't want to pleasure him, in spite of my mess of thoughts.

He hisses, arching his back. "What are you doing?" he repeats, his voice strained. His eyes lock on me, even more uncertain than before.

I continue to stroke him, my grip tight.

His moans bring me back to him slightly, and I start to feel my sexual frustration from before. The low ache in my tummy warming. His eyes roll back, and his lips part as I stroke him, adding to my sexual torment. My body thrums for him, but I'm still of the mindset that we can't live our life this way. He can't continue to leave me in the dark.

His eyes flutter closed as he groans, his hips thrusting into my fist. "Persephone..."

I pump his cock faster. I lean over and lick one of his nipples before sucking on it, biting it.

His hips buck, and he bites his lip, hard. It takes everything in me to not lean in and bite it for him. I continue to fuck him with my fist, knowing his release is coming.

I move my lips to his ear. "I want you to come, demon. Inside of me. I crave it. I crave you."

"Never," he grates out. His body tenses, and his jaw clenches, as he finally finds release, spilling over my hand and his stomach.

Did he say never?

My stomach sinks. Would we never share this with each other? Did he simply not want me like that? I release him and climb off of the bed. My body aches, clit and pussy throbbing with need, but I know I need to put some distance between us. Need space to consider his admission. To mourn this closeness that we'll never experience together.

I feel his eyes on me. He reaches out for me. "Time for you."

I easily dodge his grasp. He moves to grab me again, and I flick my wrist, vines appearing seemingly from nowhere and wrapping around his wrists and ankles, holding him in place.

He snarls, his eyes flashing, like a man possessed. "What are you doing? Release me. Now."

I don't look back as I leave the room wordlessly and go for a shower.

I press my back to the bathroom door, my chest heaving, my eyes stinging with the threat of tears. I love Hades. I am completely in love with him, but I can't live like this. Not anymore. For my whole life, I have been kept secret. Decisions have been made for me and about me. My destiny, widely known by many, kept hidden from me.

My heart breaks as I consider my life without Hades, my fated one, and I consider my gratitude for him. He unlocked another side of me. One previously viciously locked away by my mother.

A rose with a bite...

Never merely the dainty, perfect Goddess of Spring.

Hades *likes* that about me. Embraces my darkness, entwines it with his own.

But he is destroying me in his own fated way.

I stand from the floor and walk to the mirror. I sigh at my reflection. This is the closest I've ever been to knowing who I truly am. It seems the closer I get to my true self, the less willing I am to accept less than I deserve. And I deserve the truth.

I wipe my tears, my eyes dim from the internal turmoil, from the thought that Hades and I might be fated

358

but might also be doomed. Just like on Olympus, this cage is gilded with lies, omissions, and half-truths. It strikes me then…

A prison is a prison, no matter the jailor.

Chapter Seventy One

Hades

IYANK AND TEAR AT THE VINES, BUT THEY JUST GROW BACK. My shadows do nothing. She doesn't understand. My mouth is tied by a stupid choice I made so long ago.

The home of the Moirai on Mount Olympus is a place shrouded in darkness, a feeling of mist oppressive on my skin. Yet the fog isn't there. Only the sensation. I refuse to rub my arms against it. I stride forward into the main room, my hands tucked into my pants, looking around. There's nothing in the room, at least to me. Only void. I keep my composure, even as a voice from seemingly nowhere speaks to me, "God of the Dead seeks the counsel of the Fates?"

I keep my eyes straight ahead, not looking around, searching for the source of the voice as I want to. "I have."

Another voice echoes, "You know the cost of knowing your fate."

A third voice speaks before I can. "You will be helpless to change it."

I stop myself from smirking. As if I could be bound by such a trivial thing. It's merely a puzzle to be solved. A trick to be deciphered.

"I understand," I reply coolly. "I still wish to know."

The Fates murmur, "Then we shall tell you."

I wait patiently. Even as the voices sound around my head, ruffling my hair.

"The lonely god," one sneers.

I grind my teeth for only a moment before relaxing, I won't give them the satisfaction of knowing they provoked a reaction from me.

"Lonely no longer," another adds.

"Explain," I snap.

I shouldn't have demanded they tell me. I should have never gone to them in the first place, should never have been so foolishly arrogant to believe that fate was a game for me to play. A game I could outwit. If I hadn't gone…I wouldn't be here, bound by vines to her bed, naked, waiting for her to return.

The heels of my feet dig into the bed, and even as my shadows attempt to unwind the vines, they only grow back stronger. Fucking arrogance. Pride goeth before the fall.

I don't know how much time passes until she returns. She completely ignores me as she drops her towel and sits in the armchair in the corner of the room. Her body makes me hiss immediately, as it always does. She's my every fantasy made flesh. She lifts one of her legs over the arm, opening herself so I can see her glistening pussy. Her hand starts wandering down her body slowly, only locking eyes with me, her fingers sliding between her legs, teasing herself.

I snarl at the sight, my shadows moving to tend to her pleasure even as I fight the vines. That is my job. To pleasure her. My treasured responsibility. She's taking it from me. It feels like a dagger in my gut. She knows exactly what she's doing too. She's dealt the blow with precision.

She stills her fingers and growls at me, "No shadows. I want you to watch me."

I hiss, my cock hardening again, struggling against

the vines. "Why? Let me pleasure you."

She remains still, her eyes hard. "No. Shadows."

My hands fist in the vines. A precise blow, leaving wounds in its wake. A queen who would take no prisoners. Iron Queen. Destroyer of Worlds.

My shadows drop and move to fist my cock, since my hands are held. It aches from seeing her.

Her eyes narrow. "No. Watch. Nothing else."

My arms strain in the bonds, snapping at her. "So you intend to torture me?"

She slides a finger over her clit, my eyes locked on her movements. "Yes."

I flinch for a moment, trying to understand why she feels the need to hurt me so deeply. She won't be kept in another prison, full of half-truths and omissions. Though I know why, I still ask, "Why?"

She slowly slides a finger through her pussy, pushing it inside. I hiss, fighting the vines, but they only grow back. "How you're feeling right now is how I feel every time you don't come inside me. And I don't get a reason either."

I shrink back into the bed, my eyes locked on her fingers, whispering, "This isn't comparable, and you know it."

She moans, working a second finger inside herself. "No?"

I close my eyes, but I can still hear her. "I'm still giving you almost all of me. This is you teasing me with what you let me enjoy."

You're spurning my touch. The sound of her pleasuring herself stops. My eyes open slowly, seeing her walk to me, sliding her fingers over my lips. I moan, licking her fingers.

"And there lies the problem, demon. I have given you all of me." She sighs and turns from me, releasing me from the vines finally.

I scan her face, my body still tense, despite being released. "And I've given you my heart and soul. But that's…not enough?"

She pulls on a large t-shirt. Cold. "You say you've given me your heart, Hades and yet…the secrets. I've had a life of being kept in the dark. No more."

I want to tell her. I need to tell her. But…

"I'm bound," I whisper. Even the words are a strain. Torn from me.

She blinks. "Bound?"

Fate tightens around my throat. Keeping the words from passing. I open and close my mouth, fighting. "I can't…I can't speak of it."

Those who know their fate are unable to change it. Bound by my own arrogance. My foolish pride in believing that I could know my fate and not feel its effects.

I touch my throat, hissing in frustration.

"Who has bound you?" she asks, her eyes mistrustful.

I try to answer, but only a strangled sound comes out, and I growl in frustration.

She moves to me, pressing a hand against my chest. "Okay. It's okay."

I exhale, covering her hand on my chest. "Just…I have a reason, I'm sorry."

Pathetic. All that I can offer her.

She sighs, nodding, pressing her lips to my head.

I close myself for another moment, steeling myself. "If…what I can offer you is not enough, please tell me now." I'll be shattered. But I'll keep moving forward, even if I'll never feel it again.

She cups my cheek, her eyes flickering. "I love you."

The words should fill me with joy, but, instead, make me more tense. "Is that…do you mean that as a goodbye?"

Chapter Seventy-Two

Persephone

AGOODBYE? Doesn't he understand the depths of my feelings for him? Doesn't he know that he and I are inevitable? Have I been mistaken?

No.

My thoughts from the bathroom fade when I realize that he physically can't tell me, when I see how much keeping this from me is wrecking him.

I see the pain in his eyes, the longing, the sadness. I never want to be the one that makes him hurt.

I shake my head. "I mean it as 'I don't know how to breathe without you.'" I slide my thumb over his cheek, feeling him relax into my touch.

My God of the Underworld, so uncertain.

It makes my heart squeeze.

"Even if I can't...give you...that?"

I nod, sighing. Truthfully, I'm not sure I'll ever get over the fact that he'll never give himself to me fully when he owns me so completely, but I am kidding myself. If the choice is most of him or nothing, I would always choose him. I *will* always choose him.

"Do I bring enough pleasure without it?"

He nods, his eyes softening. "More than I've ever known."

My lips twitch. Maybe this will be alright. Maybe

364

I will grow used to it in time. We can be close in every other way. We don't need this experience to cement our bond, because we are inevitable.

Lie.

"Alright."

I feel him relax even more against me. "It's almost impossible to remember to pull out."

I brush my lips over his. "Do you think about it? How it would feel to fill me...to watch it slide out of me?"

He groans, pushing away from me. "Don't tempt me with this." He clenches his fists, his anguish clear on his face. "I fantasize about it more than I should."

I step forward, moving into him, kissing him softly. "Fine. I won't mention it." I slide my tongue along the seam of his lips. "But just know...I fantasize about it too."

He groans into my lips. "Please..."

We're both pulled from my maddening teasing when my phone starts ringing from across the room.

My lips pull into a half smile. "Saved by the ring." I step away from him, before grabbing my phone and answering the call. "Hello?"

"You're running late." Jackson's voice is barely recognizable, edged with malice and anger. Not the happy, soothing voice I'm used to from him, but the one I've been hearing more of recently.

I glance at the clock. My eyes go wide, seeing the time. Fuck, I am late. I summon vines to pull my outfit out of the closet and start on my hair and makeup. "I'll be there in ten minutes."

"You better be." He hangs up and a chill travels down my spine. How could I have been so wrong about a person?

I pull on my outfit as my vines continue to get my hair and face ready. The tight red dress sits high on my thigh, and while it wouldn't ordinarily be my first choice for a dinner with a spurned ex-boyfriend with a vendetta against me, I know how much he loves it and hope it'll distract him enough for me to collect intel without seeming too suspicious.

I bend, pulling on my sky-high black heels, depending on them to give me the confidence I'll need to face off with my mother's mortal minion. I curse colorfully, frustrated with myself for my poor timekeeping.

Hades's gaze remains on me the whole time, watching every movement, as I prepare to see Jackson. His eyes do nothing to ease me. They only make me feel as if I'll burst into flames at any moment.

"You're wearing that?"

Self-conscious, I pull at the bottom of the dress, trying to stretch the small amount of material wrapped around my body. "You don't like it?"

He groans, once again trailing those deep blue eyes over me.

My skin tingles under his gaze.

"I do. I hate that he's getting to see it."

I walk to him, my vines still teasing my hair into perfect long, dark curls. "But you…" I brush my lips over his jaw, "…you get to enjoy it."

He sighs, his hands going to my hips. "You sure I shouldn't just kill him?"

I shake my head, chuckling. "I have to go."

He squeezes my hips, pulling my body against his, groaning. "Hurry, before I drag you back."

I wink at him before turning to leave, careful to not look back at him. I feel his heated, hungry gaze fixed to my ass, and I know that looking back and seeing those dark eyes will…lead to me being even later to meet Jackson.

I arrive at the restaurant in record time, with no idea if I made my ten-minute deadline. I immediately see Jackson at the door. Plastering a smile on my face, I walk over to him. "Jackson."

He barely looks at me, gesturing for me to enter the restaurant.

We're taken to our table, and his cold eyes bore into mine. "Sit."

My whole body tenses, not enjoying being ordered, but for the moment...he holds all the cards. Or so he thinks.

I sit in the chair opposite him, my jaw clenched as I try to hold my tongue, struggling more than usual to school my face into that darling smile my mother forced me to learn to do on command.

"She's furious. She wants you home. Tomorrow."

I lift an eyebrow, feigning ignorance. "Why is she furious? I thought you weren't going to tell her anything as long as I met you for dinner." I flutter my eyelashes. "And I'm here. At dinner." I pause. "Speaking of my mother though—"

"Someone else told her about your boss. Someone from your work," he interrupts.

I blink at him, my mind already racing, thinking of who would do such a thing, of who even knows. Mellie knows, but surely she wouldn't...plus she's dropped off the Earth, hiding from Helios. Surely, my actions are the furthest thing from her mind.

I narrow my eyes at him. "And how did you come to be so close with my dear, dear mama?"

His eye twitches, obviously irritated by my own investigation, and something flashes over his face. For a split second...he wasn't Jackson. Then he is. I furrow my brows, trying to sort through my limited knowledge of the gods.

He shuffles in his seat, and I notice his chest rising and falling as he takes a deep breath, trying to...control himself?

"We have...similar interests."

I lean in, hissing. "Who are you?"

He narrows his eyes, weighing his options before standing, smirking down at me. "Twenty-four hours. If you're not back on the mountain, she'll come to collect you."

I discreetly use my vines, forcing Jacks—whoever it is—to sit back down. They wrap around his forearms tightly, until I'm satisfied there's no way he can get free.

He smirks again, the expression looking so foreign on Jackson's kind face. "Can't hold a psychopomp."

A psychopomp? That means Jackson could...travel between worlds. *Only gods have that power.*

In a flash of gold, he vanishes from sight, appearing behind me, his lips at my ear. "Better hurry up, *Persephone.*"

Chapter Seventy-Three

Hades

I KEEP PACING BACK AND FORTH. I went back to the penthouse after she left. I couldn't be surrounded by her things and her scent without wanting to kill that mortal. At least the penthouse only retains a whisper, a phantom, of her scent. *We haven't been together long enough for her to have completely seeped in.* We never really had the moment to be together, both of us needing to fuck out all the lust that burned inside us. I need more. I need her scent around me, in my home, on my skin. Her taste in my mouth.

But I won't get the chance. The sand continues to fall. Time continues to slip past us both. I'll be back as King of the Underworld, sitting next to an empty throne. I shouldn't be thinking about her sitting on the obsidian throne at my side, her dress a waterfall of midnight silk, a crown of onyx roses sitting on her head. She was born to sit there. To rule. *Iron Queen. Destroyer of Worlds.* I could come inside her and have my fantasy. How would it feel?

Stop thinking about it.

Yet I'm thinking about ways to get around the curse, to warn her. I don't know how many times I can keep the sanity enough to stop myself from coming inside her.

One slip. And it's over. For both of us.

Will her first term be like mine? When Gaia declared me ruler, I couldn't leave the Underworld for over a year. Not once. I didn't know if I would ever see the other world again. Will it be the same for Persephone? The thought makes me ill.

How much longer does she expect me to not interfere? How much longer can I respect her wishes about it?

My phone buzzes and I lunge for it, blinking repeatedly as I read the text.

PERSEPHONE

What gods do you know who can shapeshift?

I just stare at my phone, my fingers not typing. What an odd question.

HADES

Too many, why? What's happened?

Many gods have other forms we hide behind glamours. Some can shift into animals and plants. Several can fully shapeshift, into anything, or anyone. Mostly the trickster gods. *Dangerous deities.* Most have no respect for any kind of rules or regulations. Many have attempted to slip things past me over the millennia. They found themselves *outmatched.* They could trick all they wanted, but I play every eventuality. Every possibility. Well, except in the case of Persephone.

PERSEPHONE

That wasn't Jackson.

I blink repeatedly at my phone. It wasn't Jackson, and she didn't tell me till now?!

Come home.

I can barely see the screen with the rage in my throat. I resume my pacing, likely wearing a path in the wood of the floor. I can't focus enough to shadow to her. My glamour is already flickering. The cloaking of my shadowing is beyond my reach at the moment.

It takes entirely too long for the elevator to ding and her voice to fill the penthouse. "Hades?"

I spin to face her, mid-pace, relief flooding me. "My spring?"

She looks at me for a moment before closing the distance, not speaking, burying her face into my chest with a shaky exhale.

My arms wrap around her, even as I frown at her. "What's wrong?"

She pulls back slightly, but her arms slide around my waist. "That wasn't Jackson. They said something about 'can't hold a psychopomp' before they flashed out of my hold."

I curse at her description. A full shapeshifter, who was a psychopomp, who flaunted his ability to get out of even a god's hold? "Only one psychopomp like that." *A prick.* "Hermes."

Hermes, God of Messages, Commerce, and Thieves, the only divine being besides myself that can come and go from the Underworld without having been born there. His speed and dominion over thievery make him an annoyance at best, a very dangerous trickster at worst. Never underestimate a trickster. That's how they thrive. By being passed off as *nothing*.

Persephone releases me, beginning to pace. "I have twenty-four hours to return to my mother. Plus, I have no idea where the real Jackson is."

I growl, my power rolling against my control, needing to break through and snatch back the words she just spoke. "Return?"

She continues to pace, back and forth.

Time is running out. Faster and faster. The sands of the hourglass slip, becoming a blur. Till only a small handful is left.

I watch her. "Persephone?"

She stills, but her mind is clearly still racing. "Hm?"

My shoulders slump in defeat. Demeter...Demeter could turn the world to a barren wasteland if she wanted, to get her daughter back. Even Zeus is wary of her. Probably why he was so insistent that I not pursue her daughter. This is just the beginning, I reassure myself.

I run through the various possibilities in my head. If I refuse the Goddess of the Harvest? *The world pays.* If I try to kill her? *I kill the mother of my fated queen.* If she kills me? *I die.* Clearly that's out. There's only one path forward.

"You have to go back to her."

I'll find a way to get her back. I'll have to. But for now...this was the strategic defeat of a battle in order to claim the war. I'll get her back. She is *mine*. Since my first breath, I was fated to belong to her. And her to me.

Her brows furrow. "What? No—"

"Persephone, we don't have a choice." A tactical defeat. Even though it makes my body vibrate with anger at the thought of losing Persephone, even momentarily.

She flinches, and it crashes into me. Her face morphing from anger and confusion to *devastation*. This isn't some game. And I've dealt a blow I didn't mean to.

I flush with shame, looking away. "I'm heading downstairs soon."

Time is running out.

My eyes snap up when I hear her feet retreating,

heading for the elevator. I chase after her, grabbing her wrist before she can step inside. Spinning her back to face me. "Look at me."

She yanks her arm from my gasp, her eyes hard and filled with tears.

I cup her face. "I don't *want* you to go, but what choice do I have?"

She blinks at me, a tear sliding down her cheek. "You already made a choice. To give me up." She turns away from me again, stepping into the elevator, looking back at me, another tear falling. "Goodbye, Hades."

Time isn't running out.

It's gone.

Chapter Seventy-Four

Persephone

I FEEL HIS LARGE WARM HAND WRAP AROUND MY WRIST AGAIN, and he yanks me against him, until our bodies are flush. He seals his lips over mine in a desperate, earthshaking kiss.

He begins pulling me back into his apartment. "I'm going to…give you everything, Persephone."

My brows furrow, but I begin to relax into his kiss, my body melting as his firm lips move over mine.

He turns us, walking us back into the apartment, not letting me go, his fingers digging into my waist, and his mouth locked to mine. He pulls back after a moment, his eyes shining with emotion. "Everything. Promise you won't…" His voice cracks, and he squeezes my waist, unable to say whatever it is he desperately wants to. He swallows thickly and moves to the bed, laying me down. He climbs over me, pressing his lips to mine, the kiss so deep, so intimate, so…anguished.

I tangle my fingers in his hair, holding him to me, not knowing if this is the last time we'll ever see each other. I moan softly into his lips, "Hades…"

He kisses down my neck, tracing his fingers over the tight red dress. "Beautiful." He curls his fingers into the plunging neckline and rips it open, right down the middle.

My breath hitches. I look down, watching him. Trying to memorize the planes of his face, every angle, every expression.

He continues to kiss down my body, seeming to worship every curve and crevasse. I arch into his touch, moaning as I feel his shadows sliding over me, repeating Hades's ministrations. He doesn't stop, continuing down my body to settle between my thighs. He kisses my inner thigh before pressing his lips to my core, sucking my swollen clit into his mouth. I glance down at him, meeting his glowing gaze. His eyes shine with the flames of desire.

My lust-filled cries fill the room, and I grasp at the sheets, fisting them.

He flicks my clit with his tongue and drops his glamour. I shiver as his wings trail along my arms, his tail wrapping around my ankle in that primal, possessive way I love, oh, so much.

Following his lead, I allow my glamour to drop, knowing how much more sensitive my skin is in my true form.

Gods, I love the feeling of being completely free.

I feel my orgasm coming, feel that tight spiral of tension coiling in my stomach. But he…he pulls away.

Before I can protest, he crawls up my body and thrusts his cock inside me, the feeling of fullness making me cry out. "Hades!"

He growls, pulling out of me before thrusting back in, hard. "All of me." He thrusts again. "Nothing held back."

I drag my nails down his arms, lifting my hips to meet his every thrust. "I love you."

He nods, his brow covered in sweat, moving his hips faster, harder, pounding into me over and over.

I move one of my hands, dragging my nails along the sensitive body of his wing.

"Hades…I'm going to come…"

He nods, groaning. "So am I."

I pull his face to mine, kissing him deeply, his lips swallowing my moans. Warmth floods through me, and my pussy clenches his cock as I come hard, my release coating him. I arch my back as waves of pleasure ripple through me.

His hips slam into me, through my orgasm, and I wait for the dreaded feeling of emptiness. For him to pull out…but it never comes. He thrusts again and again, driving my body up the bed with the force, before his body tenses. His roar practically echoes in the room as he comes, filling me with his release, the liquid heat exploding inside me, so powerful I feel my climax continue as he fills me, seeming to go on endlessly, until my body quivers beneath his.

He pants, shuddering, and collapses on top of me. His lips press against my neck, making me shiver. "Everything…"

I tangle my fingers in his hair holding him close. Needing him to always be this close. I blink up at the ceiling, smiling, the realization of what just happened finally sinking in. Hades and I joined, completely.

I was right. I knew that the feeling of closeness would be overpowering. What I did not anticipate was the feeling of claiming. Finally, I was his and he was… mine.

Hades is mine.

Did I feel different? Yes.

I finally feel…right. For my whole life, I've felt as if I was half a being, never fitting in, never meeting expectations, and yet, the second Hades claimed me, it felt as if that other part of me, the one that's been gnawing at me, begging to be released, finally has been.

It started the second I met Hades, the awareness of…something. The ability to localize the feeling was facilitated by him. I never anticipated that he would also be the key to unlock it.

And yet, my surprise is unfounded. Hades has unlocked so much of me, why not this too?

I exhale, relaxing into the darkness that seems to be winding its way through my body, mingling with the light, the goodness, the spring. My muscles tingle as they marry together, relieved as they are reunited at last.

Hades shudders, his body still covering mine, his weight crushing me in the most delicious way. "No going back."

I moan softly, basking in my newfound freedom. My eyes flutter closed. "What do you mean?"

He pulls back before kissing me. "All of me."

I smile into his lips, kissing him back. "What changed?"

He sighs, and his mouth opens, as if he's about to reply, but no sound comes out.

The binding.

My lips twitch. "Never mind."

He sighs, pressing his face into my neck. "I'm sorry for what's...what's..." He struggles again. "Argh! This stupid chokehold."

I nuzzle into his shoulder. "I trust you."

He pulls back, looking at me. "Maybe you shouldn't."

And, with those three words, my peace is shattered.

Chapter Seventy-Five

Hades

MAYBE YOU SHOULDN'T. Even that was a struggle to say, as if speaking past a vice clenched around my throat. But what pains me even more is the way I see Persephone's eyes die a little at it. Worse than any blow I've ever received.

But she covers it so quickly, too *quickly*. She's too good at that, hiding her emotions from me. For how long has she needed to utilize that skill to have honed it to such perfection?

Persephone rolls me onto my back, straddling me, the twisting of my gut vanishing under the onslaught of need. She kisses me deeply before she starts rolling her hips. The words of warning, of the implications, I can't remember them. Not when she moves against me like that. The ticking clock that's now exploded...I need to warn her. How long until the curse activates? How long until she'll hate me? Till she realizes…

Gods, I did the same as her mother did. *I didn't think this through.* I think *everything* through. But this? I acted on feeling, on gut instinct. So against my typical nature, my careful counsel, my planned strategies. Everything that I usually rely upon. *Everything out of my reach since I met Persephone.*

I took her choice from her. Imprisoned her. *You've given her things to replace what you took.* I've given her a kingdom...one she never wanted. One she doesn't even know is hers. *A crown of onyx roses, golden thorns, eyes that make even the Underworld feel warm.* A realm to make her own, for our lives to intertwine together, like the vines she creates. We've only known each other for such a short time—

Her hips whip, and I forget the future, focusing on the present. I let out a husky groan. "Again? You're insatiable."

This I can focus on. Not the future. The present. Not what's coming. Not the black sands of the shattered hourglass that are all around us. A future as damned as our present.

She kisses along my jaw and down my neck. "Tell me to stop."

Her scent is deeper now, more mysterious. If I close my eyes, I can almost see the black palace in the Underworld, surrounded by the mist. I growl, "Never."

I could no sooner stop breathing.

She moans, rocking her hips, my cock already responding. Hardening inside her. I never thought to rely so heavily on my divine resilience.

I drop my head back, moaning. "Need to be filled again?"

I thought it would feel incredible. But it is even more. It isn't just marking her, planting a piece of myself inside her. It's deeper than that. It is a claiming. A searing of our souls. Burning them with a brand.

A piece of my soul. Found in another. In *her.*

The implications could be explained later. Everything could wait.

She drags her nails down my chest, sitting up on me. "You shouldn't have given in to me, Hades."

I growl, stiffening to an ache, my voice still hoarse from roaring. "Oh?"

She moves her hips slowly, riding me leisurely.

"Cause now I can't get enough."

Nor can I. Now I have an eternity to do so. Fuck. I just need to tell her.

My hands go to her hips, claws coming out, sinking in. I need to warn her. "Persephone, there's—"

She twists and thought ends.

"Fuck, so good."

She moans, throwing her head back, quickening her pace on me. Her hands cover mine, pushing my claws deeper into her, until her golden ichor spills. "Fuck."

I hiss at that, at her need for me. For the darkness that lurks inside her, that roars and meets mine in a clash. I can only hold onto her, claws grappling for purchase, as she rides me.

A queen claiming her king.

She slides one of her hands down from mine, moving it between her legs to circle her clit. "You fill me…so perfectly."

I snarl at that, knocking her fingers away. Letting my fingers replace hers, forgetting my claws. "You're to be mine. Forever."

She cries out, her hips moving faster. I feel her squeezing me tighter. "I'm going to come."

I growl, "I'm right behind…fill up that greedy cunt of yours."

She arches and screams my name as she comes. I just repeat her name over and over, following behind.

She bends when we level off slowly, kissing me deeply.

I pull my other hand from her, licking her blood from my claws, moaning at the taste. "Fuck."

She kisses along my neck, panting. "I am so mad at you."

I tense. How did she know? How could she know? "W-What?"

"You prevented this from happening for so long…

when nothing feels better than being full of you."

I relax slowly. "Really?"

She moans, kissing along my jaw. "You have no idea."

I need to tell her.

I nuzzle her neck, inhaling her scent, hoping to bolster myself. "There's...I—" The words strangle in my throat. "Stupid thing! There's implications."

She pulls back, looking at me, her smile slowly falling. "You don't enjoy it?"

I give her a look.

She frowns. "It wasn't as good as you anticipated?"

I scoff. "It was better."

She sits up. "Then I'd expect you to be...happier?"

I rub a hand down my face. "It's not that. It's that, I...I can't explain to you why I couldn't."

She moves away from me, standing, our combined release on her pussy. My eyes lock on it, licking my lips without realizing.

She looks at me, her lips twitching. "What, demon?"

I barely glance at her face before I see more of our release slip from her, again licking my lips.

She slides her hand down her body, scooping some of it onto her finger, bringing it to her lush mouth, her eyes rolling back as she sucks. "I can do that...or..." She returns her hand between her legs, taking more of our release onto her fingers, before pushing it back inside her, moaning. "Or that..."

I am so utterly *fucked.*

Chapter Seventy-Six

Persephone

HADES CLIMBS OFF THE BED, GRAB-BING ME AROUND THE WAIST. He growls into my ear, "You're going to be so fucking full of my cum by the end of tonight, my spring."

I giggle, pressing my body against his. "Is that so?"

Before I can register what's happening, he tosses me onto the bed, face down, yanking my hips up. He pulls me to the bottom of the bed, so I'm kneeling on the edge. "You should be thankful for my divine resilience."

My toes curl in anticipation and I bite my lip.

His hand comes down hard on my ass, the sting, the warmth, the loud slap making me moan, making me arch for him.

Hades groans the second he strikes me. "You feel it slipping down your legs?" He spanks me again, making me lurch forward.

"It's sliding down my thighs, baby."

His hand caresses my stinging skin, soothing, but I want him to do it again, craving the feeling of his hand colliding with my asscheek.

He lifts his palm, bringing it down harder. "Yes, it is. All over you. You like being a dirty slut?"

I cry out, panting. "*Your* dirty slut."

Again his palm comes down on me, followed by the gentlest of caresses. His moans grow lower, more guttural. "That's fucking right. *My* dirty slut. You're hungry for my cum? For my cock?"

I push my hips back after every strike, greedy for more, the sharp sting of pain spurring me on, driving me wild. "Fuck me…please…"

He spanks me again. "You don't give the orders here."

I moan. "I'm sorry, sir."

His tender massage, such a contrast from his strikes. Another follows. "You're damn right you are. What are you?"

My fingers dig into the mattress. "Your dirty little slut."

I hear him shift and then feel the tip of his cock dragging along my cunt. I flush, feeling how wet I am, embarrassed by how much that turns me on.

"You're a mess." I can hear the smirk in his voice.

Bastard. But so delicious.

"I didn't know how much I was going to like seeing me dripping from you," he hisses.

I glance over my shoulder, looking at him through my lashes. "Yes, you did. When you…let yourself think about it."

He smacks my ass again, his eyes locking with mine. He growls, once again running his cock along my slit, pushing it in slightly until it drags through my soaking folds.

I face forward again, biting my lip so hard it bleeds.

I curse when he penetrates me, just pushing the very tip in, knowing exactly how to drive me wild. My breath hitches.

He pulls out again. I almost groan in frustration, earning me a growl and a hard spank. "What was that?"

My body arches. "Sorry, sir."

He presses the tip back inside me, torturously slowly feeding his length inside of my aching pussy. I dig my claws into the sheets, hearing them tear under the strain. I try to resist pushing my hips back, trying to be good for him.

He rotates his hips, slowly. "Full of my cum."

I arch my back, needing him to thrust, needing him to fuck me. "I need it, I crave it."

He finally starts rocking his hips in shallow thrusts, not quite satisfying my need to be fucked, but easing the ache slowly. "Yeah you do. Just like the dirty slut you are."

I push my hips back slightly, trying to not push him, but showing him that I need more. "Please…please, sir…"

Finally, he pulls back, before slamming into me, filling me. "You want more?"

I cry out, tearing the sheets. "I need more. Please!"

"Yeah you do," he growls.

I lean down on my elbows, changing the angle, allowing him deeper. My back arches as the pleasure courses through me. "I need you."

He spanks me. This time, when his hand meets my ass, he grabs the ample flesh. "I'm going to come inside you."

I continue to push my hips back, meeting every brutal, punishing thrust. "Yes sir."

His hands move to my hips. He digs his claws in, and I say a silent prayer, begging for him to bruise me, mark me, brand me, own me.

"Fuck!"

"Can I…Can I come, sir?"

"Come for me," he growls.

I push my hips back once more and arch my back, my hoarse voice just managing to scream his name as I come hard, shattering around his cock.

My cunt tightens around him, and he yells as his orgasm is pulled from him. His hot release fills me completely.

I rock my hips slower as the waves of pleasure start

to ebb.

After a moment, Hades finally pulls out of me, and I feel our combined release spilling from my pussy, warm as it slides down my thigh. I collapse on my front, my chest heaving.

Chapter Seventy-Seven

Hades

I PANT AS I FALL NEXT TO HER QUIVERING BODY ON THE BED. Sweat beads on my brow, and I lean in to kiss her. It can't be like this for other fated couples, can it? How do they get anything done? Not that there were many fated couples out there. The Fates told me there were several among the gods that had yet to come to fruition, even some who were married millennia ago, but never…cemented the bond between them. The Fates even whispered about a fated match between a god and a goddess from *another* pantheon.

I let my eyes drift close, exhaustion finally setting in. "Sleep for a moment?"

She kisses my cheek. "My love."

I yawn. "Yes?"

She brushes a stray lock of hair from my cheek. "You're mine."

She curls into my chest, falling asleep, even as my chest aches. I keep her pressed to me, smiling as I finally drift off.

I smile at the golden apples that shimmer from the grove trees at the Isle of the Blessed. My fingers reach out to touch the shining fruit. The scent of haunting roses alerts me to her presence even before she speaks.

386

"You know what they say about picking an apple in a garden," Persephone muses, coming to stand at my side.

My fingers grasp the golden fruit, my fingers sliding over the hard flesh. I glance at her as I lift the fruit to my mouth, taking a sharp bite. "That's a different garden than this one."

Persephone goes to her toes, taking a bite from the other side of the apple, licking her lips when the juice slips free. "Eris would disagree."

I smile at her, my heart swelling when I see how she's dressed. The midnight gown glides around her, cut tightly to her waist, but the embroidery begins at the hem and glides all the way up to her shoulders. Golden vines and flowers, but with thorns that lurk beneath. A rose with a lethal bite.

My eyes linger on the onyx crown sitting on her head, and the ring on her finger.

My wife. My queen.

My Spring.

When I lift the apple to take another bite, I frown, seeing there's nothing in my hand. I open my mouth to ask Persephone about it, but she's gone. I look through the gardens, walking through the grove.

"Persephone?" I call, frowning when no one answers.

I duck around another tree, searching for her. "Persephone?"

My head turns to the side, looking for her at the rustle of branches. My eyes catch on the shining golden apples, my brow furrowing. I reach out to pick another shining fruit, but as my fingers brush it, the gold turns ashen. The fruit rots at my touch. I take a step back in surprise. My eyes follow as each piece of fruit begins to die around me, then the trees, then the very air.

Death everywhere. I spin around, everything around me turning barren.

"Persephone!" I scream.

There's no answer.

The scream follows me from my dream. From the

387

yawning abyss of sleep into reality. I hear the echo of my scream, but when I try to open my eyes, they don't budge. Am I still asleep? A dream within another? It wouldn't be the first time. As King of the Underworld, I had learned tricks from the Oneiroi, the gods of dreams. Sometimes, that ability leaked into my own dreams.

I focus on my eyes, imagining them opening, as if it were easy. My eyelids don't move. Not even a millimeter. There's only darkness. My hands reach to touch my face, but I can't feel my limbs respond to my mind.

My breath becomes harder and harder to pull in, air being squeezed from me. My chest caving in, my lungs held in a vice, becoming tighter and tighter. *Why can't I breathe?*

Again, I try to awaken, try to force myself into reality. But I can't. The scent of rotting roots and trees surrounds me. Am I still in that dream? Of the rotting Isle of the Blessed? *Persephone, where is she?* I try to search with my nose for her overwhelming floral scent. But I can't pick up anything. Not even the barest hint.

I flex my hands, but I'm pinned in too tight. Air isn't coming into my lungs. I can't think. I can't breathe. I can't see.

I can't awaken. Even trying to move my wrists sends searing pain down my arms. Then I realize.

This isn't a dream.

I let out a growl and try to suck in air or break free, but I can't move. Even without air, something that feels like a tree branch shoves its way down my throat. Choking me. If I had eyes, they would have teared up from the pain.

The tree branch seems to go on and on, never ending. When it finally stops forcing its way down my throat, horror and fear seep into me.

Because then it starts to *feed.*

Feeding on me, from the inside out. I can do noth-

388

ing. Nothing but *endure.* Trapped and frozen. The God of the Dead, kept on the brink of death, without being pushed over.

Persephone, I love you. I'm sorry.

Chapter Seventy-Eight

Persephone

I ROLL OVER IN BED, NEEDING HIS WARMTH, HIS TOUCH, HIS COMFORT. My dream draws me in completely, though, not letting me free from it.

Enclosed space, the smell of earth, rotting bark. I feel my heart racing, my power waning. Where am I? Why am I so weak, so helpless?

I awaken with a start, the smell of dirt still lingering. My chest heaves as I try to orient myself. A familiar smell overtakes the remnants of the one from my dream.

Hades.

I glance at the other side of the bed, frowning when I find it empty. I swing my legs over the side, leaning my elbows on my knees, trying to fight the nausea sitting heavy in my stomach. My head spins from my nightmare. I cradle my throbbing head.

"Hades?" I call into the dark apartment. I wait for a reply but none comes. "Hades!?" I call louder. The silence that greets me is deafening.

I stand on shaky legs, pulling on one of his shirts, and walk to the living room, the sun only now beginning to breach the apartment windows, casting a watery yellow glow. I stumble to the kitchen and pour myself a glass of water.

Could he be at work already?

I find my phone on the kitchen island and type out a quick message.

> Can't come to work today. Not feeling well. I love you.

My head snaps up as the elevator bell rings, notifying me that someone is waiting to be allowed in.

Who could that be at this time?

I sigh, the dreamy prospect of immediately returning to bed disappearing. I walk to the panel on the wall. My brows furrow as I observe the unfamiliar woman standing there.

The woman in question is definitely divine, like an ethereal Morticia Addams.

My instinct to let her in overwhelms me, and I press the small green accept button, allowing the elevator doors to open.

The second the doors opens she looks around the apartment, her scrutinizing gaze judging every item of decor.

She wrinkles her nose. "Hm. Time to go."

I blink at her, cursing myself for being so trusting. "Can I help you?"

She looks me up and down, as if, up until now, she had no idea I was standing in front of her. Her eyes turn yellow and feline. "My name is Hekate. I am here to escort you, Your Majesty."

I take a step back from her, surprised my mother organized anything so formal to return me to the mountain. I half expected her to show up herself and drag me by the hair. "I'm not going back."

Hekate frowns, her head tilting. "Back? Have you been to the Underworld before?"

"The Underworld?" My brows furrow. "My...my

391

mother didn't send you?" Something like relief flits through me. Shortsighted, considering there is a stranger in my apartment trying to take me somewhere. I've seen enough episodes of *Investigation Discovery* to know to never go to a second location.

Hekate gestures to her Gothic attire. "Do I look like the kind of person your mother would keep company with, Persephone?"

I clear my throat. "I-I suppose not. Wait. You know who I am?"

Hekate blinks. "I know both who you were and who you are now." She claps her hands together. "Make haste, we leave soon. The Underworld waits for no one."

I blink again, feeling like I'm missing something vital to being able to successfully partake in this conversation. "Who I am now?" I look down at my state of undress. "I can't leave. I'm barely wearing any clothes!" I pause. "Where is Hades?"

She ignores me completely, grabbing my arms. The room spins around us, and yet, it strangely feels as if we're not moving.

Within the blink of an eye, we arrive. I stumble slightly, but Hekate doesn't release me until I'm on even footing. My eyes go wide. I gasp as I take in the room.

I'm no longer in the large, minimalist space that is Hades's apartment. His scent no longer surrounds me comfortingly. Still there, but faint, like he's not been here in a long time. Black paneling lines the walls, with intricate gold detailing. The furnishings are expensive-looking and plush, not in the same way as his apartment and office, but much grander, more ostentatious. A large fireplace crackles midway along the wall, heating the room. At the top of the room, on a dais, sits two ornate thrones, one larger than the other. Both obsidian, the blackest of black, atramentous, so polished they appear to mirror the room. Large silk, black cushions sit in the center of both. The larger of the two is plain and regal, with an air of power. The smaller throne, however, has roses carved delicately around the sides.

My gaze slides back to Hekate, and I try to pull Hades's shirt down to cover myself, feeling more exposed than I ever have.

Hekate simply smiles. She bends, curtsying low. "Welcome home, Your Majesty."

HADES & PERSEPHONE'S
STORY CONTINUES IN THE
MISTRESS &
THE RENOWNED.
IN THE MEANTIME
ENJOY THIS BONUS CHAP-
TER

Inside the Club
Melinoë

THE MUSIC POUNDS AND I BATHE IN THE FEEL OF IT RATTLING MY BONES. A bead of sweat rolls down my neck and I tilt my head at the feeling. There was no sweating there. No music. No writhing bodies. Only torture and wasteland and the sounds of screams in the distance as souls pay penance for their crimes.

Persephone links her fingers with mine, bringing me back to the utter bliss of the club. My feet stick to the floor and there's at least four people touching me at all times, I love it.

Freedom is bliss....

I give my body free rein to move however it wants, submitting wholly to the music, the beat, the other bodies bumping and grinding into me. Persephone's melodic laugh carries over the deep bass and she hands me a shot glass, lifting hers to the sky.

"To new friends." Her smile seems to brighten the entire club, and I am in complete awe of my best friend.

"To new friends!" I echo enthusiastically.

The burn of the liquor makes me wince, but it warms my insides in a delicious, almost forbidden way. I'd never experienced alcohol before I came here.

Then again, I'd experienced nothing other than aimless wandering through the abyss and pain. Although after a while, I didn't mind that so much.

The alcohol loosens my limbs up more and the dance moves that come to me are outrageous and extraordinary. My movements falter a little when my gaze is drawn to the balcony, Hades' gaze is locked on the beautiful brunette in front of me. He looks like a wildcat, starved from the hunt, stalking his prey.

"Yikes." I say, grimacing.

Persephone frowns, "What is—" Her words trail off when she turns and sees what's drawn my attention and I watch in fascination as her eyes darken. My brows furrow. Feelings and interactions are still a mystery to me, I find it fascinating how emotions can be so versatile.

Hades and Persephone try very hard to dislike one another but are drawn together like moths to a flame.

I wonder if I'll ever have someone look at me with the hunger that Hades looks at Persephone. I wonder if I'll ever look at someone with the same disdain tinged desire that Persephone looks back at him with.

"I guess he had the same idea" I say, looking back up at Hades.

Persephone grabs another shot and downs it, shuddering as she swallows the amber liquor. She grins at me, dancing again, I tilt my head at her.

Why is she avoiding Hades' gaze?

The song changes, the lower tempo vibrating my bones in a way that makes my body move differently and once again I'm lost in the beat.

I'm vaguely aware of Persephone calling Jackson over, of them dancing together, but I get lost in the crowd, letting my legs guide me as they wanted, deeper into the mess of sweaty bodies. Every so often a stray hand brushes over my body, some accidental, some not.

Some *really* not. It doesn't concern me, nothing concerns me but the sounds, the warmth, the decadence of being this *free.*

I dance into someone, not dissimilar to my whole club experience but, it felt like an electric shock jolted through their body into mine and my eyes snap open. I immediately tense, my eyes going wide when I meet the gaze of Helios, Persephone's divine friend.

His lips pulled into a smirk and his bright amber eyes locked with mine, sparkling in interest. He cocks his head; the smugness rolling off him.

"Easy there, hellcat" the low timbre of his voice sent a shiver down my spine.

I blink at the pet name, I'd never had a pet name before, unless you count, "that weirdo from IT".

I step back from him, feeling uncertain. The gods are not kind to those like me, *the wanderers.* They look upon us, born from the deepest recesses of hell, with contempt and disgust.

Except Hades and Persephone. But they are the exception, not the rule.

Helios tilts his head, regarding me and my brows furrow at the gleam in his eyes. Not even a whisper of disdain in those whiskey coloured eyes, there was something... dark in them but not the sort of darkness that made me fear him, the darkness that set a fire deep in my stomach, the darkness that made the hairs at the back of my neck stand.

He was looking at me with a similarly predatory gaze that I'd seen not 30 minutes ago when I watched Hades practically devour Persephone with his eyes.

But the eyes looking back at me don't hold any of the false hatred Hades did. They are playful and the gold flecks seemed to dance in his irises and he slowly took me in.

My clothes suddenly feels too tight and the temperature in the club seems to rise by at least 10 degrees.

"So where has Persephone been hiding you?" Helios drawled, a dimple appearing on his right cheek as his mouth tugs into a half smile.

"Hiding?" I tilt my head.

"You're not divine." He states. There is no aversion in his voice, just a statement of fact. I watch him, waiting for a reaction, any reaction. "But…" Her narrows his eyes, "You're not human…"

I roll my eyes, "How observant, and here I thought you were just a pretty–." I blush, the words having come out before I'd thought about them.

Helios's lips pull into a shit-eating grin, "So you think I'm pretty?"

"No." I say far too quickly. I feel the heat of my blush spreading down my neck. I never get flustered with men., I haven't since I came to this realm. It's probably just because he's divine. And an arrogant ass.

Helios lifts his chin, his eyebrow quirking. He curls his finger into one of the belt loops in my shorts and pulls me close.

"You fascinate me…" He tilts his head, "You never told me your name."

I narrow my eyes, "That's right. I believe what I said was that I wasn't interested. A fact that hasn't changed in the past hour." The heat from his body seeps into me. It's different from that of the club, his warmth is like pure sunshine, radiating from him, drawing me in. Even the darkness inside me enjoys the sensual shadows he creates with his light.

He waits, his other hand going to my waist. *Gods he's so... hot.* His fingers practically scald me. My shirt restricts his touch, but he rubs his thumb in maddening circles along the edge, I gasp as the pad meets my skin.

"Mellie."

He grins, flashing his perfectly straight white teeth,

"Mellie. What a wild little hell kitty you are."

"I'm not a hell kitty. Don't have claws" I say, frowning at the pet name he used again.

"Maybe…" He stokes my hip again, "No one has given you a reason to use them…"

I narrow my eyes, "What use would I have for claws?"

Helios leans in, his lips at my ear, "I'd love to feel them dragging across my back while I make you purr."

My cheeks heat and I pull back, needing to study his face. *Could this be a trick? Some way to hurt me?*

But all I can see in Helios's eyes is… need. His golden eyes have darkened, the caramel color now almost black. He keeps his eyes on me, watching me with such intensity, watching me like no one ever has before. I feel myself leaning into him, his hand tightens on my hip and I can already feel that it'll bruise tomorrow. His fingerprints seared onto my flesh.

Helios licks his lips, his darkening eyes going to mine and before I know what I'm doing I surge forward, slamming my lips to his. The way his lips immediately mold to mine sends a jolt of awareness between my thighs. I wrap my arms around his neck, once again letting my body take control, but it's not the music guiding me this time. No, its lust, need, carnal desire and it feels even more freeing than dancing.

Helios pulls back and my heart sinks. *No good bottom dweller, lesser than a god.*

I pull away but he grabs me and pulls me in close.

"Why do I feel like you're going to disappear?" He asks, his gaze roaming over my face, searching for something. "Fuck." He releases me and takes my hand, pulling me through the crowds, off the dance floor. I follow behind, my brows furrowed in confusion.

Helios stops in front of the ladies' room and opens the door for me, I blink at him and he rolls his eyes, pulling me inside and locking the door.

I tilt my head, watching him, he runs his hand through his blond locks, before turning to face me.

"Mellie…" Helios whispers, looking at me, his eyes full of emotion.

I slam my lips to his, shoving him back against the door. He grunts at the impact but deepens the kiss in response, his hands moving to my hips, he squeezes them again, harder than before and I moan into his lips.

Helios's lips are heaven… or at least the closest I'd ever come to it. Soft, plump , heavenly clouds but doing all kinds of sinful things to mine. His tongue plunders into my mouth and I flick my tongue with his, needing more of him. Helios shifts, his hands going to the backs of my thighs and he lifts me, wrapping my legs around his waist and spinning us so my back is to the door. He pushes me back into it with similar force as I did to him and I groan but the small bite of pain makes me rock my hips for him. Helios presses his crotch into me and I moan at how hard he feels.

My shorts are soaked and if he doesn't relieve this ache between my legs soon, I'm going to go insane. I push him on by reaching down and unbuttoning his jeans, doing my best to push them down. Helios responds by setting me on my feet, his hands going to open my shorts.

"Are you sure about this, hellcat?"

My eyes flash in anger, another rush of desire pulsing in my pussy, "Don't call me that."

Helios smirks and the second we're rid of our bottoms, he lifts me again, slamming his lips to mine, his cock grazing my opening.

Oh, how I ache… Gods, never ached this much… How do people live like this?

Helios pulls back, tilting his head, silently asking me if I want this. I growl, the sound like a feral cat,

400

ravenous for its next meal.

Helios's eyes heat and in one swift move, he buries his cock inside me. I tunnel my fingers through his hair and kiss him deeply, wildly, desperately. His large size making me tremble in pain and pleasure, the line so fine between the two.

Never want him to stop.

He pulls almost completely out of me, leaving me feel empty, incomplete, before plunging back inside, his grunts of pleasure sending shivers down my spine. I yank at his hair, pulling his head back to look into his eyes.

Untamed, wild, feral beast. Just. Like. Me.

I lean in and lick his cheek, tightening my fingers into a fist in his hair. He growls when I pull some strands out but it only encourages him. He thrusts harder and faster into me. His hips slapping into mine almost violently.

He grips my thighs harder as he fucks me mercilessly; I feel the warm stickiness of my blood as his nails break my skin. I feel myself getting wetter; Helios's cock sliding in and out of me easier the more turned on I get. I pull back, arching my chest. My gaze locks on his and I slap him hard across the face. He snarls at me, not stopping his thrusting. He leans in and bites down on my neck so hard I scream at the pain, the fucking rapture.

I throw my head back, the sensations almost too much, completely overwhelming my senses. I move one of my hands between my legs and the second I brush my thumb over my clit, I completely dissolve into a mess of pleasure and release. Helios presses his face into my neck, muffling his roar and his scorching release fills me, his whole body quaking.

We stand there, panting, I can't tell if I'm still pressed against the door because Helios is basking in

401

my pussy goodness or if he wouldn't be able to stand without the support.

Eventually he pulls back and eases his grip on my thighs. Every single part of my body aches deliciously and I want to bottle this bittersweet agony so I can experience it whenever I want it.

Helios's eyes have returned to that whiskey, golden brown and he moves one of his hands to cup my cheek, slowly lowering me to my feet.

The realization of our realities hits me like a ton of brick at the sight of the godly being in front of me. No longer the feral animal that could also have been from the wastelands, now he is the glowing titan of the sun and I am…

"Mel…"

I tense, not that voice. Not the *"Sorry Mellie, but you're a downstairs dweller but thanks for the fuck…"*

I shake my head, "Don't."

I'm not ready to hear what he has to say, I don't want to. I already know.

He strokes my cheek, "Hell–"

I cut him off by slamming my fist into his face. Pushing all of my underworld strength into it.

Fucking gods.

Helios hits the ground, hard. Completely KO'd and I grimace. I grab his wrist and try to heave him away from the door, my one escape route.

I grunt as I pull his heavy, lifeless body and prop him against the stall divider. I nod once, appreciating my handy work and pat him on the head before leaving the bathroom.

A woman walks past me, on her way to use the bathroom and I grab her arm, "Oh, I wouldn't use that one. There's this really weird guy passed out in there."

She blinks, looking alarmed and mutters her thanks before heading away in the other direction and I skip back to the dance floor.

Printed in Great Britain
by Amazon